Cherries on Snow

Robert W. Craven

DEDICATION

This book is dedicated to

D. Michael Jones, DD

Who has pastored Independent Bible Church of Port Angeles,
Washington, for over forty years.
Like the white horse of Revelations 19:11,
you have brought the Rider to all you have met, and equipped many
others to carry Him to places you have not gone.

Nos Servo.

Revelations 19:11

And I saw heaven opened

And behold, a white horse

And He who sat on it

   is called

      Faithful
         And
      True---

     Blessings

Contents

PROLOGUE

The events depicted herein were drawn from the materials of the Great Archive of Nos Servo. They were based on artifacts, archival documents, and the diaries of past and future events written by those who have already lived them. Only material deemed to be of primary historical/prophetic resource was used in this writing. No second-degree or tertiary resources were incorporated. Relevant events are integrated into a consistent timeline for ease of reading. Information regarding ongoing operations are withheld for security reasons.

Chapter 1

Soon

Philip sat at the mahogany desk, fiddling with some paper and drawing stick figures. Monday morning surgical conferences were always tedious, but today it was literally giving him a headache. David seemed to be just droning on and on.

David paced around the room, trying to keep his staff from falling asleep. "I know a lot of you are still missing Operative Notes from the last 'stabilization effort.' Try to get them into the computer by the end of the week. If you can't remember the case, just do the best you can. I find reviewing the nurses' notes very helpful. If you are still really stuck, you might want to look at the billed supply list. If it lists that a biliary stent was billed out, then you probably did a biliary stent procedure. In any case, I want them all done by the end of the week. Oh, and remember, Philip and I will be out at the end of the month for the annual trauma conference in Boston." He looked around the room. The other doctors and surgeons had their usual look of exhausted indifference. "All right, let's move on to new business." David glanced at Philip. He had never said anything about them going to a conference in Boston. David gave Philip a subtle nod conveying they would discuss it later.

"Trauma teams one through seven to the emergency room, stat! Trauma teams one through seven to the emergency room, stat!" billowed over the loudspeakers. David, Philip, and several others sprang from the room and jumped into the express elevator. "Come on. Come on," David mumbled. He stared at Philip on the other side of the packed elevator, which was now stopping at every floor. "Aaahh, come on!" The door slid open again. The people waiting outside cringed. Several turned and ran for the stairs. David and Philip would have done the same, but they were both packed tightly in the back and couldn't get off. "Trauma teams one through seven to the emergency room, stat!" billowed again overhead.

As the door finally slid open to the emergency room, they were bombarded by the noise and chaos of what looked like a battle scene. There were wounded everywhere. David rushed out of the elevator. "I want all the triage moved out to the parking lot. Now! Red tags on the stat cases, then yellows, then greens. Just like we practiced it, people. Just like we practiced it." David looked at a charred body going by him on a stretcher. The tech looked up, shaking his head. "No." The man was already dead.

David glanced around at his frantic staff. "ABCDs, people! ABCDs!"

David shoved his way through the chaos to the parking lot in the back. Several military Armored Personnel Carriers were already there unloading more wounded. Corpsman and techs hurriedly tried to start IVs. Bags of blood were being hung on ghost-white soldiers. Patients with multiple traumatic amputations, high velocity gunshot wounds, burns, and other injuries littered the area.

A voice came from behind him. "We also have six Life Star Carriers fully loaded en route by air." It was the nursing supervisor.

David turned. "Six?"

The nurse nodded. "Yes, six." She looked silently at David.

David shook his head. "I want the hospital placed on Priority One status now. Any patient fit to walk needs to be transferred out immediately. They can go to a neighboring hospital, nursing home, or wherever. I don't care. Just get 'em out of here." The nurse nodded and started to turn. David looked up to see the first Life Star Carrier landing on the roof. Each one carried thirty patients. He pointed his finger at the military aircraft. "And I want a surgeon on that rooftop in thirty seconds, or some of those patients aren't even going to make it to the operating room." The nurse sprinted toward the hospital.

David hurried to the nearest triage station. The sheer number of the wounded was overwhelming. He went for the first patient he saw wearing a red tag. He did a quick assessment. The man had multiple pinholes in his neck. He was gasping for air. Every time he gasped, blood poured out the tiny holes like a sieve. Thick clotted blood was also building up in his neck. He couldn't breathe.

"I need a CricKit now!"

He glanced at the O2 Sat on the monitor—82 percent. Not good. The nurse handed him the CricKit. He tore open the betadine pouch and poured it on the man's neck. Then he grabbed the disposable number fifteen blade from inside the kit. His mind and hands raced. *Skin incision, spread, spread. Push the thyroid inferiorly, Cric hook…in…pull. Cut the cricothyroid membrane, spread, shove the tube in…done!* He secured the ambu bag to the connector and started ventilating. The gurney was already rolling toward the OR. He glanced back up at the O2 Sat monitor—98 percent. *Fabulous!* David finished his ABCDs. Circulation—a quick survey of the patient's body revealed blood still pumping out of the man's mangled leg. *That will need to be amputated*, he thought. He tightened the field tourniquet. His mind raced as he started to go through his OR plan in his head.

The gurney slammed into the OR door, pushing it forward. David looked down the hall. Two doors down, Trauma Team Three was rushing into the operating room en masse. He shoved the gurney into the operating room. The rest of Trauma Team One was already inside prepping the room. "We're going to be starting with a neck exploration. I may need help from vascular. Then we'll do a quick amputation of his right leg. He is going to need at least four units of packed cells to start."

The next six days were a blur. *Cut, sew, cut, sew, amputate. Coffee. Cut, sew, run a code. Amputate, blood soaks through boots, get new boots, coffee. Patient dies on table. Cut, sew, coffee. Bad headache, run code, really bad headache. Cut, sew, cut, sew...* At some point they started giving him the caffeine tablets. He really hated those. His thinking was already getting more blurred, and the rebound headache was going to be a killer. *Cut, sew, cut, sew...*

Philip hadn't seen David in days. About the third day into the crisis, it looked like things were starting to wind down. Then there was another major offensive. The casualties were literally starting to pile up. The morgues were full.

The Administration said it was just another "stabilization effort," but Philip knew better. *This is as bad as it was during the war*, he thought. Rumors were, they were receiving the same intensity of casualty delivery in New York and Baltimore as they were here in Hartford. His team, Trauma Team Six, was totally burned out. Backup trauma teams had been flown in from Los Angeles and Phoenix as soon as the skies were considered safe enough for flights. No one knew how many had been killed. Clearly it was in the tens of thousands. Still, the television media and interlink were inundated with Administration officials minimizing the extent of the conflict and touting their effectiveness in quelling the "fanatics."

Philip walked through the parking lot, looking at the sea of green tags. There was still a small line of yellows off to the left, so he headed in that direction. There were lots of other people walking through the sea of injured. A legion of medical staff were busily doing their jobs. There was also a contingent from the Administration. They were easy to spot. In a field of white lab coats and green OR scrubs, the Administration's police wore black and red.

He heard yelling off to his right. It was different from the familiar scream of pain from one of the injured. It was the roar of a hungry lion that had just found another wounded lamb to consume.

"There is a fanatic, right here! Here, among the honored wounded!" yelled one of the Administration's agents.

Philip stopped and stared as the officer grabbed a wounded man with both hands and pulled him up off the ground.

"Aaahhh...stop! Stop!" But the wounded man's cries went unheeded.

The officer made sure his loud billowing monologue was heard by every-one. "These fanatics are a cancer eating away at the soul of our great union!" he roared. His sneering face was filled with disgust. The officer unbuttoned the top of his holster and pulled out his pistol. He placed the weapon firmly against the young man's chest. He paused for an instant and seemed to glare into the young man's face. The wounded soldier started to pull away. *Bang…bang…bang…bang… bang…bang. Click…click…click.* Six loud shots rang out across the parking lot. The officer made sure the clip was emptied. The agent continued to hold up the dead body as he shifted behind it. Then he pulled out a long black knife from a scab-bard at his waist. The blade was serrated with a glistening edge. Then he decapi-tated the lifeless corpse. He laid the severed head neatly on the pavement next to the body, in a rapidly increasing pool of scarlet. The officer stood up slowly and remained motionless for a moment. He looked around at all the staring faces. He seemed to want to make sure everyone had witnessed what he had done.

Obviously, a single to the bullet to the head would have been much more effective, Philip thought. But clearly there was more to it than just killing a rebel. He had seen it before. The Administration's agents always made it a point to empty the clip.

Philip grabbed a young woman with a yellow tag and headed back to the OR. Casualties continued to flow in for at least another week. Then things just seemed to slowly peter out. The insanity level around the hospital was nearly back to nor-mal. That was a good thing, because it was time to go to Boston.

"What kind of music is this anyway?" Philip demanded.

"It's called country music."

"I thought they banned that stuff." Philip squished up his nose and hit the button to roll the car windows down.

"No, they would never ban country music!" David scoffed. Then he glanced over at Philip with a mischievous grin. Slowly and dramatically, he let go of the steering wheel, lowered his left hand to the buttons on his armrest, and raised the car windows back up.

Phillip shook his head. "Well, they should. In the last hour I have listened to three bar fights, four divorces, two truck wrecks, and at least four people trying to figure out who their father was."

"Exactly—country music!" David said proudly. He started bobbing his head and humming along with the next song.

Philip looked out the window at the passing countryside. "I assume there is more to us going to Boston than attending another trauma meeting."

"No," David said stoically. "We are going to a meeting. It is in Boston. And it is on trauma." Then he turned toward Philip with a small smile. "Oh, but we may be leaving the conference early."

Philip thought "Level Two Penetrating Neck Trauma—When to Explore and When Not To" was a great lecture.

David agreed. "It would have been much more helpful, however, if the Administration could have figured out a way to give us that lecture before the last 'stabilization operation' instead of afterwards," he scoffed. The rest of the lectures the first day consisted pretty much of the same old stuff. On day two, their favorite was "Spinal Cord Injuries and High Dose Steroids."

"I don't know about cutting out the use of the opioid antagonist though. I don't think the data really supports that at this point," Philip said. He had come over to David's room the following morning so they could take the shuttle to the conference together. "I think I am going to start with the symposium on 'Biological Weapons.' How about you?"

"When we get to the conference this morning, I will talk to all of our friends. I will mention several lectures I am planning on attending. And I will tell everyone how I am looking forward to tonight's dinner lecture." David walked over to the closet, pulled all the remaining dress shirts and slacks from the hangers, and stuffed them back in his garment bag, though the conference continued for one more day. He glanced at Philip. "You will be doing the same thing. Then we will return to the hotel, get our stuff, and leave out the back." David zipped up the garment bag.

Philip chuckled, swiveling the only chair in the room to face David. "I wondered why you parked there last night. But there is still one day left at the conference."

"Exactly. And there is clearly nothing suspicious about a couple of doctors leaving a medical conference early. Then we will head back to Hartford." David walked over to the only dresser in the room and started stuffing his socks and underwear back in his small roller bag. He looked directly at Philip. "If there is any suspicion about our trip, it will be focused on Boston. Not on Hartford. Why else would have we traveled all the way here? But our real meeting will be right back at home. Actually, not that far from the hospital."

"So we came all the way to Boston so we could go home early, to a secret meeting where we already live?"

"Exactly." David slipped on his leather dress shoes.

"That's diabolical." Philip chuckled.

"Yes it is." David smirked. "And that is why I am head of Trauma and you are not." He laughed.

"Yeah, I'm the honest one!" Philip shook his head and grabbed the day's program listing. "OK, I think I know which programs I would've gone to if we were actually staying. I'll make sure I mention them to whoever we talk to."

The two men walked downstairs to the hotel dining area and went straight over to the breakfast buffet. Most days at the hospital, they were too busy to enjoy a casual meal, so the men made it a point to stuff themselves to the gills. David piled up the pancakes. Philip forked on the French toast. Both their meals were floated in a sea of syrup and buried under a mountain of bacon. As they returned to their tables, each man glanced at the plate of the other.

"I put myself on a statin drug a couple years ago," David said with a happy grin.

"Me too." Philip laughed.

They each loosened their belts before heading to the conference center. Both men heartily greeted everyone they knew at the meeting and tried to be as visible as possible. They stood in the back of the lecture hall, where several experts were giving the talk on "Biological Weapons." They chatted with some friends for a few minutes about how nice a day it was outside.

"Great day for golf," Philip chimed.

"Yeah, I think you're right," David seconded. A few minutes later they snuck out the back. They jumped into a cab back to the hotel, paid cash, grabbed their luggage, and were out on the road back to Hartford in less than ten minutes.

Philip drummed his fingers on the console as David drove slowly through Hartford. He stopped at every stop sign and even at the yellow lights. He said he did not want to draw any attention. Near one of the local parks, he pulled the vehicle to the side of the road. He left the engine running. He looked at Philip and spoke in the same serious tone he used in the operating room. "The order you are joining is very old. The war has continued. And as we were told in God's Word, the enemy has been allowed to prevail, as man chooses it to prevail. Still, God is in control, and Satan's purview is not complete. There are places that are protected. We call them 'Hedges.' One of those is located here."

David took the engine out of park and drove the car around the corner. Philip sat up, frantically pointing his finger. "That's a church!"

"Yes," David said, "that *is* a church."

"But they were outlawed years ago. And look. That one still has crosses on the tower, and there on the sanctuary!"

"Yes, it does." David sighed with a big smile. "This is the Church of the Good Shepherd. I do not know how or why it was chosen. But it is one of the Hedges. Perhaps it is because of the unique legacy behind its construction. It was built by the Colt family. You know, the ones that made all the guns. Maybe it was that. The irony of a beautiful church rising up out of a sordid history of bloodshed and violence. God does that. Takes the things of man and flips them around."

David pulled the car into one of the many white-lined parking spaces. As the two men walked through the lush green grass surrounding the church, Philip suddenly stopped. He looked surprised. "Did you feel that?" His eyes glistened with wonder.

"It's the Hedge." David closed his eyes and took a slow, deep breath. "That feeling signifies its boundary. Everything inside the Hedge is protected. None can see. None will know. No torturer can drag out of you anything that happens here or whatever you may learn here."

"But it's a church, right out in the open." Philip stopped on the grass in disbelief. "Surely the Administration—"

"Oh, they know all about it. But as I said, it is outside their purview."

Philip looked around in disbelief. He glanced at the people walking on the nearby streets. "But what about all the people? Surely they—"

"They what? See it?" David shook his head. "People drove by churches a hundred times a day before they were outlawed and didn't see them for what they were. Now that they are outlawed, why would it be any different?" David continued walking. "Come. There is a lot we need to talk about."

Philip looked up, admiring the beautiful gothic architecture. He loved the high tower, the different colors of the stone, the small flying buttresses, and the stained-glass windows. He relished the sense of age permeating from the stone. But most of all, he admired that it was church. Still standing. Still with crosses raised to heaven. Still on mission.

The church's front door was made of stout, thick banded wood. It was not locked. They entered and found themselves in a small foyer. As the door closed behind them...

"David, David...and this must be your friend Philip. Welcome, welcome." A smiling monk rushed toward them, pulling his robes up as he scurried across the tile floor of the entryway. Before they could move, they were both engulfed in the monk's outstretched arms and loose, baggy robes. He was a hugger. "I'm so glad you made it. I wasn't sure if you would be coming or not."

David awkwardly tried to make introductions. "Yes. Philip, this is, ah, brother..." He looked at the monk, trying to get some help.

"Brother Pentral. I am so glad to meet you." He put out his hand and shook Philip's with excited vigor.

David looked at Philip. "What he hasn't told you is that he is one of a set of identical triplets. And I mean identical." He looked over at the monk. "Thank you for helping me out. I thought it was you, but I just wasn't quite sure."

"No, I totally understand. We are truly identical, which does make it hard. Even our names can be confusing sometimes." He put out his arm and motioned for them to walk down the hall. "Pater, well, he has been here from the beginning. Actually, we are all the same age but… Anyway, he oversees pretty much everything around here. Then there is Prognatus. He got here a little before I did. He is the real advocate for the Order, and well, all the Iredenti. And then there is me, Pentral. I guess you could say I'm the most recent addition. And well, I'm just here to help. So there you go. Once you get to know us though, you will find that we are totally different. But please, please, come in." He guided them out of the foyer and down a long hall. "I know the two of you do not have much time, so I would like to get started."

Pentral whisked them through the beautiful old building. His loose robes billowed behind him as he hurried them on. Philip caught a glimpse of the old pipe organ constructed into the aged stone, and a gothic lectern with a carved, broad-winged eagle holding an actual Bible. He would have given anything to just stop for a moment and hear the fullness of the music and turn the pages. Still, as he looked at all the empty pews, he was filled with sadness.

Brother Pentral placed his hand on Philip's shoulder. "Not to worry. More are being called. Please, you are with me." He ushered them to the back and out onto a covered portico, where there was a large round oak pedestaled table. He motioned for them to sit.

Pentral sat with his loose robes fluttering around him. "Well, I'm not really sure where to begin," he said, shaking his head. "With all the stuff going on in Rome and with the war, things are getting pretty complicated, really fast. Perhaps…"

Philip saw David's face flash with the same shock probably now showing on his own. Pentral stopped talking.

"What stuff?" David asked. "We haven't heard anything." Philip offered a confused look of agreement.

"Oh. Ah…" Pentral fumbled, clearly trying to organize his thoughts. "Let's start with Rome. First, we are not supposed to call it that anymore. The Administration has officially changed the name to 'The City of the Seven Mountains.' They said they wanted to give things a fresh start. It seems there was too much of a stigma associated with 'Rome.' Oh, and because the new name is so long, the city can also be called 'Sedem H^or.' This is a Slovakian name in honor of the many European members of the Administration."

Philip snuck a quick look at David. He too looked dumbfounded.

"She is still the same city though," Pentral added with a not-so-subtle frown. "The EU has made an announcement that they will be moving their capital there. And the UN is moving its headquarters there from New York." Pentral looked at the two men's blank faces. "And as for the war—"

"But the war is over. It's been over," Philip interjected.

"Yes, that war is. But the Alliance of the Ten Nations is really… Well, maybe it is in need of a new name. It seems that three of those ten nations have had some second thoughts about things. All those 'stabilization efforts' we keep hearing about are not just battles against 'fanatics.' They are really major battles within the Alliance. At least one of the three nations has already declared war. I am sure the other two will be doing the same thing very soon."

Hours passed as Pentral gave the men updates on the world around them. Sometimes he paced. Sometimes he sat. Most times, he waved his hands.

David sat shaking his head. Philip's mouth hung open until his lips dried out.

"I'm flabbergasted, absolutely flabbergasted." David shook his head with his mouth now also agape. "I can't believe the media have been able to keep all this a secret. There have always been rumors, but..." He turned toward Philip. "But this, this is inconceivable."

Pentral rose to his feet. "The world has very little time left." He walked reassuringly over to the two friends. "There is so much more I would like to tell you. But I think it is time that the two of you go to the Great Archive of Nos Servo. There you can meet the others and be told of what is happening around the globe. I think the time has also come when they will begin giving you your own mission assignments."

David had started to rise when the monk headed toward him. He sat back down and looked up at the monk. "One of the other stewards mentioned the Great Archive to me a year or two ago, but I really have no clue as to where it is located."

Pentral put his hand on David's shoulder. "It is just outside of Seattle. The two of you will need to find an excuse to go there. Then let me know, and I will make all the contact arrangements."

It was late, and the two friends needed to leave. David and Philip each gave Pentral a big hug. They were again engulfed in flowing folds of his loose robe. As they left, David turned and stopped in the door. "Oh, I just remembered. Philip and I will be attending the Northwest Trauma Conference in Seattle next month. I think it's around the seventeenth." A big smile lit his face.

Pentral chuckled softly and nodded. "I will make the arrangements. Some people will meet you there and take you on a tour."

The two friends dashed back to their car. Traffic was heavy. It was going to take David over an hour to drive Phillip back to his apartment. They would get a good night sleep at home and then go into the hospital together in the early afternoon the next day. They agreed they would be very open about leaving the conference early...that morning.

"So, earlier you were telling me about the founders of the order. Whatever happened to them—Dryados and Talmun?"

David sat up and started to roll the window shut. "We are no longer in the Hedges," he said pointedly. "The Administration can monitor speech even in a moving vehicle, but not with the windows up and music vibrating the glass." The window glided slowly closed. The country music came back on. "Well…"

Chapter 2

A New Star

Dryados kicked the roan stallion hard in the flanks and leaned forward in the saddle. "Heyaah! Heyaah!" The horse raced down the road at a full gallop. The landscape flew past. It was almost sunrise. Dryados could see the road clearly now. He pitched the torch to the side of the road and leaned down closer to the horse's back. He glanced to his left. The angel was still there. The warm glow of the angel's presence enveloped both him and his horse. Beyond that layered barrier of angelic light raced an army of demon Black Voids. The angel's gaze was fixed straight ahead. They had to make it to the river.

As he leaned forward, Dryados could feel the heat of horse's neck against his own cheek. The horse's mouth was foaming. Dryados surged forward and back in the saddle in synchrony with the pounding of the horse's hooves. They were almost there. He glanced to the side. He could see a small smile growing on the angel's face. The angel was as miraculous to behold as all the other angels Dryados had seen. The only difference was the small crown he wore upon his brow. It was a delicate filigree of gleaming silver. At its center burned a small brilliant star. It modulated in color and brightness like a rainbow in a rainy breeze. The variations of the light spoke to Dryados as clearly as any voice. "I am Pergama!" it declared. It shined with all the hope and promise that the city embodied. For the angel beside him was an Ecclesia Custos, a church angel.

It was so light now. He remembered the warning the angel with the great chain had given him. "Dryados, you must be out of the lands of Pergama before sunrise." He ground his teeth. The sun's rays would soon touch him, and the church angel would be gone. And without the church angel, so also would go his provision of escape. "There!" he screamed. The river was just ahead. The angel had already seen it. "Heyaah! Heyaah!" Dryados flicked the reins frantically. The horse seemed to sense the urgency of the command and gave a final burst of speed. The Black Voids surrounding them buzzed like a nest of angry hornets. They too seemed to understand the end of the chase was now at hand. They slammed into the layered light of the angel's presence with peels of thunder. But the barrier of the angel's purview held. As the front hooves of the horse's feet crashed into the water, the Black Voids seemed to race into a separate tunnel of existence—and vanished.

The cool water cascaded up around Dryados and his horse as they careened into the river. Dryados sat back in the saddle and let go of the reins. The roan stallion instinctively slowed and then stopped in the center of the river. The horse lowered its head into the quiet flood and started guzzling up the water. The cool flow of the river caressed Dryados's cramping legs. He moaned a loud "aahhh" as the stress drained from his tight muscles. The angel walked in the water beside them, though the water did not seem to actually touch him. The angel's eyes slowly closed, and he stood motionless in the gentle current, obviously enjoying the feel of the water softly embracing his form. Dryados's fear washed away like a leaf on the surface of the stream.

The angel drifted slowly over to Dryados. A subtle gin blossomed on his face as he breathed in the cool morning air. "For now you should dwell in Philadelphia," he reiterated.

"Yes, but for how long?" Dryados asked in desperation.

"For as long as the season is upon you." There was a sense of sadness in the angel's voice.

"Can I ever return to Pergama?"

"No, you may not." He looked at Dryados with sympathetic eyes. "A great battle is rising up around you. The darkness tries to hide the path and turn humanity onto a wrong one. The Way must be lit and the battle fought to show the earth of a greater battle yet to come."

"But I am just a small-time merchant, and now, not even that."

"Yes, that is true." The angel seemed to sit down on the surface of the water. His eyes were filled with wonder. "But just like Gideon as he hid in a winepress or Mosses as he fled to the desert, you too have learned to hold The Sword and become part of its dance." A great smile erupted on the angel's face. "And anyone who can dance, can fight."

"I didn't fight. The Sword did."

"Exactly, but you carried the Sword where it needed to go."

"And when will this battle come?"

"It is unfolding around you now. Like Elijah in the cave, you too have been given a moment's respite. But even still, you must help the hidden king. You must come to see that which is right in front of your eyes. And finally, when the scepter is presented, you must say, 'Yes.'"

Dryados was tired and confused. "I'm not sure what…"

The angel walked slowly out of the water. He turned again, facing Dryados.

"Dwelling in Philadelphia is a journey, not a place. The River is not disturbed as it runs its course. Where many are buried, a gift and a purpose will be born." He smiled. "Your pure hearts will be rewarded."

"But…" Before he could finish, the angel was gone. Dryados sat on the exhausted horse staring…at nothing. He pulled the horse's head reluctantly up out of the water and urged it forward. He and the horse moved slowly through the cooling water toward the other bank. He steered the horse around some of the submerged rocks and patted the horse's still-warm neck.

As he glanced up at the other shore, Dryados sat up in his saddle. Waiting there on the other side of the river stood another angel. The angel's face was smiling and eager. His iridescent wings fluttered as though he were taking in the warmth of the glowing sun. Like the angel before him, he also wore a small filigree crown. The pulsing radiant star in its center, however, was completely different. It was a new star. It was the star of Thyatira. Its pulsing presence pronounced its glory like a horn of battle.

The angel waited patiently as Dryados and the exhausted horse approached. The splendor radiating from the angel was as invigorating as Alesia's smile. As Dryados and the reluctant horse drew closer, the angel began to stroke the horse's neck. The roan stallion whinnied and stood taller. The angel looked at Dryados. "I am here," he said softly. It was almost like a whisper. After a few moments, the angel turned and walked down the road. His spirit quickly faded into the distance, and then he too was gone.

Dryados nudged the horse forward. The stallion's gait seemed refreshed and eager. The road continued south, paralleling the river Lycus. Thyatira was only a few more miles. Farms quickly popped up around him. Houses grew closer together, and there was a steady increase in noise as he approached the city. Dryados paid no attention to any of it. He stared blankly as he rode. *The first angel says to live in Philadelphia,* he grumbled to himself. *I have no idea why. Makes no sense at all. And the second angel's instructions were…clear as mud. Yep, clear as mud. This is all just…* His mind was lost in a hundred different conflicting feelings and ideas. He stopped at the first inn he came to. A nice place called the Purple Ram. The building was clean, with elegant marble. The lobby inside boasted an extravagance of ornately carved and gilded wood. Dryados was too tired to worry about the cost.

"One silver and two copper dinars per night," announced the stout innkeeper. "The room comes with breakfast and dinner." It was a lot of money for a room. Dryados didn't care. He gave the innkeeper the money and asked for directions to the nearest livery. Then he trudged back outside to his waiting horse. As he untied the roan stallion, he noticed it was favoring one of its hind legs.

"Great!" Dryados muttered. He could barely keep his eyes open, and his backside was killing him. He moaned silently and plodded into the city, pulling the limping horse along. The city was not as big as Pergama, but even from a glance it was clear it was equally as wealthy, if not more so. Dryados trudged his way through the crowded streets.

One of the street merchants held up a beautifully tooled urn. "Alabaster vases." He grinned eagerly. "Thin as papyrus and translucent as a morning fog." The hawker placed a lit candle inside the vase, which began to glow like a night moon. The delicate image carved into its surface came instantly to life. It was absolutely fabulous, but Dryados was too tired to care. The crowds pushed against him. The smell of the cinnamon permeating the air was overwhelming. He bought a honey roll and plodded forward. He weaved his way through the throngs of people filling the streets. Soon he could hear the familiar banging of a blacksmith in the distance.

The banging grew louder, as did the usual smell of the smithy's forge. He entered a large square. The livery was on the other side just behind the smithy. He muddled his way through the many shoppers and then stood outside the livery by the rail fence and waited. He watched as the heavy armed smith worked the red-hot metal at his forge. The only interruption of the loud *bang, bang, bang* of his great hammer came from the steady whooshing of the bellows. A large barn was in the back, attached to a big corral filled with horses. He was quickly approached by two young workers. Dryados pointed them to the horse's hoof.

One apprentice took a cursory glance at the roan's leg. "Yes, the whole hoof work will need to be taken down and the shoe replaced with a new one. We will need to fit it exactly. Otherwise, the other three shoes will be out of balance."

"Yes," the second reiterated. "It will need to be replaced." He gave Dryados an examining look. It wasn't the kind of look to see if Dryados would agree to the work, but to see how much money he thought he could get out of him. It was the look of a crooked merchant.

Dryados reached for his horse.

"What's that you say?" bellowed a loud voice from near the forge.

"The shoe will need to be replaced and a new one smithed. Probably take two or three days to match the others," yelled back the older apprentice.

The smith clamored his way out of the cluttered smithy and walked over to join the others. "Hold there. Let me take a look at that." He wiped his hands on his leather apron as he approached. He was a bit taller than Dryados, but solidly built. His hair was coal black, and he had a tightly trimmed beard. He had the biggest arms Dryados had ever seen.

"Now let's just see what the problem is here." The smithy bent down and meticulously examined the horse's hoof. He grabbed the shoe and began pulling and twisting it back and forth. The horse whinnied and snorted. "There's a good horse," muttered the smith. Consternation crossed his face. "The shoe is fine." He looked up, shaking his head. "The nails are loose, and the inner flange is bent into the hoof." He took out a thin iron rod from inside his apron and slipped it beneath the shoe. His thick arms flexed even wider as he held the hoof and bent the metal. The stout smithy seemed to enjoy the momentary battle with the forged shoe before it bent back to normal.

"There. Now you boys hammer those loose nails tight and add two more on each side." He looked sternly at the two apprentices and then nodded for them to go.

The apprentices stood motionless for a moment.

"Now, be quick about it!" bellowed the smith. "We have plenty of orders to get filled today!" He rose to his feet and shot his apprentices a short-tempered gaze.

"That is completely against the guild rules, and you know it," muttered the older of the two. "The rules specifically say—"

"Yes, yes, yes," growled the big smith. "The guild says this. The guild says that. And I say, get the shoe hammered on. Now!"

The two young men glanced at each other for an instant and then quickly led the horse over to the barn. The older apprentice looked back over his shoulder. "I'm going to bring this up to the guild at our next meeting, Ascalon, and you're already in enough trouble with them as it is." He continued to grumble as he jerked the horse across the yard.

Ascalon turned back toward Dryados. "Good apprentices, just got their heads on a little crooked when it comes to things like hard work, is all. Now, that'll be three copper dinars. They'll bring the horse out over there when they are done." The thick-armed smithy pointed to an area over to the side of the corral.

Dryados handed the smithy the coin. He hesitated for a moment. "I'm sorry, but I'm really not even sure how long I'm going to be here in Thyatira. Would it be possible for me to board the horse with you until I depart?"

Arrangements were quickly made to board the animal. Dryados paid Ascalon another ten copper dinars to cover up to three days of boarding. With the horse finally situated, he trekked slowly back to the Purple Ram. He was up the stairs and asleep in bed before his feet were actually off the floor.

Dryados woke up several hours later. His headache was gone, and he felt at least somewhat rested. He went downstairs and was surprised to find his men had still not arrived. It was getting late. He hoped they would make it into the city before the gates closed. Still, he felt refreshed and decided to go out and explore the town. He also desperately hoped to make contact with the local Iredenti. The fatigue his body still felt was overwhelmed by the excitement bursting inside him. He had seen angels! And Black Voids! And Shards of Light! He had been in the River! He needed to tell someone, everyone!

He walked the heavily trafficked Cardia to the city's agora. There was more shoving and jostling as he pushed his way through the great throng. Hawkers yelled their wares. The enticing aromas of roasting chicken and lamb pulled at his mind. His fatigue, however, commanded that he mainly focus on hot tea. The roasted dove and pomegranate jelly he ate were just to liven up the beverage. He scanned the streets. He wasn't even sure what he was looking for. As he walked among the crowds, he noticed a vague inscription lightly chiseled into the stone of the road. It looked as though some kids had scratched it there to play a game. But no, he had heard of this. It was an eight-spoked wheel, and it was Iredenti.

He purchased a snack of bacon-wrapped peppers and smoked fish from a passing street vendor. It was a beautiful afternoon, and there were crowds of people just sitting in the sun, enjoying the day. He sat down by the subtle inscription and quickly became just one more. After downing the smoked fish, he decided that just sitting there might be interpreted as simply coincidence by other Iredenti. He bent down and scraped up some dirt from the road and placed it on the stone wall beside him. He looked around. There were no Romans. He drew the eight-spoked wheel in the sand. He could quickly wipe it away if any Romans approached. It was as much of a risk as he dared take. He sat there picking his nails. *This is really stupid*, he thought. He got up and took several steps away and then turned and sat back down. Soon he fell into his own nervous routine—he picked at his nails, stood and stretched, sat back down, recited some verses Gaius, his Iredenti friend in Pergama, had shared, and then ran through different scenarios in his mind on how the Romans would kill him. Soon he was back picking at his nails, and the cycle started over again. Time passed slowly. Throngs of people hurried by, but none took any notice. He drank more tea. Ate some more of those delicious bacon-pepper things. And just watched the people. Hours passed, and the sun began to sink on the horizon.

Dryados noticed a young man who had passed by him several times. The young man now stood looking at him some distance away. During a furtive glance, they made brief eye contact. Dryados turned away and picked at his nails. The young man remained motionless for a moment and then approached.

"Hello, I don't think I know you, but you look familiar," the man said. He glanced at the symbol in the sand and then back at Dryados.

"No, I'm new to Thyatira. I arrived just this morning from Pergama." Dryados glanced at the symbol in the sand and then back at the young man.

"I see," the young man responded. There were several seconds of uncomfortable silence.

Dryados wiped away the symbol in the sand. "You see, well, I was lost, but now, well, I guess I'm found."

The young stranger smiled and started tapping his foot. Dryados looked down. The man's foot was right by the symbol etched into the stone. The symbol was almost invisible in the fading light. But both men knew it was there. "Perhaps you would like to walk with me, to see Thyatira?" the young man asked.

Dryados was terrified. He looked up nervously at the young man, "Yes, of course."

The two men walked nervously down the Cardia. The shops were starting to close for the evening. Dryados glanced frequently at the young man. His mind whirled. *Is he a Roman spy? Is he taking me somewhere to rob me or kill me?* Dryados panicked. He stopped in the road and turned frantically at the young man. "Oh please, I hope you are not a Roman spy. But I am Iredenti. There, I've said it. Yes, I am Iredenti." Dryados looked at the young stranger with expectant terror.

The look on the young man's face was hard for Dryados to figure out. It was either the look of a man about to kill him or the unrestrained look of youthful shock. Fortunately for Dryados, it was the latter.

"Oh...well, good...yes..." the young man stammered. "But let's not talk about that here." There were still many people scattered about the busy Cardia. He led them farther down the road and off onto one of side streets. Soon they were away from the diminishing crowds and alone in a quiet residential area. The young escort scanned the street again and then spoke. "My name is Barda, and I too am Iredenti. There are others of us here in the city." Barda was very nonspecific. He suggested that he would meet Dryados at the Purple Ram the following night and then take him to meet some of the others.

"I am hopeful that the men traveling with me will arrive in the morning. They are all Iredenti. May they come as well?" Dryados asked.

"No." The young man shook his head. He glanced cautiously around the street. "We are slow to welcome strangers, and a group of new people will cause panic among the others. Tomorrow it must just be you."

"I understand."

"Tomorrow then." And with that, the men parted ways. Dryados headed back to the Purple Ram. Barda disappeared into the darkness.

Dryados lay in his bed. His mind spun in a hundred different directions. Alesia, Talmun, Ivoluntas, leaving Pergama, and on it went. The morning had come hours before. He eventually crawled out of bed and went down stairs for breakfast. He picked slowly at his meal. The same thought ruminated over and over inside his head. *I have lost everything.* The hard-boiled pickled eggs had been peppered and were just spicy enough to help wake him up. The bread was fresh and the butter soft. He had seconds, then thirds. He played with some stray green olives as they rolled around on his plate. The innkeeper whipped his table again and gave him a sour look. Dryados decided it was time to go outside. He stood at the front of the Purple Ram and looked out at the streets crowded with people. He recognized none of the faces. Still it looked like any other of the great cities. The people rushed noisily about doing the ordinary tasks of daily living. He decided to go out and do some more exploring.

Thyatira was smaller than Pergama, but the trappings of wealth were evident everywhere. The buildings and temples were elegant marble. The streets were spotless. The citizens were well dressed. Purple was the color of the town. Textile merchants stood on every corner. There were entire streets that appeared to be cut from the same purple cloth. As he explored the shops, Dryados spotted a beautifully cut woman's tunic. The purple color was rich and deep. The textile tightly woven and soft. Alesia—his lovely betrothed, still in Pergama—would love it.

The merchant at the shop had a friendly smile. "Twenty-five silver dinar," he replied. Then he launched into the expected sales pitch about the quality of the cloth, the color, the texture, and so on. But the price was ludicrous.

Dryados was still tired and feeling a little punchy. "Five," he responded. "You do know the value of silver is going up. Mining problems in Macedonia, I think." Dryados continued to babble on about the need for mining regulation and improved underground ventilation. The merchant quickly realized Dryados was merely being cynical. The man's friendly smile returned. He seemed to bond with Dryados instantly.

"Twenty-two—any woman would love such a magnificent garment."

"Eight."

"Twenty. It is the finest weave that can be made."

"Ten."

"Eighteen, and the color is vibrant."

"Eleven." And that was really as high as Dryados wanted to go.

"Fourteen, and that is the guild price. It is the lowest price I can give you." The merchant held up the garment, waving it in the bright sunlight to catch the color. It was stunning.

Dryados shook his head. "That is just way too expensive." He looked at the merchant with honest disappointment. The merchant continued to smile. Then an idea crossed Dryados's mind. *Perhaps I could sell them in Pergama.* He looked back at the salesman. "What if I bought five of them, and I would go to eleven, with three copper dinars each. What would you say to that?" That was a lot of coin for a tunic.

"Sir, I'm afraid it wouldn't matter if you ordered a hundred of them. That is the guild price. Honestly, fourteen is the best I can do."

"That doesn't make any sense." Dryados moaned in frustration. "Clearly there is far more money to be made selling a hundred of them at twelve than there is to sell one at fourteen. Surely this is basic math."

"That is why they are only sold here in Thyatira." The merchant seemed an honest man and truly disappointed in what he was saying.

Dryados stared at the purple tunic. It truly was spectacular. Alesia would love it. He begrudgingly paid the fourteen silver dinars and continued on. He was sure he had just paid the ransom for some captured king somewhere. But it was for Alesia. Out of curiosity, he approached other garment merchants at the agora and haggled the price for similar tunics. The results were always the same. The guild price for a purple woman's tunic was fourteen silver dinars, and that was that.

He bought some mint tea and spiced lamb from one of the many street vendors and slowly walked back to the Purple Ram. As he rounded the corner, he recognized several men milling around outside Inn. Dryados stopped and counted his scattered escorts. Then he counted them again to be sure. There were only seven. Five were missing.

"We couldn't go a hundred yards without losing a horse or rider," Lassus explained. "Even with torches. Even with the men dismounted. It didn't matter. The horses were frantic." He shook his head. "So we ended up walking all night. The darkness was unnatural. Then at sunrise, everything seemed to change. A couple hours later we got up the courage to get back on the horses and try to ride. Even then we didn't go much faster than a quick walk, for fear of calamity. But the rest of the journey passed without incident, and we arrived here just a few moments ago." Lassus glanced up toward the inn. "The innkeeper here said a man of your description arrived yesterday, so we were planning to just settle in and wait."

The men's faces all had that cheerful look of having finished a hard journey, mixed with the fatigued look of having completed the same experience. "We will be spending the night here," Dryados said encouragingly. "Have the men livery the horses and grab some food." Dryados gave them directions to the livery run by the big smithy and how to get to the main agora. "I'm going to lay back down for a while and take a nap. I will meet you all later here at the inn for dinner."

Back in his room, the call of sleep quickly claimed victory. He stirred a little as he heard the clamor of the men coming up the stairs to their rooms. Otherwise, he slept soundly.

Bang, bang, bang. Dryados lurched up in bed. "Dinner!" the innkeeper announced from the other side of the door. Dryados sank back into the refuge of his covers. He heard the innkeeper pound on all the other doors, making the same proclamation, and then plod back down the stairs.

A few minutes later Dryados dragged himself out of bed and went down for dinner. The men looked more refreshed and were cheerfully enjoying their evening meal of roasted fish. Dryados told them of his upcoming meeting with the local Iredenti and his need to go alone. The men understood. Some of the older men were planning on going back to their rooms and sleeping. The younger ones wanted to go out and see as much of the city as they could. As the plans were being discussed, Dryados noticed a nervous young man glancing into the hall.

"Excuse me." Dryados pushed back his chair and stood up. "I think I will be going out for that walk I mentioned." He smiled at his men and turned to go.

The young man slipped back out the door as soon as Dryados stood up. The two men met outside on the darkening street and began their journey. Barda spoke very little, but his eyes never stopped moving. He wove them in and out of the alleys. At every intersection, he would stop and search cautiously for soldiers and then motion Dryados forward. They worked their way through the city to an exclusive neighborhood of large residences. There were no Romans. They came to a palatial home with a large white wall surrounding it. Outside the entrance were two large men with matching house armor. They looked at the advancing pair like two snakes assessing some distracted field mice. The swords at their sides looked well used. Barda moved courageously forward. Dryados hesitated but followed cautiously several feet behind. His eyes remained focused on the swords and the guards' hands. One guard reached backward…and casually opened the door.

Barda nodded at each of the huge armed men as he passed and marched boldly in. He led Dryados on an unescorted tour through the home. "Our prophetess always meets with us in the Grand Receiving Hall," he said, smiling. They walked down a wide corridor leading outside to a large garden courtyard. Just past a corner sitting area they curved back around and came to the great hall. It stood as a sanctuary enclosed on both sides by a dozen thick, large marble columns. The columns were covered with flowering vines that climbed up to the high ceiling, which was painted with a luxurious fresco of playing nymphs. The floor itself had a sky-like quality in an elegant brocade marble of light gray and blue. The whole effect was like turning the world upside down. Scattered around the hall was a squad of young men serving refreshments. Dryados could see perhaps forty guests milling about, but the room could have held several times that number. At the far end of the hall rose an elevated dais. To its right Dryados could see two sets of stairs. One set went up, the other down.

Barda ushered him into the noisy hall and began a series of introductions. Everyone was friendly and eager to chat. As the men grabbed some cheese and wine from one of the servants, a chime sounded. The room quickly quieted. A woman made her way out of the crowd at the front and sat down on the dais. Even from a distance Dryados was taken by her attractive features. She was…voluptuous. She wore a fine elegant blue tunic, which covered her modestly, while the small belt she wore high on her waist declared her womanly figure. Her hair was long, shiny black, and flowing. The silver pin she wore in her hair was wide with inlaid garnet. It shone in harmony with her raven locks. Moments later an older man also made his way out of the crowd. He wore a modest workman's garb but had a wide smile and friendly face. He sat down beside the prophetess and motioned for the guests to sit. The other Iredenti in the room quickly drew closer and seated themselves near the dais.

Barda motioned smilingly toward the dais. "She is our prophetess, Jezebel. The older man beside her is our teaching elder. His name is Jakotrudi. He was discipled by John in Ephesus. He still gets letters from him sometimes."

Jakotrudi rose and began to speak. "A hammer is not a hammer until it is used. It can be used to pound a nail or to break a chain or forge a shield. It can be used for many things. This is true with every tool. Until it is used, it is just an object of odd shape or form. Only in its use does its purpose and nature become evident. You are the tools of the One who made you." He got up and walked closer to the crowd. "A man can claim to be a fruit tree, but until he bears fruit, he is a liar." He looked questioning at those in the crowd. The guests seated before him did not speak. "Yet I tell you, I rejoice every day—for I have seen many of you blossom and bear a great harvest!" Jakotrudi's face glowed as he spoke of the things he had witnessed, the fruits of his fellowship. "I have seen widows, orphans, and strangers blessed. I have seen alms given to the poor, words of hope shared with the dying, and great courage shown to even speak the truth. The candle is lit, and the darkness flees."

He spoke for some time longer and then sat down. Those in the crowd began to ask questions. The prophetess remained silent on the dais. One man in the crowd asked, "I have walked the road with the path lit at my feet, yet temptation still calls me, and I am torn to go with it."

"The desire to submit to temptation arises first of the mind. The body goes where the spirit leads. You hear what—" Jakotrudi began.

"Yes," interrupted the prophetess. "The body serves its own desires. The spirit can remain pure even if the lust of the body demands to be answered." She rose and walked out into the crowd with a look of concern. She gently held the arm of the man who asked the question. "Your soul can remain pure even if your body forces it to an undesirable place. Prayer and fasting will keep the spirit pure and allow the body its natural failings and tendencies. Such things are below and separate from the redeemed spirit."

Dryados was confused.

Jezebel smiled and walked among the people as she continued to speak. She was a congenial host and always seemed to have her hand on someone's arm or shoulder, giving a motherly touch. "Your body is the temple to a clean and redeemed soul. But the body itself is separate and fallen. Its passions only allow damage when we allow them to impact our spirit. Discipline the soul to keep these separate so that you are pure no matter what the passions of the flesh demand it to do."

The young man who asked the question earlier seemed relieved by her words.

Jakotrudi raised his head. "We are the temple of the spirit. But it is important to ask—do the walls rule the spirit, or does the spirit rule the walls?" He smiled fatherly at the young man.

The prophetess sighed loudly and walked back to the dais. She looked at the crowd. "Some spiritual mysteries are hard to grasp in a physical world. I think it is enough for one night. Let us enjoy some time of fellowship. I will be happy to talk with you individually if you would have questions." Before Jakotrudi could say a word, the chimes sounded again.

The party atmosphere quickly resumed. Dryados and Barda socialized around the room. Barda introduced Dryados to his friends. More refreshments were served. The musicians began to play. Barda pulled Dryados by the arm. "Here, I want to introduce you to my uncle." The two men approached a group of people talking near the front of the room.

"Uncle…" Barda touched a large stocky man on the shoulder. The man turned.

"Ascalon?" Dryados questioned. The stocky blacksmith was almost unrecognizable, completely washed and dressed in a white tunic. The smithy looked equally surprised. "Master Dryados?"

"Just Dryados." Dryados laughed. He shook his head in shocked disbelief. "It is so good to see a familiar face." The two men were quickly engaged in conversation.

"Most of the work at the shop is pretty much your standard smithing—horseshoes, farming equipment, wagon repair, and the like. We also get lots of orders for weaponry, of course." His smile grew as he spoke. "Holding my hammer is like holding my wife's hand."

"Well, I will promise not to tell her that," Dryados said, smiling.

Barda apologetically interrupted. "Uncle, I am sorry, but I would really like to introduce Dryados to Jakotrudi before it gets too late." The men politely excused themselves. "Uncle Ascalon can be a bit of a talker." Barda laughed.

They made their way to the front of the hall, where several young men surrounded the prophetess. Jakotrudi was busy nearby with a mixed group of people. He had a warm smile and a passion for people that was evident even across the room. He seemed to know everyone's name and who each was as a person. The glistening in the people's eyes and smiles on their faces made it clear that the members of his fellowship also loved him. As Barda and Dryados drew closer, they were stopped by several more of Barda's friends. Dryados never got the chance to speak to Jakotrudi or the prophetess.

It was late by the time Dryados got back to the Purple Ram and dragged himself up the stairs. What little sleep he had garnered over the last several days made no dent in his fatigue. He closed the door to his room, threw his tunic on the floor, and flopped onto his very comfortable bed. But sleep did not come. The events of Pergama replayed over and over in his mind. He stared at the ceiling. Regrets, loss, and questions danced in a giant frolicking circle in his brain. He rubbed his burning eyes. He needed to sleep. Still, his past brought only thoughts of sorrow, and his future...was blank. He flipped over and over in bed and hid under the covers. Nothing helped. He got up and lit the lamp. He pulled some of his parchment from his satchel and wrote letters to Alesia, Talmun—his closest friend and business partner—and Gaius, a friend and mentor. They remained in Pergama. Then he went back to bed. He stared at the ceiling. He wrapped himself snugly in his covers and then took them off again. After about another hour, he got back up and also wrote a letter to Titus, his future father-in-law.

"Wake up, little princess." The joking laughter at the door told him he had overslept again. He was quickly dressed, packed, and downstairs eating breakfast with his men.

"Tonight we will camp near Sardis. The following day we will press on to Philadelphia...my future home." His forced smile was unconvincing. His men were refreshed and ready to go. Dryados dispatched one of his men to ride back to Pergama and deliver the letters. With the letter to Alesia, he would also deliver the purple tunic, a bouquet of rosebuds, and...his love.

They camped just north of Sardis by the river. Some of the men wanted to venture into the city. "I have seen plenty of big cities before," Dryados told his men. "I will stay here and guard the camp. We will leave as soon as we have eaten in the morning, so I suggest you make it back tonight." The other men left for the city. Dryados sat by the river and caught up on his journal. It reminded him of a place by a river he and Talmun had stopped years ago. He watched the water drift slowly past. He stared at the trees and the birds. "Why do I have to live in Philadelphia? Why can't I stay Pergama? Why can't I..." And so the evening passed.

Chapter 3
Rude Awakening

Dryados looked up at the inside of his tent. He actually felt rested. The sun was up. No one else in the camp seemed to be in any hurry to get out of bed either. The air was crisp. He snuggled in his blanket.

"Unclean, unclean." The yell filled the camp. The warning cry was quickly echoed by Temarius, who was standing watch. "Unclean! Unclean!" He sounded frantic. The clamor of men grabbing their weapons and jumping out of their tents exploded around him. Dryados scrambled to find his sword. Then he remembered he had left it packed with the horses. He jumped out of the tent and raced toward his roan stallion. The other men had already gathered at the center of the camp by the fire. Their swords were drawn. Temarius had his bow out with an arrow nocked in place. The men stood gazing up the river. On the riverbank about a hundred yards away was a group of lepers.

Their leader stood in front and continued to call out the requisite warning, "Unclean, unclean."

The lepers had already stopped along the riverbank. Some were already in the river bathing. Others were just beginning to disrobe. Some did their laundry.

Dryados stopped and walked back toward the center of camp. He motioned for his men to lower their weapons. "Mitesco, you and the others wait here. Temarius, you are with me." Dryados walked closer to the diseased monsters. Temarius followed nervously just a few feet behind. They walked silently like two men stalking an angry bear. As they got closer, Dryados cupped his hands to his mouth and yelled, "Do not approach any closer to the camp!"

One of the lepers moved toward them. "We are unclean. We mean you no harm. I shouted the warning as soon as I saw the camp. We only wish to bathe ourselves, and then we will be on our way. We are unclean," he yelled back.

Dryados had seen lepers before. He knew they were safe to approach but not to come in contact with. Their leader seemed to appreciate Dryados's understanding and walked closer.

"Hold fast!" Temarius screamed. "One more step and I promise you I will loose this arrow straight into your demon chest!" His bow was up and the arrow shaking as he strained against the pulled string. He had taken several fearful steps backward.

The leper froze and then began to edge slowly away.

"Put that arrow down before you put out an eye! We are safe, and he means us no harm," Dryados scolded. Temarius looked angrily at Dryados but lowered the bow. He kept the arrow nocked and the string tight.

Dryados motioned for Temarius to remain calm. "Just relax. Everything is going to be fine. I can handle this." He glanced back at the men by the campfire, still holding their swords. He flashed a confident smile at Temarius. "Just head back to camp. We don't want to panic the lepers, and the men will feel more at ease with you back by their sides with your bow."

Temarius glared at the leper and then stormed back to his gathered comrades.

Dryados edged slowly forward. The leper did not move. Dryados glanced at the lepers in the river. What he saw made him physically nauseated. Disrobed, their bodies were hideous and distorted. There was no gentle way to frame the living death this disease embodied to its poor victims. Yet, they washed themselves and played in the river. What they wore was little more than rags. A woman sang as she did her laundry. Several of them were obviously blind. There were probably twenty-five or thirty in the group.

Dryados stalked closer and then stopped. The leper leader was still some distance away but bowed graciously. "I am Decima Pratti," he said softly. His voice was young. He kept his face hidden in the hood of his tunic. What Dryados could see of his one hand appeared pale but normal. He was probably early in the disease. "I gave the required warning as soon as I saw you. Your presence took the others by surprise. Our colony bathes here daily, and there are rarely travelers along this section of the river."

Dryados was growing quickly more anxious as he looked at the putrid frames of the unclothed lepers. "My name is Dryados. My men and I will be leaving in a short time." He glanced back at his escorts. The men were gathered by the fire with their swords drawn. Temarius still held his bow with the arrow nocked. Dryados smiled at the leper. "It would be better if perhaps you came back later, after we have gone." Dryados's eyes were pulled back to the lepers in the river. It was odd that his eyes would be drawn to look at their hideous form. *Morbid curiosity*, he thought. He looked back at their leader. "When we depart, I will have my men leave you some supplies." Dryados glanced around. There was a hollow log not far away. "We will conceal them there, within the hollow." He looked back and forth between his panicked men and the bathing lepers. "It might be best if you could hurry your people along. I think—"

"We are accustomed to staying away from the living. I will have my people move off into the hills. We will not return until after you have departed." The leper bowed again and moved off slowly toward his group. As Dryados looked toward the river, he noticed three or four in the colony appeared to be children.

Dryados returned to his camp. The men stood by the fire with their jaws clenched and faces ready for battle. They held their swords tightly. "Put those things away! It's just a bunch of lepers. They'll be moving along in just a few minutes. Let's eat and get going."

"Who could eat after looking at that? They are an abomination!" one man muttered as he spit on the ground. He sheathed his sword and walked back to his tent.

"Fine. More food for the rest of us," Dryados said cheerfully. He was hungry. The meal was quickly prepared. The smell of spiced goat sausage and the crackling warmth of the fire soon drew the other men back out of their tents. Though the men ate heartily, they spoke little. Every eye seemed fixed on the retreating leprous monsters. The men sipped their tea and munched on assorted dried fruit, nuts, and dried bread. Dryados noticed whenever one had a free hand, it would slip instinctively to his sword.

The morning chill continued to hold the men by the fire. The lepers moved on, and the men's spirits were quickly restored. Soon a new sound of clamor filled the camp as the men took down their tents and packed for the journey ahead. Dryados hid some supplies for the lepers in the hollow of the fallen tree, just as he had promised. As he placed the gifts inside the log, he thought of their disrobed bodies. He was generous with what he left. Most people would not buy or sell with the lepers for fear they would catch the disease. It was not uncommon for lepers to simply be killed and their bodies left to rot. People would not want to come near enough to even bury them or burn the bodies.

Chapter 4
Caravanserai

Dryados and his group rode on with their weapons at hand. The section of road they traveled today to Philadelphia was part of both the Royal Road and the Post Road. It was wide and well traveled. Roman security was tight, with frequent patrols and watch posts. Still, each encounter on the road aroused a great deal of anxiety. Robbers often disguised themselves as fellow travelers, which allowed them to get close before they attacked. They usually killed those they robbed and simply put the ill-gotten belongings in with their own. Dryados's men had their hands on their weapons any time they passed someone. Those they passed could be counted on to maintain a similar tense posture.

The valley itself grew wider as they trekked south. They occasionally caught sight of the snow-covered peaks of Mount Tmolus almost straight ahead in the distance. They passed grape vineyards with local merchants trying to sell wine to the many travelers. Occasionally one or two of the men would stop, purchase a small bottle, and then race to catch up with the others. They also encountered many Roman watch posts as they pressed on. The Roman soldiers rarely spoke but could be counted on to give their typical threatening scowl. Most of the watch posts were fairly small, perhaps a dozen soldiers. Some, however, were much larger with upward of thirty or forty men. The larger ones usually had their own "Garden of the Dead"—criminals the Romans had captured would be impaled on wooden spikes and placed in rows like a field of corn. The crop was a silent reminder of Roman intolerance for those who broke the law. Occasionally Dryados and his escorts passed a stalk of corn that was still alive. Between the Romans and the threat of bandits, the men did little talking.

Philadelphia itself sat on a hill about eight hundred feet above the river Cogamus. As they rode up the hill, they paused frequently to take in the view of the wide valley below. The locals called the area "Katakekaumene," the Burned Land. The land was made of rich black volcanic soil, with abundant water. From their vantage point on the hill they could see the prosperity of the region. They gazed out at countless fields of worked grain and vast vineyards. Strangely, its most renowned product was the *rasen soldani*, or the sultana raisin. They were not black like other raisins, but golden. For generations they had been reserved only for the sultans, hence the name. Now they were available to everyone.

As they rounded the final corner up the hill, Vodica brought the group to a halt. The city spread out in the foothills in front of them. The white Acropolis stood higher up the mountain behind the city. The ruggedness of the foothills and gray stone of the mountain accentuated the sharp smoothness of the buildings and whiteness of the marble temples. The ruggedness of the land here was different than that of Pergama. Still, Dryados found it stunning. Yet what caught his eye the most was a bulwarked fortress just outside the city wall. It was four stories tall with thick walls and high corner towers. Like all caravanserai, it had an array of battle ports all along its top and only one way in or out.

Vodica waited until all the men had gathered close beside him. "The rules of the caravanserai are the same throughout the empire. The gates open at sunrise and close at sunset. No exceptions. If you are late in your arrival, or want to leave early, it will not matter. The gates are never opened at night." He turned his head, looking sternly at the men. "As we approach, security will be very tight. Do exactly as you are told, or they will kill you where you stand." He looked slowly around the group, meeting each man's gaze to make sure everyone understood and would heed his warning. After an affirming nod from each, he kicked his horse forward. "OK, slowly, slowly."

Dryados had been to a caravanserai before on a business trip with his father. They were as secure as the strongest Roman garrison and located exactly one day's travel from each other across the entire length of the Royal Road from Sardis to Susa, a distance of over sixteen hundred miles. They had been built by the Persians, connecting the markets of the East to the rest of the world. Because they were so critical for trade, any violation of caravanserai law, trust, or protocols was met by death. They were totally secure and completely trustworthy. A fact Dryados was counting on.

At the first of the caravanserai's outer markers stood a large squad of men. All had their swords drawn or spears in hand. "You will dismount your horses and walk in from here. If you so much as touch your weapons, we will kill you." The squad leader raised his sword high above his head and motioned the blade toward the caravanserai. Dryados could also see the archers in the high towers raise their bows with arrows nocked and ready. The squad leader stood gripping the sword above his head like a man at the hippodrome with a flag getting ready to start a race. It was clear if he lowered his arm, the archers would loose their arrows, and his men would attack. For a moment no one even breathed, and then the men dismounted their horses. The squad leader circled his sword above his head before slowly lowering the blade. As Dryados's men stood beside their horses, they were quickly engulfed in armed men. The guards were abrupt.

"No, we are originally from Pergama… No, we spent the night in Thyatira and then Sardis. No, we have never been to Assyria. Dryados is a citizen… That is for self-defense… Yes, these are the only weapons we have… Those products are for a store I am planning to open…" They were questioned extensively. All their goods were thoroughly searched. Once assured they were not a raiding party or other security risk, they were allowed to continue to the other checkpoints. Each of the remaining checkpoints served a different purpose—shipping inventories, tax regulations. At the final checkpoint, they were assigned an area to sleep and a place to secure their horses. Once inside the men settled in to their assigned spot. Dryados went to find the caravanserai manager. He quickly made arrangements to rent a space to store his goods until he could get his business up and running in the city. The men unpacked the horses and stored all of Dryados's merchandise in the secured storage area.

After a brief discussion the men decided to rush out and try to see the city before the caravanserai closed. Most had never been this far south and probably never would be again.

"Remember what Vodica said," Dryados cautioned. "They secure the gate at sunset, no exceptions."

Vodica threw his bedroll onto some hay and looked up. "Not to worry," he said with a big grin. "I too will be going with them. I have not come so far to return home and tell my family that I did not even walk the streets of Philadelphia." He shook his head. "No, that would not be good. Still, we will be back before the gate closes."

"Well, I will probably be living here the rest of my life, so I am in no hurry." There was a sense of defeat in his tone. "There are also some letters I would like to write for you men to take back with you when you leave in the morning."

The men hurried out the great gate at the front. Dryados found a nice spot in the sun and began to write. Caravans from the East were arriving almost every hour. Wagon masters were barking orders to their men. Small cooking fires sprang up all around him like shoots of grass. He had never seen so many loud, snorting camels. The place was a kaleidoscope of smells and colors and languages. It was all just too alluring. Dryados sighed and folded up his journal. He made his way eagerly among the caravans, snooping to discover he hidden treasures they might be carrying. His heart beat faster, and the excitement in his spirit grew with each merchant he passed. There were products from all around the empire and places he had never even heard of. And all of it was expensive. Caravans did not travel hundreds of miles with simple pots or basic foodstuffs. This was the cream of the crop of retail.

As a merchant himself, he was pretty comfortable talking to just about anyone.

He engaged in conversations with traders from all over empire. There were people from as far away as Assyria and even beyond. There were many Parthians. Few spoke Greek and none Latin.

As he ventured around, Dryados came across a caravan with bright flags and dark-skinned people from beyond the Indus River. Such caravans were very rare. The merchants among it spoke no recognizable language. Despite that, Dryados had somehow gotten himself engaged in trade negotiations. He wasn't even sure exactly how it happened. He had noticed the merchants moving a large package of saffron. Dryados knew its value and had simply pointed at the package and smiled. The chief merchant immediately held up two such packages in one hand and ten silver dinars in the other. Perhaps the Indus trader was short on cash or simply did not know their local value, but that was an incredible bargain. Dryados knew he could get at least ten times that amount. But he had not come to buy saffron. He smiled and waved to the merchant and started to walk along. The Indus trader waved, shaking his head no, and removed two of the silver dinars. Dryados stopped. The price was ridiculous—eight silver dinars for that much saffron! *The saffron must be tainted*, he thought. *Then again...* Dryados motioned to see if he could open the bag. The merchant indicated it was OK and opened the bag for him to inspect. Dryados sifted through it. *Pure! Absolutely pure saffron!* Dryados's mind raced. A hundred different scenarios played out in his thoughts. The Indus trader clearly could see Dryados's mind churning. While Dryados stood there, the trader motioned for his men to bring out more bags of saffron.

Dryados pointed to three bags, then gave the man a questioning look.

The man flashed his hands—10, no, 12 fingers. Then pointed to a piece of silver. Twelve silver dinars.

Dryados and the man stood there flashing fingers at each other, 12-10-12-10-12-10, then Dryados finally flashed 11. The Indus man smiled. It was agreed.

As the man moved toward the bags, Dryados stopped him and pointed to the three remaining bags. A total of six large bags. Again their fingers flashed, 20-22-20-22-20-22-20. The Indus man flashed 21. Dryados's fingers echoed the number. It was agreed. The two men smiled broadly. Both were happy with the sale and equally amused they had completed the deal without speaking a word. *Money, math, business, and people*, Dryados thought. *They're all the same wherever you go.*

Dryados pointed toward where he and his men were stationed in the caravanserai and motioned that he would be right back with the money. The Indus man smiled, nodding his head in understanding. As he turned, Dryados noticed the glowing lamps now filling the caravanserai. It was after sunset. He hoped his men returned in time.

He worked his way back through the lumbering camels and crowded wagons to where he and his men had been assigned to camp. As he approached, he could see his men already had a small cooking fire going. The saffron was quickly paid for and secured. Dryados would keep two bags to sell locally and send the other four bags to Talmun in Pergama. Talmun could sell them at the Upper Agora for an even greater profit. His escorts cooked some rabbits they had purchased on spits over the fire and spoke of their adventure in Philadelphia. The clamor in the caravanserai slowly died down to a low roar. When Dryados and his men finally laid down to sleep, they slept hard.

Braying mules and snorting camels served as the men's wake-up call. Most of the caravans packed up quietly in the dark. Once packed, they formed an orderly line down the center of the caravanserai to leave. At sunrise the huge sealed gates of the caravanserai were opened. Caravan masters barked orders, reluctant animals heard the crack of whips, and an armada of wagons leaped forward. Dryados's men rode out an hour or so later. Dryados stood alone at the gate, watching his only connection to his past leave without him. As the last smiling face turned away and kicked his horse, Dryados's heart dropped. He was truly alone.

Dryados did not know the city, its people, or the local customs. Philadelphia was not his home. He rented a room at a shabby inn just inside the city gate and tried to just get oriented. He learned the layout of the city. Where the agora was located. How to find the nearest public toilet. Where to buy food. Each day became just a collection of tedious hours away from everyone he loved. He spent much of his time in his room. After a few days of staring at the ceiling, he decided it was better to be exhausted than lonely.

The next day he got up and negotiated to rent a large stall at the city's main agora. He quickly had his business up and running. He set up his tables and organized his wares each morning. He was the first merchant to open his shop and the last to close. He adjusted his lines of merchandise, he networked with local merchants, he smiled, he talked, he traded, and he worked and worked and worked. In the midst of all that, he managed to rent a room at a nicer inn called the Open Hand. The food there was better. The bed was cleaner. And there were several friendly taverns located nearby. Each night he returned to his room completely spent and stared at the ceiling. Several weeks later he cut a deal with another merchant to acquire the adjacent stall at the agora and expanded the shop. He added copper and silver bracelets, earrings, and necklaces. He displayed a shipment of intricately carved ivory from southern Egypt. And expanded the line of parchment, paints, and bright-colored inks from Talmun in Pergama. Soon after that, he stopped going to the taverns. There simply wasn't enough time in the day. But each night he returned to his room and stared at the ceiling. Then it hit him. He had made a terrible, terrible mistake. He suddenly realized, *You can actually be completely exhausted and still horribly lonely!*

Each day he ate his noon meal alone just outside the main entrance to the agora. Each day he would draw the eight-spoked wheel in the sand. And each day no one noticed. He was too busy to make friends, and he had been unable to find Cleopas, the Roman centurion that Aeolis, the Iredenti Roman captain in Pergama, had mentioned.

Disappointed, he finished his noon meal and returned to his shop as he always did. His sales steadily trickled in the rest of the afternoon. It was getting later in the day when a little waif of a girl approached the shop. She was about eight. At first Dryados took her for one of the many street orphans. She was a scrawny child with no shoes, but she was clean and so were her clothes. She had gangling arms but a sweet face. She walked nervously into the shop.

"I would like to see something," the young girl pronounced.

"What would you like to see?" Dryados asked as he leaned over the counter.

The girl looked around. "Some string."

"I don't sell string."

The girl looked around the shop. "Maybe a candlewick or some yarn or… something like that."

"I'm sorry, but I don't sell any of those things either," Dryados said, sounding disappointed. The little girl was the cutest thing he had ever seen. He could tell she was trying very hard to be brave in the big shop.

"Fine," she said. Then she paused looking around. "OK, just watch my finger." Then she stood on her tiptoes and placed her finger onto the counter. Slowly she traced out the eight-spoked wheel. "There!" Then she looked up proudly at Dryados. She was Iredenti, or at least sent by them.

"I see," Dryados said. "And where can I find that?" he asked.

"My mother said to tell you they would meet you over there." The young girl pointed to a large food stand under a group of trees. There were several people nearby eating and relaxing in the shade.

"Thank you," Dryados said. The little girl smiled and then turned and sprinted out of the shop, running toward the food stand.

Dryados worked in the shop for another two or three hours before closing. He walked over to the food stand, not quite sure what to do. He stood there awkwardly for a brief moment, when a woman came out from the cooking area in the back. "Your roasted chicken will be ready in just a few minutes. Please relax just there under the tree."

"But…"

"Just there." The woman nudged Dryados toward the spot she had indicated. He obediently sat down. As promised, a few minutes later she returned with a beautifully seasoned roasted chicken with grilled olives and tomatoes. "Three coppers."

"What?"

"Three coppers for the dinner."

"Oh, yes." Dryados reached into his tunic and handed her the coins.

"At the sound of third watch, we will meet you at the east end of the center bridge."

"What?" It was too late. She was gone. Dryados jerked up to go after her but then immediately sat back down. Confused, he relaxed and slowly ate the chicken. It was moist, and the aroma of the spices filled his nostrils. It was too early for dinner, but it didn't matter. He cleaned the carcass of its tiniest morsel.

He took his usual route back to the Open Hand and then tried to get caught up in his journal. He sat on his bed. *The timing will be everything*, he thought. *I really do not want to get stuck milling around by arriving too early or too late.* He left the Open Hand, praying nervously as he walked. He sped up and slowed down, trying to judge the timing. Mostly he worried. *I barely got a look at her face. How will I even recognize that woman?* He fiddled with his cloak and walked anxiously to the bridge with the rest of the crowd.

Third watch sounded. He was just a few yards short of the bridge. Almost perfect. On the other side of the bridge, playing down by the river—or rather, fighting with her brother—was the young girl who had so bravely ventured into his shop. The woman from the food stand stood on the bridge, yelling unsuccessfully for them to come back up. "OK, kids, we need to go home. Kids, it's time for dinner. Time to go. Kids, you need to get up here!" They looked as ordinary as any other family with children. Dryados made eye contact with the woman. She looked back down at the children by the river. "Sarah, Reuben, it's time to go." The children immediately stopped their fighting and scrambled up. She knelt down and wiped the mud from the children's clothing. There was an almost imperceptible glance at Dryados. Then she stood back up and started to walk on. Dryados followed the three, making sure not to get too close. He didn't even break stride. Perfect.

They walked farther from the city into the surrounding fields. Dryados kept his distance. They were surrounded by countless farms. The mother and two young children veered off the road and entered an old stone barn. Dryados glanced casually around. No one else was nearby. He entered the barn through the same small door on the side.

He closed the door behind him and edged cautiously forward into the large barn. The smell of wet hay permeated the air. The lighting inside was dim. No lamps had been lit. As his vision adjusted to the darkness, he could make out several people gathered in the shadows. Everyone stared at him without speaking.

Dryados stood motionless. The air was dank and stale, and he could barely see. His heart now pounded in his chest and he started to hyperventilate. He threw his hands from his sides and turned slowly around so all could see he was unarmed. "I was invited—I assure you." He stopped spinning and stood with his arms still held out into the air. No one moved. The barn was silent.

Finally a figure approached from the darkness. It was the woman from the food stand. "I am Justinia. It was I who invited you. I saw you make the sign a few days ago as I left the agora to get more chickens for the restaurant."

The others in the barn remained quiet. Several shifted about in the shadows. One drew closer. Dryados's heart raced. Something wasn't right. Maybe this was an ambush. He took a step back and stopped. "I am Dryados. I am just moved to Philadelphia." The room remained silent. "And I am Iredenti."

"Dryados of Pergamum?" spoke a voice in the darkness.

"Yes, I am he." Dryados could not see who had spoken. He turned to face the shadows. Cold sweat dripped down into his eyes. He felt like he was standing on his own grave. Was this a setup? He had just admitted he was Iredenti. What else did they want him to do?

A stout man strode out of the darkness. His jaw and cheek were thick and his nose tortuous. He looked to be a brawler. He was about forty. "We are all Iredenti here." His voice was hushed but firm. He had a long cloak covering him down to his ankles. Dryados noticed the man's sandals were Roman issue. Even under the cloak his large frame was not well concealed. As he moved, Dryados caught a glimpse of a uniform. He was a Roman soldier.

"You remind me of a man I know in Pergamum. His name is Aeolis. He said he had a brother in this area named Cleopas." Dryados looked questioningly into the man's face.

The stout man broke stride and walked closer with a small but growing smile. "No, we are not brothers of blood, but brothers of soul. And if you know him, you are a brother as well." The Roman put his thick hand out for Dryados to shake. "Welcome, welcome." He placed his other hand on Dryados's shoulder. "Join us now. You are among family. I am he. I am Cleopas."

Lamps were quickly lit. As they were going around the room introducing themselves, the front door of the barn slid widely open. There was a sudden burst of light from the front of the barn. Panic gripped most as they ran to the shadows. Cleopas's hand went instinctively to his sword beneath the cloak.

"I'm sorry. The door just got away from me. I'm sorry." Another man entered from the front of the building, sliding the barn door closed behind him. He had a smiling face. "I am so sorry." He stood squinting at everyone as his eyes slowly accustomed to the darkness. Those already gathered paused, and then everyone started talking again.

As soon as the new arrival's vision adapted, he spotted Dryados and walked over. "I am Cantus Cresiti. I welcome you." He pulled Dryados close and gave him several warm pats on the back. Being hugged by strangers still made Dryados feel very uncomfortable. He was glad when the man finally pulled away. Cantus was older, perhaps sixty-five or seventy, clean shaven, with thinning brown-gray hair. He had most of his teeth and friendly eyes.

After several more warm greetings, Cantus gathered several sheaths of hay and put them in a small pile in the front of the room and sat down. The others quickly followed suit, throwing similar sheaths of hay or horse blankets in small piles in front of him, and they too reclined. Several lamps were lit, and the room glowed in golden hues reflected off the hay and straw. Cleopas welcomed Dryados to sit down beside him.

Then Cantus began their lesson. "God loves us and pursues us like a young man after his bride. He redeemed us so that we may know Him. And knowing God, we love Him. And if we love God, we love the people He created. Loving God and loving people become the center of our being, and how we live our lives." The gathered Iredenti listened expectantly.

"How many of you would like to learn a new song?" Everyone looked sheepishly around and then raised their hands. "OK, it goes like this." Cantus started to hum a beautiful melody. He mumbled some words and la-la-la. It reminded Dryados of the song Talmun and Sarina sang to each other each night at the Askeplion, where she had cared for her sick father. "How many of you like the melody?" Cantus asked. Everyone smiled and nodded their approval. "OK, now I shall teach you the words." It was an old love song. Soon couples in the room were looking into each other's eyes and singing or humming the tune. Dryados thought of the moment he would be able to sing it to Alesia.

Cantus let everyone enjoy and share the song with each other for some time. As some of the couples began to blush, Cantus got up from his spot and started to dance with the members of his fellowship. Just a step or two or even a little twirl. "Here is tonight's lesson. Love is the melody we teach the world. We know that if they like that melody, then they will want to learn the words to the song. And then they will come to love the One who wrote it. Even on days they cannot remember the exact words, they will still know the meaning of the song. Just as you continued to hum it to each other when you too had forgotten. If you want to teach the world about God, first love them, and they will be eager to learn why."

As the lessoned ended, Dryados looked around the room. There were perhaps twenty people. They looked to be laborers, farmers, and simple craftsmen. There was no wealth here. He felt stupid as he thought about it. *This is why I could not find them. These people would never shop at the agora. They would use the cheaper street merchants and barter for whatever they could.* He shook his head. *I was just looking in all the wrong places.* They were friendly, unpretentious, and warm. He felt at home. The meeting went on for several hours. As in Pergama, they staggered their departures to reduce suspicion. Dryados was one of the last to leave.

He met with the fellowship whenever he could. There were only about thirty Iredenti in the whole city. But secretly, they waged a covert war. In a world full of cruelty and hate, they offered mercy and grace. In a world that constantly doled out death, they offered life. Unseen by those around them, the light was spreading. New people joined them regularly. At the same time, many of their most mature members seemed to leave to take the light elsewhere. As Cantus had taught them, "They were the yeast in an unleavened world." It was exciting to experience but it kept their numbers low. Soon Dryados was teaching. He used the copies the gospels and letters from John as the foundation of every lesson. He wrote pleadingly to Talmun, *Send more copies!*

At his shop, he only sold the highest-quality merchandise. Every day he adjusted how he displayed his products to give the shop a crisp and fresh appearance. He eagerly approached each customer with a friendly smile. And he made a lot of money. But still, each day became more dreary than the one before. It just wasn't the same. Slowly he began to realize that much of what he loved about what he did, was really about whom he did it with. With no Alesia and no Talmun, the spark was gone. It was just work. He often found himself closing the shop early. He wasn't sure how it happened, but most days he ended up at the caravanserai. It was filled with exotic people, animals, foods, smells, and merchandise—everything! It was like the entire world was all smashed together inside its thick walls of stone.

As Dryados shuffled into the foyer of the Open Hand, the clerk waved another letter at him. He wore a mocking smile. "Another letter, Master Dryados." The clerk's grin was mortifying. Dryados got at least one letter every day. It would not have been that embarrassing if the letters were from Alesia, but they weren't. Most were actually from Titus.

The situation here in Pergama is intolerable, Titus began. *Foxes and Hounds is no longer any at fun all! Alesia never lets me win. And the faster she wins, the more she gloats. It's just intolerable.* Dryados smiled as he pictured it in his mind. When it came to Foxes and Hounds, Alesia was merciless. Dryados laughed and continued reading. Titus mostly complained about his work as quartermaster. *The backlog on our supply orders has grown totally unacceptable. Pergama is the capital. We can't have outdated or tattered weapons. We have the highest-ranking officials in the region, and they all want decorative armor, ceremonial swords, spears, and all the trappings. The local artisans just can't keep up. It's beyond frustrating! They take our needs completely for granted. Just yesterday…*

Dryados sat back and read the letter over and over. His mind seemed stuck racing in a loop. There was something there…he just couldn't figure out what it was. He decided to go for a walk. The sun was still up, and it was getting cooler. It was the perfect time to stroll outside. He wasn't going anywhere in particular, but somehow, as always, he ended up at the caravanserai. He stood outside watching the caravans entering for the evening. Titus's words were like a spark. Now a wildfire consumed his mind. So many thoughts, plans, and preconceptions just seemed to burn away. All his ideas about his business were incinerated. His ideas of how he would spend the rest of his life blew away like ash. The anxiety in the back of his mind was frightening. The pounding in his chest distracting. The decision was enormous, yet it seemed to be made before he had even truly formulated the question. He stood there for a very long time. The last caravan entered. The sun set. The caravanserai doors were sealed and locked down for the night. He watched as the tower torches were lit.

He was suddenly cold, and awakened from his dreamlike state. He turned and walked slowly back to the inn. In his room he wrote two letters. One was to Titus in Pergama. The other to Ascalon in Thyatira. He paced the room. About an hour later he wrote two more. One to Alesia and one to Talmun. He would send them out in the morning. He would hire couriers. They would be more expensive, but it would be well worth it.

Ascalon raised his hammer. "Drives me crazy!" The hammer fell hard on the heated metal. *Bang, bang, bang.* He rotated the bronze shield he was repairing. He laid his hammer down for a moment to work the billows. "Guild rules say blah blah blah." He slammed the billows down hard. "This is my shop! Not the guild's. These are my laborers, my apprentices!" Flames shot from the forge. The metal had gone from a nice malleable red to almost white. "Dag nab it!" He rotated the shield. The muttering continued. "Not their risk or reputation! No, that's all mine. Drives me nuts." He raised his hammer again. *Bang, bang, bang.* "There. Perfect." He immersed the shield into the large bath of water. As he looked up to watch the rising steam, he saw a man standing at the fencepost, yelling and waving his arms, trying to get his attention. He moved the bronze shield over with the others.

"You Ascalon?" the man asked.

"Yes, that would be me. How can I help you?" Ascalon dried his hand on his apron and looked curiously at the lanky man. He was clearly not there to get something fixed.

"I have a sealed letter for you from Philadelphia," the man said politely. He handed Ascalon the letter.

Ascalon did not recognize the seal. It was a triangle inside a circle. But the seal was intact. He broke the seal and examined the written parchment. He stared at the page. Then nodded his head with vigor. "Thank you. That will be all." The lanky man turned and walked away. Ascalon looked back at the page. That of course did present a problem. Ascalon could not read. He would have to go get his friend Malachi, the scribe.

Ascalon started closing up the smithy. Dryados's plan was scary, bold, and brilliant. He wasn't sure what to do. He stacked the iron rods back over in the corner. He brought in more dry wood for the forge and stacked it in the pile. He swept the floors. It was time to leave. He held up his hammer. He thought about his father.

"Now, son, you must hold the hammer at the end of the handle, not in the middle. Then just before it hits the metal, give it one last flick of your wrist. That way you use every muscle from your shoulder down to your fingertips. The hammer will fly faster, and you will not tire so fast. Work smarter boy, not harder. That is the key." Ascalon remembered looking up and seeing his father smiling at him. He thought how much he loved his father's smile. It had always made a dimple in his right cheek. His mind flashed ahead to a day that soon followed.

"Ascalon! Hide! Quickly, there in the woodpile. Don't come out no matter what!" Men started screaming. He remembered diving into the woodpile and pulling wood over himself.

"You there, smith, hold fast and do not move!" The sound of the charging soldiers was tumultuous. They flew into the smithy like a flock of vultures after a dead corpse.

"I am just a smith. I have done nothing wrong. I have been here at my smithy all day." Ascalon watched as his father laid down his great hammer. Two soldiers grabbed his father's arms. His father did not resist.

"You are conscripted into the emperor's service. Take him!" barked a centurion. The centurion looked at his father with distain.

"I have done nothing wrong! I have a family! I have a family! Please…" His father glanced at Ascalon, still hiding in the woodpile. His father's eyes filled with tears. He grimaced one more small smile. Ascalon saw the dimple in his father's cheek. Then the soldiers dragged him away.

Ascalon continued to put his tools and bits of raw metal away. He never saw that smile or his father again. He kissed the great hammer as he hung it back in its place for the night. It was still heavy, but not so much as it was when he was a boy. He started to walk home.

He thought about his newborn son. His father's words *work smarter, not harder* kept echoing in his head.

Dryados started receiving the responses back in just over a week. He was amazed at the speed of the couriers.

Titus—yes.

Ascalon—yes.

Alesia—yes, absolutely.

Dryados wasn't sure if he was excited about the responses or terrified. The letter from Talmun was the most reassuring. It arrived two days later along with six men. Talmun's note was brief. *Yes, of course. As always, it is all 100 percent ours.*

Do with it as you please. Hope to see you soon. Although the six men who delivered the letter looked much like any other travelers, they carried a fortune of coin hidden within their baggage.

Back in his room, Dryados paced the floor. He sipped on his goat's milk. *It is such a big change*, he thought. *But God does big things. Sometimes wild, crazy, don't-make-sense kind of things. This is just one of those.* He had prayed about the plan many times. The concept itself was simple. He would taper himself out of retail merchandising and focus on imports/exports, shipping, and bulk sales. As a merchant he knew what the other retail sellers could get for their goods. He knew the profit margin they would be looking for and what they would be willing to pay. From there he could work through his own costs and determine all of his price points. He would also work with Titus and try to develop a business relationship with the Romans for major sales. His knowledge of business and financial risk had been growing his whole life. *I am totally prepared*, he thought. He continued to pace the floor and began biting his lip. *I have only had a few major setbacks. Well, not that many.* He drank more goat's milk. But there was that time… He started to run the financing problems, shipping concerns, cash-flow issues, and other complications through his mind again for the hundredth time. His stomach really hurt. He drank more goat's milk and wrung his hands. Then he laid down and started praying again.

The noise inside the guild hall of Thyatira was loud and raucous. Ascalon stood outside silently, mustering his courage. He prayed, "Oh God, please…" He sighed and opened the door. The noise and clamor hit him like a hard slap to the face.

"Ascalon, welcome, welcome! Would you…"

"Ascalon, come join us…"

"Ascalon, do you know…"

Someone shoved a large goblet of wine into his hand. Someone else draped an arm around his shoulder and babbled senselessly. His breath stunk. Ascalon turned. "So good to see you again. Here, let me go fetch some more wine." Ascalon turned and escaped into the crowd. He had no idea who the man was. Everyone was nodding and smiling at him as he passed. The heavy drinking had obviously been going on for some time. No one else even seemed able to walk straight. Men shouted across the hall. Raucous laughter erupted all around as men told bawdy jokes and boasted of the prowess with the ladies. He tried to make his way over to the side of the hall, where he wouldn't be so out in the open. He sipped on his tasteless wine and put on a moronic smile. "So glad to see you. Nice tunic. Excuse me." He nudged his way through the crowd. There was a man near the front who looked only mildly inebriated, so Ascalon decided to start up a conversation with him. He walked up and flashed a smile. "Fabulous night for a guild meeting," he said, smiling at the man cordially. Unfortunately, the gentleman was far more intoxicated that he appeared, and their conversation quickly became a series of confused ramblings. Ascalon hated drunk people.

It was an act of mercy when the meeting finally started. "Order! Order!" The guild master stood atop a dais, pounding with his gavel. The drunken rabble slowly quieted down. Business matters were quickly addressed. All the votes were passed with a loud, slurring cheer. "Now we will move on to any new business. Does anyone have anything new to present before the guild?" Ascalon had moved himself to the front of the room so he could be first to speak.

"I would like to make a motion to extend the working hours for the laborers at my business for one month to get caught up. We are way behind and—"

"Motion denied!" chided the guild master.

"Wait. Don't we have some discussion?"

"No. Guild rules are very specific on this matter. There are no exceptions," the guild master pronounced firmly.

Ascalon had anticipated the denial, which helped him to stay calm. "In that case, I would like to bring in some outside workers, just for the next month. It is an incredible opportunity for all of us. It—"

"Motion denied. All workers must be members of the guild to perform any work in the region of Thyatira." The guild master shook his head at Ascalon in disappointment.

Ascalon smiled to himself. He had known from the beginning it would ultimately come down to this. "Oh no, I'm sorry. Of course they would be guild members. I thought that was understood. I would never consider using anyone who was not a member of our guild. In fact, I will pay their guild dues immediately, so we are all in agreement on that." Ascalon walked up to the dais holding up a large bag of coin. "It is my privilege to sponsor ten new members of our glorious guild," he said proudly. Then he pulled out forty silver dinars and laid them on the guild master's counter. That was enough to cover the guild dues for ten men for a year.

"Motion passed!" The guild master quickly swept up the coin. No one in the crowd even noticed. The guild master looked over to the oblivious rabble. "If there is no further business for our guild, we stand adjourned!" His declaration bellowed over the noise of the crowd. The inebriated throng miraculously lifted their heads. The guild master smiled widely as he raised his hands, motioning to the doors on the sides. The attendants flung the doors open. The mass of waiting prostitutes flooded in. The room exploded into riotous cheers.

The men hooted and screamed as they scrambled for the women. Ascalon headed inconspicuously for the exit. He moved slowly, still holding up the same goblet of tasteless wine. He watched as one of the younger men grabbed a rather eager prostitute, stripped her clothes off, and started to have sex with her. The man's comrades cheered him on wildly, waiting their turn. It was the same everywhere in the hall. Ascalon pressed on toward the exit. He hadn't moved ten feet when he was embraced by a thin young woman no longer wearing a top to her tunic. She kissed him madly and pressed her breasts hard against his chest. In his younger days, he would have had her where she stood, but he was no longer that man. He motioned her for the doors. She smiled, eagerly pulling him along behind her to the exit. Just outside the door, she shoved Ascalon behind some landscaping and started to rip off his clothes. She was young and eager. Her body slender and firm. Ascalon was not immune to the arousal that came from witnessing what he had just seen inside the hall. She was beautiful and thin, with Kashmiri eyes. No one would ever know. Still, there was no magic to what he did. He just said, "No." Ascalon apologized, acknowledged the young woman's beauty, and gave her a few copper coins. She smiled at the coins, gave him a coy giggle, and then ran back into the guildhall. The "guild meeting" would go on for several more hours.

The walk home was quiet. The extra workers would start in the morning. He hoped it would be enough. This plan of Dryados's had to work.

Ascalon put his hand to the side of his brow and started to rub his temple. His head was killing him. The scribe read him the new orders from Dryados. More swords, more helmets, shields, arrow tips, gold leaf, and on it went.

"Axheads? Who needs all these axheads? This is crazy. I'll never get this through the guild. They are crawling all over me the way it is!" He stood there shaking his head. "We are too far behind already." Ascalon looked at the scribe, shaking his head blankly. "I need some water."

He and the scribe walked over to the shaded barn in the back and sat down at a small worktable inside. Ascalon drank several large glasses of water. He went over to one of the stalls to feed his favorite horse, Sunrise. She was so fast. He still enjoyed taking her for rides. He rose, grabbed an apple out of the bucket, and let the horse nibble it out of his hand. He rubbed the mare's head. Standing there, he looked back at the scribe. "Let Dryados know that we will do it. I have no idea how, but we will make it work." Malachi got up and flashed a reassuring smile toward his friend and then left. Ascalon retrieved the horse brush hanging on the stall wall and began to brush down the happy mare. He let the issues wade through his mind. He was pushing his suppliers at the mines to the maximum. His men were exhausted. The guild was going crazy. And his budget was busted. He felt like getting up on Sunrise and just riding off into the sunset.

Ascalon fed the horse another apple and returned to his forge. The hard work gave him more time to think. He worked at making swords and axheads until his great arms finally failed him. It was long past dark. He dragged himself home. He had just enough coin to see him through the end of the week. Dryados said after that they would have to wait until the large sale to the Romans was completed. But he couldn't think about that either.

The fellowship meeting at Jezebel's was crowded. Ascalon let his deep baritone voice blend with the other voices around him. He let the music carry his soul. It was weird, but somehow singing to God brought the rest of his life into tune. He felt a little guilty, but he often found the music as refreshing as the message.

Jakotrudi and Jezebel stood together on the raised dais, leading the others in song. Jakotrudi was much like an old shady tree. His smile glistened like wet leaves on a sunny day. His hands rocked above his head like branches in a soft spring breeze. Jezebel was almost motionless beside him. She wore no smile, and her eyes always conveyed a sense of hungry discontent. Yet in her own regal way she also appeared happy. As the song finished, the two sat down and Jakotrudi began his report.

"The philosophical discussions we are having in the community are being greeted with amazing public support. The people consider them to be very Greek and enlightened." Jakotrudi chuckled. "During these forums we can sometime get a sense of who is searching, who might be open. Then we cautiously approach them later." Jakotrudi continued his update. The small fellowship was fully engaged.

Some were active in nursing the ill. Others, feeding the poor. A smaller group had also been meeting with aliens from other lands and helping them integrate into the community. Ascalon smiled.

He grabbed a goblet of wine from one of the attendants and took a small sip. That was one thing he had to say about the fellowship meeting at Jezebel's—she did serve good wine. Tonight Jakotrudi was teaching about focus.

"Set your mind on things of the spirit. Keep that focus. There is no temptation that has overtaken you that is not common to all of us. God is faithful, He will not let you be tempted beyond your abilities. It is hard sometimes. But we can do all things by the power of the One who has redeemed us. So walk in Him. Be rooted and built up in Him. Lay these other things aside…"

"No, no, no," Jezebel touched Jakotrudi softly on his sleeve and rose to her feet. "Temptation creates tension, and it is that tension that is evil. It grabs our thoughts and pulls us away from God. How can our minds focus on Him when tension pulls us away? Surely eliminating the tension that separates us from God should be the goal. God desires a relationship with us that is unencumbered and undistracted."

Ascalon thought that made sense. He knew his mind did wander sometimes.

"Yes, this is true Jezebel, yet how we do that is just as important as the goal we seek to achieve. To flee, to pray, to study, to seek godly wisdom. These are all right ways. To—"

"You are so right," she interjected. "These *indirect* approaches might be helpful, at least for the moment. Yet even these methods require effort, and that effort then becomes its own distraction, and again, the relationship is hindered. Sometimes the best solution is the simplest one. Address the distraction fully, completely, until it is exhausted and gone. Then when it is gone, it is completely gone. Then the relationship can flourish, unencumbered and undistracted." She smiled at Jakotrudi and walked into the crowd and began to answer questions. She was soon surrounded by a group of young men.

Jakotrudi smiled at the crowd as well. "Yes, flee the obstacle that blocks the path." Then he followed Jezebel into the crowd.

Ascalon thought it was a good lesson. A little confusing, but it made him think about how out of control his priorities were at the moment. He glanced around the crowd. Their numbers were growing, and there were many in the fellowship he did not know. New people were always easy to spot. They always seemed to hang in the back or by an exit, looking nervously around. Ascalon knew what they were thinking. *Is this a mistake? Am I going to get myself killed? Are these people crazy? Could what they believe actually be real?* Ascalon always sought them out first.

Time passed quickly. Jezebel left early, taking some men downstairs to tour the estate. Ascalon spoke with Jakotrudi about the lesson. As he did, Jakotrudi motioned for a young woman to come and join them. The two men kept talking as she worked her way through the crowd.

"Ascalon, I don't believe you've met Jezebel's assistant. This is Daravaza." The young woman turned toward Ascalon. She was beautiful and thin. She had Kashmiri eyes.

Chapter 5
Mooring Rope

"We are out of time!" Ascalon yelled. "He arrives tonight!" The other smiths were busy at all five forges. The apprentices ran around frantically with swords, spears, axes, or whatever they could carry. Tempers were short. Ascalon paced around the smithy like a giant looking to crush an ant.

"No, that wagon is for steel!" Ascalon stormed over to the wagon. "No! No! No! I told you, the helmets...the helmets are separated and then boxed! Not wrapped!" Ascalon grabbed a polished helmet and shoved it into the man's chest. "Now! That wagon over there!"

Ascalon ground his teeth. He had combed the streets of Thyatira for days looking for any laborer willing to work. The guild was furious, but it didn't matter. He was out of time. He would pay the extra guild dues at the next meeting and make a very large "contribution" to buy the guild's approval.

The day passed by in a heartbeat. Four of the wagons were completely loaded. The fifth was almost out of room. "What else could possibly go wrong?" he roared. He stormed over to two men waiting in line to load the wagon. "I don't care if we have to borrow a wagon from the lowliest farmer. I don't care! Just get me another wagon!"

"We've already tried—"

"I don't care," Ascalon yelled. "Just—"

"They all want cash up front," the workman interrupted, shaking his head. "They won't even rent us one."

"Aahhhhh!" Ascalon clenched his jaw and shook his fists in the air. He was completely out of coin. He couldn't buy a snack from a street vendor, let alone pay for a wagon. "Promise them double."

The workmen shook their heads and kept their place in the line. "They all want cash."

Ascalon looked at all the swords, shields, and other products still lying in the street waiting to be loaded. The wagons were full. "We will just have to go short," he moaned. "Just load what you can."

Ascalon turned and walked away. It was a disaster. It would destroy their credibility with the Romans. And worse than that, Dryados would have a complete mental breakdown. But they were out of options.

Bang-bang-bang. Dryados lay in his bed in Philadelphia, dreaming. He walked toward the familiar sound of Ascalon hammering. There was nothing else in the dream. No people, no roads, nothing, just the sound of the hammer. The landscape around him was utter blackness. But Dryados could tell he was getting closer. *Bang-bang-bang.* It was louder now. He could see Ascalon standing at a great forge. His body was red and glowing. It pulsed with color as the fire surged with each pump of the billows. The hammer collided into the metal. White sparks erupted around him with each impact. Yet what Ascalon was fashioning was small. The object he forged glowed radiant white and forced the surrounding darkness farther and farther back. Ascalon stood, holding the object in his tongs. The glow reflected in his eyes. He…

Dryados woke up again. He was closer this time. He had dreamt the dream many times. Each time he had gotten just a little closer. But he still could not see what the powerful smith was making.

It was time to get up. The air outside the tent was cool. He walked over to the fire. The cook quickly brought him some food. The men in the camp were already up, checking the wagons. There was one final burst of noise as the tents were taken down and repacked. They had camped just north of Sardis at his usual spot along the river. He checked the hollow in the log. It was empty, so he assumed the lepers were getting the supplies. He filled it again with some old clothes, food, and a net for fishing. He was careful not to touch the sides of the hollow. He wanted to help, but he didn't want to take any chances either. He threw some fresh brush and leaves over the opening.

They pulled out of camp not long after daybreak. Dryados rode his roan stallion at the front of the train of wagons. He watched anxiously as the extra men he hired rode security around the perimeter. They sat alert with their swords strapped to the fronts of their saddles. He looked behind him at the rest of the caravan. They had left Philadelphia with eight heavy wagons and four strings of pack mules. The family of one of the blacksmiths he had sent to Thyatira had joined the caravan to move to Thyatira and be with their loved one. Dryados had placed their wagon in the center of the caravan for security. The day quickly grew hot again, and soon Dryados was wiping sweat from his brow. The road to Thyatira was dusty. There was no shade. Anything close to the road bigger than a blade of grass had long been pilfered by the many travelers for firewood. Dryados was thankful when it finally started to cool down again.

The day was tense, but they encountered no problems with the Romans or with bandits. Still, Dryados felt a sense of relief as they approached the city walls. He could see a flurry of activity at the city gate as they drew closer. It was almost sunset. Dryados turned and motioned for the lead wagon to pick up the pace. As they entered the city, the great gates were sealed behind them. From then on they moved forward at almost a crawl. The streets of Thyatira were packed with people now out enjoying the coolness of the evening. Dryados led the small caravan through the shifting streets directly to Ascalon's smithy. As they rounded a corner, Dryados brought the wagons to a stop. He sat on his horse in shocked dismay. There in the middle of the street in front of the livery, he watched Ascalon. The smith's face was red, and the veins bulged in his neck. He yelled at anything that moved. Several large crates still lay in the middle of the road. Men ran around strapping things to the sides and tops of wagons.

"No! No! No! Not the axheads," Ascalon bellowed. "I said, take out the battle shields! We need to make room so we can get in all the swords." Ascalon was yelling so loudly he didn't even hear the caravan as it pulled in behind him. Ascalon finally turned and saw Dryados already dismounted and standing beside him. His face went from beet red to ghost white.

Dryados glanced at the crates on the ground and then back at Ascalon. Dryados's mind raced.

The big smithy's face was now sickly pale. "Dryados, we will make this work. I don't care if we have to make litters and drag this stuff all the way to Pergama. We will make this work. We will leave tonight if we have to—"

At that moment a woman ran out from one of the wagons in the center of the caravan. She glanced around and then changed directions, with a growing smile on her face. She waved to one of the men standing in line with his arms full of merchandise. She sprinted toward him. "Simeon! Simeon!"

The man looked up in stunned disbelief. "Kathryn?" He dropped everything to the ground and ran toward the woman. "Kathryn! I can't believe it." The couple raced across the courtyard, greeting each other. Their kiss was long and deep. They were obviously married.

Dryados turned, smiling at Ascalon. "I believe that young couple may have just solved our small dilemma." The couple's goods were quickly unloaded. It was dark. Torches were lit. All the remaining crates were loaded into the newly borrowed wagon. The streets were quiet and empty as the last of the goods were finally packed onboard. Ascalon and Dryados both stood in the center of the road with smiles. Nothing would be left behind.

Bang! Bang! Bang! Dryados rushed through the vacant blackness of his dream. He knew his way there by heart. He ran faster and faster. He knew he had little time. "There!" He pivoted just to the right. He could see the great forge just ahead of him in the distance. Dryados could feel the grit of the soot in the air around him. The smell of the heated coals filled his mind. The bellows pumped. The forge pulsed with power. He could hear the roaring of the blaze in the heart of the forge. The busy blacksmith shimmered in the glow of the pulsing light. The long tongs he held in his hands grasped a small object at their tip. It was glowing white. Dryados could almost see it now. It was just there. It pulsed brighter and brighter. The blacksmith held it there in iridescent wonder. It was…it was…a key.

Dryados woke up and got dressed. He hurried downstairs, wolfed down some food, then shuffled down the street to join the others. The roads of Thyatira were still dark. Yet there was a smoldering commotion around the gathered wagons. Family members had to say their good-byes. People rushed to get something to eat or a hot drink. Ropes needed to be retightened. Forgotten treasures needed to be shoved in at the last second. Despite the frantic moments, the caravan lumbered slowly out of the city at sunrise just as planned.

The journey to the river was short. Dryados watched from the bank as the caravan sloshed its way through the cool flow. The river marked the boundary between the lands of Thyatira and Pergama. It also delineated the extent of the protective hedge placed around him and served as a liquid wall separating him from those he loved. He sat atop his horse and watched the wagons pass. He prayed for the men as they crossed through the rippling waters. He prayed they would all return home safely. He prayed that the journey would go well. As the group disappeared down the broad road, Dryados turned and headed back down to Thyatira. He looked, but this time there was no angel to greet him.

Ascalon could feel the stress melt away as soon as they crossed the river. He looked at the security guard sitting next to him in the front of the wagon. "You know, he is a good partner, Master Dryados is," he said, nodding his head. "He is just too smart to drop your guard around, is all. You just can't relax around the man. He looks at you with that look of his, and you know he is thinking five steps ahead of you." Ascalon shook his head and sighed. "It's just exhausting. He is demanding, meticulous, and never stops asking questions. Oh, and he is very particular about everything." Ascalon sat up on the wagon bench and grinned at Bellator. "Beyond that, he's a great partner." Ascalon kept nodding. "Yep, best partner a man could have…great partner…" Bellator looked at Ascalon with a confused smile.

The caravan moved steadily forward like a mouse in a cornfield full of cats. The roads were relatively safe, but there was no sense in dropping their guard this close to the finish line. The tension dropped when they saw the Roman checkpoint just ahead of them.

"Hoo…" Ascalon pulled the first wagon to halt in front of the waiting soldiers. A cloud of dust followed close behind and momentarily obscured the faces of the hardened men. Ascalon made his best imitation of a Roman salute. "To Rome and our emperor, Domitian. Peace and good fortune." Ascalon flashed a friendly smile. The soldiers did not smile back. The lead centurion looked up blankly and gave a slight nod to his men. The soldiers quickly fanned out, surrounding the wagons. The clatter of their armor was loud. The dust rising from their feet was worse than that from the horses. Ascalon's eyes felt gritty. The soldiers did not speak, not even to each other. The only noise was the sound of clanging armor and the shuffle of their goods as the soldiers searched through the caravan.

"We are delivering a large quantity of merchandise to the Roman quartermaster himself, Titus Justinian Dociles, in Pergamum," Ascalon said boldly. He hoped it would make the caravan seem more official.

The Roman centurion was not impressed. "You have thirteen heavy and one light wagon as well as nine strings of mules. It is much wear on the roads and demands greater security. There is a toll of thirty pieces of silver." The centurion's voice was firm and his face expressionless.

It was a shakedown. No different than that done by any thug on the street. But this was a Roman centurion with the might of the entire empire behind him. Clearly he thought a caravan of this size would be flush with coin. Dryados had given Ascalon extra silver to keep for just such an encounter, but he had been forced to spend that to keep the guild off his back. Now he had but a few coppers left in his purse. His gut tightened. Then he nodded smilingly at the centurion. "Totally understandable, great sir. Totally understandable. But our coin is all tied up in these goods. We are just from Thyatira. We will be paid in Pergamum and return this way tomorrow." Ascalon grabbed his coin bag and gently tossed it to the Roman centurion. "I assure you this is all I have. My men will have even less. We will happily pay you the rest tomorrow, as well as any additional tolls or fee, of course." Ascalon smiled but could feel the sweat now beading up on his brow.

The centurion looked up at him with expressionless eyes.

"I assure you this is all the coin I have," Ascalon said honestly, "and I will pay you tomorrow, here on this same road when we return."

The centurion gave the smallest nod to his soldiers. Two men leaped into the front of the wagon and dragged Ascalon to the ground. Ascalon put his hands out in surrender and did not resist. "Please, please…it is all the coin I have." The soldiers threw him crashing to the ground. The other soldiers standing nearby held their ground, flanking the caravan. None of Ascalon's men moved. The two soldiers grabbed Ascalon again and held him kneeling on the ground beside the wagon.

"Sir, there is no need for this...take what goods you want! There is no need..." The centurion slammed his fist into Ascalon's face. Ascalon instinctively drew back, trying to raise his hands. The blow took him hard on the left side of his head. Things started to go black. The centurion hit him hard again in the mouth. Ascalon felt his teeth rattle and tasted blood. As his senses cleared, he found himself halfway on his side, with the centurion pacing in front of him.

"You are a liar! Some of your goods are from far to the east. Much of it even imported from outside the empire!"

"Yes, yes, that is true. We—"

The centurion leaped at Ascalon and slammed his fist full force into Ascalon's face. Ascalon's head whipped to the side. His body crashed sideways to the ground. He spit out several teeth. His nose and mouth poured with blood.

"Take what you want. Just take..." He saw the centurion shift. He saw the heavy shod boot race toward his face. Then blackness...

Ascalon's men raced to their fallen leader. The other Roman soldiers drew their swords and stood motionless to meet the tide. Ascalon's men stopped in their tracks. Some began to back quickly away. Bellator watched in horror as the centurion began to beat Ascalon to death. The kicks were merciless. Ascalon's heavy muscled frame rocked like a log in the pounding surf with each blow. Kick after kick. Bellator watched as Ascalon's left arm took the brunt of the attack. Soon it was broken in so many places it looked like a thick mooring rope undulating in the surf.

One of Ascalon's men was screaming "No! No! No!" The others stood in shocked silence. Bellator slid closer across the buckboard of the wagon to see. The Roman soldiers did not move. The Roman centurion continued the merciless beating with his boot.

Soon the Roman centurion started to tire. After a few more labored kicks, he stopped. He was covered in sweat and breathing heavily. He took off his helmet and wiped his brow. He paused for a moment to catch his breath. He stood there looking at Ascalon's lifeless body. "You want this lying thief—take him." The Roman soldiers parted silently like the opening of a well-oiled gate. They held their swords drawn, with their eyes fixed on Ascalon's men. The men stood motionless.

"Take him, I said!" The Roman centurion stood wiping his brow and staring at the misshapen body. "Then be on your way." He cinched his helmet back on with a firm tug and then turned and walked back inside the checkpoint with Ascalon's meager bag of coin.

As the centurion disappeared inside the checkpoint's small shack, the men raced forward. They paused by the body, unsure what to do. Bellator jumped down from the wagon. He was a former soldier and gently rolled the body over. Ascalon's face looked like a black swollen pile of baker's dough. His left arm was like a giant dead snake. Bellator placed his fingers on Ascalon's upper neck to the feel for the pulse of his heart. No one else breathed.

"He lives," he whispered softly. "Quickly, get a litter. Do it quietly." Two men leaped up and rushed back to the wagons. In seconds they returned with a litter fashioned from two long iron spears and some thick woven under armor. They rolled Ascalon's heavy body onto the litter and carried it back to the wagons. No one made a sound. The Roman soldiers stood silently in their lethal poise. The sharp edges of their swords glinted in the sun. The men slid the litter on top of some crates in the last wagon. The former soldier squeezed in beside Ascalon. "He could still live…" His eyes betrayed his doubts, and his words were unconvincing. He placed cool wet rags over Ascalon's face. The other men raced to their posts, and the train of wagons moved forward.

The Askeplion, Pergama

"On three. One, two, three!" The large foundation stone slid slowly forward on the skids. "Push, push, push, push!" The men groaned, and the great stone slipped into position with a soft *thud*. There was a chorus of heavy sighs. Talmun smiled broadly at his men and patted the newly seated stone. "We will let this and all the others settle overnight and then begin the new masonry wall over them in the morning." His men smiled back with exhausted grins. They all stood for a moment staring at the long line of foundation stones they had spent the entire day struggling to get into position. "Now *that* was a good day's work!" Talmun proclaimed. He was a lord, and rich, and powerful, and knew lots of people. Yet in the end, none of that mattered to him. He was a worker. He loved to make things. But most of all, he loved working at the Askeplion, where he knew his wife was nearby caring for the sick and dying.

Talmun excused himself from his men and went to the back of the construction site and rinsed himself off. He put on a clean tunic and then headed out across the city. Aeolis had made arrangements to meet him at the East Gate to escort Dryados's caravan up to the Acropolis. He was especially looking forward to meeting Ascalon. Dryados had written so much about the mighty smith and his monstrous big arms that he was looking forward to seeing them for himself.

Talmun climbed onto his chestnut mare and rode across the city. He generally liked to walk, but he had come to realize that horses did occasionally have their uses. He pulled the horse's reins and headed south. It would be faster for him to skirt along the outer part of the city and then come back up to the gate rather than try to weave his way through the back streets. Aeolis and a handful of soldiers were already there waiting when he arrived.

"Hail Lord Compitavitae!" Aeolis put his hand to his chest, standing at attention with the rest of his men. Talmun smiled and dismounted. He gave Aeolis a commanding nod. Aeolis and his men then went at ease. The area around the gate was crowded and busy. There were several small shops nearby. Aeolis and his men moved off and tried to find some shade.

"Come, captain of the guard. Let me treat you and your fine men to some wine. The day is drawing to a close, and I am sure you and your fine soldiers deserve at least that in the service of our emperor."

Aeolis and his men were extremely hesitant. "If anyone asks, tell them Lord Talmun insisted."

Aeolis put up some token resistance but eventually allowed his men to sit with Talmun and enjoy the wine. He knew it would help Lord Compitavitae earn the friendship of the Romans. He and Talmun had become close friends. As captain of the guard, it was not unusual for him to be seen with powerful community leaders like Talmun. It was the perfect cover for their friendship.

They had been relaxing in the shade for about an hour when the caravan appeared in the distance. Aeolis formed up his men. Talmun rode out to meet the string of wagons. He kicked the chestnut mare and trotted out the gate.

A large dust cloud followed in the wake of the approaching wagons. They were riding in fast. The closer he got to the wagon, the more confused Talmun became. The wagon driver was nothing like Dryados had described at all. He was stout, but nothing unusual. Yes, he had good-sized arms, but only above average at best. They were definitely not the biggest arms he had ever seen, as Dryados had gone on and on about in his letters. The driver suddenly started to wave frantically.

Talmun kicked the mare and raced to the side of the lead wagon. The frantic pilot lashed at the horses as he tried to quickly explain what had happened. The driver forgot to even give his name.

"Understood!" Talmun pivoted his mare and pointed to the city gate. "I will meet you there." Tallman kicked his horse hard in the flanks and flew back to Aeolis and the waiting Roman escorts.

Talmun gave a brief explanation to Aeolis as to what had happened. "I will take the last wagon carrying Ascalon directly to the Askeplion. You and your men will escort the rest of the caravan directly to Titus at the Acropolis."

"Agreed."

The caravan was there in less than a heartbeat. The men separated. Clouds of dust filled the roads, going in two different directions.

After seeing the men off at the river, Dryados rode back to Thyatira. He knew it would be several days before he heard anything. He decided to walk to the Textile and Dyers School and see Lydia. She could always be counted on to be there spending her day with the young students. The school was an active weavery and produced a large variety of dyed cloths. And she too was Iredenti.

As he walked in, he could see Lydia at the front of the hall teaching the students. She had met Paul and many of the others in the early days when she lived in Philippi. When she had grown older, she returned home to Thyatira to be with her family. She had discipled Jakotrudi and many of the others. But the bond she shared with Dryados was unique. They had both witnessed the unseen universe of angels, Shards of Light, and Black Voids. At the same time, she was also a guild leader and had been influential in convincing the guild to allow Dryados to join the guild and export their products.

Lydia could also be counted on to always wear a smile. No matter how bad things seemed, she always made him feel happy. Dryados stood in the back of the hall and watched Lydia as she pulled a big root out of a bucket. "This is the madder root," she said. Her face filled with the smile he so desperately needed to see. "This is the source of our famous purple dye. The plants are very difficult to grow. Its secret is known only to a handful within the guild. Other cities had tried to grow them, but none had been successful." She saw Dryados standing in the back, and her smile grew even larger.

She and Dryados waited until after her students had started their work before they talked. "And what news have you from Lord Compitavitae?" she asked. "Is he in agreement with the plan and all its restrictions?"

"Talmun is actually as excited about it as I am!" Dryados spoke eagerly. "We can never thank you enough for all your help."

"Well, it doesn't hurt that the guild has been hoarding the madder roots for years to help keep prices high. Now that our warehouses are filled to the brim, well, it is good timing."

Dryados nodded in agreement. "Please reassure the guild we will not in any way affect local demand or prices. We will sell the dyed products only in Greece. And with the sale of their excess madder roots, the guild will make even more coin." That was where Talmun came in. The House Compitavitae had many estates in the Greek lands. Each estate had trade agreements in place for the sale of their products. Adding a new product as rare and valuable as the madder root would be easy. Everyone would make a great deal of money, and the new Lord Compitavitae would be immediately seen as a genius.

The two walked outside to enjoy the day as the students continue their assigned tasks. Dryados had to steady her every now and again, as her balance was poor. They stopped in a nice spot to just sit and catch the warmth of the early sun. "Sometimes he still shows himself to me, you know," she said quietly. Her voice trembled with the timbre that only came with age.

"Who?"

"The angel of the church of Thyatira," she said, smiling. "He shows himself to me, sometimes as a beggar or lost child. One day I was sharing my story with a stranger I had befriended…it was him. After he revealed himself to me, he smiled and just sat there and let me continue to share my testimony, even though, well, he had already heard it. He told me it was his favorite story and that he just loved to listen to it over and over again."

Dryados thought of the many angels he had seen. He closed his eyes and breathed in a slow, deep breath. He remembered…the River…and started to drift away on the memory.

"The star in the crown they wear—it's not really a sparkling jewel, you know," she said quietly.

"What?"

"The star in their crown, it's a Shard of Light," she said. "Like the one in your chest, or mine, or even in the angels." Dryados watched as Lydia softly smiled and closed her eyes. She was praying. Dryados closed his eyes and began to pray as well. In the silence of the moment, he could feel the Shard of Light in his chest. It seemed to reach out and melt into the Shard of Light resting in Lydia's frame. It was like joining hands in a circle with a third person they just couldn't see. And all three of them were one. They prayed.

Dryados returned to the Purple Ram an hour or so later. He had stayed there many times over the last several months when he came to check on Ascalon's work. As he lay down to sleep, he thought of Lydia and the madder roots. He thought of shipping the roots to the Greek lands… Then he began to worry. It all came down to Darius. Could he really do it?

Smyrna, near the warehouses by the docks

Darius the fishmonger left the Iredenti meeting. His thoughts were entangled in the turmoil…of nothing…and everything…confused. They had been praying…a whole family had been taken. And again, Suistus, the Jewish chief priest, was behind it. They had to stop him. He walked slowly toward the docks. *He wouldn't be that difficult to kill*, Darius thought. *I could do it myself*. He grinned. It would be completely unexpected. *Simply approach him and gut him like a fish*. Darius thought that would work. *He always has a large retinue with him, but never really any guards. It would be a good trade. One for one*. He nodded. *Still, it is not our way*, he thought. It was a difficult decision. *Yes…no…yes…*

He arrived at the docks and stopped. He allowed his thoughts to return to the immediate problem at hand. He was about to buy a cargo ship. Dryados had been very specific: The boat must be exactly the right size—not be too big, not too small. Fast, but not a racer. Inexpensive, but not cheap. Not new, but not too old, and so on. Darius's heart pounded faster with each step. *That man can be a real pain in…* Still, Darius had an idea. There was a nice ship that fit the bill almost perfectly. It was a good ship but had not been making any money for its owners for some time. The ship's captain was lazy and already had made plenty of coin. He simply didn't care anymore. In truth, the man would much rather stay at a tavern and drink than take the ship out. Yet the man enjoyed the title of Captain. The ship's owners had no idea how bad of a captain they had in charge of their vessel. Darius had toured the ship earlier on the pretense of hiring it for a job. That would in fact be the case if the purchase did not go through.

Darius walked slowly down the creaking dock. He had been given full authority by Dryados to negotiate the shipping fees or the sale price, depending on which way the deal went. The sound of the gulls was soothing. But inside, his gut was tight. He felt like he was clinging to a raft, watching the sharks circling him. He had done that once when he had been blown overboard in a storm. Spending this kind of money without Dryados here to give his approval felt exactly the same.

Dryados sat at his table at the Purple Ram, eating his dinner of spiced fish, when the courier walked in asking for him by name.

"I'm Dryados," he said as he got up, motioning to the man. The letter was brief. It bore the seal of House Compitavitae. Dryados scanned the message. *Ascalon severely injured… Taken to Askeplion… May not survive. Pray…* Dryados couldn't breathe. Memories of Ascalon flashed through his mind. He sat back down with his mouth agape. *Breathe…breathe…breathe.* He forced his mind to slow down, then looked again at the parchment. *Sales completed with Titus… Funds en route…* The letter went on. Dryados sat in the chair and read the letter over several times. The courier stood waiting next to him. Dryados glanced up.

"Lord Talmun bid me not to leave without a reply."

Dryados retrieved some parchment from his room and jotted down a short reply. *Will wait in Thyatira as long as is necessary. Am praying desperately for Ascalon. Miss you all dearly. I really just want to come home.* He handed the man the letter.

"I was also instructed to give you this second letter after I had received your response." The courier held out a second sealed letter, also marked with the seal of House Compitavitae. Dryados quickly opened it. This letter was even shorter. *Sarina is pregnant.*

Late every afternoon, Dryados made his way to the north gate of the city. There was no courier or caravan from Pergama the next night, or the next, or the next. With each passing day his feelings of guilt grew worse. His stomach was killing him. He was drinking so much goat's milk the innkeeper at the Purple Ram had started to tease him, "You drink more goat's milk than a baby kid!" Then he would laugh.

Now Dryados's skin was starting to itch. He racked his brain. He wanted his days in Thyatira to count for something. He wanted to meet with other local businessmen and the city's guild leaders. He wanted to lavishly entertain them and make generous overtures to them. He wanted to make amazing business deals that would cause his enterprises to explode! But none of that was going to happen. He was broke.

Instead, he spent most of his time with Lydia. She was much like Gaius. She was old but sharp of mind and fit. Everyone in the city seemed to treat her like their favorite grandmother. She introduced him to the members in the dyers' guild and weavers' guild. But what he enjoyed the most was Lydia's teaching. Dyers, weavers, students of all different levels—it didn't matter.

Lydia was always hands on when she taught. She worked the madder root. She spun yarn, worked the looms, and tied knots for rugs. And as she worked, she taught her trade. Dryados would always stand in the back and listen. "Dryados, no, please go back to the inn," she would chide. "What I teach is of no interest to a man of your high education. It is ordinary knowledge."

Dryados would just smile and shake his head. Lydia was mistaken. What she taught was as new to him as morning. He knew everything there was to know about running a retail business. But what he needed to know now was far different. He needed to understand growing conditions in Thyatira, manufacturing requirements for different products, how much weight a camel could carry over a long distance, shipping taxes, the statistical probability of a bandit attack along every section of the trade routes. He needed to know all of it. Dryados sat in the back of the class just like he had when he was a youth. It made him chuckle.

As he did every afternoon, Dryados excused himself just early enough to head to the northern gate. Ascalon and the others could return any day. Standing there waiting in the late sun, the anguish of what had happened would careen with the hope of his friend's return. He picked at his fingers. Today he arrived in time to see a small caravan approaching the city walls. It flew tall banners of the Roman legion. It was flanked by a large contingent of Roman horsemen riding its perimeter. Within that rode a second layer of elite house guard. Dryados climbed the inner stairs of the city wall to get a better look. The caravan itself was obscured by the cloud of dust raised by its wagons and cavalry. The horsemen closed their perimeter tighter as the caravan approached but held their positions as the caravan entered. A string of scarlet and golden banners led the way. Dryados did not recognize the driver of the first wagon, but he did recognize the old statesman riding on the horse beside the driver. The older man looked up at Dryados on the city wall with a broad smile.

"I have brought my Foxes and Hounds with me," Titus yelled with a smile. "But you must promise to let me win at least a game or two!" Dryados spun and ran down the steps. He pulled up his tunic so he could run faster and not break his neck. As he ran down the stairs, he wasn't sure if he wanted to cry or sing. Dryados watched as the column of valiant soldiers entered the city. Despite the dust and the obvious long ride, Titus's polished armor still glistened. He entered right behind the tall banners, with the first wagon.

"Alesia sends her love," Titus said as he dismounted his horse and gave Dryados a big hug.

"Yes, she does…"

Dryados spun. The first wagon had pulled over to the side. The driver held Alesia's hand as she exited. She looked poised and magnificent. She wore the purple tunic he had sent her. She paused as she dusted the garment off with her hands. "Do you like it? It fits well." She turned around several times, allowing the fabric to float out beside her. Dryados did not even realize she was talking about the dress. He thought she meant her hair. It floated like a halo around her. She had woven tiny rosebuds into her thick blond hair. It was the image of her that he had always held in his mind. It was the image of her that day at the Upper Agora in Pergama. She was a dream taken form.

"And that, Mr. Dryados, was your last hound!"

Dryados had totally forgotten how annoying she could be. "Fine, three out of five."

The innkeeper at the Purple Ram, who had stood nearby watching the last of the game, gave out a little chuckle and shook his head embarrassingly at Dryados. Then he walked back into the kitchen. Now they were again alone in the dining area. Alesia bent across the table and started to arrange his game pieces. Her blonde hair fell against the board, moving the pieces around as fast as she tried to set them up. He knew if he lunged to kiss her, she would be too fast for him. He didn't care. She was the smartest person he knew, but he had learned a thing or two as well.

"Your hair is so…" He lunged to kiss her. She was ready and snapped back across the board and into her chair like a catapult, just as Dryados had expected. Her coy giggle suddenly stopped, however, as he shoved the entire table aside, crashing the board and pieces to the floor. He threw his hands out wide and loudly roared "Rraahhhh!" He jumped across the vacant space as the table crashed to the ground and wrapped both his arms around her. She was hard to surprise but now sat there in his arms, unmoving. The game pieces rolled around on the floor. Dryados snuggled his face into her hair. The couple did not speak or move for several moments. Dryados pulled away just enough to take in her face. "You see, sometimes the hound does catch the fox."

She smiled and laid her head back. "Yes, it does." He expected her to bolt out of his arms at any moment, but she did not.

She kept her head nestled on his shoulder as they breathed in the moment. "April twentieth" was all she said.

"April twentieth?"

"Yes, it is a Sunday."

Dryados smiled. "OK. April twentieth." And with that, the date for their wedding was set. Just over a month away.

Chapter 6

Home

Dryados ran to Ascalon's smithy. He had already returned to the Purple Ram when he got the news. Ascalon was back. He had not anticipated any more travelers arriving this late to the city. By the time he arrived, the wagons were already there and unloading. The men were quiet.

They lowered a litter slowly out of the back of one of the wagons. Dryados assumed it was Ascalon. He really couldn't tell. The man on the litter was laying rolled over on his right side. The left side of his face was black, purple, and yellow. His black swollen eyelid merged with the rest of the face. Even accounting for all the swelling, the face looked misshapen. The left arm had been splinted from the fingertips all the way to the shoulder. There was a leather shoulder brace that wrapped around his neck and back. His chest was wrapped tight with bandages. The man groaned with every breath.

The four men at the ends of the litter adjusted their grips. Their leader nodded, and the litter rose smoothly off the stone road. Slowly they began their deliberate shuffle down the narrow streets toward Ascalon's house. Two men with torches led the way. A handful of other men followed with some of Ascalon's clothes and personal property. Dryados stood stunned for a moment, staring as the men carried the deformed body away. Then sprinted to catch up with the litter.

He walked nervously beside the litter. "Ascalon…oh God…I am so sorry." He started to reach out to touch him but then stopped. There was no place he could see on Ascalon's mangled body he could touch without causing him more pain. "I am so sorry…" The men continued down the cobbled street, trying not to shake the litter.

"Has anyone talked to his wife?" Dryados asked. The men looked up blankly and shrugged unknowingly. They continued their slow, steady pace toward the house. Dryados ran ahead. The roads were dark now. He had been to Ascalon's house many times on his trips to Thyatira and knew the way there. He could hear Ascalon's newborn son crying inside the house as he approached. He knocked softly and tried to quickly compose himself. He breathed slowly. *Calmmm…*

Sperta opened the door cautiously and then smiled as she recognized his face. She invited him inside. Dryados and the other men had updated her regularly when any news arrived about her husband. She had been told he would be returning soon, but she had no idea he had arrived and was nearly outside the door. Dryados tried to get her to sit down, but she continued to walk around the room, swaying with the baby in her arms.

"He looks really bad, Sperta. His face…well, he looks really bad. Just try to be supportive. He will need you to be, well, ah…" Dryados fumbled.

Sperta turned, rocking her son. "One of Ascalon's men got kicked in the face by one of the horses. The other women and I from the smithy tended to him." Sperta bounced her son up and down. He was so small, only a month or two old. His arms and legs shot up and down with each bounce. She steadied the boy's head. Then she slipped him beneath her tunic to feed him. "This will be no different," she said calmly. "The other women will help me. When that man returned to work, Ascalon insisted that the entire event had actually improved the man's looks. I am sure it will be the same for Ascalon."

"I just want to make sure you are prepared…he looks really bad. I mean, it's just terrible…"

Anger filled her eyes as she spun to face him. "I know!" she snapped. She stared him cold in the face. Dryados decided to stop talking. She took her son, Lautus, from her breast and led Dryados back to their bedroom. She placed Lautus quietly in his crib and gently kissed him on the head. She pulled the blankets down on their bed. "Just have the men lay him here."

Dryados glanced around the room. It was very clean and uncluttered. The shelves were lined with bandages and oil. A wash basin and a large jug of water were already waiting. She had obviously readied the room every day for his return.

"I will send for the other wives when he gets here. We will be fine." She bent over and pulled Lautus's blanket up to better cover him and then led Dryados back to the living room. She was as calm as a quiet mountain. They did not have to wait long.

The men came up the front stairs slowly with the litter. Dryados looked for the expression on Sperta's face as she saw her husband for the first time. He watched her take a deep breath as if to brace herself. That was all. She bent over and kissed Ascalon's face as he was shifted onto the bed. She whispered softly, "You are home, my love."

Dryados made arrangements for Ascalon's money to be dispersed throughout the city. Some would go to the banks, some would be protected by the Romans at their garrison, and some would be held by the guild. All were safe places, but none was impenetrable. Money was best protected by spreading it around.

Titus had brought the fortune with him concealed in the wagons. The Roman contingent he brought made sure the coin was taken safely to the different locations. Titus also made arrangements for half of his Roman soldiers to escort Dryados safely back to Philadelphia. They would protect him from robbers, vandals, and equally importantly, from other Romans.

Despite the darkness that filled the world around him, Dryados found himself shooting out of bed and eagerly embracing each new day. Every morning after breakfast, he went to Ascalon's and tried to cheer him up or make him laugh. Every night after dinner, he would do the same. But his days belonged to Alesia. He showed her the beautiful artwork at the Temple of Apollo. They toured the Dyers School and spent time with Lydia. They searched through the entire city to find the most beautiful purple cloth. And they took long horse rides to see the countryside. Sperta insisted Alesia ride Ascalon's horse Sunrise to keep it in shape until her husband got better. Dryados found a hundred things to do that allowed him to spend time with her. He also made it a point to play Foxes and Hounds with Titus, and let him win on occasion. But then like a quick afternoon shower, Alesia was gone.

The morning sky was red and brilliant blue the day she departed. Dryados laughed to himself as he looked out at the dawning colors. He thought they matched him well. Red for his tear-filled face and blue for his broken soul. Dryados fussed with the horse's bridle and strappings over and over. Anything to keep her just a moment longer. Then she rode away.

Dryados, his men, and the remaining half of the Roman contingent departed soon thereafter. The journey south was empty. The Romans insisted they stop at the Roman post inside the city of Sardis. It was the first time Dryados had been through the area and not stopped and left something in the hollow log for the lepers.

When they arrived in Philadelphia, they unloaded a treasure trove of merchandise from Talmun's estates in the Greek lands, as well as several crates of parchment from Pergama. Almost all of it would be shipped to the East. The gold and silver coin they had concealed was dispersed to several locations within the city. The contingent of Roman soldiers Titus had loaned him departed back to Pergama. Dryados walked to the Open Hand. He lay in his bed and stared at the same ceiling he had stared at a hundred times before. He had many friends among the Iredenti here, but somehow he had always managed to keep them at arm's length. Staring at the familiar defects in the ceiling, he realized the only things he had ever really allowed himself to have in Philadelphia were his businesses and a place to sleep. And he made up his mind—that was going to change.

A noisy bedroom in Thyatira

"Aahhh! Stop it, woman. I just want to lay in bed!"

"There's nothing wrong with your legs, you big ox! You're going to get up… *now!*"

"My whole side is killing me. It hurts just breathing!"

"Yes, and the doctor said today was the day you were to get up and move around." Sperta tugged on Ascalon's good arm. It was like a butterfly trying to lift a boulder. Ascalon started to laugh.

"OK, stop…stop! You're making me laugh, and that makes it hurt even more!"

"Then get up or—" Lautus started to cry. Sperta let go of his arm and picked up the crying boy. She bounced him gently on her shoulder and patted his butt. "I cannot take care of two babies at once. You need to get up," she said passively. She had learned—with Ascalon, the softer she spoke, the more likely he was to actually hear her. She let Lautus nurse and walked out into the living area.

A stream of loud grumblings continued from the bedroom. Sperta paced the floor and continued to quietly nurse Lautus. Ascalon walked out and sat in the chair across from her. Most of the yellow and purple was now gone from his face. There was still a hint of it in his neck, which looked a little odd. His left cheek and eye were sunken in. The side of his face hurt when he tried to move his jaw. Most of his teeth in front were gone. "Everything is still double when I look up or down," he said dejectedly. "It's OK if I look straight ahead though."

"The physician said it will not get any better on its own at this point. He and some of the other men will be coming by tonight to work on it." Sperta walked over beside him. "I bought several bottles of strong wine."

Ascalon sighed deeply. He knew the wine was for him. "Well, I'm going to need to be able to use my jaw better, especially now that I am missing so many teeth."

Sperta took Ascalon for a walk outside. He struggled to walk the cobbled streets with his double vision. Still, the morning air felt cool and crisp in his nose. He watched as the streets grew busier with people. As they walked, he spied a ragged blind man struggling down the road. Soon the man sat down in the dirt and started to beg. Ascalon squeezed Sperta's hand. "I can still see out of both eyes." He smiled.

"Yes, you can," she replied. "And I will always be here beside you." She squeezed his hand even tighter.

When they got back, he rested in the living room and watched as Sperta worked on a new baby blanket for Lautus. It was white cloth with raised embroidery. The blanket was almost completed.

The couple sat with their first child. "He has gotten so much bigger since I left." Ascalon smiled with pride. "Look, he can even hold his head up now." The young boy continued to flop his arms up and down and kick his legs randomly. His head bobbled, but he held it up all on his own.

As the day came to a close, Ascalon started drinking the wine. He was not one to drink heavily. But he wanted to be very drunk when the physician and other men arrived. He hoped the strong wine would help.

Ascalon waited quietly in the center of the bed. They had bound both of his arms down, even the broken one. Then they bound his legs. They pulled out a smooth wooden gag for him to bite on. The physician showed him the instrument he would use on his cheek. It was shaped liked the pincers of a scorpion's claws. It had two long, sharp, curved needlelike iron spikes. The spikes could pierce through the flesh, then be clamped together in position and used to move bones. They would pass the needlelike spikes beneath his cheekbone and pull it out.

"It will be important that you do not move. It will only hurt more and take longer. Do you understand?" The physician looked expectantly at Ascalon.

"Yes." Ascalon began taking slow, deep breaths.

"There is also a chance that none of this will work." The physician stared at him with confident uncertainty.

Ascalon nodded that he understood and continued to breathe deeply.

"You two men hold his head down." The two men were smithies like Ascalon. Their arms were strong. They grabbed his head and chin. "You other two men, on his chest and shoulders." Two large men moved into position. "And the rest of you, put you weight on anything that moves." The other men in the room shifted around the bed. Sperta waited in the living room.

"Ready?" There was a final pause as the physician glanced around the room.

Ascalon panted loudly and then silently nodded.

The others in the room each gave a subtle nod. Someone put the wooden gag in Ascalon's mouth.

The physician readied the instrument. Then took a deep breath. "OK…*now!*"

Ascalon could not help but scream. The sound was muffled as he bit down on the gag in his mouth. He felt the two spikes in the side of his face just in front of his left ear. He heard the snap of the clamp.

"Hold him down…*now!*" Each threw his weight onto Ascalon's frame. He felt the immense jerk on the side of his face. He felt the bones in his face snapping and popping as they moved out. There was a scream and what seemed to be a white explosion inside his head…then blackness.

Sperta was pacing the living room as the physician walked out. "The cheek is partly done. He has passed out. While he is out, I would like to do more."

Tears rolled silently down her face. Sperta nodded yes. Lautus was still in her arms, wrapped in his white blanket. He had started crying when all the shouting began but was beginning to settle back down. She bounced him a little faster.

The physician wiped the clamp clean and then placed one of the curved spikes inside Ascalon's nose, pointing down. He placed the other spike inside his mouth behind the ridge where his upper teeth had been. He struggled hard on the clamp before it finally snapped closed. Ascalon's body instinctively writhed in pain. The doctor slowly started to pull out harder and harder on the clamp. His muscles flexed. "Steady…steady…" The men all held their positions, holding down Ascalon's unconscious body.

Ascalon's body still knew the pain even though it was asleep. The unconscious moans were sickening. The left side of Ascalon's face and palate moved slowly forward. The doctor stopped when it looked like the cheek lined up with the other side. There was surprisingly little blood. They rolled Ascalon's body onto his stomach so he wouldn't swallow any of it.

The doctor looked at the other men in the room. "The shoulder is in the joint, but I must work on it now while he sleeps so it does not fix itself solid." The doctor moved the shoulder around. There was an odd popping noise inside the joint as it was freed up, like the breaking of small bones.

Perhaps it was the odd noise from the shoulder, or the steady drip, drip, drip of blood onto the floor from Ascalon's mouth, but one of the men holding Ascalon suddenly slumped onto the bed and then slid onto the floor, unconscious.

"We are done here," the physician pronounced. He pointed to the man lying beside the bed. "Let him stay on the floor. He will awaken on his own in a few minutes. Ascalon should be fine as well."

Residential area, the Acropolis of Philadelphia

Dryados felt guilty, but what else could he do? Time was running out. He stood in the backyard, admiring the stunning view. He could look out across the river and see the cultivated fields of the Katakekaumene stretching off into the horizon. The yard was big enough for a large garden and even a small vineyard. The house was well inside the Acropolis wall and just west of the theater. It was safe, beautiful, and close to everything. It was perfect. Alesia would love it.

After about an hour of negotiating, he and the seller settled on the price. He really did feel guilty. As soon as the price was settled, he and the seller walked out to the front of the house. The seller's mouth dropped open. Outside on the road stood an army of workers waiting for the signal. Dryados smiled and waved to the cohort. The workers flooded it. He looked at the seller. He really did feel guilty.

"Wedding guests will be arriving next week," Dryados shouted. "The garden is the top priority. I want that done first. We can worry about the vineyard later." He knew Alesia loved gardens and that she would want to plan it all out herself. But he couldn't bear to have her come to their new home without at least some kind of garden and flowers waiting for her. "Yes, and lots and lots of roses. Every kind! I want something always in bloom for her." He took the workers to the back-yard. "I want a tree right here, and a table with chairs, and a board of Foxes and Hounds set up and ready to play." He knew he would never really capture his fox, but he hoped she would at least slow down enough for him to hold her once in a while. He imagined the game board and his stalwart hounds on the hunt. A big smile grew on his face. He had an idea…

In Thyatira, the weeks passed.

"Seriously, I think it actually improved your looks. Yes, I think it did." Sperta moved Ascalon's head back and forth, inspecting his face. "Yes, much more mas-culine looking now." She nodded with an affirming smile. She stood on her tiptoes and kissed him.

"Well, let's hope the men down at the smithy don't think so," Ascalon chided. "I'm telling you, I will bust their heads wide open if so much as one of them makes a pass at me—me being a married man and all." They laughed. She was glad his sense of humor was intact. Many other things were not.

Despite the best efforts of his doctors, his left shoulder was frozen and couldn't move. His arm was still in the splints, but it was already clear he would never be able to use his hand properly again. The whole appendage was now more like a club. His right arm was fine, but he and Sperta knew the truth. Life was going to be forever different.

Ascalon stood up to go. Today was supposed to be his first day back at work. He rubbed his right hand up and down his shattered left arm, his eyes full of dread. "There is no such thing as a one-handed blacksmith," he moaned soberly. He looked at Sperta with empty eyes and sat back down.

Sperta sat down on the floor in front of from him. "That might be true." She sighed. She held Lautus in his white blanket. The embroidery was almost finished. She kissed her son on the head and then looked up at Ascalon. "It might be true. I don't know. But you are twice the man that most men are, so I guess losing one arm will just about make you, well, even."

"What are you talking about?" He looked at her, puzzled.

"It's a math thing. You were never good with your figures." She snickered.

Then she shook her head with a growing smile.

"I am a blacksmith! Not a scribe," he grumbled loudly.

"Exactly." Sperta stood up directly in front of him. "And how many men were working for you before all this started with Dryados?"

"Six."

"And how many lately?"

"Twenty-three or twenty-four, I think."

Sperta looked at him with mocked confusion. "So is it your job to fix every broken bit or pound out every shield, helmet, or rivet? Do you muck the stalls?"

"No, I have good men for that!" Ascalon said stubbornly.

"Yes, you do, my love." She leaned over and gave him a gentle kiss on his head. "Maybe there is more to you being a blacksmith at this point than lumbering around pounding on things. Maybe, since you are the boss, you could even come home early and spend time with me and your son?" She placed Lautus in his lap. They both smiled at their baby. As Ascalon played with him, Lautus grabbed his finger.

"Did you see that! He reached out deliberately and grabbed my finger." Ascalon wiggled his finger. "He has a strong grip." He pulled his finger free and held it still. Lautus's tiny hand shot just past it and then grabbed the finger again. "Did you see that…he got it!" Ascalon started wiggling his finger again. Lautus held on to the finger with all his might and giggled.

Ascalon glanced back at his beautiful bride. "But I really love being a black-smith." He sounded defeated.

"Then do the best you can and as much as you can. And let your men do the rest. It will be different, and that might be a good thing." She gave him a long, passionate kiss. As she pulled away, she gave him an equally passionate sly grin.

"OK, coming home early could be a good thing." He said, looking longingly at his wife. "But today I think I would rather go in late."

Sperta placed Lautus back in the crib.

Philadelphia

Dryados stumbled over to the next caravan. He already had a headache. This was the fifth caravan he had visited today, and it wasn't even noon. He had just finished purchasing a large quantity of exotic furs and sculptured ivory from a caravan from beyond the Indus River. This one was from nearby Syria. They were carrying cedar wood to the markets in the West.

"Bulk product, hard to ship, labor intensive to move—no real profit there." Dryados started to move on. His translators thanked the caravan leader for his time.

"No, no, no. Please wait. Let us sit and have tea." The Syrian's Greek was poor but understandable.

"Tell him we would love some tea but that we are really not interested in the cedar."

Despite Dryados's obvious lack of interest, the caravan leader still insisted they sit down. Magnificent rugs were quickly spread, and a small feast of nuts, fruits, and various breads were spread out before Dryados and his translators. The tea was aromatic and dark. Dryados decided to stay. He would not be making any kind of deal, but it did give him a chance to meet another merchant for future business. The spicy meal was refreshing. He especially loved the tea. Dryados's headache even felt better. As the meal wound down, Dryados and his two men waited patiently for the sales pitch he knew would come.

The caravan leader's sales offer was as spectacular as the meal. In years past, Dryados might have even gone for it, but he was older now. "As I said, we really are not interested." Dryados had his translator explain his honest and real concerns. There was no profit for him to make here. Dryados and his men rose to their feet. There was no sense in dragging things out.

"Please sit," the caravan leader said as he motioned back again to the pillowed floor. The words held the same tone of honesty that Dryados had heard earlier. Dryados looked at the merchant and sat back down. "You are correct," the caravan leader said to Dryados. "And we both know it. But we are also both businessmen." The man started to puff on his large water pipe. "I have heard of you, Dryados." He took a long drag on the pipe. "You are an honest man." Then he paused, raising a finger at Dryados. "And a shrewd businessman. I know that too. But there is money here for both of us. Your concerns are real. For me, if I sell these goods here, I can return to Syria and bring another shipment back in less than a quarter the time it would take me to complete the transport and sale of the timber I have here now. That would mean at least three or four full shipments here instead of one complete shipment to the other markets. If the price is right, it is better for me to sell it now." He sat silently, puffing on his long pipe.

Calculations flew in Dryados's head. There was also the opportunity cost to consider. "There are many caravans here," Dryados said, shaking his head. "I could do much trading. This will tie my capital up for much longer. Faster trades are also much more profitable for me as well."

The two businessmen sat staring at each other, neither one blinking. The moment was broken by a girl coming over and clearing the plates. The musicians continued to play in the background.

"Then it is important for us to find the right price that makes us both money and considers both of our valuable time," said the Syrian man. There was another long pause and stare. The negotiations began. The only stray thought that snuck into Dryados's mind was whether Darius had purchased the ship.

Smyrna

Darius looked sick as he walked in the door. There was no booming greeting from his lips. He dropped his cloak in the middle of the room and sank into his chair. The wood creaked from his weight. Helen, his wife, had seen that before. Someone had either been injured at work or killed by the Romans. Suistus and the Jews were now conducting raids regularly and turning their victims over to the Romans for execution. She hoped it was no one close to them. She hoped it was just an injury at work.

Helen came over and kissed him on the forehead. "I'll get you something to eat."

There was lots of noise in the house as the kids played. Their youngest son scurried over and started running a toy animal up and down Darius's leg. It tickled a little bit, even to his leathery body. It made him smile. Still, he sat unmoving in his chair.

Dinner came and went. The family seemed to sense his mood and let him sit silently. He played with the children, but with vacant eyes. He helped with the dishes. That was their usual time to talk. Every effort Helen made to get him to speak was answered with a smile and an incomprehensible mumble. Soon the kids were sent off to bed, and they sat down at the kitchen table.

"Every copper…I spent every copper Dryados gave me." His voice was quiet and distant.

Helen tried to conceal the shock that she knew had overcome her face.

"He said that was his limit…less was better…but that was his absolute limit." Darius let out a sigh. "I hope I have not ruined the man."

Helen touched his hand. "If he said that was his limit, then that was his limit. Dryados is a smart man. He will be OK. He would never set a price that he knew was going to ruin him." She tried to sound confident and reassuring.

For the first time, there was a hint of a smile on Darius's face. But more than that, there was a glimmer in his eye—of pride. "Helen, you should see the ship. She is big and grand. She can hold more cargo than even Dryados could possibly ship. And she is fast. The ship was built wider than most, so the draft is shallower. She will sail safer in the reef-filled Aegean than any other ship of her kind." His smile edged a bit wider. He rested his heavy head on his raised hand. "At the end, I just told the owner it was all the money I had. Take it or leave it…all the money I had. The owner was furious. I could tell he wasn't faking to negotiate a better price. He yelled that I had wasted his time. Then he cussed me out. He demanded half again as much money as I had. He just kept yelling at me. I apologized to him…honestly, Helen, I did. But he was enraged. So I just got up to leave. When I got to the door, he stopped me. 'The ship is yours' is all he said. I started to thank him, but he threw me out and told me his men would write up the sale and arrange for the money to be exchanged." Darius sat there staring at his wife. "It was a great deal and a great price. But it was every copper I was given…every single one. I feel sick."

Helen looked at her poor, confused husband. He was a good man. "Dryados will be proud of you and happy for what you have done for him. It is a good and wondrous thing." Darius sat silently at the table. "Like you have told our children, 'Rough seas lead to big catches.' It is just a big catch, that's all." She gazed at him teasingly. "I guess you are just getting too old to sail out into the deep waters." She stood and started to walk into the kitchen.

"What?" He looked up at her defensively.

"You heard me." She looked at him challengingly.

Darius rose to his feet. She started to run. He clamored around the room after her. "I'll show you who can still sail in the deep water around here."

Philadelphia

One of his men woke Dryados from his nap. He had purchased a small office with a large warehouse near the caravanserai. His headache was gone. Eight caravans this morning and five deals. His mind started racing the instant he woke up. Some of the trades would be fast. His quickest one was just going to Sardis. That would flip his money quickly. Cash flow was always a priority. Maybe his headache wasn't gone.

They headed to the caravanserai to meet the new arrivals. Some caravans would stay a few days. Others would leave in the morning. Those morning departures were the ones he would still try to negotiate with before the caravanserai closed. It could get busy if too many new caravans arrived at once. He had to be sure not to get stuck too long, or he would be spending the night inside the caravanserai…again.

The first caravan had arrived from the East. Marble going to Ephesus. Five minutes into the discussion, Dryados realized the deal was never going to happen. He spent the next hour showing the caravan leader around and treating him to some tea. He never passed up an opportunity to get to know another businessmen and get his name out there.

A second caravan could be seen arriving from the North. From what Dryados could see, it looked small, perhaps travelers. Dryados decided he would go lay down. He instructed his men to awaken him in an hour or so. That would give the small caravan a chance to settle in. They could always wake him sooner if another caravan approached.

Dryados walked back to his small office, pulled off his sandals, and flopped onto his cot. The curtains were already closed, but he still stuffed his feather pillow over his face to block the stray beams of penetrating light. In two heartbeats, he fell asleep.

"Dryados! Dryados, come…" One of his men was pounding on his door. "A large caravan is coming…very large."

"Aahh…you're kidding. I just laid down." Dryados threw his legs off the cot and sat on the edge of his small bed. "From which direction?"

"West."

"West, ah, that's even worse." Dryados put his elbow on his knee and propped up his head. They had been having little luck with the caravans coming from the West. Most were fresh out of Ephesus or Smyrna and were not eager to trade this early in their travels. But still, it was always worth a try. "Give me just a minute." He dragged himself to his feet, slapped his face with some water from the basin by the door, and then walked outside.

"Surprise!" Suddenly he was wide awake and surrounded by a large crowd of smiling people. He knew all their faces. In the center stood Alesia. She wore the purple dress. But today her hair was braided with purple lace and lavender blossoms. She wore a large shell necklace with iridescent mother-of-pearl. But her smile and eyes stopped his heart. He leaped across the distance, kissing her and holding her tightly all at once. There was shocked surprised on many of the surrounding faces. Dryados had always been…reserved.

A large hand patted him on the shoulder. "I've learned you need to pace yourself at that, brother." He knew the voice. He turned to see Talmun. "Surprise."

Dryados's heart exploded. He cried in stunned confusion. He couldn't let Alesia go, but he had to hold Talmun too. He grabbed Alesia even tighter with his right arm and wrapped his left arm around Talmun. Then just squished them all together. "I have missed you…" was all he could say. They stood there for a moment. Silent, unrestrained tears washed down Dryados's face. Alesia held her cheek against her future husband. They all just waited for Dryados to end the moment.

As Dryados looked up, he could see Titus, Gaius, and Antipas's older children. There were his old workers from the parchment factory, Stephanos, and of course, Sarina. She wore a puffy tunic, and the baby within her was already showing. Luculenus stood behind Alesia.

Dryados's workmen from Philadelphia were completely stunned. The Dryados they knew was quiet and focused, a businessman, brilliant and detached. For the first time they saw him for whom he really was—a loving man, alone and separated from his family.

Dryados turned and noticed a Roman statesman sitting on a horse. He held up a burning torch. It was early in the afternoon with the sun still high in the sky. Dryados stared at the torch. Then he smiled broadly as understanding flooded his mind.

"This torch shall burn until the ceremony," Titus said proudly. It was fire from the hearth at Titus's home in Pergama. He had carried the fiery torch all the way to Philadelphia. The fire was an important part of the *Aque et ignis communicatio* ceremony. The ceremony of sharing fire and water that sealed a marriage. The fire was supposed to be from Alesia's father's home. It was an incredible gesture. Titus spoke loudly above the now silent crowd. "So there is no question of how proud I am to have you as my son and that she is yours." He sat tall in his saddle. All those gathered looked up at the burning torch, and the two men now locked in a father and son gaze of pride.

Housing arrangements were quickly made for all the guests. Once the other guests were situated, Dryados, Titus, Alesia, and Talmun headed to the Acropolis. Titus had secretly made arrangements for him and Alesia to stay with the Roman garrison in the dignitary quarters. Talmun and Sarina would stay at Dryados's new home. And Dryados would stay at his office by the caravanserai. But tonight at his home there would be a feast!

Dryados had been alone in Philadelphia long enough to know who made the best food. Best chicken—Justina by the Agora. Best roasted lamb—that small shop by the theater. Best honey rolls—Mama Joanna's. He knew them all, and he ordered everything. With the other guests engaged in the party, he made up some excuses to sneak Alesia outside and show her the garden. The plants had all taken well, and the flowers were blooming in a kaleidoscope of colors. Off to the side stood a young transplanted tree. Beneath its branches was a table with a game of Foxes and Hounds set up and ready to play. Alesia grinned as she looked at the game. He walked her slowly around the garden, pointing out all the details. He deliberately said nothing about…

"What's that?"

"What's what?" he asked innocently.

"Those, right there." She started to smile. There by the back wall was a special gift he had made for her. A life-size ceramic hound that had a beautiful ceramic red fox trapped in the corner. Alesia stopped and smiled. She lovingly squeezed Dryados's hand. They stood in the cool twilight, staring at the ceramic self-por-trait.

"Oh, so that is how you think this marriage is going to be, is it?" Alesia said in mock disdain. She walked over and hid the ceramic fox in the rose bushes. Then she pointed the ceramic hound looking in the opposite direction. Dryados smiled at his future wife. At that moment he realized, that was how the rest of his life was going to be—chasing Alesia. And he knew no other life could be better than that. He was home.

Chapter 7
Quest

*B*ang! Bang! Bang! Dryados raced through the blackness of the void. He watched the great smith working at the blazing forge, as he had done many times before. Ascalon held up the pulsing white key. Dryados felt its power slamming into his soul with each pulse. It was like feeling the heartbeat of a giant. There was a pause in the flow of the dream. Things did not fade. Events did not race past him. This was different. He had…a moment. For the first time, he could really look at the scene. He could see the one forging the key. His eyes glowed with fire, but it was not reflected from the forge. His legs were like finished bronze. His arms were great, but it was not a strength of muscle or sinew. Dryados suddenly realized he had been mistaken. This was not Ascalon. This was an angel. Dryados could not see the angel's face, for he wore a hood. But somehow he knew this angel was different. It raised…

Dryados woke to a clamor at the door. "Another caravan has arrived."

Dryados rolled over on the small cot in his office. "If it is not from the beyond the Indus, then I told you, I don't care! I'm getting married. Now let me sleep."

Dryados's mind drifted back to the dream at almost the exactly same spot where it left off. The power of the key knocked him staggering backward. At the same time it was like a team of horses pulling him closer. His soul felt like it had to leave. Like there was another place it needed to go. He had to… The great angel turned, holding up the key. As the key pulsed with light, Dryados could see an army of Black Voids charging at them in the darkness. They scattered in the light's mighty current like sparrows in a hurricane. Then the white key began to sing. There was no sound. Still, Dryados could feel the voice of God in the entrancing melody. His senses were confused. He tasted the colors of a summer's day and heard the fragrance of roses. The Black Voids disappeared. The great angel turned…

Crash! Bang! Bop-bop-bop. Dryados jumped to his feet. His heart raced as he glanced around the small office. His mind was muddled from the sudden awakening. He couldn't see anything. He went to the hearth and struggled to get the fire going again. He threw some straw on the coals and blew. As light burst into the room, he saw a raven that had crashed through the window flopping about on the floor. He opened his door and shoved the thing out into the night with a broom. He sank back into bed. As the straw burned away, the night returned, and the tiny cot welcomed him back to sleep…

Suddenly he was dreaming of being chased, then he was dangling precipitously over a cliff, then he was lost… The rest of the night his dreams were filled with tension and fear. But in the morning when he awoke, he remembered the key.

He needed to talk to Talmun and Gaius about his dream. He would need to get them alone, to pull them away from the others. Dryados shook his head. He knew that was never going to happen. Every day more and more people were arriving for the wedding. Dryados's parents had recently arrived with a large group from Ephesus. The next evening a small caravan had arrived from Pergama, composed entirely of Alesia's friends and relatives. She had relatives Dryados had never even heard of—second cousin's nephew's sister-in-law…and relatives like that. They were literally running out of rooms in the city. His biggest problem, however, still remained. Gaius had agreed to perform the wedding, but Alesia had yet to pick a spot.

Dryados decided to steal away and take his friends to meet with his fellowship. There were six of them, including Gaius and Titus. The fellowship, which still met at the barn, welcomed them warmly. Cantus told the story of Abraham and his concubine. As the other members of the fellowship departed, Dryados had his friends linger to speak to Cantus. Once all the other fellowship members were gone, Dryados chose to share the visions of his recurring dream.

"In the dream, you said the Black Voids were vanquished by the light of the glowing key. That tells us the key has power and authority," Cantus explained.

"Yes. The ancient texts refer to the Key of David. This key is much like we would envision the 'key to the city' that is given to us by a great ruler," Gaius began.

"Exactly." Cantus continued, "It is the authority and power to command. Just as was given King David to rule over the Israelites. It is…"

The two men then engaged in vigorous debate about the ancient text, symbology, eschatology.

Dryados focused on the dream. He had seen the Black Voids. He had fought them. They were real. Perhaps the key was real too? Perhaps that was the next step in the battle—to retrieve the key?

Dryados forced the question aside as they began the journey home. It was chilly outside. Sarina kept snuggled close to Talmun. Dryados held Alesia's hand. The view of the city improved with each step they took up the Acropolis road.

Near the top, Dryados asked permission from Titus to take Alesia on a short walk, just the two of them. Titus smilingly nodded his approval.

The engaged couple walked quietly together under the stars. There was a large public garden just above the theater. They strolled through the aromatic trails of the garden and stopped along the east wall. They could see the firelight of the city and the moon dancing on the river. Beyond that glistened the tilled soil of the valley filled with patchwork fields. The view of the twinkling stars lit memories in his soul. Dryados told Alesia about the wonder of his encounters with the church angels of Pergama and Thyatira.

"Their stars sung to my soul. They…just filled me. It was like, well…" He stopped and smiled. "It was like snuggling with you." Alesia squeezed his hand. They stood staring up at the stars. Dryados bent over softly and kissed her hair. "You are my heart's star, Alesia…I love you."

She did not flee. She did not toy with him. She looked out at the city and the stars dancing in his eyes.

She spoke softly, "We shall get married right here."

Bang! Bang! Bang! Dryados raced through the darkness. He saw the forged molten white key. The angel…

The darkness shattered as his dream suddenly shifted. It was a bright noonday sun. He stood on a cliff…no a waterfall. He screamed as he plunged off the waterfall. The rocks were jagged and…

Bang! Bang! Bang! Dryados could see the angel and the key. He…

He woke with a sudden stabbing pain in his back.

Bang! Bang! Bang! And on it went all night. He was up all night, in and out of countless dreams. Half of them about the key. The other half about something terrifying. He never saw anything more in the dream beyond the white key. He threw his legs over the bed and sat there with his elbows on his knees holding his head. He wasn't sure if he had a headache or not. The key was important. *The Key of David,* he thought. *Power and authority…and David was a king…and the kingdom grew… Perhaps the Key of David was like the Staff of Mosses?* He got up out of bed and wandered in circles. *Or…perhaps it is like the Banner of the Bronze Serpent? They held it up in the desert to drive out the serpents. Yes!* he thought. *The Black Voids are invading my dreams and the world around me. The great angel must be trying to show me where it is…but they do not want me to see it!* Dryados continued to pace. The last several nights had all been filled with nightmares. He was positive now—he definitely had a headache.

The others would be leaving soon, and he really wanted to speak with them again. *But what if he did?* he thought. He couldn't ignore the dream. He couldn't delegate his responsibility regarding the dream to them. *And it is my wedding! Do I really want my friends focused on Black Voids and battle?* He got dressed. *No. I must address this quietly by myself,* he thought. *Then I will surprise them all when I have the key in hand. The answer is simple.* He smiled. *It is time for a quest.*

It was nothing like Alesia had dreamed of as a little girl. She had dreamt of a grand wedding at the Acropolis, with Roman guards in polished armor, the sounds of trumpets echoing off the great temples, and lots and lots of flowers.

It was nighttime. She was surrounded by an army of people who loved her. Each held a sparkling candle to reflect their smiles. The stars twinkled just as they had the night Dryados had taken here there for a walk. There was a low din of city noise, subdued by the sound of a gentle breeze and the hush that had fallen on the crowd.

Dryados was there just ahead of her waiting at the altar. Behind him were the lights of the city. To his right and left were two great arbors. How Dryados had done it so quickly she did not know, but each arbor held a thousand candles. They shone like the heavens. Alesia remembered she had told him she wanted lots of candles—she started to laugh.

Titus walked proudly beside his daughter. His jovial face glowed.

"Who gives this woman to this man?" Gaius asked loudly.

"I do, and my father, and my father's fathers." Titus placed Alesia's hand into Dryados's. He gave Dryados a smiling nod and stepped away. Then he too joined the gathered crowd and held up a bright candle.

There were no trumpets echoing off the mountains. Yet in the quiet starlight, eternal vows were shared. The soft delicate words "I do" echoed through the halls of time. Sacred bread and wine were offered. As tears filled the eyes of many in the crowd, a veil of separation was lifted, followed by an eternal kiss of new be-ginning. Soft "oohhs" and "aahhs" filled the crowd. Married couples nudged and squeezed their spouse's hands. An ancient chant, "Quando tu Giaus, ego Gia," was met by an explosion of cheers and a firestorm of celebration by the army of friends and family.

Dryados and Alesia walked among their family. It was bittersweet for both of them. A great new life awaited them, as their old one would be left behind. Like the birth of a child, the most wondrous things often seemed to be born in pain. But now the joyous party reigned. Old friendships were renewed. Stories of days past shared. And smiles given for the hopes of days to comes. Yet in all too brief of a time, the moment came for the groom to leave and go to their new home and await the arrival of his bride. Talmun decided to accompany Dryados. The walk was short. Dryados considered telling Talmun of the quest, but he decided against it.

The jubilant wedding party arrived a few heartbeats later. Titus carried the burning torch he had lit at his home in Pergama. The rabble of supporters quieted as Titus proudly handed the torch to Alesia, who took it inside and lit the hearth. There was another explosion of cheers as she returned back outside, doused the torch, and threw it to the crowd. The party streamed into the home, at least as many as could fit. There was more food and wine. Dryados served exotic dishes from beyond the Indus River.

But as was tradition, within the hour all the guests were gone. Fire and water were shared. *Aque et ignis communicatio* was completed. They were a family. Alesia walked outside to the garden in the back to look at the stars once more. Dryados walked quietly with her and held her hand softly. It was a clear night with a shallow moon. The stars shone brighter than they ever had before. Alesia stopped as something in the garden caught her eye. The ceramic hound had the fox trapped against the far wall again. She smiled at her husband.

"Sometimes the hound does catch the fox," she said softly as she turned, kissing him. "But I wonder…if the poor hound has any idea what to do with the fox once he does?" She looked questioningly into his eyes and then led him back inside.

Thyatira

"All right, boys, time we finished things up." Most of the men had already started putting things away. One of the new hires was still pounding out some late steel for a sword. "No, no, no. You got to keep the steel hot. Work smarter there boy, not harder!" He put the blade back into the forge, burying it deep in the coals. Then he worked the bellows. He pulled the glowing blade out of the furnace and laid it on the block anvil—just using his right hand. Then he pinned the glowing steel blade onto the bock anvil, using the forked steel arm brace he had fashioned for himself. The brace was secured with thick leather and wrapped around his hand and forearm all the way up to the elbow. It was lashed on tightly with leather straps up its length. It had a flat steel shaft down the back that came out in a curved *T* above the elbow to brace against his upper arm. The steel extended out like a fork about nine inches past his clubbed hand. With the harness on, he could pin things down and hold them in place. That was about all. But that was more than enough. With an object pinned, he could pound it with his hammer. He could not handle anything delicate, but he did fine with the larger piecework. Unfortunately, his double vision had gotten worse. His left eye seemed to slowly sink into his head as it healed. He had taken to wearing a patch over the eye when he was moving about. He would take it off when he was working. Otherwise he lost his depth perception. He made do. It wasn't pretty. He did what he could. And as the owner he delegated whatever he couldn't do to the other men. In truth, he really didn't have to do anything if he didn't want to.

He raised his big hammer again. *Bang! Bang! Bang!* An explosion of tiny comets flew in every direction. "Yes, boy, like this. Like you mean to do it some serious harm. Ahhh!" *Bang! Bang! Bang!* The steel slowly molded to the force of his will and power of his arm. The sparks flew. The metal rang. The forges roared. Ascalon glanced around the smithy. He felt himself again. And another ordinary day passed. The smithy closed for the night, and Ascalon walked to the busy street kitchen now being run by his fellowship. They fed the poor there twice a day. The people living on the streets and in the wild areas outside the city clamored to it. The Romans for their part looked the other way. Petty crime had gone down in the area, which was probably why. *Whatever works*, he thought. Yet the Iredenti were still extremely cautious.

As the fellowship meeting that night wound down, Jakotrudi watched as Daravaza led a small group of men down the stairs at the front of the meeting hall. He felt apprehensive as he watched. Daravaza had a playful giggle and seemed to be flirting with some of the men. The men also looked…eager. The fellowship meeting had ended, and everyone else was leaving. Jezebel was already speaking with several other men just off to the side. For some reason the women of the fellowship did not seem to care for her. With a sinking feeling in his gut, Jakotrudi decided to try and catch up with Daravaza.

He scurried quickly down the stairs. Daravaza and the men had vanished. At the bottom was a heavy bronze door and a large house guard. "I'm sorry, sir. Mistress Jezebel's guests are not allowed beyond this point," muttered the well-muscled guard. He had a friendly smile and wore a bright house uniform.

"Oh, I was just trying to catch up with Daravaza and the others." Jakotrudi flashed a reaffirming smile as he edged toward the door.

The guard stepped in front of him. His friendly countenance did not change. "All guests must be escorted beyond this point."

"Of course. In that case it would be fabulous if you could escort me in to catch up with them. I would be very grateful."

"Regrettably, sir, I may not leave my post. Please enjoy the rest of your evening." He motioned for Jakotrudi to head back up the stairs from whence he had come. The guard was still smiling.

"I see." Jakotrudi sighed. "I am so sorry." He nodded graciously and walked back up the stairs.

The great hall was almost empty now except for the group of men gathered around Jezebel. Some looked deep in thought, obviously contemplating what she was saying. The talk appeared friendly, as others wore soft smiles. The house stewards continued to generously distribute more wine.

"It is about being effective in your work and ministering to others. That takes focus and clarity." Jezebel paused as she noticed several of the men glancing at Jakotrudi as he approached.

"Good words, Jezebel. Life is so busy and filled with distractions." Jakotrudi smilingly patted one of the men on the shoulder. Then looked to Jezebel to continue her teaching.

She flashed a terse smile in return. "Yes, a man cannot do one thing if his mind is somewhere else. Now, if you will excuse me, we will talk more next week." She turned toward two young men on her left. "And I will see you two men Tuesday during third watch. Now, please excuse me." She smiled and walked gracefully down the stairs and disappeared.

Chapter 8

Hot Springs, Hot Meals

Dryados looked at his wrinkled skin. Any longer in the hot pool and he was sure it would never smooth out again. Alesia was so much more self-disciplined. She was already out and waiting patiently in the shade off to the side. He really wanted to join her, but the steaming waters of Hierapolis felt so good. He sank lower in the pool and looked at the cascade of white steaming pools stairstepping down the mountain. It was such a paradox to behold. The side of the mountain looked like a white snowy glacier. Yet each of the many pools was steaming hot. The ones at the top just a smidgen more than those at the bottom. As each pool filled with the heated mineral water, it spilled down into the pool below it. He leaned against the side of the pool and played in the layer of mud at the bottom. He squished mud in his hand and between his toes and thought how much Talmun would like it if he were here. Still, the moment had come for him to get out. He forced himself to his feet and reluctantly fled the heated pool.

Alesia handed him a cool glass of water as she helped dry him off. "The skin on your back is starting to peel."

"I really don't care," Dryados said with some degree of finality. He took the towel and started to dry his legs. "I'm never leaving here. I don't think I have ever just relaxed like this." He smiled up at Alesia. "It's truly just perfect." He sat down in the shade beside her. "I'm serious. I really don't want to go back." Alesia threw a towel over his legs to block some random rays of the sun penetrating the shade. He looked at her and sighed. "We will go back, and it will all be busy again. I will be exhausted, and I will miss out on life. I can't help it—I have always been that way. I just hate it."

"Then don't do it," she said as she muffed his head with a towel.

"But I have too. I have so much going on. I've got to…"

"No, you don't," she interrupted. She bent over and kissed his cheek. She looked at him with determined eyes. "No, you don't." She sat down on his legs right in front of him. "That architect you are always blathering about, Raperius…"

"Raberius?"

"Yes, that one. Does he cut every stone or lay every brick? Does he hoist the great scaffoldings they use or mix the concrete? No, of course not." She handed him a platter of grapes and cheese.

"But this is different."

"No, it isn't." Her voice was soft but determined. "Sometimes you have to let one thing go so you can grab on to something better." She put her towel over his stomach where the sun was shining through the leaves. "Why has Talmun been so successful at the Askeplion? Did he draw the plans or cut the stones?"

"No." Dryados started to laugh. "He was so far in over his head he didn't know up from down."

"And yet he succeeded greatly and made a name for himself."

"That's true, but he had a lot of help." Dryados chuckled.

"Exactly. Exactly, and so does my father and that Raperius fellow."

"Raberius."

"Whoever. But you…you are…too arrogant!" She laid down the platter of grapes and looked at him with convicting eyes.

"What? No I'm not!"

"Yes you are. You think you are the only one who can do it."

"No, I just want to make sure everything is perfect."

"And no one could possibly do it as well as you, right?" Alesia asked rhetorically.

"No, I'm not saying that. I just don't want any mistakes," he answered defensively.

"Oh, so in that case, it is because you're afraid."

"No, I'm not saying that either."

"Then what?" Alesia sat there waiting for an answer.

"Well…" Dryados looked her, feeling dejected.

"Dryados, what do you want? I mean, really want?" She leaned forward, touching his hand.

"I want a life with you." He grabbed her hand tightly. "I want a life with you… like my father had with my mother." He closed his eyes and shook his head. "But I have so much to worry about…" He sounded completely exhausted

"So did Talmun." She looked at him encouragingly.

"But he got a lot of help." His voice faded out like he had just said something impossible.

"Yes, and that will be hard for you. It is always hard for driven people to learn how to let things go. But if you do, maybe you can pursue something better." She flashed a loving smile and got up to leave. "I am heading back to the room now."

Philadelphia, Dryados's villa

The weeks passed. The seasons changed. The power of Rome continued its unrelenting growth. Emperor Domitian's persecutions increased.

"Domitian and the others know some manner of the truth. They know that men whose souls are saved are not cruel and unjust. They know that such men will not support an empire that is. And they know that when there is enough of such men, cruel and unjust empires will fall." Dryados spoke like he was speaking in front of a great army. But it was just he and the two young men seated together in his living room.

"So you are saying our quest to obtain the key is so that we might conquer Rome?" Chaim asked.

"No." Dryados shook his head. "I'm saying that the fallen nature of man will consume the earth until none are left but those who hold absolute power, in absolute cruelty. That when man thinks he is god, he is a cruel one. He is fallen. There can be no other outcome. In that way, Ivoluntas is as fallen as man is. He prowls the earth. He can only be at one place at one time, so he uses his time wisely. He is drawn to seats of power to amplify his influence. Rome to him is just a tool, nothing more. The greater Rome becomes, the greater influence he may exert. If there was one government controlling all the world, he could use that tool to influence the whole of humanity. Right now, Rome is the closest thing to that there is. He will do what he can to facilitate its growth. He will use Rome as long as he can. When it falls, he will find another. He will do this until he controls all the world. The key is not to conquer Rome. It is to conquer the fallen."

Chaim and Jankel knelt in the living room. Dryados stood between them with one hand on each man's shoulder. He prayed an ancient prayer. "The Lord bless you, and keep you; the lord make his face shine on you, and be gracious to you; the Lord lift his countenance on you and give you peace." It was just the three of them. After the prayer of blessing, the three men reclined on the floor. "Once you get to Smyrna, Darius will make passage for the two of you to Jerusalem. If the key is to be found, that is the best place to start." Dryados rose and brought over a platter of smoked meat from the table. "The key still may even be there. Tell the leaders of the Iredenti in Jerusalem of the dream and the need we have of the key. Beyond that, tell no one of the quest. The Qui Malaam will do everything in their power to stop us." The three men prayed again and then went out into the dining area to join Alesia. She was the only other person who knew of the quest. The two young men looked nervous.

"The journey to Smyrna should go very smooth," Dryados said, smiling. "My dear friend Cleopas has arranged for the caravan to be accompanied by a sizable contingent of Romans." Dryados glanced smilingly over at Alesia. "Yes, apparently they have been wanting to make a more ostensible show of force along the road, so, well, the timing just worked out." In truth, Dryados had begged Cleopas for the extra security, and that had been the excuse he had used with his superiors to deploy the troops.

"Just three more days," Alesia said graciously. "I'm sure the two of you are busy tying up any loose ends and saying your good-byes." She slid a plate of spiced fish closer to the two young men.

The young men smiled back politely. "Yes, we are," Jankel replied. "But we are also excited and prepared for whatever lies ahead." Then he leaned across the table and tore a juicy section of meat off the cooked delicacy. He had a young, eager face. He and Chaim were both about the same age, eighteen or nineteen.

"Yes, we are," Chaim added.

They both seemed too nervous to really hold much of a conversation. Perhaps it was the journey. Perhaps it was the fact that Dryados was one of the most powerful businessmen in the city. But it was to some degree humorous. Most of the boys' conversation seemed aimed at reassuring themselves. "Yes, we have been studying and are ready for anything that might come our way," Jankel reiterated. Dryados smiled as he watched the bravado of youth crash head-on into its own inherent cautiousness.

Dryados did what he could to encourage the younger men. "You will be well funded, so that should relieve some stress. Oh, and try not to be too overwhelmed the morning the caravan departs. My new warehouse manager is, well, a very cautious man, much like me. He may be particularly…passionate that morning. So just try to ah, well, avoid him."

The two young men glanced silently at each other.

"And my new caravan manager, well, he yells a lot. I think he enjoys his job way too much." Dryados laughed. "But he is harmless." Dryados looked at the two youths' blank faces and forced a smile.

The young men stopped talking.

"Come to think of it, you might want to avoid him too. Yeah, I think that would be a good idea." Dryados forced another smile onto his face. Then decided to add a forced laugh. "Ha-ha-ha…"

The young men started to look a little pasty.

"What I'm trying to say is just, well, find a good spot, and just try to blend in. Yeah, that's all." Dryados smiled, shaking his head. "Oh, and have fun."

Alesia looked aghast at the now ghost-white young men. "I believe what my husband is trying to say is that there have been a number of changes in his import/export business over the last few weeks. So if there are any ruffles, just take it all in stride. Everyone knows exactly what they are doing, and you will be fine, despite the excitement of the caravan's departure."

"Yes, exactly what I was saying…" Dryados said, nodding. The two young men looked silently at each other. They seemed unable to talk.

Chapter 9
Svistvs

The docks of Smyrna

"Hold there!" Darius bellowed. "Keep those ropes tight, and hold!" He walked over and checked the pulleys. Everything was holding fast. "Get those men out of there, or they'll be flatter than a halibut's underbelly. And you boys, be quick there!" The extra dockworkers scurried out of the second hold. The *Rose Fox* was a stout ship. She had four wide holds going deep into her hull. This lowered her center of gravity and added stability. Still, her draft was less than that of narrower ships, which allowed her to go into shallower waters without running aground. That was a helpful trait in the reef-filled Aegean and Mediterranean Seas. She had three shorter masts instead of the usual two taller ones. This created less of a lever arm on her hull in high winds, making her more stable. "Now, lower that pallet slowly. No! Slowly, slowly…" The ropes in the high pulleys creaked from the weight of the heavy pallet. The men on the side ropes threw their weight into shifting the pallet a little more to port. "Slowly, slowly…yes…just about…there!" The pallet settled into position.

Darius continued to pace the deck. The ship rocked gently in its dock. Men checked the canvases. Fresh foodstuffs were being brought into the galley stores. Heavy pallets were being hoisted off the dock. Everyone moved with purpose. A heavy freight wagon rattled to a stop on the loading dock. It was followed by many others. Darius stared blankly at the line of wagons with his jaw agape. Darius had been told the caravan was big, but… His heart fluttered in panic. *Dryados is insane, absolutely insane. There is no way the ship is going to be able to hold all this cargo.* The army of dockworkers stopped to gawk at the rich caravan.

The abrupt silence brought Darius's thoughts back to the moment. "Just more work to put food on the table, men," he yelled loudly. "It loads just like all the rest of it, one piece at a time." He turned back, looking at the partially filled hold. "I told you boys before—pack it tight! Now slide that pallet hard against the one aft. No, no, no. I said tight!" Darius stormed back across the deck. "And you boys there, lash those pallets down…"

Hours passed.

Jankel and Chaim stayed out of the way. The dock was packed with wagons, work animals, cargo, and quick-tempered dockmen. The air was filled with language not fit for gentler ears. Men raced in a hundred different directions doing a hundred different things. After several barrages of "Get the %#$@& out of the way!" and "Move your lazy %#$@&!" the two men found a little corner off to the side. They had spent the night at Darius's home and had been invited to join him down at the docks. Jankel was athletic and a born leader. Chaim was quiet, a hard worker, and very inquisitive. Despite their differences, both men thought it would be fun. Darius had taken a short break at lunch and then went straight back to work. He was planning on booking the two men passage to Jerusalem as soon as he had seen to the *Rose Fox*'s departure.

The two young men stayed in their little corner. The main loading tackle to the third hold had snapped. Two of the men were hurt, but not seriously. The loading had come almost to a complete stop. Tempers got even shorter. The language, more flavored. The two travelers offered to help. "Ha, your mommies might get mad if two young girlies like yourselves got bruised up a bit. Now move your %#$@& over to the side!" The two men decided it might be best to meet Darius back at his home.

Darius was in the middle of helping to move a heavy crate of Roman armor. "Get a wheel under that! You're gonna tear the deck! No! No! No! Not like that, man!" Darius raced over and shoved the wheeled skid under the pallet. "Now swing the hoist."

Jankel waved his arms, getting Darius's attention, and yelled up, "I think we are just going to head back over to your house. We will meet you there." Darius looked up and nodded an affirming grimace as he continued to fuss with the stuck pallet. The two young men quickly left the dock.

They headed for the Fountain of Poseidon and Darius's home. The streets were busier than those back in Philadelphia, and the shops filled with amazing products. The smells of the street were inviting.

It was still early in the afternoon when they arrived at the Fountain of Poseidon. "We are going to be as much out of place with Helen as we were with those dockworkers," Jankel grumbled as he loosened his satchel and sat down beside the bubbling sculpture.

"No, it will be fine," Chaim answered. "We can have some tea and relax in the small garden in the back. We can play a game of cards outside or just read." Chaim smiled and let out an honestly tired sigh. "It has been far too busy the last couple of weeks. It will be great to just relax."

Jankel looked at him in frustration. "Look, it is still early in the day. We can go see some of the temples and still be back before Darius even gets home. We will be much less of a bother that way." Jankel spoke confidently.

"No." Chaim shook his head but wore his ever-present smile. "Darius would not want us roaming about the city by ourselves. Let's just head back to the house. I'm sure Darius will take us to see the sites here in the city before we leave."

Jankel started putting his things back in his satchel. "You are like a child," he scolded. "We are just going to go for a walk. There's plenty to see. The city is easy to navigate. And if we get lost, we will just ask directions to the fountain."

Chaim groaned with a sigh of exhaustion. "I'm really tired. It's hot. Let's just head home."

Jankel rose to his feet. "I'm going into the city. You can do whatever you want. I personally do not need to be babysat. Nor do I want to impose myself on everyone we meet." Jankel turned to go. "This is going to be a long trip, and we have to learn to take care of ourselves."

Chaim scrambled to his feet. "That's true, but Darius is our host, and we need to respect that."

Jankel threw on his satchel. "I'm leaving." Then he stormed away, heading into the city.

Chaim hurried after him. "You don't even know where you're going."

"No, but that doesn't mean I won't get there." Jankel stopped a random man on the street. "How do I get to the Golden Way?"

The man paused briefly. "Straight ahead to the end of the road, about a half mile, then turn left. Then take your first right. Should be less than a mile. Most of the temples will be up to the right." The man turned and continued on his way.

"Left, right, right—simple!" Jankel flashed a confident and well-practiced smile.

Chaim shook his head.

They followed the directions without difficulty. They entered the Golden Way just a short time later. It was the main thoroughfare of the city and was packed with people. Jankel pushed his way through the crowds. Chaim followed close behind. "Excuse me…pardon me…I'm so sorry…" After a hundred polite overtures, he realized in the midst of the noisy masses his words were probably not even heard. Soon, like everyone else in the crowded throng, he stopped his shallow apologies and just shoved his way along. The attire of those surrounding him spoke of a hundred different places, from the stone-jeweled ephods of the Egyptians to the hats of leopard skin and red-gold feathers of the black Nubians. Exotic animals and birds squawked in a hundred cages from dozens of shops. Incredible smells filled the air. They grabbed some shredded spiced chicken from one of the shouting venders, and honey tea from another. Chaim struggled to stay as close to Jankel as he could. In no time at all they arrived at the Temple of

Cybele. It sat on a raised dais of seven or eight stairs. Its great marble pillars were tall and majestic with ornate Corinthian tops. Entering the temple was like entering the throne room of an Olympian goddess. In the center sat Cybele, mother goddess and protector of the city. She rested on a grand sculptured throne flanked by two great chiseled lions. It was the largest work of carved stone Chaim had ever seen.

He looked at Jankel. "Have you ever seen the like of it?" he asked, shaking his head.

Jankel's eyes were just as wide as he slowly shook his head. "No."

There were paintings, and tapestries, and rows upon rows of smoldering incense burners and lamps. Chaim would have been content to spend the rest of the day just looking at the paintings. Jankel, on the other hand, wanted to see "everything," and almost physically dragged him out.

The two youths continued up the broad road. They were jostled about in the thick crowds. They had heard of the small altars that the Romans carried about the city and were quick to skirt around any they saw. Their movements went unnoticed in the busy tumultuous crowd. They stopped at shops selling every conceivable product they could imagine, as well as some they could not. Jankel found one selling giant carved ostrich eggs and gold-leafed alabaster. They ate hot buttered rolls drenched in cinnamon, and spiced honey chips. In what seemed like no time at all, they came to the Great Synagogue of the city. Roman soldiers were everywhere, but they saw no more of the small portable altars.

It was getting later in the day, but they still had at least an hour or so before they had to head back. They pressed on. The crowds were dense, loud, and impolite. The walkways in the square were blocked by the praying Jews. Some had cubes strapped to their heads and arms. They had carved out sections of the road to ensure their rituals were seen by all the trapped crowds. The two men thought about going around on one of the side roads, but they were almost through.

"You are strangers to the city—is that not true?" asked a tall Jewish man.

"Yes, just visiting from Philadelphia," Chaim replied.

"Are you Jews here to worship at the synagogue?" The tall Jew smiled.

"No. We are just here to visit the temples and admire the grandeur of your city," Jankel answered nonchalantly.

The three men struggled down the road together like fish swimming a rocky stream. The tall Jew was bumped inadvertently against Jankel. "I am so sorry," he said apologetically, grinning. "Which temples do you wish to see? Which gods do you worship?"

There was a brief moment of silence. "We would like to see all of them. We have heard the Temple of Aphrodite is exquisite." Jankel continued walking.

"Yes, it is one you must see. I find the benches in front the most entertaining to watch. And if you are looking for a conquest..." He smiled broadly. "Though

I would never say that to my wife." He laughed, slapping Jankel on the shoulder. "And what gods do you serve? Dionysus? Apollo? Or perhaps Cybele?"

"And the temple of Cybele…was spectacular." Jankel shook his head in awe. "I loved the carved lions and the detail in the sculpture of Cybele. Amazing!" Jankel smiled and tried to press forward in the crowd. But the street was packed—they were going nowhere.

"So are you followers of Cybele then?" the tall man asked.

"No, but the temple was amazing to see. Good day, sir." Chaim nodded and tried to move forward, but the crowd was dead stopped.

"Don't worry. You will not offend me. We Jews have grown accustomed to you Romans and your pantheon of gods."

"We are not Romans," Chaim corrected. "We are from Philadelphia." The crowd was starting to move.

"And which gods do you serve?"

Neither man responded. They simply pretended not to hear as they pressed forward into the weakening wall of people.

Progress was slow. It was like being hip deep in mud. Despite their best efforts, it was clear they were not going to make it to the Temple of Aphrodite and still get back to Darius's in time.

Chaim looked at Jankel with his usual smile. "Darius will take us another day. We do not want to be late. Besides, we have already seen so much." Chaim's tone was positive and upbeat.

"I suppose you are right." Jankel sounded reluctant, but the two men turned around.

The crowd was moving much better heading south. They soon found themselves back at the Central Synagogue. The praying Jews still obstructed the road. The two men veered off to the side. Jankel felt a heavy hand on his shoulder and a sharp poke in his side. The tall Jew stood beside him. Jankel looked down to see a slender blade pointing into his left rib cage. "You and your friend will come with us. This way!" The tall Jew jerked him off to the side of the road.

Chaim was a few steps back as he watched Jankel grabbed and shoved off the road. He pushed against the intervening people, trying to surge forward and help. "Follow your young friend or die on the street." He felt the stab of a knife tip in his back. "No one would even see who stabbed you." Chaim instinctively stopped on the road. His sudden stop was met by an even sharper stab in his back. Someone seized him by the shoulder and shoved him to the side. "Don't make this difficult. Just follow your friend." The tip of the blade pressed more firmly into his back as he was quickly ushered off the road.

Darius looked around the deck. The workers had all finished for the day. *We'll have to get some new ropes, a bigger block and tackle, new pulleys…* There was still cargo to be loaded. He was disappointed, but they would easily have the loading completed tomorrow. He stared at the nearly filled holds.

The two young lads had left hours ago. He hoped Helen was not too mad about having to entertain them all afternoon by herself. She was usually pretty good about that sort of thing. On the other hand, she might give him an ear full when he got home. *Could go either way*, he thought. *Maybe I'll bring her home a little something. Yes, that would be wise.* He had the last of the dockmen put some extra lashings on the heavier pallets. Finally he headed home.

Helen greeted him with a big kiss as soon as he was inside. She smiled happily as she looked at the box of dried fruit and sweet cakes he had brought home for dessert. "Where are the two boys?" she asked cheerfully.

Darius's heart stopped. "What do you mean? I sent them home hours ago!"

Helen's cheerful demeanor vanished. The color left her face. "I haven't seen them since they left with you this morning." She laid the dessert on a counter. Her face filled with rage. "What do you mean you sent them home hours ago?" She glared at him in heated silence. He didn't answer. "Why didn't you come home with them? Or have one of your men bring them here? You sent them home alone? They are new to the city! They don't know!" Despite the tone in her voice, her face was now more terrified than angry.

"No, my love, I told them everything. I told them all about the Romans and the altars. I told them about all of it! They said they were coming straight home." Darius wandered around the room and then pulled out a chair at the table and sat down. "That was hours ago." He sighed.

Helen sat down beside him. There was no more anger, just dread. "What do you think happened to them?" It was like asking how they died.

Darius sat quietly breathing. "I don't know." He glanced outside. "It's dark out now. It's not safe to be out. They may have gone over to see the temples and visit the Golden Way. Any of those areas that are still open will be teeming with Romans." He looked at Helen. It was the look of a man about to go to a funeral. "I will eat a quick bite of food. Then I will head over to the fountain. Perhaps they are lost or forgot how to get home from there." His head sank slowly into his hands. "I just don't know."

Helen rose and quickly dished up a plate of food she had prepared for their meal with the young men. Darius wolfed it down. He put on his night cloak and paused at the door. "I will try to find them." Then he turned and walked out into the darkness. He and Helen both knew the unspoken truth. They would never see either of the young men again.

The two young men were ushered down a flight of stairs to the lower level of the Central Synagogue. The torches flickered as they were shoved through the narrow stone corridors. They could hear the noise of the crowded streets outside and the soft sounds of their own sandals on the stone floor. No one spoke.

Their captors shoved them into a large room at the end of the hall. Jankel stood motionless with the knife still in his left side. Chaim staggered into the room beside him, struggling to breathe. His captor held his tunic from behind and had tugged the collar up tight around his neck. He stood on his tiptoes, pulling at his tunic, choking and coughing. At the front of the room was a raised platform on which stood a thick gilded table. Behind the table were three ornate chairs. The two smaller chairs on the sides were empty. In the large seat in the center sat a man wearing the pure white linen tunic of a high priest. He wore an elegant sash embroidered in blue, purple, and scarlet. And beside him on the table sat a large flat-top turban he had removed from his head. He had a thin face and a hooked nose. He sneered at the two men with disgust. His eyes were hard.

"Bind them!"

Chaim's captor let go of his collar and began to bind his arms behind him.

"You have no authority over us," yelled Jankel. "This is not a Roman court. We are both Roman citizens. This is an affront to Roman justice." Neither of the men was actually a Roman citizen, but it was all he could come up with. His words had no effect.

"The Romans do not rule here, young citizen of Rome. They merely look over us, like a dark cloud," said the smiling thin-faced man at the table. "And like any other storm that has come before, they too will pass, and we shall remain. If, as you say, you are citizens of the empire, this will be quickly finished, and we will compensate you for any inconvenience we may have caused. Now, Romans, which gods do you serve?"

"The Roman Empire has many gods. The…"

The thin-faced man flashed a twisted smile and a small nod. *Bam! Bam! Bam!* Jankel fell to the ground. Blood flowed from the back of his head. He glanced up just quick enough to see the thin-faced man nod again. *Bam! Bam!* Jankel slumped to the floor. The cudgel fell onto the back of his legs. *Bam! Bam! Bam! Bam!*

"Stop it! No, please stop it!" Chaim took a step forward. His arms were bound behind him, and he was held securely by two large Jews. He could see at least three or four other armed men walking about the room. "We have done nothing wrong!" he cried. "We are citizens of the empire!" One guard yanked upward on his bound hands. Both his shoulders burned like fire. He screamed. The right shoulder tore out of the joint. One captor grabbed him behind the neck and drove him to the floor. His face smashed into the stone.

Both men lay pinned to the floor. "Get them both up!" snapped the thin-faced man. The captives were jerked to their feet. Jankel's legs were shaking as he tried to stand. Chaim stood hunched over, favoring the dislocated shoulder. Their labored breathing filled the room.

"My name is Suistus," sneered the hook-nosed Jew. "I am a patient man, but a busy one. Perhaps you do not understand. I will ask a question one time, and you will answer. It is very simple. Now, which gods do you serve?"

The two young men froze. Neither knew what to do. Their bluff had been called. They remained silent. Moments passed.

Suistus pushed his chair back and rose to his feet. "As I said, I do not ask questions a second time. If we meet again, I can assure you, you will be more than eager to answer my questions." Suistus pushed his chair back and rose to his feet. "I will simply need to delegate the task of persuading you to someone with perhaps a more convincing skill set." Suistus walked down from the dais and turned, smiling to the guards. "Take them to Bellua. If they are still alive in the morning, bring them here. Not too early—I was planning on sleeping in." Suistus walked casually out the door without so much as giving the two men a second glance.

Chaim and Jankel were shoved and jarred along a darkened corridor. They came to a broad door with a heavy bolt. The door was quickly unlocked, and the well-oiled rod slid free like the axle of a king's chariot. The men were dragged through the door and shoved down a steep irregular corridor of stairs. The passage was too narrow and serpentine for the men to even fall. The guards lit more torches as they went. There was another heavy door at the bottom, which opened with similar ease. They entered a damp passage. After a maze of turns they came to a three-quarter-sized door carved into one of the stone walls.

The door creaked loudly on it hinges as it opened. As it did, the entire group lurched backward. The stench of death and corruption coming from within was overwhelming. The two men were thrown forward. The room inside was well lit. There were torches burning everywhere. Yet it still seemed dark from the blackness of the soot coating on the walls. Over to the side was a stack of corpses in various stages of decay and rot. Some looked fairly fresh. Others were covered with armies of maggots. The room was filled with implements designed to torture, maim, and kill. Off to the other side sat a large fat man covered in sweat, drinking from a waterskin.

"I was just getting ready to leave for the day," said the sweaty fat man. The guards shoved the two men forward so Bellua could see them. "Aahhh! You have got to be joking!" Bellua rose to his feet. "I will just run them through and be done with it. You men can help me carry out their bodies." He paced over to the wall and pulled down a tattered sword and then turned and stormed determinedly toward the two young men.

One of the guards stepped into his path and put up a hand to the fat man's slick chest. The fat man glared at the two young prisoners. The guard gave Bellua his instructions.

The torturer flung the old blade across the room and roared with profanities. "Aaahhhhhh %^&#$@(^%$^$#%%!" He sulked away into the darker center of the room. The thick black hair on his stomach was wet and matted down. It camouflaged his frame in the limited light. He grumbled and then growled angrily. "Fine! But I am not dragging this out all night!" He turned and walked over by the wall. "So Suistus wants them to talk, but doesn't want them killed?" Then he looked at the guards and chuckled. "And I'm ready to leave this %#$@& hole!" He seemed to stand there just staring at the wall. But no. It was not the wall. It was the torch. He watched the flames dance undisturbed in the breezeless room. He seemed mesmerized by the movement. Then he pulled the torch from the wall.

He sneered as he approached the two men. His jaw was clenched. He looked at the guards. "Bind their arms across the top with those long rods." He nodded toward a stack of iron shafts lying near the mound of corpses. "Bind them on about every two inches with those leather ties, no further apart than that." He nodded again toward a large stack of leather ties hanging on the near wall. "Soak the ties in the bucket there first."

"Both arms?" asked one guard.

The torturer laughed. "No, just the right ones."

The iron rods were tied to the men's right arms from their shoulders to past the tip of their middle fingers. Bellua inspected the bonds. "Bind them several more times across the palms, wrists, and elbows! I do not want any movement! None! I don't want them flopping about like some dying pigeons and knocking things over." The jiggling fat man gave one final inspection to the wet leather bonds. "Now chain them to the wall."

The guards were distracted as they scanned the walls looking for the chains. Jankel attacked. He swung the iron shaft bound on his arm with all his might. It struck one of the guards hard in the head. There was a loud *crack* as it hit the man's temple. The man dropped to the ground, unmoving. He would die several hours later. Chaim threw all his weight at one of the other guards. His bound arm was tangled in the leather strappings, and he couldn't lift it. He tried to strike with his left fist, but he was never a fighter. The blows were embarrassingly weak. But he struck as hard as he could. The struggle ended quickly. They were both subdued and beaten severely. "Don't kill them! Don't kill them!" screamed the lead guard. Bellua stood back, eagerly waiting for the men to be chained to the wall.

Once chained, Bellua took his time. He waited for the room to grow silent. The words he was about to share were clearly important. "This is a little lesson I learned from our Roman hosts," he said. His words were cold and filled with bitter sarcasm. He held his torch up level to his eye. Slowly, he raised his right hand. He held it there for a few moments for the men to look at. He rotated it slowly from side to side. There in the light of the dancing flames, his right hand looked like melted wax. All five digits had been burned away as well as the lower half of his hand. The flesh was smooth, red, and warped.

"Grab that sheet of metal," he yelled to one of the guards. He motioned his head at a thin sheet of metal about a foot square leaning against the base of the wall. "It will protect their other fingers as we move along," he said flatly. "Here are the rules. Rule one—we stop when one of you answers the questions I have asked. It doesn't matter who answers. Rule two—whatever I have to do to get one of you to talk, I will also do to the other. So the sooner one of you speaks, the better it is for both of you. Rule three—everybody talks. No one has ever *not* answered the questions I have asked." He moved the torch closer as he raised his mangled hand. "I have never met a man who has lasted as long as I did," he said with pride. "But rule three is true for all of us." He sneered at Jankel and Chaim. "We all talk." His eyes seemed to go blank as his face filled with disgust. "After I talked, the Romans killed all my friends, all my family, everyone I loved. Everyone I betrayed." He stared at his disfigured appendage.

"I will start with your fifth digit. You will scream. When the fire has burned it completely dead, the pain will end, and you will stop screaming. When you stop screaming, I will move the torch to the next digit, and so on. None have lasted as long as I, but if you do, remember, you have another hand, and two feet, and arms, and legs." He waited for a few moments.

"Grab this one!" The guards grabbed Chaim and held out his hand. They slid the metal sheet between his pinky and the ring finger. "Answer the question Suistus has asked, and you will both be spared a great deal of needless pain," Bellua growled. Chaim shook his head no. He was already sobbing.

Bellua waved the torch in front of his own hand again and examined his tortured appendage. "Sometimes I feel them—my fingers, I mean—like they were still there. It is an odd feeling you too will come to experience." Then he moved the torch.

Bellua left an hour or two later. Both men lay in their prison cell, unconscious. They were each missing four fingers from their right hands. The two boys woke up several times during the night. They cried. But their tears were not from the pain in their hands.

Suistus slept in late just as he had planned. His breakfast was marvelous. The pomegranate juice was sweet. The fruit was at the peak of its season. He had toasted bread and cheese. He liked the honey-soaked prunes and almonds. He left home, kissing his wife and children good-bye. The morning air was brisk as he walked to the synagogue. Many along the way greeted him with humble bows. He was the chief priest; it was his due. Everyone in the city knew him.

After some brief meetings, he went to the secret rooms below the synagogue. He took his seat on the raised platform. He had been informed the men were harder to break than most. But like all the others, they too had learned the truth of rule three.

Bellua gave his report. Suistus was impressed with how much information Bellua was able to get out of the two young men. Once they were broken, they were truly broken.

"And they told you it was this merchant Dryados?"

"Yes, Rabbi," Bellua said humbly.

"I have heard this name before…" Suistus sat on the raised platform in his ornate chair, thinking. "I'm just not sure, but I have heard that name." Bellua waited patiently for Suistus's thoughts to come together. "Yes, now I remember." Suistus nodded. Recognition flooded his face. "This man is a phantom. I have heard many of the businessmen in our congregation speak of him, never favorably. They complain to one another about him all the time. He is almost a legend. But I have heard nothing specific about him, nothing of disloyalty to Rome or hatred for our people. Now to come to find out that he is Iredenti!"

Bellua remained motionless, waiting.

Suistus shook his head, befuddled. "And the quest you say was for the Key of David?"

"Yes, Rabbi."

"Surely, it is a myth." Suistus rose and started pacing behind his chair. "Could such a thing still exist?" He shook his head in disbelief. "Yet…David was a king. A mighty king." Suistus walked to the front of the room, thinking. A myriad of possibilities raced in his mind. Was this a tool used of King David to conquer the land? Like the great Ark of the Covenant that went before David's armies to destroy all who stood against them? Suistus stopped and looked questioningly toward Bellua. "David's armies were unstoppable. His kingdom expanded and his enemies were conquered. Perhaps this is the tool God has prepared for us to rid ourselves of the Romans." Bellua remained silent.

Suistus walked closer and stood by the torturer. "You have done well. The information you have discovered is invaluable. If this Key of David does exist, I know the one who will know where to find it." Suistus turned and started to walk out of the chamber, then stopped at the door. "Have the two Iredenti tortured daily, but keep them fit to travel. They will soon be going on a little journey. In the meantime I must determine what to do about this…Dryados."

Chapter 10
Perceptions of a Ghost

"Cash flow! Cash flow! Cash flow!" Dryados stood mumbling to himself in his empty warehouse. Part of him looked at all the empty space as a vast land of opportunity just waiting to be filled with amazing products from across the empire. The other part of him remembered his flaccid money purse and other empty coffers about the city. "Stupid! Idiot! Moron!" he mumbled. He thought about the caravan they had sent to Smyrna. A small fraction of the goods could be sold almost immediately there in the city. That would flip a little of his cash back to him right away. But most of the goods would be shipped on to the Greek lands and then to the more distant markets around the empire. He would make several fortunes in this single voyage, but it would come at a cost. Most of his wealth would be tied up for several weeks at a minimum. He had reinvested and reinvested and reinvested. But this, this was the biggest undertaking he had ever attempted. "It had to be done," he muttered. "It had to be done."

Against his better judgment he decided to go over to the caravanserai and just take a look at the new caravans. As he walked in, he was greeted by the caravanserai's typical beehive of early morning activity. Some of the slower caravans were just leaving. There was the routine noise of grumpy camels, braying horses, and small herds of goats and sheep. People were washing. Others were cooking. The smell of the caravanserai was always a perpetual contradiction of cooking delicacies and livestock manure.

"Master Dryados, please come. Have some tea with my humble family..."

"Master Dryados, I have been looking so forward to trading with you. Come, let us sit and have tea..."

"Master Dryados..."

"Master Dryados..."

"Master Dryados..."

He was confronted by a hundred smiling faces, and all he could do was say, "No thanks." "No, I'm sorry." "No..." His face grew redder and redder with each feigned apology. Soon he was hunched over and doing everything he could to avoid contact with everyone.

"Oh, Master Dryados, I almost didn't see you there. Please…"

Dryados kept his head down, nodded, and politely waved them off. Three steps later he turned and raced out of the caravanserai like a man with loose bowels running for a toilet. Several of the merchants actually laughed as he raced by, thinking that was in fact the case.

Back in his small office he resumed his pacing. "How could I have been so shortsighted!" he moaned. He remembered his father telling him a hundred times, "Always sit and have tea when you are asked, and *never, ever, ever* destroy your cash flow!" Now he was stuck violating both. "Stupid, idiotic, shortsighted!" He wished his legs were longer so he could kick himself in the butt.

Smyrna

"You said Dryados?" Suistus listened closely to his complaining friend as they walked down the steps of the Central Synagogue.

"Dryados! Yes, Rabbi, that is his name! Truly, the man is a genius. But more than that, he is a ghost. He appeared out of nowhere just over a year ago. The power he wields is astounding. We do not know how, but he has forced many of the great merchants of the East to sell their goods to him. Yet they speak highly of him. He seems to control limitless wealth. He rules the caravanserai system like a king upon a throne. His sway among the caravans is unparalleled. And he seems to have an army of spies. His forces are everywhere. We have heard he has dealings as far away as the Greek kingdoms."

The two men stopped at the bottom of the stairs. "Do you think this man is a Greek then?" Suistus asked, confused.

"No, he is known to be a citizen of the empire," explained the complaining merchant.

"The Romans have come to be our friends of late. Perhaps this Dryados can be swayed? Perhaps—"

"No, Great One. No." The merchant's face was growing more flushed by the second. "This one is not our friend. He attacks us mercilessly! But he is also subtle and wise. He knows to attack us openly would be met with immediate reprisals. No, he attacks our business interests, not the synagogue. He undermines our wealth and power. I tell you this is not simply a business matter. No, he attacks us because we are Jews! He destroys our businesses to weaken us before the Romans and to ultimately destroy us. I know this to be true!"

"The Romans will insist that this is merely a business issue. They will not intervene." Suistus looked appraisingly at his friend. "And you are sure that it is not that he is simply a better businessman than you? You said the man was a genius."

"Yes, he is. But I tell you, this is far too much for one lone man to accomplish. This is clearly part of a greater conspiracy. Somehow he has brought our enemies together. Somehow he has integrated them into a weapon to destroy us financially. And in so doing, destroy the synagogue and our very faith! But *he*...*he* is at the heart of it!" The man looked at the now silent chief priest. "It is not just me. He has attacked the interests of many others. Surely you have heard of this before?"

Suistus stood, nodding his head. "Yes." He was finally convinced. "I have spoken to many of our people over the last few days. Like you, they have all said the same thing. It is clear that this ghost is a brilliant man, and his plan is equally so. He has waged an invisible war at the financial foundations of the synagogue." Suistus sighed deeply and began to guide his friend through the ever-dense crowd of people along the Golden Way. Suistus nodded and exchange pleasantries with many people as they passed. He stopped at one of his favorite venders and purchased a tall goblet of pomegranate juice. Imbibing on the sweet nectar, he looked confidently at his good friend. "There was a nest of scabby rats like that at my villa," he said, smiling. "I had them all killed!" He nodded confidently at the beleaguered businessman. "Our relationship with the Romans remains strained. Perhaps this man, Dryados, is a genius. Perhaps he is a phantom. Like a great general in a war, perhaps he has mistakenly thought himself safe by staying hidden in the background." Suistus stopped in the roadway. "In either case, the Romans must not know of our involvement with anything that might happen to this man." Suistus patted the harried businessman on the shoulder. "Even phantoms can have accidents...and be killed." He smiled again and then went his separate way into the crowd.

Chapter 11
Room of Keys

It was dark when they moved Jankel and Chaim out to the wagon. The long cloaks they wore over their tattered tunics ensured that no one would recognize them. Only the tinkling of their chains on the stone gave a clue that they were prisoners. But in the cold hours before dawn there was no one around to hear even that. Suistus had insisted they be kept fit for travel. They walked to the wagon on their own accord. Bellua made sure not to injure their legs. But from the waist up, that was a different story. In truth, even if someone had seen their faces, it would not have mattered. They were no longer recognizable for whom they once were. Now, men of sorrow.

They were pushed into the back of the wagon and then chained in place. The back gate was drawn closed behind them. They had not spoken in days. They passed back into unconsciousness as the wagon started to move forward. It moved slowly down the street, unnoticed in the early morning darkness.

Dryados read the letter over and over. He sat in his chair, stunned. He looked out the window of his beautiful villa, across the garden, to see a flawless blue sky. Yet there was no consolation to his soul over the disappearance of the two young men. He had picked them. He had sent them out. He had seen the love in their spirit and the excitement in their eyes when he asked them to go on the journey, on "the quest." Now all he could see was what they would never be—never grow up, never find a wife, never have children. He had robbed them of all of it!

"It is not your fault, Dryados," Alesia said softly. She stood beside him, running her hands lightly through his hair. "They chose to fight knowing that it might cost them their lives. They both had friends and family that had been killed. They knew."

"No, they didn't. Not really." Dryados turned, looking into her beautiful eyes.

"They were so young. They never thought it would happen to them."

Alesia shook her head. "Dryados, you are wrong. They knew it could happen to them, and that is exactly why they went. They knew it could happen to any of us. And they knew the world needed...to be saved." She leaned over and kissed his face.

"They were so young..." He spoke like his own life had washed out of him, like it surely had theirs.

Alesia sat beside him. "Yes, they were." They snuggled together. Dryados put his hand on Alesia's stomach. It was softer now since when they had married. Her cheekbones and jawline were more rounded. He half smiled. Alesia laid her head softly on his shoulder and closed her eyes.

The men of sorrow knew nothing of the journey they were taking. They were kept chained in the sealed darkness of the back of the wagon. They had only been awoken one time. It seemed it was at night, and it felt as though the wagon had stopped for a while. The guard opened the back of the wagon for the men to urinate, and then to beat them mercilessly with a chain. They no longer yelled or screamed. Only their bodies moaned. After the beating, they just slept.

The next thing they knew, the back of the wagon dropped open, and they were dragged out onto a street. They could each see out of the one eye they still possessed. For Jankel, it was his right. For Chaim, his left. They could see it was a big city, at an acropolis. A large contingent of Roman soldiers surrounded them. There were people on the street staring, trying to see what was happening. The Romans formed a wall of bodies around them so that no one could catch even a glimpse of them. They were shoved quickly off the street into a palace with a long, narrow entry corridor. There were new guards. They were enormous. Great bronze doors...a carpet! They could not raise their heads, but looking at that carpet...it did not matter. The carpet was...

They stood in an amazing room. Their bodies and wills were broken. But the carpet...it seemed to infuse...something...

The two men could hear the weight in the great bronze doors as they swung closed behind them. There was a lone shadow standing beside them. The shadow bowed and then kneeled. "These are the two Iredenti seekers, my lord." Like a reflex before a beating, both men braced themselves. It was Suistus's voice.

Something slammed into the back of their knees. They both crashed to the floor. Only the *thud* of the strike to their legs and the rattle of their chains disturbed the peaceful silence of the room. They did not speak or groan.

"There is no need to be so harsh to our guests," said a cheerful voice from deeper inside the room. "I can tell they've had a rough few days as of late. Please, help them up." The voice was calm and gentle.

The men were lifted up from the floor like weightless scraps of parchment. Their cloaks were removed. Then their chains. One of the large guards brought them cool water in gold-and-emerald goblets. For the first time, the men looked up at their host. He nodded politely for them to drink. The goblets were refreshed as quickly as the men drank them. Perhaps it was rude, but the men kept drinking for some time. It was the pure biological instinct of their dying bodies. Eventually they paused to catch their breath. They stood there panting.

Their host was as amazing and beautiful as the room in which they now stood. He was tall and muscular. He wore a garment of arrayed gems, almost like a fighting harness. His features were as chiseled as his body. He stood motionless and let them stare at him for a few moments.

Suistus stood silently, patiently beside them. Their host nodded, and the two large guards left the room.

Their stunning host waited patiently until the great bronze doors had been sealed. "Now, you will tell me of this quest Lord Suistus has reported to me in his many letters. He tells me you have been sent on a quest to find the Key of David?"

"Yes, Your Majesty," they responded in unison. There was no longer even the hint of hesitation in their voices. They were as broken as two old nags at a riding stable for children.

The governor's eyes remained fixed upon them. But his hand went instinctively to a platinum white chain around his own neck. He stood holding the chain, seemingly unaware of his altered posture. It made him look...unsure. "And for what purpose would you seek it?" There was a momentary silent pause. Neither young men could tell whom he was taking to. "You there, the taller one, answer the question!" barked the governor. His cool demeanor was gone. He looked at Jankel.

"We believe it to be a tool, like the Rod of Moses," he panted. "That it will wield the power of God...to fight our enemies...and expand His kingdom. That it will unlock the prison that holds the souls of men." His words were halting and labored. His body was near death. His soul was ready to leave.

The governor stood silently in front of them. His hand toyed with the platinum chain around his neck. His eyes had grown completely blank. His thoughts were obviously in another place.

Ivoluntas walked with God. He rejoiced in the relationship he had with his Creator. He could feel God's love for him physically flowing through him. That love was no different than the blood flowing in his veins or the air he breathed. His existence was bliss and fulfillment. He dwelled with his Maker in heaven, the Great Eternal Kingdom. It was the reference point of all creation. It was the center of every universe, dimension, and scale. His existence was joy beyond measure because he was with God.

He remembered a day the Holy One had taken him for a walk in one of the Perpetua Occultis. They were so many, and each one more glorious than the one before. It was as though there were an infinite number of new heavens all within the one. In that place there were many wonders Ivoluntas did not understand. It was a living place for the Chayot Ha Kodesh, Ophanim, and Erelim. It was like the garden that was in Eden, but it was just for them. On that day the Holy One took him to something different. To call it a place did not seem to capture the essence of where they went. It was a…community of strange objects. They were made of every fashion and occult composition. The objects there were alive, though they were not. In one room were mounted many keys and nothing else. The Holy One took one key and placed it around Ivoluntas's neck. It was opalescent and moved with living color. Ivoluntas tried to hold the key in his hand, but the key passed through his being as though he were a ghost. Only the chain to which it was attached could he hold or move. As he moved the chain up and down, the key itself stayed tight against his flesh. He could not remove the chain from his neck or the key from off his skin. He was helpless to do more than move them up and down against him. As the key slid down his chest onto his upper abdomen, at its lowest point on the chain, he could read an inscription honed into its substance. It read, *Otvoriti*—to open. He could feel a roughness on the back of the key. He thought something else was inscribed on that side as well. But he could not move the key off the surface of his skin no matter what he did. The words inscribed on the back of the key, he did not know.

He had smiled proudly as the key was placed around his neck. "What is this for?" he asked.

The Holy One had responded blankly, "When the fifth trumpet sounds, you will know. Then it will return to another." The Holy One never spoke of that day or of the key again. The key had hung upon his neck for millennia.

The memory faded from his consciousness as his thoughts returned to the moment. He still stood holding the chain around his neck. He looked over at Chaim dripping blood onto the carpet. "And you, puny one, what do you have to add?"

Chaim lowered his head. "It is as he has said, Great One." His voice was vacant.

Ivoluntas looked puzzled. "This does not make sense. The Long Expected One has come." He turned toward Suistus. "The power of death remains in the law, but the law has been fulfilled?" He sounded confused. "Now we must also battle this Novitate Unum, the Unexpected One. What more does He think he needs to do? What use has He of symbolic tools of ages past, when that which they represented has come in carne?" He shook his head as he stared at the two men. "These things have no meaning now. Like Nehushtan, they were but shadows of the coming sun, which vanish upon its arrival." He looked totally perplexed as he walked closer to the men.

Suistus seemed shocked and even more confused than his master was. "Great One, forgive my boldness, but what do you mean, it has been fulfilled?"

Ivoluntas looked at him and laughed. "Suistus, Suistus, you are obsolete." He motioned toward the two young men bleeding on his carpet. "Even these dying bags of dust know that. The curtain is torn, the temple remade." He looked at Suistus like he was an idiot. "In the beginning, dwelling among you. Now He has come full circle, in carne among you again." He shook his head as he paced the room. "You, your temples of stone, none of it is needed any longer." He looked at Suistus for some indication of understanding, but there was none.

He walked toward the young men. "But perhaps these useless things can be made useful." He stopped now in front of Chaim. "Tell me all you know of this Key of David, *now*!"

"It is a gift to the Iredenti, to walk through doors He has opened, to fight the darkness."

"No!" Suistus yelled. "It was given to the Jews long ago. It is our heritage! It is our gift! It is ours to control and wield against the shadow! I claim it for the Jews!"

Ivoluntas laughed loudly. "Like a great tree growing over a lesser one, the Iredenti will grow and overshadow that which came before. They will transition the imperfect to the perfect. They will destroy your synagogue of stone and law just as they will try to destroy me! They are both our dooms"—he smiled wildly, shaking his head—"but not today!"

Ivoluntas breathed in. He seemed to inhale everything around him. There was the sound of a mighty storm. He grew bigger and brighter like a lamp hidden in sackcloth. His physical body seemed to be swallowed up by a greater one of glorious light and power. Wings of sun-white snow unfolded from his back and shoulders. They sprouted, unencumbered by his flesh or armor. The chain around his neck grew longer in proportion. As his magnificence filled the room, he pulled the chain around his neck upward. There at its end hung an opalescent key of dancing glowing color. The light of the key filled the room in a myriad of white and variegated brilliant hues.

As the wonder culminated in Suistus's and the captives' eyes, bilious vomit seemed to curdle in their stomachs and filled their mouths. The smell of pus and the sound of violence overwhelmed the room. The men began to wretch.

He held the chain and let them gaze at the Great Key about his neck. "You speak of fighting that which you do not know. There is no darkness! There is no shadow! There is *only* choice! And I am that choice. *I* am the Key of David!" The magnificent angelic being reached down across the room, grabbing Chaim. He raised Chaim's body off the floor and held him up like a hungry man looking at an overripened tomato. "I am the one given power and authority to rule. There is none but me." Ivoluntas spoke loudly. Chaim's legs kicked in the air, and his arms flailed against the angelic hand holding him aloft. The hand tightened. Chaim screamed. Ivoluntas suddenly jerked his hand closed. Chaim's body snapped like a handful of twigs. Blood dripped onto the floor. As it hit the carpet, the angelic fabric rippled like the surface of a lake being hit by a pebble. The blood vanished into its substance like a drop of rain into the ocean.

Jankel stared emotionless as the crumpled body of his friend slipped to the floor. Within less than a heartbeat, he met the same fate.

Suistus did not move.

Ivoluntas stood proudly in the center of the room, his form of eternal perfection dazzling to behold. "They are our enemy, these Iredenti. They wish to destroy us both." He looked fatherly at Suistus. "Your star is fading quickly. But mine is eternal. You and your people must join me. If you wish to save the law, if you wish to save the synagogue, then there can be no 'Qui Salvum.'"

Suistus had dreamt of a fire. All the confusion in his life was suddenly burned away. He knew the law encompassed all things. There was no arbiter. No grace. No mercy. Nothing but the law. He looked up at the magnificent angel of light standing before him. He knew in his heart the law was what made him and the other Jews so holy. "I will fight them with all that I have," he answered. "I will fight their false message. I will fight for you."

Ivoluntas smiled. There were already several Black Voids within Suistus's frame, but there was room for more. He silently called across the firmament for a few more of the Qui Malaam. The room filled with Black Voids. They circled the room, basking in the openness of their master's angelic form. They gazed at the carpet and its incorruptible image of home. They were so close to being at peace. Then they noticed a tiny mortal in his shell of congealed dust. Like warm clay along the banks of a slow river, it looked so inviting. Ivoluntas nodded his approval. They swarmed into Suistus like bees to a hive. His soul tasted like sweet honey.

Chapter 12
Parceiða

Suistus lay in bed, eyes opened, his mind reviewing the day. It had been a long night. He had recited the law over and over. But he still couldn't fall to sleep. He had to save them…the law, the temple, the Jews, everything! But how? He looked at a crack in the wall beside the bed. The paint was starting to peel. *That wall needs to be painted.* The stray thought raced through his mind. The cracking wall was like his whole life—the perfect exterior was starting to crumble.

I am an educated man. I am the chief priest of the synagogue. I know all the answers! He pulled the blanket up over his head. *There must be a way!* His thoughts galloped like the thunderous horses at the hippodrome. *Great men have faced impossible problems like this before. What have they done?* He looked out the window. The sun was just coming up. The mountains to the northwest reflected the scarlet colors of the sun rising in the east. Beyond those rocky giants was Telmissus. He was so tired…he drifted back to sleep and began to dream…

He saw the young man driving the oxcart. It was an odd site because an eagle had perched itself on the back of the cart for a ride. The youth was of no particular note, a peasant.

The oracle stood on the side of the road with the gathered royalty of Phrygia. "That one, he shall be king!" The long bony finger of the oracle pointed at the young peasant lad.

"His name is Gordias," someone proclaimed from the crowd.

Suistus watched as the gathered royalty crowned Gordias as king of Phrygia. The oxcart Gordias drove was tied to a post. The knot that was tied to secure it was the most intricate and complex knot ever tied. The oracle then raised his hands high above the crowd and prophesied, "Whoever frees the cart from the undoable knot, he shall be the king of Asia."

Ages passed. The mysterious knot still held the ancient cart to the post.

Countless men had tried to undo the undoable knot. All had failed. Then one day a proud young Macedonian arrived. He too had heard of the prophesy. He too tried to undo the undoable knot. And like all those before him, he too began to fail. Then without warning, he pulled out his sword and sliced the impassable knot in half. It unraveled to the ground. The young Macedonian held the freed yoke of the cart high above his head like a trophy. His name was Alexander.

Suistus awoke, the dream still vivid in his mind. It was still early in the morning. The servants had stoked the hearth, and the house was beginning to warm up. Breakfast was always his favorite meal. He sat listening to his wife chatter about her plans for the day. His servants brought him his pomegranate juice. The juice was deep violet red, viscous like wine, and cool. It was perfect. His subtle nod instantly conveyed to his servants his desire for another goblet of the delicious beverage. *Servants are such a blessing,* he thought.

His thoughts drifted back to the impossible challenges confronting him. *These Iredenti and their secret leader, Dryados—they must be stopped!* He sighed deeply. It was impossible. He sipped on his juice. *How to kill the Iredenti? How to kill Dryados? And how to do it without the Romans knowing and the Jews getting blamed?* He stared into his goblet as he swished around the last of the juice.

The servant brought out Suistus's second glass of the pomegranate juice. He slid his crooked nose into the goblet. He breathed in slowly. The juice had an amazing bouquet. He savored the moment. Unbridled pride filled his thoughts. *I love being rich,* he mused. *I love having servants. It is so nice to be freed from the mundane activities of life. If only my servants could...* His thoughts crashed to a stop. He laid the goblet slowly down on the table as the solution solidified in his mind. *Yes... paid help,* he thought. *That is exactly what I need!* The impossible solution galloped across the finish line like a horse at the races. *They just need to be the right kind of help.* He smirked. The smile on his face slowly grew as he finished the second glass of pomegranate juice. *I can save them all,* he thought. *All I need...is Parceida.*

It was a hot day. The glare off the walls of the amphitheater was annoying. "More wine, and in the name of Apollo, put up the shade!" Parceida yelled. The sunshade was quickly raised. It was like a large flat umbrella, but it lay low enough so it did not block the view of the hundreds sitting behind them. To return the festive mood, the servants quickly brought out chilled wine from the wet hay in the back of the view box. Parceida leaned forward in his chair. The roar of the crowd came to a crescendo. The executions had begun. Today, the Iredenti captives would be sawed in half.

The first young woman screamed as they dragged her across the dusty dirt of the amphitheater floor. She clawed at the ground like an animal trying to escape its slaughter. The crowd booed and hissed its displeasure. The other captives were chained to the side walls and forced to watch as their own gruesome futures unfolded before them. Their hushed silence was as terrifying as the tormented screams now filling the amphitheater. Everyone in the stands had come to watch the executions. Everyone except Parceida.

The woman was quickly chained in place. Then they brought out the saw. It was long and splattered with the blood of its previous victims. It looked rusty and dull. There was no sheen to its edge. The Roman executioner raised the saw high above his head and wiggled the blade. The crowd burst into raucous cheers. He lowered the blade and taunted his victim. Then he slowly...started sawing. Parceida watched the man's face. The executioner was enjoying his work. *Yes, he might be a good candidate*, Parceida thought. He glanced at the other men helping with the killing. There were four, one at each of the captive's limbs. Two looked stern and professional. One appeared to be getting sick. The man by her right leg was smiling, engrossed in the gruesome killing. *Yes, that one too*, he thought.

The executioner did everything he could to prolong the torment. The victim's screams were unfathomable. A woman in the box next to Parceida's started to wretch and vomit. It was hard for Parceida not to watch the captive's gory end, but he had work to do. Good help was so hard to find. He would talk to the executioner and his assistant later. But now he had to stay focused. Perhaps there were other men here today who could be of use to him. They dragged out the next screaming Iredenti. It was a young boy. *Perhaps the woman's child*, Parceida thought. He pushed the stray thought from his mind. He needed to keep on task.

"Your lordship..."

Parceida spun like a coiled snake. "What!" His face was as red as the blood on the amphitheater floor.

The servant cringed back. "Your lordship, there is a courier here to—"

"Bring the man here, and be quick!" Parceida straightened himself up in his chair. "And for all the swords in Smyrna, bring me more wine! The day is scorching!"

"Yes, Great One. Immediately." The frightened servant bowed several times as he backed quickly away.

Parceida relaxed back in his chair. His eyes darted back and forth as he watched the young Iredenti boy getting sawed in half.

"Master Parceida, Lord Suistus sends his greetings and—"

"Now! This very instant?" Parceida pulled his short sword halfway out from its sheath.

The startled messenger stumbled backward and tripped onto the marble floor. He scooted frantically backward as Parceida glared at him. "I am just the courier, just the courier, for Lord Suistus. He sends his greetings and asks...no, begs...

begs that you would honor him with your presence." The courier cringed on the floor several feet away, with his head bowed so hard down into his chest, his chin was making a dimple in his sternum.

"The chief priest has need of me?" Parceida laughed loudly, spilling some of his wine. "Well, I suppose I should go and thank the old sourpuss for today's entertainment. I hear he was the man who brought most of our honored guests here to justice." He glanced back at the amphitheater. The Iredenti boy was already dead. "But I do not wish to miss such excellent festivities. Tell your master I shall be along as soon as the entertainment has come to an end."

The frightened courier looked up nervously. "I believe my master was hoping to see you now, as his schedule is quite—"

"Ha-ha-ha." Parceida rose to his feet and walked toward the young messenger. Parceida was over six feet and close to 290 pounds. None of it fat. He dragged his sword loudly across the view box floor behind him. The young messenger's eyes bulged with fear. He shuffled backward until he collided with the far wall. He stared up at the towering monster in front of him.

Parceida stopped directly in front of the quaking youth. "Don't worry, child. I lost my penchant for young boys years ago." He slowly raised his sword and lightly poked the boy in the stomach and upper arms. "But you do look tender enough." He glanced at his cohorts gathered in the viewing box. The hardened guards laughed loudly. The boy remained frozen in place. "Tell your master not to keep me waiting." He waved his sword toward the exit at the back of the view box. "Go!"

The young man jumped to his feet and raced for the exit. Parceida slapped the boy on his butt with the flat of his blade and then roared raucously in laughter. The boy fled with the jeers of Parceida's men echoing in his ears.

Parceida walked slowly over to the buffet in the back. A smorgasbord of roasted dove and lamb was laid out on a wide table. There were grapes, sultana raisins, fruits, breads, and cheeses. He filled his plate. Then he sat back down and became entranced with the entertainment.

Suistus was bored. "Why don't they just kill the Iredenti scum and be done with it. Must they truly appeal to people's basilar instincts?" His servants brought him a pewter plate of grapes and cheese. "It is simply more darkness that the Iredenti have brought into the world." The flowers his servants had brought into his view box looked lovely. He stood, smelling a nice bouquet as he continued to watch the entertainment. *I have so much to do*, he thought. *I can't simply fritter the day away on some well-intended executions.* He watched as they dragged a dead Iredenti adult male across the amphitheater floor, well, half of him. It made Suistus smile.

Parceida was supposed to have joined him over an hour ago. But Suistus could still see him drinking and cheering wildly in the view box across the way. He decided to sit down and just watch the rest of the executions while he waited. His eyes grew wider and wider with each execution. He watched as they applied tourniquets to saw off extremities, admired the assortment of dull instruments they used, and enjoyed the frenzy of the hungry animals being fed the leftovers. The Romans' methods of administering justice were enlightening. He was particularly impressed with the executioner. He appeared to be a man of a particular education. He had an amazing understanding of the importance of drama and rising tension—and anatomy. The last two or three dismemberments of the day were simply glorious.

The Romans had paused to drag out a young married couple they would execute together. Suistus stared impatiently across the amphitheater at the growing party in Parceida's view box. Several women had joined them, and he could hear the small group of musicians playing even from here. They all seemed to be having a particularly good time. Suistus smiled. *Perhaps I have been going about this the wrong way.*

Parceida sat in his chair, kissing a giggling young woman. The executions had just ended, but that didn't mean the party had to. They would move it back to his villa eventually, but there was no hurry.

"Master Parceida, Lord Suistus and his entourage humbly request a moment of your time," announced the young messenger boy loudly from the other side of the view box.

Parceida continued to kiss the young woman. "What does that stiffed-necked bureaucrat want with me? Tell him I will meet with him…in a couple of days."

The messenger cleared his throat coarsely. "Uh, Lord Suistus and his entourage are here now to beg an audience with your greatness."

Parceida glanced over to see Lord Suistus and his two escorts standing at the entrance of the view box. He continued to caress the woman as his thought strayed to what the infamous Jew might want of him. Begrudgingly, he raised his head off the woman's bosom. "Aahh…what do you need, priest?" he moaned loudly.

Suistus edged his way cautiously into the view box. "I am Suistus, chief priest of the synagogue and your humble servant. I am—"

"Aahh…" Parceida nudged the young woman off his lap and rose to his feet. "I know who you are, priest." He walked menacingly across the view box floor. "And I am Parceida," he said sternly. "Everything you have heard about me is true." He pulled his sword out from its sheath. He waved the sword toward the young woman who was still adjusting her tunic. "If that young maiden leaves before you finish talking, I will kill you where you stand." The young maiden smiled wryly at her master.

Parceida made sure Suistus felt the tip of the sword in his belly. The priest's eyes bulged with fear. "I would suggest you speak quickly," Parceida growled. "I do not select maidens based on their attention span." Parceida looked smilingly back at the young maiden and twinkled the fingers of his free hand in a childish wave. Then he looked blankly at the chief priest.

"I need to hire you," stammered the priest. "And probably a large number of your men, for a job." Suistus tried to edge backward, but Parceida kept the blade pressed sharp into his belly.

Parceida looked back at the maiden. "Please, my darling, sit and have some more wine. I will return to you in just a few moments." Then he turned back, glaring at Suistus. "You have five minutes."

Suistus looked around at the many eyes staring at him. "Perhaps issues such as this are best discussed with some degree of discretion."

Parceida smiled at his men. "Why? As soon as you leave, I will just tell it to them myself. Save me some time and speak of what you want."

Suistus looked at the musicians and the woman scattered about the box. "And these others, are they as disciplined, and worthy of your trust?"

Parceida glanced around the view box and then back at the priest. He nodded for Suistus to continue. "Well," Suistus said slowly, "it involves killing…perhaps a large number of people."

Parceida pulled his sword away from Suistus's belly and glanced around the view box. "You others are dismissed. Take the women and the rest of my guests up to the villa. I will be along shortly." The view box was quickly emptied of everyone except Suistus, his escorts, Parceida, and perhaps a half dozen of Parceida's personal guards. Parceida took his seat. Cool wine was brought to both men. "Now, priest, how can I be of assistance?"

Suistus explained his plan.

Parceida did not speak for a few moments. Then he asked several specific questions. Suistus's answers were blunt and as accurate as his spies had told him. Parceida swirled the wine in his goblet. "That will take a lot to accomplish. I anticipate many of my own men will die." He drank a deep draft of the smooth beverage. Then he looked at Suistus with blank eyes. "It will be expensive."

"Yes, I am well aware of that," said the priest, nodding. "I have been planning accordingly." He flashed a smile.

"Good!" Parceida sat up in his chair, staring at the priest.

Suistus rose to his feet and bowed. "I will let you take care of the details." His face wore a subtle sneer, and he spoke as a man who did not want his fingers dirtied by such vulgar undertakings.

Parceida had not yet given the priest permission to leave. His face was blank as his eyes shifted form Suistus back to the chair where he had been seated. Suistus bowed, clearly forcing a smile, and returned to his seat.

Parceida groaned as he stood up and walked to the edge of the view box. He looked at the blood-soaked arena floor, then he turned toward Suistus with eyes full of hate. "Tell me, priest." He sneered. "Which is worse—the man who kills with his own two hands, or the sniveling coward who pays him to do it for him?"

Suistus did not answer.

"My spies tell me of secret places beneath the synagogue. They tell me they are not for religious purposes." Parceida walked closer to the chief priest. The two men stared blankly at each other.

Suistus showed no sign of emotion.

"Give me two months. Then we will be ready." Parceida took another sip of his wine and nodded for the priest to leave.

Chapter 13
Moments

Dryados returned home. There was no sense humiliating himself further at the caravanserai or beating himself up at the warehouse. He changed into an old work garment and went out into the garden with Alesia. He had discovered that working with her in the garden relaxed him. He enjoyed just digging in the dirt and trimming the flowers. He and Alesia had a constant battle over arranging the ceramic fox and hound. Usually she would hide the fox in the strangest of places and then just wait for him to find it. Today was different. They had worked outside for over an hour when he finally took notice of their ceramic companions. Alesia had strangely placed the fox and hound together. This was odd. The two ceramic figures seemed to be looking at a small blossom she had just planted.

Alesia paused when she realized that Dryados had noticed the ceramic pair staring at the blossom. She didn't say a word. She just looked at him and waited. He glanced at the fox and hound and then back at her. She just smiled.

Dryados glanced back and forth several times, trying to figure out what was going on. Alesia just kept working with some flowers, with a strange smile.

"What are you up to?" he asked accusingly. Alesia was entirely too smart, and anything out of the ordinary could mean, well, almost anything.

"I don't know what you mean," she said innocently.

"You know what I mean."

She looked back at him with a mock look of innocent confusion.

"The fox and the hound, they are together," he said, again accusingly.

"Yes, they are."

Dryados's mind whirled. What was she up to? Then it occurred to him. *I have come home early…we have worked together in the garden…we have had a great day…we are married…maybe she is feeling a little…*

Alesia hit him with a small clod of dirt. She could obviously read his mind. "Is that all you think about!"

"Well, actually…"

"Oh!" She got up and walked over to their ceramic companions. She stopped directly in front of them and stood there. Dryados quickly followed suit.

They both turned, looking at the ground. Now that he was closer, Dryados could better see what the fox and hound appeared to be staring at. It wasn't a small blossom that Alesia had planted at all. It was something else. Hidden in the low grasses there in front of the ceramic companions was something tiny. It was a small fox…a baby fox. Dryados looked into his wife's eyes. "We are going to have a baby," she whispered. She took his hands and placed them to her stomach and held them there. Suddenly the world stopped spinning.

Ascalon sat in the living room watching Lautus. As he watched the playing child, he began the nightly routine of *working* his left arm. The appendage was now more like a battle club than a human appendage. The upper arm could move out away from his body, but not up and down or rotate. The elbow had scarred and flexed almost ninety degrees. He could extend it a little bit from there, and that was about it. But the wrist, hand, and fingers had fixed almost solid. The lower arm seemed to have all healed together into a solid rod of flesh. The physician had warned him that he had to keep working it or sections of the limb would start to bend off in obtuse angles. He worked the arm every day. But in opposition to his best efforts, tight scar bands had formed in the arm nonetheless. By stretching them out daily, he had at least been able to keep the limb usable. Wearing his brace at worked seemed to help the most. Sperta helped him strap it on every day.

Ascalon watched as Lautus scooted around on the floor. The infant boy could really crawl fast. But he crawled in an odd kind of way. He used both his hands and right knee in the typical normal crawling way. But he held his left leg out straight like a wooden crutch. It was really more halfway between a walk and a crawl. It looked weird, but the kid was fast. He had also learned to stand up holding on to things in the house. The boy would shoot across the room and then bring himself upright using the chair Ascalon was sitting in for help. Then he would stand, balancing himself using the chair. He would waver back and forth for a moment. When he was steady, he would smile and giggle at himself. Then just as quickly, he would drop to the floor and shoot across the room to the other side.

Ascalon sat in his chair watching his young son scoot back and forth across the room. Then it happened. Lautus was on the other side of the room holding himself up and looking over to Ascalon. He moved his hand away from the chair and balanced. He stood there for a moment all on his own!

"Sperta! Sperta! Come quick. Look! Look! Look! Come quick!"

Sperta raced in from the kitchen. "What's wrong? What's—"

"Look! He is standing! Just watch!" Ascalon pointed to Lautus on the other side of the room.

Sperta's smile seemed to encourage the boy on. He giggled loudly and again awkwardly let go of the chair. His whole body wobbled...and he stood!

"Good boy! That's mommy's good boy!" She sat down onto the floor beside Ascalon. "Good boy! Mommy and Daddy are so proud."

Lautus took an unsteady step toward them and then crashed soundly on his butt. He didn't cry. He just got up and started doing his crazy crawl thing back and forth again across the room.

"Did you see that!" Ascalon bellowed proudly. "Did you see that!" He looked back toward Lautus, now creeping up the chair on the other side of the room. He stood again, braced against the chair. "Come to Abba...come to Abba..." Ascalon leaned forward, putting both arms out toward his excited infant son.

Lautus stood away from the chair, balancing precariously. He stood and stood, and then wobbling, took a step, then a second, then almost...almost...crash!

"Lautus! What a good boy!" Ascalon raced across the room and swooped up his son. "You are Abba's little man!" Then with a playful "rrraahhhh," the big muscled smith kissed him all over and started tickling him.

Sperta raced over. "Lautus, Lautus, Lautus..." She kissed him over and over on the head. Soon the little boy was wiggling to get back down on the floor and practice his new achievement. Mother and Father sat watching their baby boy starting to grow up.

Chapter 14
Another Jaunt to Laodicea

City of Laodicea, south of Philadelphia

Dryados nudged his horse forward and glanced back at Jo-El, shaking his head. "I really just hate that guy."

Jo-El chuckled with a small smile. "Well, not every business deal is going to go through. You have told me that yourself a hundred times."

"That's true. But that guy is just annoying." Dryados directed his horse off to the side of the busy road and into the Nymphaeum. The *Rose Fox* had returned much earlier from her first voyage than anticipated and had quickly turned around for a second. His cash flow problems were long over, and now all he had to do was continue to expand his businesses. But he had discovered that Laodicea was going to be a tough nut to crack.

It was an exceptionally hot day. The Nymphaeum was packed with people, who seemed to be doing everything they could to deal with the heat. Children raced around splashing and playing in the fountains. Women collected water in skins, amphora, and large jugs. The mist blowing off the frothing water was wonderfully cooling. Dryados dismounted and guided the horse through the crowded people. He winced as he was suddenly drenched with water splashing up from some of the playing children. He guided his roan stallion to one of the large pools on the side of the fountain and let it drink its fill. "Every aspect of my proposal is financially sound, and we will both make money. What could possibly be wrong with that?"

Jo-El's horse nuzzled alongside of Dryados's and began to guzzle down water streaming from the fountain. Each man stood there holding his horse's reins. Jo-El's skin was red and starting to burn. "Because it is not enough money, Master Dryados." Jo-El wiped heavy beads of sweat from his brow. "And I am not sure, but I think that is what he told you the other three times we have called on him... sir."

"But that doesn't make any sense at all. How much money does this guy have to make in a deal?" Dryados shook his head in frustration. "I'm telling you this will work. Aurum is already shipping the black wool to the East. He is selling it as far away as Sousa. I'm telling you the better market is to the north...in Rome and Venice. The winters are colder, and people have a sense of fashion. Styles change. The black wool of Laodicea is soft and elegant. It will sweep the empire. I can feel it...black is going to be the new purple!"

Jo-El wrinkled his nose. "Black is a dreadful color. It's the color of funerals and assassins. People of fashion wouldn't be caught dead in it. And that is never going to change...sir."

"OK, stop with the sir stuff. I always appreciate your opinion. Even when it is overly honest and blunt. You are a wonderful servant and a good student." Dryados handed his reins to Jo-El and walked over and took a long drink from the fountain. The water was stale and tepid, but it didn't matter. "And what kind of name is Aurum anyway? Who names their kid that?" He dunked his head in the pool and then walked back over, taking both sets of reins from his manservant.

Jo-El drank deeply from the fountain and similarly doused his head. Then he filled up both of their waterskins. "It is really hot today." He sighed. "And there is no shade up on this plateau." He tossed the waterskins back on the horses and then helped Dryados onto his roan stallion. "Well, I suppose if you are the richest family in all of Asia, you can name your oldest son and heir anything you want. I think Aurum is a perfectly legitimate name for a family that is practically made of gold. The Nicostrate family built a brand-new amphitheater for this city, for goodness' sakes, and they paid for it in cash! Besides, maybe his parents just thought he was 'priceless' as a newborn baby..." Jo-El smirked.

Dryados stared at a passing aristocrat and his wife. Both were attired in colored tunics with bright-colored sashes. And each of their ensembles had accents of black wool, even in this sweltering heat. "I think the next time I come here I will contact the local shepherds who raise those elite black sheep and try to get a contract with them on my own. That way—"

"Master, I think that is a very bad idea. That supply chain has been controlled by the Nicostrate family for generations. It will never work. All you will do is anger them with your failed attempt...and create a very powerful enemy. Better to stay on their good side, and as you have taught me, just keep trying to work the deal. At some point they will recognize your tenacity and the infrastructure you have created. Then they will bring you into their business dealing." He looked at Dryados, hoping he had not stepped too far out of line. "Master, for now I think you are better off biding your time."

"So what you're saying is that I am a mite laying in the dirt, and I am simply not worth his effort to bend down and pick up?"

"No, Master, I am saying that..."

Dryados shook his head at his freeman. "No, Jo-El, you are right. With all their wealth, it is not worth Aurum Nicostrate's time to get involved with a merchant like me." Then he smiled confidently. "At least, not yet. I will simply need to keep doing what I am doing until it is. Still"—a sly grin grew on Dryados's face—"who gives a kid a name like that? If I ever have a son…" Dryados looked over at the workers chiseling the hard stone to expand the Nymphaeum. They were dripping with sweat. Each man's skin was as dark as the plowed, fertile fields of the Katakekaumene, and they each looked just as ragged. A sweet memory of Talmun working at the Askeplion flashed into his thoughts. Dryados brought his horse to a stop. He reached down into his money purse and pulled out five silver denarii. He turned his stallion and worked his way back through the crowded people. Staying on the horse, he motioned his hand toward the foreman. "You there…"

The surprised work boss looked up at the wealthy merchant and his aide. The two wore clothes of fine white linen and rode magnificent steeds. The one calling him was younger but… "Yes, my lord? May I help you in some way?" He lowered his head, fearing that his men had caused some offense that was about to bring the merchant's wrath down upon him.

"Y-yes," Dryados stammered, "you may." He edged his horse a little closer to the gang supervisor. He could see the anxiety now rising in the nervous work boss's eyes as he finally looked up. The other workers had gone equally quiet, waiting for Dryados's next words. "You and your fine crew are doing an excellent job improving this magnificent structure. I just wanted to thank you for your service to the city." He threw the five silver denarii to the foreman. "Have your men buy a large sunshade to cover the area where they are working. And if there is any coin left, have them buy a bottle of wine to share."

The gang boss looked up in shocked relief. After a moment's pause, he turned toward his men. "Saba!"

A thin man with a weathered face moved away from the stone figure he had been chiseling into the monument. Sweat was now pouring down his face from his altered position. "Yes, Boss?"

"You and your son do as this fine lord has instructed, and be quick about it. I think the lot of us are about to melt like cheap wax out here in this awful sun." He passed the coin to the worker.

Dryados watched as the worker stared in awe at the five silver coins. It was probably the most money he had ever held in his hand at one time.

Saba glanced over at his boss, "Yes, Master, yes." Then he looked up at Dryados still seated on his horse and nodded his head. "Thank you, my lord. Thank you." He motioned toward the other workers. "We all thank you." In the meantime a young boy of perhaps ten had made his way over and stood nearby. Saba smiled at him as he approached. "My son Jacob and I will leave right now and do as you have commanded." Saba glanced again at the crew foreman with a look of hesitation. The gang boss gave him an approving nod. Saba squeezed the coins tight in his hand and then began to run quickly toward the city agora, with his son racing along by his side.

Dryados turned his horse back toward the street and nudged the animal into the rest of the slow-moving crowd. He turned toward Jo-El with a big smile growing on his face. "Just imagine, the *Rose Fox* with her cargo bays filled with black wool…"

Chapter 15
Sharks in the Water

Smyrna

The *Rose Fox* lowered her mainsail. The canvas furled closed. The deck men lashed the sail tight as they spun the spar aft. Slowly she pulled in along the dock. The ropes were thrown, and the muscles of the deckhands flexed as the ship creaked loudly into dock. There were swarms of seagulls looking for a free meal from the new arrival. The crew scoured the dock, looking for familiar faces. Finally, the captain walked to the top deck. "Unloading crews to the aft starboard holds. Those on shore leave…are dismissed." The entire crew erupted in to raucous cheers.

The wharf was quickly filled with men of purpose. Some running into the arms of waiting families. Some moving carts and wagons. Others working the hoists to lift out the pallets from Greece and Rome. One man walked aboard against the exiting tide and took his spot on the platform amidships. The old fishmonger knew it would be the best spot to oversee all the loading and unloading.

Darius marveled at the amazing stout craft. *Every last cent*, he thought. *Every last* cent…and worth every one. Though she was made of wood and rope, he had somehow formed a bond with the beautiful lady of the waters. She seemed to carry more than just products to distant lands. She carried the hopes and dreams of his youth.

The dance of loading and unloading the ship began. He barked orders the same as he did with any crew. Still, he couldn't shake it. The first time he loaded the ship was the day the two young men had disappeared. He knew it was his fault. He had searched the city. He had asked all the questions. He had done everything he could do without arousing suspicion. But there was no trace. The boys had simply disappeared. Maybe they had been robbed and their bodies thrown in the harbor…or buried outside the city. Maybe the Romans had captured them and taken them somewhere. No one really knew. But somehow, Darius knew the ultimate truth. They were now long dead.

"Be careful with those! That ain't no ship anchor...careful!" The hoist slowed as the pallet lowered gently onto the wharf. Even under the packing rags, Darius recognized the components to several new looms. It made him smile. It had been his idea.

Darius received instruction letters regularly from Dryados. He was getting pretty good at reading. Now he would only take the letter to the scribe if he had questions. And that was happening less and less. Dryados always had new plans, new ideas, new...problems. It was exhausting. The man was just so compulsive. Still, they were partners. Darius wasn't even sure exactly how or when it had happened. But now, well, they were. Others had told him Dryados had a way of doing that. "One day you are doing business with him. The next thing you know, you are neck deep in some wild scheme of his as his partner." He stood there shaking his head. He had heard the warnings before. Had he only known!

Darius watched the hoists lifting more pallets from the holds. The cargo would be taken to one of their nearby warehouses until the next caravan arrived, which could be any day now. They tried to time the shipments from Thyatira and Philadelphia to coincide with the ship's schedule. That way the merchandise could be loaded directly onto the ship and not require them to tie up any additional warehouse space. Dryados did not like the ship to be idle—something about his cash flow.

As the hoist moved the lifting spar toward the wharf, Darius noticed several men arguing on the dock. Strangers had stopped a few of his workers. His dockmen were yelling, trying to get back to work. Darius couldn't make out the words. The strangers seemed to be very persistent. Darius headed to the dock. One of the strangers grabbed a dockman by the collar. Darius began to run. As he crossed the boarding ramp, one of the strangers spotted him. The stranger let go of the dockman, pulled his own tunic up to cover his face, and ran. The other two strangers followed suit. From the distance, all that Darius could discern was that they were Jews.

Darius hurried down to the dock. He intercepted the dockmen before they could get back to work. "What'd they want, those strangers you were speaking with? Jews, were they?"

"Odd you should ask, as a point they was, and downright rude at that. Had several questions about you. But mostly they asked about that partner of yours, that Master Dryados." The dockman raised his brow. "Seemed they had taken some exception to the way he was a-doing his businesses...him being a thief and all...how he was stealing their livelihood."

"What? That doesn't make any sense," Darius said, confused. "What exactly did they want to know?"

"Well, who you was and what kinda business you'd run. Stuff like that. They was also interested in exactly what was in them pallets we was taking off and where they was from." The dockman scratched at his chest and then spit out a large wad of…something. "They weren't no dockmen nor overseers, as we could tell, so we told um nothing and that they could just go…" The dockman's insult was imaginative, although Darius thought it to be anatomically impossible.

"And what of Dryados? What did they ask about him?"

"Well, that was a bit more no nothing kinda stuff. You know, like where he lived, was he married, was he a Roman. That kinda stuff." The dockman spit again. This wad appeared to be a thick green. Seemed he had a sinus infection. "Course I told them the whole lot of them was a…" Darius blushed. Still, he was impressed with the way the dockman was able to insult the lineage of all three of the strangers and their livestock at the same time. "That seemed to hit a nerve." The stubbly dockman smiled proudly. "So then I told 'em that Master Dryados lived in Philadelphia and they could go and just takes the matter up with him. And course on the way there they could just go and…"

Darius's jaw dropped open. The dockman's final suggestion was so disgusting that it probably violated Roman law! "That was pretty much the same look the tall Jew give me…ha-haaa!" The dockman's laugh was loud and full of salt.

"You told them what? That Master Dryados lived in Philadelphia?"

"Yep, and on the way there they could just…"

Darius did not wait for the man to give a second rendition of his graphic suggestion. Darius's heart raced. He thought about the two young men. He thought about the Romans, and the amphitheater, and Thad…and… His gut sank. He knew Master Dryados had to be taking the business away from somebody. But it was just business, and he was a genius. But no one had ever come looking for them at the docks before or asking questions. He needed to leave.

He hurried to his nearest warehouse. *There are always sharks in the water…don't mean you can't go for a swim or go fish'n'*, Darius thought, trying to reassure himself. He glanced around the streets. He thought about an incident a few years back when one of his men had fallen overboard. They were hauling in a good catch of fish, and there was a pack of sharks in the water. The man splashed trying to get back to the boat. The water frothed and churned around him. Darius remembered watching the familiar blueness of the sea turn to red. The sharks tore the man to ribbons. He walked faster. *Always sharks*, he thought. *Always sharks.*

His eyes darted quickly around the road as he approached the warehouse. He knew there was parchment and a quill there. He stopped at the door and took one more quick glace behind him. No one followed. He fetched what he needed and sat down. He wrote Dryados a fisherman's note of warning—about sharks.

Jezebel looked at the monotonous faces of the people she passed on the street. Vendors loudly hawked their goods. Shoppers crowded their favorite butcher shop. Someone shoveled horse manure off the road in front of his shop. They went about the routine tasks of their mundane lives. *Thyatira is so…prosaic,* she thought. She had just returned from Pergama. *I met generals and visiting dignitaries from around the empire. I met great merchants and priests from every temple.* She smiled wryly to herself. *And I met Diotrephes.* Her smile broadened.

Everyone greeted her as she walked the streets. She had many followers. Clearly, some of the women had a sense of what was going on, but they remained silent. She was powerful and was rumored to have a darker side. They all knew that as well. For Jezebel, eliminating the evil in the world was not just a figure of speech. Her enemies did not last long.

Her mind wandered. She was pregnant again. She smiled and greeted the people on the street. At the same time she contemplated what to do about the baby growing inside her. She had absolutely no idea who the father was—there were far too many possibilities to even try to figure that out. Her voluptuous figure would hide the pregnancy until she had made a decision. She had become good friends with a "midwife" who had developed the skills to kill the child while it was still inside her. Over the years the midwife had continued to hone that skill set. She smiled as she walked. *I hardly bled out at all the last time,* she thought. She had already decided that she was not going to let this child live either, but it was fun to think about it. *I will try the poultice first.* They were safer. But now, it was time to get back to work.

She had been grooming one of the elders for some time. It had been rumored he had been a womanizer before he had become Iredenti. She hoped those embers had not gone out and had been slowly trying to fan their remnants. She had recruited several women from within her circle to help. He had been hard to crack at first. She had also recruited several others to help embitter his wife. All the pieces were coming together. The wife had become more and more unhappy and was starting to nag. Just one more blow and the chain would break, and he would be free. Wine and a low-cut tunic would be the hammer. Her body would be the chisel. Demas would be arriving any minute, so she needed to hurry home.

She arrived just minutes before he did. Just enough time to get ready. She wore no perfume. She had learned that always came across as too obvious and only hampered her success. He had been invited over on the pretense to discuss helping others in the city. They would start with that…

"No, Lady Jezebel, I just ate my evening meal just before I left home. But thank you." Demas nodded courteously at his host.

"Well, then you must at least come and sit with me. I am quite hungry. You can have some wine."

Jezebel led him to the dining room. It was set for two. The servants brought in a seasoned roasted dove. It had been slowly smoked. It looked and smelled delicious. They also brought in some salted nuts and pickled vegetables for Demas to snack on. He was given a cavernous goblet of wine.

"Deacons? Yes, I think it is a marvelous idea," Jezebel said, smiling. "We have so many needs in our fellowship that are going unaddressed." She edged closer, sincerely interested in his idea.

"Yes, Prophetess. The deacons would mainly work with the widows and orphans." Demas explained the plan as he sipped on his wine.

"They are such a lonely group. Their only companionship is fear and depravation. They lack the simple joys of a warm bed and soft touch." She ate slowly. Demas began snacking on the salted nuts and pickled vegetables. She sipped her wine. The smells of the kitchen filled the dining area. He was hungrier than he thought. The snacks were addictive. The servants made sure his goblet remained full.

Jezebel leaned across the table. "You have something just there." She wiped his mouth with her hand. Her leaned posture and low-cut tunic always had the effect she desired. "There, that's better."

She made a few toasts. The servant filled Demas's goblet again. She noticed the occasional drifting of his eyes.

"Let's move over to one of my receiving areas and continue our discussions there." She started to get up. "Oh, finish your wine first." The goblet was full. He downed it in a few gulps. She smiled. A large traditional seating area was made out on the floor. Demas sat down. Jezebel sat right next to him, pressing her thigh firmly into his. "Oh, Demas, let me just get this…" Her long hair fell into his face as she reached across him. As she began to sit back down, she kissed him deeply.

There was a moment when he started to back away, but it was gone in an instant as she pressed her body hard against him. The kiss became more passionate. She leaned back to untie the belt she wore. Before she could the belt broke apart under Demas's siege. It was like the breaking of a chain.

Demas was quickly lost in the pleasures of her body. She would invite him downstairs after the next fellowship meeting with the others. She would ensure that Daravaza had him that night. From then on, he would be free to choose whomever he wanted.

Chapter 16
The Spirit, the Water, and the Blood

Philadelphia

"They knew and they chose," Alesia said for the fourth time. "No, they didn't choose! How could they? In order to choose, they had to have the ability to say no. They didn't!" Dryados wasn't angry with Alesia. He was just angry, and sad, and confused, and a hundred other things. He rolled closed the papyrus ledger he was reading of the *Rose Fox's* current cargo and trade route. He would make another fortune with this run just as he did with all the others. His whole life was filled with blessing. It just wasn't fair. "Those two young men I selected for the quest lost their lives before they even had a chance to live them. I robbed them of everything." Tears formed in his eyes as he laid the ledger on the desk and walked out into the living room.

"Dryados, this has been going on for months. I think you need to go talk to the elders about this." She was tired of arguing with him about it. It didn't matter what she said. He didn't listen. "Let them know what has happened. They are good men. They will be honest with you and help you find the answers." She walked closer, kissed him, and then walked outside to the garden.

Dryados sat down in his favorite chair by the window. He looked out over the city. He could see a hundred people living out the simple tasks of their daily lives. He tried to let his mind go blank. There was a gentle knock at the door.

He had many servants, but he was in no mood for the meaningless trappings of social status. He got up and answered the door.

"Master Dryados? I was not expecting..." The courier bowed deeply. Dryados recognized the man. He was a private courier Dryados and his business associates had used many times for sensitive communications. "I carry a letter for you."

Dryados examined the letter. It bore a strange seal he had never seen before. It was that of an eagle. But not a Roman eagle. It was a great eagle in flight. He had heard of this before but had never thought it possible... "Thank you. Please come in." Dryados motioned for the courier to enter. "I will have my servants prepare a room for you."

The courier nodded. "No, your lordship is gracious, but—"

"Lordship? Now that's a first." Dryados chuckled. "Please, just call me Dryados. Come in. Come in. You look exhausted." The fatigued courier hesitantly stepped inside. "Please rest the night in my home." The courier was obviously far too tired to argue and waited for the servants to take him to his room. Dryados examined the seal expectantly.

The servants directed the courier up the stairs. "Thank you again. You are—"

Dryados interrupted, "Were there others…I mean of the letters? I mean… how many of these letters have you delivered?"

"There were seven, sir. One to each of the great cities of the Post Road."

Dryados nodded a fervent *yes*. The courier again bowed graciously and was escorted off to his room. Dryados hurried to his chair by the window. He sat down in disbelief. *It couldn't be…it really, simply…couldn't be*, he thought. Dryados broke the seal.

Ever so gently, he removed the contents. The first appeared to be a cover letter. The remainder was a larger writing. Dryados read the cover letter quickly. It was addressed specifically to him.

Dryados, grace to you and peace in the name of He who was and is to come… The letter was from John in Ephesus. The cover letter included an update on all that was going on in the fellowship in Ephesus and some personal information about what was happening with Dryados's family there. *But these other writings are of Tresdi Sintunus, by His inspiration. They are for you and all who call themselves Iredenti. That you may know…*

As he unfolded the other parchment, he began to feel strange. His spirit eyes returned. The words began to sparkle and then grow. They grew off the page like a plant sprouting out of a pot much too small to contain it any longer. They leaped into the air. Soon he was surrounded by pulsing bands of white power. His pulse beat in synchrony with theirs. He found himself back in the River. It flooded over him, surrounding him, filling him. He could not help but rise to his feet. He read the words out loud. The entirety of the universe flowed through his substance. He looked back to the beginning. There were three white Stars that were the heavens. They were everything. They were One. They spoke the Word that was the universe, and it leaped into existence. Those words danced around him and in him. Like a great pipe, the Living Waters flowed freely through his being. "That which was from the beginning, which we have heard, which we have looked upon, and our hands have held, concerning the Word of life—the life was manifested, and we have seen…" The universe and all its meaning unfolded before him. "God is light and in Him there is no darkness at all." He felt himself like a little child whose Father had wrapped His arms tightly around him. In those arms he could see that all that was in the world…was passing away. That the darkness itself was passing away. That the true Light was already shining.

He could see a grain of sand along the shore, trying to overwhelm the limitless ocean the River formed. It was too tragic to be comical. This tiny blemish spoke as the world, and the world heard its voice. And the whole world fell under its sway. Yet the ocean was undisturbed. Not so much as the tiniest wave was altered.

Dryados looked into the Great Waters. It was filled with myriads upon myriads of souls suspended in its joy. Little children dwelling in the arms of their father. Two tiny lights approached him. They were infinitesimally small. Yet they radiated a joyous light. As they moved closer, he realized it was two human forms. Their faces were familiar, though now they were made perfect and without blemish.

As they stood in front of him, Dryados could see their eyes filled with wonder and joy. Their faces were like brides on their wedding days. One smiled broadly. "Behold what manner of love the Father has bestowed on us. That we should be called children of God!" He held out his arms and spun around, displaying his living being.

Dryados could see the two young men standing before him. Even still, he had a hard time believing. He felt like Thomas. He reached out in silent confusion, touching their arms. It was the same flesh as his, though now clean, untarnished, and eternal.

Chaim and Jankel nodded in confirmation. "Yes, it is us," Chaim said happily.

"I am so sorry…" Dryados said as he started to cry.

Jankel shook his head. "Do not be surprised that the world hated us. The world did not know us, because it did not know Him. But now we are like Him, for we have seen Him as He is." His smile glowed.

Dryados continued to weep bitterly.

Chaim walked up, putting his arms around him. "You weep from the torment of your own fear. Fear that we were harmed. Fear that it was your fault. Fear that…fear of so many things."

"Yes," Jankel continued. "Because your understanding of love is imperfect. Because there is no fear in love." His glowing smile lit even brighter. "For from love comes trust. From trust comes faith. From faith comes confidence. And just as light casts out darkness, confidence casts out fear. So you must come to better understand His love." Jankel touched Dryados's arm. "For perfect love casts out fear."

"But I am always afraid," Dryados whispered.

"Well, the first part of fixing a problem is admitting you have one," Chaim joked.

That brought back the memory of a smile to Dryados's face. "Yes, but the world is filled with terrible things to be afraid of. How do I have victory over the whole world?"

Jankel held Dryados by his arm. His grip was strong, and his touch was warm. He nodded at his own living presence. "This is the victory that has overcome the world—our faith!"

Chaim and Jankel smiled at him softly and then turned and drifted back into the ocean from whence they had come. Dryados looked at the waters around him. The waters seemed to mix with blood. The Shard of Light in his chest moved into the sacred flow. The Spirit, the Water, and the Blood agreed as one. For these three were one.

Dryados opened his eyes to find himself sitting in his chair. He smiled...and cried.

Pergama

Fire and smoke billowed from the great altar in Pergama. In his royal chamber across the way, Ivoluntas, in the human flesh of the governor, stood motionless in the center of his carpet. He was almost at peace. He read the letter over and over again. Slowly he breathed in each syllable. He remembered the words...like an old friend he had not seen in a long time, so familiar, so loved. The words had always been there—always. Though the humans thought the words to be new, they were old. Older than everything. Older than Ivoluntas himself. Then he suddenly clenched his jaw. "Aahhhhh!" He stormed across the room, holding the parchment in his hand. He had promised himself a dozen times that he would tear the letter to ribbons, but he just couldn't. He had thrown the parchment to the floor and stormed away, only to come back moments later and read the missive again. The Word was part of home. Even in his fallen state, they brought him peace. Still, they were also his enemy. They were the Old Farmer, incarnate in the Word. "This is intolerable!" He groaned in confusion.

He gazed deeply into the carpet and its living portrait of home—and held the written Word in his hands. It was a sweet moment. He had the words already memorized. He had always known them, but even he could forget things for a time. He watched the changing light of the carpet. He let his spirit enter the image. He watched the silver river splash past him. He heard the song of the ancient runes etched in its surface. He was home.

"No!" He threw the parchments into the air and burned them to ash with a single thought. His face withered in anguish as he raised his hands, frantically trying to catch the bits of falling of ash. "Aahhhh!" Sorrow overwhelmed him as he watched the charred remnants disappear into the depths of the carpet. "This is intolerable! Absolutely intolerable!" The two guards outside the great bronze doors glanced in nervously.

Ivoluntas nodded to them that all was well and then sank to his knees on the angelic carpet. He ran his hands through the fabric of the rug. "John! John is at the center of this. He is the last of them." He got up and stalked closer to the nervous guards, his rage growing with every step. "I want him dead. I want him killed, murdered, butchered, slaughtered! And I want it to be slow and agonizing. Perhaps the hedge around him is still there—perhaps it is not. It is time for us to test it again and find out."

The two brutish guards nodded and turned to go and fulfill his orders.

Ivoluntas stormed out the door and yelled down the hall behind them, "You will find him in Ephesus—his location is no secret."

Chapter 17
Life with the Dead

"You know if your friends knew about this they would think you were a very strange man or you had a death wish."

"Well, why should they be any different? Half the time I think that myself."

"Well for me, it is a blessing. My conversations with you are the only times I feel normal." The leper sat on the large rock, which had become his unspoken *spot* for when they met.

"Well, Alesia has told me on more than one occasion that I'm not normal, so there you go…" Dryados sat on a small stump. "I guess I don't need to camouflage this stuff in the log when I leave," Dryados said as he looked down at the stack of supplies he had brought.

"No. I will gather them up as soon as you leave. I wasn't even sure you would still be here today. At first I thought I saw you ride off with the others."

"No, I told them I was going to stay and do a little fishing and they could just go on ahead. I will either catch up with them on the road or meet them back in Philadelphia. The road between here and there is fairly secure." He smiled up at the leper. "And I have a very fast horse."

The two men chuckled. Decima still never showed his face. Only on occasion would he reach out from under his cloak with his right hand to grab or move something. The hand appeared normal, other than being whitely pale from being hidden from the sun.

Dryados had no idea how his conversations with the leper had begun, but they had. Now he looked forward to them as much as he did a conversation with Gaius, Talmun, or Titus. The leper was broken, outcast, dying, and yet…Dryados didn't know. "So tell me the news on your people. What happened with that family you were telling me about last time? Is the father still alive? You said he was close to the end."

Decima repositioned himself on his rock. "They all live. The young boy, Felix, is learning to fish from his father. He is getting pretty good. Maria has been making eyes at Vasilis. But he is still too shy to make a move…" Decima updated Dryados on all the news among the colony of lepers. None had died. A few more had joined them. Their lives went on. Dryados saw them down by the river, bathing, washing clothes, resting, playing. He had no idea why he even cared, but he did.

"Now it is your turn. Tell me what is happening in the land of the living?" Decima asked.

Dryados took a deep breath. "Well…Alesia is pregnant." He couldn't help but smile.

"That's wonderful! What a blessing!" The leper pulled himself up higher on the rock. "So are you hoping for a boy or a girl? Do you have names picked? How is Alesia doing? How far along—"

"Alesia is doing fine," Dryados interrupted, smiling. "She is just starting to show. As for the rest of it, well, it is still pretty early."

"Yes, yes, but what do you really want, a boy or a girl?" the leper asked eagerly. "And don't tell me, 'Well, as long as the baby is healthy…' Everybody says that."

Dryados felt very uncomfortable talking about his blessings. He didn't know how old the leper was, but he had an idea they were both about the same age. *How would the leper know love? Who would marry him? Surely he would never know the blessing of children.* "Well, I think both would be fine," he answered nonchalantly.

"You mean you want twins?" The hood of the leper's cape moved subtly as he shook his head. "I always took you for a man who has aimed high, but—"

"No, no, no. I don't want twins."

"What? Twins would be wonderful. I can just see it now—"

"No, it's not that. I just…" Dryados got up and paced awkwardly among the underbrush.

There was a brief silence.

The leper interrupted the awkward moment. "Well, I have known since the beginning that I would never have children of my own. Well, not in the biological sense at least. But I have had many others whose lives I've touched, children of a different sense, which is just as much of a blessing. Actually, I have a very large family." The leper fidgeted a bit on the rock. "You can see some of those I love there in the river, so please don't be afraid that you might hurt my feelings."

Dryados looked up at the hooded figure. Somehow he thought the leper was smiling. "Well, to tell the truth, I am leaning toward having a girl."

"A girl? I'm shocked!" The leper moved himself higher on the rock. "Men never seem to want a girl for their first child. Maybe later, but usually not the first. Too much self-interest, I think. Men always seem to want somebody to play with or take fishing and such." Dryados could see the leper's hood shaking. "I'm shocked. So, why a girl?"

"For Alesia," Dryados stammered. He kicked some leaves loose from the ground and stared at a bright-colored beetle as it scurried under the next leaf. "I think it would make her happy. I think it would be…like a special gift." Dryados kicked some more leaves. "I don't know. I think…for her it would be…it would make her happy. It's hard to explain."

"No, I think you have said it well. You love her, and you want to bring joy to her. And this is a special way you can do that."

"Exactly!" Dryados looked up from the ground with a surprised look on his face. "Yes, that is exactly it." Dryados walked back and sat down on his small log.

The leper continued, "To love someone is no cause for embarrassment, nor is telling them. It is a blessing for those around us to know," the leper began.

"Oh, I almost forgot," Dryados interrupted. He stood up and started rummaging through his tunic. He had several hidden compartments made inside the fabric of the cloth. One held his extra coin. "No, not there." Another held a sculptured cameo he had commissioned, which bore the image of Alesia. "No, not there." And one held… "Got it!" Dryados pulled out a neatly folded stack of parchment. "This is a letter we have received from John in Ephesus. He has sent it out to all the Iredenti across the lands. We are making as many copies of it as fast as we can." Dryados walked about halfway to the leper and laid the parchment on a flat, clean stone and then returned to his position on the small log. After he was comfortably seated, the leper climbed down from his perch on the large boulder and retrieved the missal. Then he too returned to his customary position.

The leper fidgeted for a moment to get comfortable and then slowly unfolded the stiff parchment. He looked like a proud father opening an invitation to his daughter's wedding. "I am sure you have already studied these words many times, but would you like me to read them to you again? I can read them later myself if you have to go."

"No, I would love it if you would read to me." Dryados was somewhat taken aback. He never imagined the leper could read.

The leper sat up tall on his rock. The forest around them seemed to go silent and embrace the fullness of the words as he spoke. "What was from the beginning, what we have heard, what we have seen with our eyes, what we have looked at and touched with our own hands, concerning the Word of Life…which was with the Father…"

His words flowed as smoothly as the nearby river. They were as penetrating as the summer sun. *The leper clearly must have been a scribe,* Dryados thought. He stared at the hooded figure on the rock. *He must have been rich and powerful. And now…he is reduced to this.*

The silence of the wooded clearing again filled Dryados's ears. "And these things we write to you that your joy may be full…" He could hear the babbling of the nearby stream. He could feel the River. "I write no new commandment to you, but an old commandment which you have had from the beginning." The leper sat silently for a moment and then took a deep, slow breath in. "I have heard these words before." He sighed.

"No, these are new," Dryados interjected excitedly. "Yes, the literary structure and syntax are consistent with earlier writings, but the content is clearly of a different subject matter. You can see…"

The leper roared with laughter.

Chapter 18
A Dream and a Backache

Ephesus

John rolled over slowly in bed. His bones were old. They ached when he was awake. They ached when he slept. He did not sleep very well anymore and awoke frequently. Tonight he would sleep more deeply than he had in many years...

The boat rolled to starboard, hit by a great wave. The men clung to the ropes tied about the deck. The wind whistled through the rigging above them. Someone had already pulled the sail's holding pins, and it now hung low and unfurled, draping parts of the deck. Men scurried to try to secure the wind-whipped canvas. There was no room for error.

"John, quickly, man, we need you to starboard!" He scrambled across the deck. Terror gripped him as he slipped on the wet deck and started to slide over the side.

A hand caught his tunic by his shoulder. "John, grab my arm...grab my arm!" He could feel the fabric of the tunic slipping off his frame. "Now! Grab my arm!" His body was drenched. He could barely see through his soaked hair and the battering rain. He grabbed the arm holding his top cloth. His grip slipped on his rescuer's wet flesh. His feet slipped into the crashing waves. The man lunged forward and grabbed him with his other arm. "Got ya!"

"Matthew, I owe you one, brother."

Matthew smiled broadly. John always remembered Matthew's big smile. He had missed it now for many years. "Just help them with the mast."

As the two men scrambled to their feet, a strange silence covered the deck. They both froze. The wind still blew and rain slammed against them, but there was no other sound.

"There!" Someone was pointing to the tossing waves. A Spirit was walking on the water.

"It is a ghost!" screamed someone. "It is the lost souls of the dead come to claim our lives!"

"It is the angel of death…"

"It is…"

Then a voice came from out of the sea. "Take courage. It is I; do not be afraid." As John watched, the ghost became a man…then a friend.

Even in his dream, John smiled, knowing what lay ahead.

Peter ran to the rope rail along the side of the deck. "Lord, if it is You, command me to come to You on the water."

The voice that followed seem to fill the earth. "Come!"

John watched in dismay as Peter leaped over the side of the ship and landed solid on the waves. John gasped and chocked on the inhaled drops of rain as he watched Peter walking on the water! He edged closer to the side of the ship. Still there was no sound. He could hear his beating heart and the blood flowing in his veins. The wind railed. The waves tossed in their fury. Peter hesitated as he looked at the churning water now beneath him. Bewilderment filled his face as he thought of the miracle that he had now become an integral part. He began to sink. "Lord, save me!" he cried.

Immediately Jesus stretched out His hand and took hold of him and said to him, "O you of little faith, why did you doubt?" Peter rose out of the water like a whale breaching from the depths. The two walked among the waves and climbed into the boat. As Jesus's feet hit the deck, the wind and rain stopped.

John and the others fell and worshiped Him there on the calm sea. "You are certainly God's Son!" they proclaimed.

The boat sailed on and landed at Gennesaret.

That segment of his dream ended. John continued to lay there dreaming…and remembering at the same time. A familiar voice filled his mind. *I am in the storm. Churning waters will not harm you.* He awoke. He lay in bed a little longer, thinking about what he had just seen. He remembered the great churning water of the storm that day so long ago, and being afraid. He was not afraid anymore. He got up out of his warm bed. His bones still ached, but perhaps a little less. He did his business in the toilet, washed himself up, brushed his teeth, and combed his hair. He got on a clean tunic and started to walk to the kitchen. Suddenly, someone pounded on the door.

Ascalon smoothed out Lautus's baby blanket. The cloth was still as white as when Sperta first sewed it together. The embroidery was still crisp. Lautus was sound asleep. They had all spent the day down at the river for a picnic. Lautus had found a frog and chased it around in the grass for hours. He had fallen asleep in

Ascalon's arms on the way home. Ascalon stared at his peaceful son. "Even great lions must sleep," he mused. He gave Lautus one more good-night kiss and then blew out the lamp.

Sperta plopped down in the living area. She laid her head against one of the pillows and looked over at Ascalon. "I am just exhausted."

Ascalon plopped down beside her. "As am I," he moaned.

"Perhaps we can go to bed early. I can work on your arm. And then we can just snuggle for a while. Lautus is already asleep."

Ascalon gave her a tired nod, and they both forced themselves to their feet. The two walked back to the bedroom, and Sperta began to work on Ascalon's crumpled extremity. She began at his gnarled fingers and slowly worked her way up. His wrist had only the slightest degree of flexion and extension. The elbow could flex inward but would not go straight no matter how hard she worked on it. Ascalon wore his splint every day, even when he wasn't working. That had made a huge difference. Sperta reached down and got some olive oil from underneath the bed. She deeply massaged her husband's shoulder.

Ascalon sighed softly as Sperta worked his aching flesh. "Ohhhhh, that feels soooo good," he moaned.

Sperta smiled, happy with her success. "Now lay on your stomach," she instructed. She jumped to the side of the bed and started pushing on his heavy frame.

Ascalon immediately obeyed. The bed creaked as he shifted his weight and tried to position himself comfortably. She poured more oil across his back and down his spine. Then she leaned all her weight into him as she began to deeply massage his aching muscles. She started on his upper back and worked her way down.

"Ohh...that's perfect," Ascalon moaned. She pushed even harder. She massaged his back slowly down his spine.

The only sound filling the room were Ascalon's "oooos" and "aahhhs." Then, seemingly way too soon, Sperta announced, "There! All done."

Ascalon groaned in disappointment and laid motionless for a moment. "Sperta please...would you walk on my back?" he begged quietly.

"Ascalon, you know I hate that." She gave him a squeamish look of comical disgust.

He looked up at her with little-boy eyes. "Please?" He sounded like he was begging for a new puppy.

Sperta shook her head and groaned in defeat. "All right." Then she moved to the side of the bed. "Now slide to the center of the bed and hold the sides."

"Thank you...thank you..." Ascalon responded eagerly. Then he shimmied his large frame over to the middle. Sperta lifted his left arm up and helped him to move it to the other side.

"You know I really hate this." Her face still grimaced in bewildered disgust. "And don't wiggle!" she scolded. Sperta slowly balanced her way up onto his back. She stood there motionless for a second, "This is so weird…" Then she slowly started to creep her feet slowly forward.

Ascalon moaned even louder. "You have no idea how good that feels on my back…*aaahhhh*!"

Sperta slowly edged her way up and down his spine. Ascalon moaned with each shift of her weight. Then she stopped, unmoving on his lower back. "Oh… just there…don't move."

Sperta wiggled ever so slightly. "*Ooohhh*…that's perfect…it's just perfect." She jiggled her feet for just a minute longer and then stopped and stood there unmoving again.

"All right, that's enough," she declared and then gently started to glide off his back.

"Nooo. Please?" he groaned pleadingly.

"No, it's too late. We're done." Sperta scurried off his back and crawled under the covers beside her husband.

Ascalon rolled over onto his right side and settled into the bed. Sperta snuggled closely up against him. "Oh, I've been meaning to tell you—your uncle Amahanz came by yesterday. He keeps coming by to visit. You really need to go talk to him."

Ascalon laid there shaking his head. "I have just been really busy, is all," Ascalon said. "And he is just…so different."

"He is the closest thing you have to a father," Sperta whispered. "And he really cares about you. The two of you are so much alike it is scary."

Ascalon rolled over, looking at her. "We are nothing alike. He is a potter. I am a blacksmith. I think that about summarizes it," Ascalon scolded.

"Yeah," Sperta scoffed. "You both make things with your hands. You both do things exactly your own way. And you are both uncompromising. As I said, it's scary." Sperta sat up in the bed next to him. "He was here every day when you were unconscious. He has called here several times for you since. And now… you're too busy."

"I guess you're right." He sighed. "I promise I will go by his pottery shop sometime next week when I have a break." He rolled back over onto his side, smiling broadly in the dark. "That was a wonderful day," he said softly. "Did you see when Lautus tried to catch that frog?" The couple lay reminiscing about the glorious day they had just had and how their young boy was growing up.

Chapter 19
A Choice and a Cup

Ephesus

John knelt down in the kitchen. It took an extra few seconds as his creaky knees forbid him any speed. He folded his hands in front of him. The loud pounding on the door was no surprise. He had always been amazed they had waited so long. His prayer began as it always did. "God, thank You…"

He paid no mind to the yells of the Roman centurion outside. "John, son of Zebedee, you are arrested for blasphemy and treason." He took little notice as the front door was kicked off its hinges and crashed into the front room. It was a stout old door. He knew he would never be back to fix it. He hurried his prayer as the pounding of the metal-clad feet of the Romans got closer. His prayer ended when the heavy hands of the soldier grabbed the back of his tunic and slammed him to the floor.

His head smashed into the tile. "I am he…I am John," he stammered. He opened his eyes to see a Roman spear held at his throat. He lay on the floor, his knees still tucked beneath him. The soldiers clambered through the home, tossing things about and crashing things to the floor. No one else was there. His assistant, Prochorus, was not scheduled to arrive for another hour.

"The house is empty," reported one soldier.

"Good. Now get him on his feet!"

The spear swerved away from John's neck. "You heard him, old man." A large soldier grabbed John's tunic and jerked him off the ground.

"Aahhh…" John moaned. The sudden jerk sent pain surging into his old frame. He had arthritis in every joint. His body was bent. He really needed his cane. He stood there trying to stand but continued to wobble, embarrassed by his own frailty. His skin was thin. His head was bleeding from a cut off to the side from where he had hit the floor.

"Take him to the prison," ordered the leader.

John started to shuffle toward the door. "I just need my cane. I will be of no bother…"

The centurion glared at the large soldier who had just jerked John to his feet. "Carry him if you have to," he snarled.

"Yes, sir." The soldier nodded to his commander and turned to John. "Come along, old one." He bent forward and threw John over his shoulder like a sack of grain.

"Aahh!" Pain shot through John's back as each of the joints in his spine popped in sequence. "Aahh!" He tried to relax and let his joints loosen, but every step taken by his lumbering captor was like being hit in the back with a mallet. He lay across the man's large shoulders and moaned every step of the way to the prison. It was a long walk.

Bang! Bang! Bang! Dryados found himself in the familiar vacant landscape of his dream. "*No!*" He shouted. "I don't want this! I'm not moving!" Dryados hunkered down, flexing his knees. *Bang! Bang! Bang!* It was like the pounding at your front door from an unwanted visitor who simply would not go away. Dryados clenched his fists tightly. "No! *I will not move!*" Dryados hunkered down even more. Still, the vacant landscape around him was changing. Though he did not move, the dream world around him did…

Dryados watched as the angel pounded the glowing white object. The massive blows of the hammer seemed to slam into his chest. Heat filled his mind. The forge was like the sun. The angel held up the glowing white object. It looked like a key. The angel held it there before him, examining his work. Then he turned, looking at Dryados, and smiled. Dryados smiled back. The angel returned the glowing key to the heart of the blaze. He stoked the billows. Dryados tried to move away, but his legs refused to obey. Blow upon blow. The radiant blanched implement was changing, becoming something new. *Bang! Bang! Bang!* The key morphed slowly and was starting to look familiar. It was starting to look like…

"And you are sure it is the same dream?" Alesia asked.

Dryados couldn't read the expression on her face. "Yes, I told you. I have dreamed that dream a dozen times. It is the same one…only different." Dryados got up from his favorite chair in the living room and started to pace again. "It was only different because I refused to go forward, so the dream just…carried me along."

"But you said you saw more?"

"Yes. In this dream the key was transitioned into something else."

"What was it changed into?" Alesia sat calmly in her chair as Dryados continued to pace quickly about the room, wearing a path in the flooring.

"It wasn't changed into something…what it was…was refitted or retooled. I don't know the right word. The key was still there. It just wasn't just a key anymore. It was something…in addition to that." Dryados glanced at Alesia's calm visage. "It's hard to explain."

"I can tell." She chuckled. "But do you think that was all of the dream? Or was there more for you to see?"

"I don't know…but I think there was more. I just kept fighting it. I didn't want to be there…I didn't want to see any more. All I kept thinking about was Chaim and Jankel."

"Even in your dream?" Alesia's face flushed with concern.

"Yes, even in my dream!" Dryados's words came out more forcefully than he intended. He stared blankly at his wife. "I have seen them in the River. Alive and complete. Yet I couldn't live with myself if I was responsible for anyone else's death."

Alesia rose and walked slowly to her husband's side. She gave him a long hug. Dryados's arms hung limp at his side. Slowly his arms wrapped around Alesia's frame, and his head leaned softly against hers. He snuggled his face into her hair. They both stood silent.

After a moment he whispered softly, "I don't know what to do." Dryados breathed in. "All that dream has done is led to sorrow and death. I'm done."

Alesia looked silently at her husband and then nodded. "The question is, do you trust Him? I understand how you feel. But don't you think your fears are getting in the way? You just said you hadn't seen the end of it. You have no idea what else it will show you, or what it will all mean."

The words jarred him back. "I'm not afraid. I'm just…" Dryados let out a deep sigh. "When I was sent to Pergama, I thought God was calling me there to become a great and successful merchant like my father." He chuckled lightly to himself. "But I was wrong. He called me to Pergama to meet you." Alesia squeezed his hand. "It wasn't what I thought at all. Since then, it has happened many times. I think God is planning one thing, and it turns out He is doing something completely different."

Alesia moved in front of him. "Put your hand just here." She reached over and placed Dryados's hand on her stomach.

His face glowed. "The baby is kicking!"

"Yes," she said, smiling. "He has been doing that all morning."

"He?" Dryados asked.

Alesia looked at him with a flustered grin. "Well, with all the kicking and fussing, I am just assuming it's a boy. Either that, or she is going to be as stubborn and pigheaded as you are. So, better if it's a boy." She reached down and moved Dryados's hand off to the other side. "This is the baby's head."

Dryados rubbed his hand softly across the growing bump in her abdomen. "There is always blessing," he murmured.

"Yes, there is," she reaffirmed. "And you need to see that blessing within the dream." She looked down at Dryados with an oddly surprised expression. "Now with all this kicking...I have to go pee." Alesia turned and ran down the hall.

Dryados tried not to chuckle too loudly.

The next evening Dryados crossed the river Cogamus and headed out into the Katakekaumene. The elder meeting would be held in the late afternoon at Bondicola's home. He was a farmer not far into the plain and one of Dryados's favorite elders.

Dryados scanned the area for Romans but saw none. There was a lone man working a field just a little off in the distance. He looked up frequently, obviously a sentry. So was the man selling wine. He moved around in his little shack rearranging the carafes far more often than was necessary. The children playing in the tree... *I don't know*, Dryados thought. *Could go either way. Great view from up there, and if one of those kids ran off to go tell someone, no one would suspect a thing.* Dryados noticed the oldest one kept his eye on Dryados a little longer than just a curious gaze. *Yep, they're sentries too*, Dryados thought. *Well, can't fault Bondicola for being cautious.* Dryados waved at the kids.

The farmhouse was nondescript and looked like a hundred others in the area. Old tools leaned against the side of the house. Chickens scurried in the yard. Several kids played in the dirt with their toys. He could smell some meat smoking in one of the small outbuildings.

Dryados gave the coded knock on the door to the large tool shed attached to the barn, even though he was sure those inside were already well aware of his arrival. He shuffled quickly indoors.

The elders in Philadelphia always sang. They never had any music, so it was always sung a cappella. The deep voices of the men filled the cluttered tool room. Sometimes Dryados thought the men were secretly competing to see who had the deepest voice. He was more of a tenor and had absolutely no chance of winning that competition. But still, the deepness of their voices resonated with his soul and warmed his spirit. Many times he would stop singing and just stand there and listen.

When the songs ended, the elders sat down in a large circle using the many workbenches scattered around the room. Different men rose in turn and shared their news. No one had been arrested in months. The ministries in the city were expanding. And they had sent three young men to join a growing fellowship in

Armenia. The news was all good.

"And you, Master Dryados, what brings you to the meeting tonight?" Dryados was not an elder, but the meetings were always open to anyone who wished to come. Dryados rose from his bench and stood on the hard dirt floor. His face filled with all the sorrow his heart was bearing. He knew Chaim and Jankel were in the River. But still, it hurt.

"I think I have killed two good men," he said solemnly. He couldn't help it. He had already started to cry. The tears rolled silently down his face.

Dryados shared the story of how he had sent the two young men to Smyrna and that they had been killed. He did not tell of the quest. "I was the one who sent them. They were so eager…I have killed them both." He sobbed bitterly.

Silence filled the old barn.

"Dryados…" It was Bondicola. He looked up at Dryados with a smile, but then his countenance slowly fell. "The men we have sent out, do you think they are all still alive?"

The question took Dryados off guard. He had always assumed…

Bondicola looked at Dryados and shook his head slowly. "No."

Another elder asked, "Do you think if we all stay here, then we will all be 'safe'? That we will all be alive this time next year?" He looked at Dryados and waited for an answer.

"I…I'm not…"

"Why is that? Who is to blame? Are they here in this room?" asked a different one.

Dryados grew silent.

"We have seen children killed who were still playing with toys. We have seen pregnant women sawed in half, people burned alive, beaten to death, hung…" The elder paused for a moment. "It is never the fault of the victim that they are murdered. It is never the fault of the sheep that it is hunted by the lion."

Dryados lowered his head. "I struggle to just go on," he said as his silent tears continued down his face. He wiped his face and started to regain himself. Then he nodded to the gathered elders. "You are righteous men…"

One elder started to laugh.

Dryados looked up.

It was the head elder. He was an older man with weary eyes and a thin white patchy beard. "Well, I do not know so much about how you measure a man, but as to being righteous"—he laughed again—"there you are mistaken." He looked around the room. "Let us each share *briefly* with Master Dryados the testimony of who we were and who still tries to come back out when we are alone." He took a deep breath, "I will go first." He rose to his feet and leaned on a thick wooden cane. "I am Vocatus." He shared the story of his life and the lives he had destroyed. His wife, his children, his friends, his business—all had fallen to his unquenchable thirst for alcohol. "My children feared me. Everyone else hated me, even the ones who loved me. One day God…"

Around the room the elders went each in turn. There was no modesty or shielded secrets. "I do not know how many men I have killed" one shared solemnly. "I have fought with sword and spear and armored hand. I know many I fought were maimed and gutted. I do not know how many died. I do not know how many widows or orphans I have created in this world. One day God…"

Around the room the testimony of redemption was shared. When they finished, Vocatus again rose to his feet. "There are none righteous here—only the Iredenti."

Someone started to lead the group in another song. The men all rose to their feet, and soon their deep voices filled the old tool room once again. Dryados looked around the room. Some of the men there were very old. Still they were children singing a love song to their Father. It made him smile. He did the best he could to hit the low notes like the others. Eventually he gave up and decided to harmonize. Others followed. Soon they became a choir. He did not know if he could see everyone who was singing. Somehow he knew there were others there he did not see.

The song ended, and they all sat down. Bondicola's wife arrived and started to serve communion.

Each man broke off a piece of the loaf and ate of the bread.

Then too the cup was passed.

Dryados held the cup. Alesia's words slammed into his mind. *Do you trust Him?* Dryados froze for a moment as the answer flooded into his mind. He raised the cup.

The leper's camp outside Sardis

"Why do you think God hates you?" Decima asked. He bent forward and carefully whipped the man's forehead with a cold rag.

"Because I am a leper!" the man barked. Then he grimaced and shoved Decima's hand away.

"Every person here in the colony is a leper," Decima said reassuringly. He picked up the wet rag and softly placed it back on the man's brow. "Just listen outside—you can hear the children in the river. And there in the distance, do you hear it? Emmaus and his mother-in-law are fighting again." Decima smiled broadly at the old man. But the old man was blind and could not see its glow. Decima started to clean the old man's scab-covered arms. The lighting in the small cave was poor, but Decima did not need more. The old man had chosen to stop eating and drinking. He lay on the rocky cave floor and would soon die. Not because of illness, or at least not directly. He was just done. He was tired of being a leper, tired of hurting, and tired of even living.

"Long ago I took care of another man." Decima smiled to himself and then continued. "He too was afraid. He had been brave once…but…well, I guess it all just got to be too much for him too." Decima shifted and started to wash the man's festering feet. "I suppose it is a common feeling."

The old man rolled over on his side, trying to get comfortable. "Tell me about this other man," he said, half grumbling.

Decima smiled again. "He had fought a great battle. Actually, it was quite miraculous. And the victory that day would be recorded for all generations to know. But even after he won, he started to think about all the things that could go wrong. All the bad possibilities. So he ran away. Actually, the first time I met him he was quaking in fear, hiding himself under a juniper tree." Decima scrubbed out some of the dirt between the remaining stubs of the man's fingers. "He thought he was the only one left, that he was all alone. He just wanted to die." Decima chuckled. "He was wrong, of course. There were still many others just like him. But with all that was going on, he lost his perspective." Decima shook his head. "You wouldn't believe how much good some hot food, a cool drink, and a good night's sleep can do sometimes. That, and learning the truth." Decima wrapped a relatively clean rag around the man's ulcerated hand. "Sometimes I think that is the worst. To feel all alone…in a world full of people. That is why I love our colony." Decima got up and moved to the other side. "Every person here is in the same boat. And I think when you come to that realization that the people around you are just like you, it makes it a lot easier to show them some grace and just love them. I mean, why wouldn't you? They're just like you, right?"

The old man shook his head. "Yes, I suppose…but what use am I?"

Decima started working on the other arm. "Well, for me, you give me someone to talk to. Of everyone here in the colony, you are closest to my age. For me, as I clean your arm, I am reminded that all flesh will fail. That it is not to be envied. That it is a gift, but an imperfect and temporary one. For me, you are a reminder of purpose. As I clean your arm, I am blessed to share compassion. I am blessed to…"

"Yes, yes, but what good am I? I am a dying old leper, of no use to anyone."

Decima held the man's arm. He wasn't even sure the old man could feel his touch. One of the tragedies of leprosy was that it caused much of its victim's extremities to go numb. "What makes you think people need to be of use? That if the people around you can't use you for their purposes, that you have no value? Do you think your parents loved you when you were a crying, peeing, pooping infant for what you did?" Decima shook his head. "That is not how love works." Decima got up off of his knees and pulled his hood up loosely over his head. "I need to go get some fresh water. I'll be back in just a minute."

Decima returned a little while later. He took off his hood and sat down.

"That smells marvelous!" the old man forced himself up on his elbows.

Decima laid a still-warm bread cake by the old man's head. Then he placed a large jar of cool water beside it. The smell of the fresh cake filled the dark cave.

"Decima, that's just mean…"

"What?" Decima asked, feigning his innocence.

"That bread cake…here I am, trying to starve myself, and you bring that thing in to fill the whole cave with…temptation."

"Temptation? Trust me—that is definitely the wrong word." Decima chuckled. "This is just a reminder…of how I feel about you. And to tell you it is time to make a choice."

The old man breathed in the aroma of the warm bread cake. "I am feeling really hungry." He sighed. "And I could use something to drink and soothe my parched throat." Though he was blind, he looked at Decima with tired eyes.

Decima smiled his invisible smile. He walked over to the man and placed the cup in his hand. "It is your choice…but know that I love you, and so do many others in the colony."

The old man paused, holding up the cup as he decided his fate.

John rubbed his hands up and down his arm and walked around the small cell. There was no fire. He could tell it was early morning. There was a metal grate high above him to let in some light, but the sun had not yet truly risen. He could see the stone of the walls surrounding him. They were cold. *Better to keep moving*, he thought. He hoped the Romans would let Prochorus bring him food and maybe let him start a small fire or get some blankets. He could hear the guards shuffling about down the hall and the rattling of their keys. The small slot at the bottom of the door slid up, and a wooden bowl of gruel was shoved into his cell. There was a suggestion of steam rising from the small mound. It looked warm, or at least warmer than he was. He picked up the old worn-out bowl and devoured the contents. This was a treat. He didn't know why the guards were being so good to bring food. *Last meal*, he thought.

Hours passed. He continued to pace about the cell. When the first few rays of the sun finally trickled into his cell, he moved to take in the tiny flow of heat. The morning passed. Noon came and went. It was early afternoon when he heard keys rattling at the keyhole in the door.

"Put this on!" One of the petulant guards threw John's favorite cloak into the cell and then tossed his cane in on top of it. Apparently Prochorus had been by.

The snarling guard waited as John creaked his way over and threw the cloak over his shivering bones. As soon as the cloak was on, the guard yanked him out of his cell and shoved him down the hall. "Move quickly, old man! You have a lot of people out there waiting."

John didn't know what to make of that. He assumed there would not be a trial. At the same time, he didn't think they would be executing him so quickly either. *Better a quick death*, he thought.

He struggled up the stairs. "Come on, old man. Come on!" The guards knocked him to the ground over and over, only to help him up a second later. At ground level he was taken outside and surrounded by a small contingent of soldiers. They marched him slowly through the city. Many of the people gawked and stared. Others just scurried out of the way of the Romans' swords. When he slowed too much, he got a sharp poke in the back with a spear. He was exhausted and covered in sweat when they entered the great theater carved into the western side of Mount Oreosus.

The large theater was not as full as it often was for executions. Perhaps the death of one old man was not as entertaining as hours of blood-bathed horror. Yet there were thousands present. The crowd rose to its feet with jeers as he entered. Even with his poor hearing, the noise was riotous.

He was marched to the theater's center. The Roman guards parted around him as the high priest of Diana approached.

The priest circled John like a lion around a wounded gazelle. He raised an accusing finger and flourished it at the old apostle. "This is John, the blasphemer, the defiler, the one who misleads, the one who has betrayed our gods and our emperor!" The crowd roared with boos and hissing. "He says there is only one way, which must be His way. Our gods are not good enough!" He walked in front of John and stood facing the crowd. He raised his arms and stretched them out broadly. "But we, we are greater than this. We...are more merciful. And we...will give him one more chance to be a part of his community." The priest walked over to one of the guards and retrieved a large goblet of wine. He held it high above his head like an offering to the gods as he walked back to John.

"All he needs to do is proclaim his loyalty to our emperor and god, Domitian. And our god Domitian will welcome him into our community." The high priest walk over to John, still holding up the cup. "Or he will drink this cup of death!" The crowd cheered wildly. The priest walked over and spoke quietly to John. "You will declare your loyalty to Domitian and the acceptance of our gods, or you will drink of this cup and die in agony. It will be slow. You will writhe in pain in front of all Ephesus. And in that pain you will come to denounce your God and beg to be put down like a horse with a broken leg." The priest lowered the cup for John to examine. "Or you can proclaim the truth—the truth of Rome." The cup smelled like a sewer. John did not know what types of poison it held, but he thought there were many.

The priest raised the cup high above his head and began to circle John. A low murmur filled the theater as everyone present speculated what the old man would do. Then suddenly the high priest spun and ran toward John. "Now, John, follower of dead Jews, choose your fate!"

Silence filled the great theater. John did not speak. He raised his head. Some likely thought he was staring at the crowd, trying to decide what to do. The truth was, he was looking to heaven, but the arthritis in his neck would not let him raise his head any higher. After a brief moment, he reached for the cup.

The great theater erupted into cheers of affirmation. "Yes! Death to the blasphemer! Death to the defiler! Death…death…death!"

John held the goblet up like a holy sacrament. He thought of a moment long ago on the Passover. He remembered the One he loved holding up the cup, saying, *Do this in remembrance of me.* Over the years those words had taken on a whole new level of meaning. He held the cup of death to the highest his old frame could raise it. He prayed long and loud. "Thank you, God…sent His only begotten son…the visible image of the invisible God…risen from the dead…no other name by which men are saved…"

As John prayed, his vision eyes returned. He was surrounded by a great host of witnesses. Some were people he recognized. Some had died in this very amphitheater where he now stood. It made him pray even more boldly. Suddenly the Shard of Light in his chest burst from his flesh and enfolded his being. The light around him was blinding. He did not know if the earth had ceased to exist, for there was no sound that disturbed his lone voice. A whirlwind churned around him. His voice billowed over the crowd. Then the tempest seemed to collapse into the goblet. He watched as the poison in the cup congealed into a mass of living corruption. Small serpents slithered from the cup. Falling to the ground, they were immediately consumed by the earth. As the last serpent returned to the dust, John put the goblet to his lips.

Chapter 20
The Same Instant

At that exact same moment, three different men, in three different cities, held up three different cups. To one it was a choice to trust in what he already knew. To another it was a decision to live the life he already had. To the last it was a remembrance of something he had never forgotten. Each man drank deeply from the cup he had been given.

Chapter 21
Outrage

A pillar of black smoke billowed from the great altar of Pergama all day. It rose above the city like a foreboding guardian of impending doom. Now that black guardian was being replaced by one of blood red. The tarred logs they had used were removed and the living fire within the altar made unrestrained. A column of white smoke formed as a mountain of wet leaves was thrown upon the blaze. The white funnel became manipulated and twisted by a whirlwind of rage swirling around it. Unfulfilled malice stoked the flames higher and higher into the night sky. The redness of the blaze reflected in the white firmament, creating the illusion of a dancing red demon in the dark night. And at the base of it all stood Ivoluntas. He gloried in the dancing flames and sounds of death. He watched as the fire greedily consumed the streams of blood pouring from a hundred pigs being sacrificed there to his name. Yet it provided no comforting. It merely added to his frustration. He stormed across the courtyard back to his throne room. He paced across his angelic carpet and stared out the window. Black Voids floated beside him, trying to speak of days past and of previous glory. Still there was no consolation for what had happened earlier that day at the amphitheater in Ephesus. He spun, facing the cohort of Qui Malaam. He raised a pointed finger at one of the lingering shadows. "Tell me again exactly what happened after John put the cup to his lips," he sneered.

"I tell you, Great One, it was Novitate Unum," the Back Void said desperately. "It burst from his chest like the sun. The wonder of heaven filled the theater and flowed through every soul there. Even I was taken aback by it." The Black Void stopped instantly and cringed backward. "But...but only for a moment. I was taken off guard. I..."

"And what of the humans?" Ivoluntas asked blankly as he calculated his losses.

"It was terrible. They fell like wheat before the scythe. It just overwhelmed them." The black shadow shuttered nervously. "You know how it is..."

"Yes, I do." The calmness in Ivoluntas's voice caused the other Black Voids in the room to float farther away. Many tried to seek refuge hiding behind those in front of them. Ivoluntas's face turned from pink to scarlet as he paced the room. "How many...how many of the humans did we lose?"

"Almost all of them," murmured the Black Void.

"Give me a number! I need a number." There was growing anger in Ivoluntas's tone. "Was it fifty or a hundred?"

The Black Void sank lower on the carpet, bowing his headless form. He spoke as softly as he could. "It was thousands. Almost all in the great theater were lost."

"Aahhhhhh!" Ivoluntas picked up a golden vase and slammed it across the room. It careened through the emptiness of the Black Void who had spoken, and crashed against the far wall.

"And John? Did he not die in writhing pain as I commanded? Did he not perish in front of all of Ephesus to serve as warning to all who would follow his teachings?" Ivoluntas paced around the room, his voice getting louder with each step.

"No, Great Leader, he did not." Dozens of Black Voids floated in the governor's chamber. Most tried to hide. Some tried to lose themselves in the inviting images of the carpet. None spoke. "But...but...the plan was simple," the Black Void continued. "He would deny his faith in front of the city or drink the Unda Cruciatus. Either way, we would win. There was no way we could possibly lose," he said pleadingly.

"And yet you did!" Ivoluntas spoke coldly. Power began to crackle around him. Sparks and tiny stray foils of lightning trickled off his body. The unbridled energy slowly lifted his human frame off the ground. He held up a beautiful gold figurine and melted it with a single thought.

"The hedge! The hedge is still upon him," the Black Void moaned. "This is the work of the Old Farmer. It is not our failing! It is His merciless nature to...to humiliate us!" The Black Void laid his formless shape upon the carpet in a groveling plea for mercy. Then he looked up. "Here, Great One. You should bring him here, to the site of your throne. You could execute him personally. It would bring you great pleasure to destroy one of the tools of the Old Farmer."

Ivoluntas looked thoughtfully at the submissive Void. He had already considered that option. But the pain of his recent defeat at the hands of one of the Valde Beatus was still fresh in his mind. That had been nearly two years ago in this very room. The only blessing in that was that none of his myriads of followers had witnessed his downfall.

"No, this is more important than my own personal pleasure. He must be made a warning to the rest of the world like the other eleven before him. The more public and more gruesome his death, the better. Here there would be no real witnesses." As the scarlet faded from the governor's face, his body floated back to the surface of the carpet. "Here, the hedge may still be intact." The governor paused, looking around the room. "So I will have him transferred to Rome. I will have Domitian make the arrangements immediately." Ivoluntas smiled. Then his presence transcended across space to the emperor's body in the great city.

Chapter 22
Dryados Is Dead

Parceida's villa in Smyrna

The door to the receiving room edged slowly open, and the nervous courier crept inside. His presence was met by a murderous glare from Parceida. "I told you I was not to be disturbed." Parceida spoke calmly. He stood in the center of the room, wearing his white tunic with a vibrant purple sash laid exquisitely across his arm. His guest looked equally regal.

"No, that is quite all right, Lord Parceida. I know you are a very busy man, and emergencies can plague us all." The senator motioned graciously for Parceida to receive the courier and then rose to his feet. "I have stayed much too long as it is, and I am sure my aide will be giving me an earful about the inviolate nature of my schedule." The senator smiled broadly and gave a small polite bow. "As always, it has been a pleasure." He stopped near the door just before he exited, and turned. "Lord Parceida, one day you too will make a fine senator. Keep up the good work for our emperor. Good day." The senator exited and was met by his eager aide, who waited right outside the room.

As the door closed behind the senator, Parceida stormed across the room, snarling at the anxious courier. "If someone is not dead, I will kill you where you stand. How dare you interrupt me when the senator is visiting!"

The house valet dropped to one knee. "It was Sicaria. He has been murdered." The valet kept his gaze fixed on the floor.

Parceida stopped his menacing advance. "Sicaria? He was one of my best." His face filled with bewilderment. "Who...who has done this terrible thing?"

The valet kept his head bowed to the floor. "It was Dryados. He has killed Sicaria."

Parceida stood there stunned. It was impossible. Sicaria was a trained assassin, spy, and soldier. They had come up the ranks together. They had fought in the arena together in the early days as gladiators. He was the closest thing Parceida had to a friend. Parceida's face flushed with bewildered rage and fury.

The servant looked up cautiously from the floor. "But, Master, there is more. We believe he was also successful in assassinating his target." A smile quickly filled his face. "Dryados is dead."

Philadelphia

Dryados sat in the center courtyard of the caravanserai, enjoying the party. He would be getting home late. He knew that Alesia would be mad, but there was nothing he could do. The Indus man had gone to a great deal of trouble to plan the festivities and still get Dryados out the gate before the caravanserai locked its doors at sunset. Leaving now would be incredibly rude.

He had met this particular trader on his first day at the caravanserai. Over the last several months they had become friends of a fashion and closely tied to each other in their businesses. To celebrate their relationship, the Indus man had brought a special group of entertainers all the way from his homeland for the sole purpose of entertaining Dryados, for this one evening. It was a huge expense and an incredible tribute to their relationship.

As the Indus merchant's men prepared for the next show, they brought out several servants with buckets of water and stationed them around the area. The need for such a precaution became clear the instant the next performer walked out. He was a fire-breather. He took a drink of some mysterious potion and then spit it like venom from his mouth. As he did, he ignited it into a blast of fire above the crowd. Dryados could feel the heat from where he sat.

The fire-bender pulled out several batons. He lit the ends of the first one and began to make it twirl. Then he ignited another and another and another, throwing them wildly in the air. The flaming flock of phoenix danced before the stunned onlookers. It was mesmerizing.

Suddenly one of the men from the Indus merchant's troop rushed at Dryados. He held a long, polished hook blade above his head and charged forward, screaming. As Dryados jumped to his feet, one of his men shoved him to the side. Dryados saw the glint of another blade just off to his left. He spun...but it was too late. The second blade slammed into his left upper arm. The arm flung forward as the blade caught on the tendon. Dryados instinctively pulled his arm back. The blade tore through the front of his arm. Blood spattered onto the people in front of him. Dryados screamed in pain. The blade from the Indus caravan's screaming troop member sliced through the air just behind Dryados and slammed into flesh. Dryados dropped and rolled on the floor. The thick, hooked blade, however, had already found its target. Dryados looked up from the floor to see a geyser of blood shooting into the air. The man behind him had almost been beheaded by the impact of the hooked blade. The screaming attacker was small but not yet finished. He pulled the blade from deep inside the man's neck and struck again. The man's head dropped to the floor and rolled inches away from Dryados. The large corpse dropped across Dryados's legs. Dryados screamed and screamed as he scrambled to get out from under the giant headless body. Blood gushed from the dead body. Dryados looked like he was wearing a red tunic. He tried to push himself free, but he was stuck. He couldn't stop screaming.

Mayhem raged all around them. People streamed out of the caravanserai as the security forces raced to the scene. People grabbed cooking utensils and anything else they could to defend themselves. Weapons were strictly controlled within the caravanserai. Violence was punished by death. This was unheard of!

"Silence or blood! Silence or blood!" roared the centurion. He sounded like Cleopas.

The noise level dropped dramatically, but people were still screaming. Dryados was helped to his feet. He had lost a lot of blood himself and was feeling faint. "I need a new tunic. I need a new tunic. Alesia cannot see me like this…I need…" Then he collapsed.

As the crowds streamed out of the entrance, a large man blended in unnoticed among them. He would send a courier to Lord Parceida immediately. Sicaria had obviously been killed. But with all the blood, clearly Dryados must have been successfully assassinated as well.

Parceida looked down at his cowering servant. "Was there a written report? Do we have anything from them in writing?" The valet pulled the letter from his tunic and handed it to his master.

Parceida read the report several times. "It states that Sicaria attacked Dryados?" he asked with a look of confusion.

"Yes, Master," the courier answered eagerly with a smile.

Parceida ground his teeth. "They were told specifically not to make their presence known! They were told to spy! To gather information, nothing more. If Dryados is not dead, then Sicaria's impulsiveness has only made things worse."

"But it says that Dryados was killed."

"No! It does not!" Parceida snapped. Then he read part of the letter out loud. "I fled outside with the crowd and waited. Sicaria's large corpse was dragged out by several men. Dryados followed on a litter sometime later, covered in blood. He was pale and unmoving. He looked to be dead as well." Parceida spun at his assistant. "Looked to be…does not mean he is. Looked to be…means maybe. Which means—maybe he is not!" Parceida stormed across the room and pulled the rope to summon some of his men. He gulped down a large goblet of wine. "I am trying to juggle a hundred things here! I need to schmooze the senator to get his approval on the trade deal. I've got mercenaries out on at least five different jobs. And I am trying to look legitimate and run the estates I have stolen. And now this! If Sicaria has made this worse, I will dig up his corpse and cut out his dead heart and eat it! Which reminds me…"

A line of henchmen entered the room. He pointed at the second to enter. "You."

"Yes, my lord?" The burly man bowed and placed his hand upon his sword.

"I want to know everything there is to know about that chief priest Suistus. Where he goes, what he does, who he cheats on his wife with. I want to know what the man has for breakfast and how many times a day he goes to the toilet. I want to know everything. And I want to know it now."

The line of henchmen filed back out of the room. The valet remained. Parceida walked back over to where the wine bottle lay chilling in the wet straw. After he poured another glass, he noticed the motionless valet wore a confused look. Parceida nodded for him to speak. The valet again stooped to one knee. "Master, I thought the chief priest hired you for your services?"

"Yes, he did." Parceida laughed. "And anyone who would hire a man like me is not to be trusted." A malevolent sneer grew on his face. "Because I cannot trust them, they need to understand that I can kill them. That I can kill their spouse. I can kill their kids, their dog. Everyone they love, any time I chose." Parceida poured another goblet of wine and then gulped it down as the wide-eyed servant backed submissively out of the room.

Chapter 23
Bubbles and Churning Water

John stood in his cell in the bowels of the ship as it rolled back and forth on the rough seas. There was no widow. He still had not gotten used to the smell. Vomit squished between his toes. He leaned his head against the wall, trying to juggle his cane in one hand, bracing himself against the corner wall with the other hand, steadying the waste bucket with his foot, trying not to fall, and hitting the bucket all at the same time.

"*Rrraaalllllpppphhh…*"

He missed again. A fresh coat of vomit covered his sandal. The ship rocked wildly on the waves. He didn't know how much farther it was to Rome, but it didn't matter. He prayed, "Oh God, please just let me die."

"*Rrraaalllllpppphhh…*"

There were no smiling crowds of Iredenti to meet him at the docks. Only a brutish squad of Roman guards angered by the inconvenience of having to retrieve one old man for execution.

The keys rattled in the lock. The door slid open. The guards' faces immediately filled with disgust. "Oh, the man stinks!" roared one of the men. He grabbed John and jerked him out of the cell. Then shoved him away at arm's length and groaned loudly. "Ah, he is covered in vomit and stool!" John's waste bucket had toppled over early on in the journey. The guards on the ship emptied the new material once a day. But never bothered to clean him or the cell. The new guard looked frantically for a rag to clean his soiled hand. "Why couldn't they have just killed this old man in Ephesus?" he moaned.

He wiped the foul-smelling goo angrily from his hand and looked menacingly at John. "Up onto the deck, you putrid stack of sewage," he ordered angrily. John fumbled his way down the corridor and up the stairs. The guards got no closer than necessary. Once out of the ship's hold and onto the deck, the guard pulled a sail pin from near the mast and used it as a prod. "Let's go, little piggy," he jeered. "I hear they are feeding you to the lions today." Then he looked at John, laughing, "Don't worry. They won't mind the smell. They have grown quite partial to the taste of you Iredenti."

John was ushered into the back of a waiting prison wagon. The chains on his ankles made it hard to climb up the two or three small steps, and the stench ensured he got no help. When he fell on the steps, the guards waited patiently as he struggled to his feet. Normally he would have been beaten, so he considered his foul stench a blessing.

The prison wagon drove jarringly down the cobbled roads. John stared out the barred window with increasing awe as they approached the Colosseum. Even knowing it would be the place of his doom, he looked with wonder at its majestic walls and fluttering banners. He could hear the cheering crowds inside as the wagon came to a stop outside a heavy metal gate. The back of the wagon slammed open. "Come, little piggy. Time to meet the butcher," jeered the familiar guard. Apparently he was no longer encumbered by the smell and slammed the sail pin he still held from the ship hard into John's back. "Ahh…" John staggered forward, dropping to a knee. The sudden jarring of his bones hurt more than the strike of the sail pin. He fumbled quickly to his feet and was ushered directly to the prison labyrinth below the arena. The corridor was dark and narrow. The air was filled with the cries of terrified men who knew they would soon die. A couple of quick turns later, he was tossed into a cell and the door bolted closed behind him. Then he sat down, awaiting his end. The cell was small and smelled of human waste worse than he did. The straw was covered with fresh blood. He could hear the roar of the lions in similar cells not too far away. They sounded hungry. *I am old. It will be quick*, he thought.

He had been ready to die for a long time. He began to pray. As he did, the world around him grew strangely silent. Then he seemed to hear a distant song. He opened his eyes. There beside him sat one of the Valde Beatus. The angel looked at him and smiled. Then reached over and held his hand. The angel's touch made him feel young and invigorated. His clothes and his body were suddenly clean. There was the smell of spring flowers. Then the angel rose to his feet and slowly closed his eyes. He started to join in the distant song. The hymn had grown louder now. The sounds of a choir seemed to fill the room and vibrate the walls. The melody struck John like a great wind. It was a song of the great I AM. His soul flew like a white flag of surrender in a storm. John rose to his feet and let the great wind carry him away.

When the cyclone passed, he stood alone in his cell. *Now it is time*, he thought. *I am ready*. The guards slammed the cell open and dragged him down the hall. He offered no resistance. He prayed aloud quickly, "Oh God, please let me die well." Another heavy door clanged open. The sudden light blinded him for a moment.

There was no roar from the crowd. No jeers or taunts of impending doom. His vision returned just in time to see the heavy wagon gate open. The guards shoved him hard inside and slammed the gate closed behind him. The whip cracked. The horses reared. The wagon driver yelled, "Heyhaa! Heyhaa!" Then the wagon banged its way down the cobbled road back to the prison.

The jarring impacts felt like a beating. For the first time he felt a sense of despondency. Domitian had teased him, goaded him, and mocked him about his own death. That was just sick.

Emperor Domitian sat alone in his throne room talking to himself. But he was not alone. The room was filled with a host of old comrades. Black Voids circled the room, unseen by human eyes. Many in the senate and the rest of the empire thought Domitian insane. Perhaps he was. But today he was not arguing with imagined phantoms or hallucinations of a diseased mind. He had known these unseen compatriots for millennia. He found himself in an all-too-familiar position. "Now, tell me again exactly what happened. No exaggerations. No omissions." Ivoluntas tried to remain calm inside his human host.

"The games in the Colosseum were going fine. We held John waiting in one of the cells down below in the labyrinth. The Iredenti captives were loosed on the Colosseum floor, fighting hungry lions. The females had already gutted several and were fighting over the body of another. We let the female lions out first. They are incredibly fast. Then we let the larger male lions in later. Their roar is so majestic as they shove the females to the side and claim possession of the fresh—"

"Get on with it!" Ivoluntas yelled.

"Yes, great one." The Black Void hovered closer to his leader. "Then it started happening. It was like bubbles…bubbles of Him…were seething up into the stands. People started screaming. At first we thought their screams were from watching the lions feast on the arena floor. But the screams were different, and they seemed to occur randomly around the stands. The people seemed to see them before we did."

"The people saw who?" Ivoluntas asked quizzically.

"The Valde Beatus. A whole section of people in the stands would leap to their feet, screaming, 'There is an angel! There is an angel!' We all looked but could not see them. The people in the stands would scream the same proclamation and point to other places in the Colosseum. Still we could not see them. Then suddenly the angels all seemed to materialize out of nowhere and were visible even to us. There was one down in the arena with the captives. The lions were drawn to him as though he were a wounded buffalo. The lions raced across the arena floor. They roared. They moved and circled to attack."

Domitian leaned forward in his chair. "Yes…"

"One of the lions sprang. It flew in the air, landing just in front of the first angel. It raised its head, roaring ferociously. And then…it rolled onto its back." The Black Void's voice trailed off. "The smiling angel walked over and played with it like it were a small kitten. The other lions swaggered slowly over and lay down beside him. It was like a moment captured from the beginning. The angel rubbed the lion's thick mane and spoke to it. The words seemed meant for everyone's ear and filled the Colosseum. The words struck the people in the stands like a renewing flood in the desert. Everyone smiled. Some started to cry. The oldest more than the young. Then even more of the Valde Beatus arrived. They seemed to be bubbling up from the holding cells below the Colosseum floor. Then the angel kneeling by the lions rose to his feet and began to sing. The song began low, like one singing to a baby curled it is mother's arm. Then one by one the other angels too began to sing. The voices filled the Colosseum louder and louder. Soon the people too had risen to their feet and began to sing. Their faces glowed bright as a noonday. Every soul was filled with His presence. It was like the air in their lungs—"

"Every soul?" Ivoluntas interrupted.

"Yes, Master, every soul." He bowed his formless head. "All of us were…just taken off guard." Then he quickly added, "But we did not falter. It was then that Dicax noticed the Valde Beatus seemed to be originating from the underground labyrinth where John was being held. We didn't know what to do. Veloxa suggested we move John as quickly as possible to stop the contamination befalling the crowd. We flew instantly to the hidden maze below the floor and seized whatever possessions we had there. We commanded them to move John immediately. It was obvious to all of us that the hedge around John was still intact and that we would not be able to execute him today. So we—"

"No! It does not mean that at all," Ivoluntas roared. He jumped to his feet and clambered toward the formless Void that was speaking. "John will still die! He will be publically tortured, humiliated, and killed. The light that shines through the Valde Beatus may steal some pathetic sheep from our grasp, but John…John is mine!" Domitian paced about the room. "Where is he now?"

"We had him moved back to the prison cells by the Forum," answered the fallen Void. "But—"

"That will be fine," Ivoluntas said quickly. "And what of the Colosseum? Were there any significant losses there?"

The Black Void spoke slowly, choosing his next words extremely carefully. "The song rocked the people like waves of joy. Then a great angel arose in our midst. He grew like an enchanted seedling into a behemoth taller than the great cedars of Lebanon. His arms stretched from one side of the Colosseum to the other. His face glowed white upon white, and his wings were like rainbows. He sang 'Sanctus…sanctus…sanctus…' The other Valde Beatus joined their voices to his. Then likewise did the people. It was like—"

"Yes, but how many? How many did we lose?" Ivoluntas asked in dismay.

"I think…I think it was everyone in the Colosseum," stammered the frightened Void.

Domitian's face went blank. He rose and walked silently around the room. The immense presence of Ivoluntas filled his frame. Both beings shared the same concerns. "It does not mean the hedge is intact," he said. "Perhaps the Valde Beatus came to carry his spirit to heaven after the execution? Perhaps it was a distraction to give John more time? There are many possibilities. Yet we cannot take the chance of another such setback." He walked around the room, deep in thought. "And we cannot throw away the opportunity that the public execution of John represents. We must find a way to balance the risk."

The two beings paced the throne room together in one frame. Domitian's intellect was but a spark compared to the sun of Ivoluntas's consciousness. Ivoluntas was taken by a pleasant memory still fresh in his host's thoughts. Domitian had recently seen his old wet nurse, Genetrix, here in the palace. They had spoken only briefly, but it was a pleasant memory for Domitian. She lived in the south of the city by the Porta Latina, or Latin Gate. Domitian had spent a great deal of time there as a child. He remembered a large plaza just inside the city's wall.

Ivoluntas spoke. "Tomorrow, take him to the plaza of the Porta Latina. He is to be executed there at noon." Domitian smiled victoriously. "And this stunt by the Valde Beatus has given me some inspiration as to how we shall accomplish it."

Dryados's villa in Philadelphia

The mysterious water bubbled vigorously as they poured it into the wound. "Ouch, that hurts," Dryados groaned. He sat up in the bed. "Why can't we use the regular water like we always have?"

"Because this is not a scraped knee or a bruised shin. Now lay back down and let the physician work," Alesia scolded.

"Master Dryados, this is the healing water from the secret Pools of Galliae. There is none like it anywhere else in the empire. The people of Galliae have used it for hundreds of years on their wounded. It expels the evil humors that cause the skin to burn and the flesh to rot after a wound such as this. I have only this little supply. Please sit still and let the water bubble the evil humors out of the wound." The physician continued to clean the wound. He had sutured the wound tightly closed at the beginning. But with the one tendon cut, the rest of the muscle seemed to wiggle around too much inside and pulled the wound open. The physician decided to let the area stay open and allow the evil humors a way out. He cleaned the wound three times a day. First with a clean-water rinse. Then with the bubbling waters of Galliae. After the cleaning, he covered the wound with a damp cloth and then a dry one. The wet cloth under the dry cloth seemed to dispel the evil humors in confusion. The wound was healing nicely.

Cleopas stood next to the physician, watching the magical bubbling waters. "That was the fourth time in as many months," Cleopas whispered harshly at his friend. "The first three were obviously amateurs. We think they were probably sent by the Jews. But this…this was the work of a professional assassin. If it were not for the sharp eyes of that fearsome little warrior of the Indus peoples, you would be dead." Alesia walked into the room as the dressing change was completed. Cleopas moved out of the way so she could get closer. As she stood beside him, Cleopas turned, facing her. "My lady, I would again request that you let me station a few of my men here by the house. Just for a short time."

"No!" Dryados sat up in his bed again. "We are not turning my house into an armed camp. I—"

"You are sick and obviously out of your mind!" Alesia snapped.

She nodded gracefully toward Cleopas. "Your kind offer is most appreciated, and we accept with our humblest gratitude."

Then she turned back toward her wounded husband. "And you! If you go and get yourself killed while I am pregnant…I will…I will murder you twice!"

Dryados smiled. "That doesn't even make sense."

"No, it doesn't. And it doesn't have to. I am pregnant, and I don't have to put up with this!" Alesia placed her hand onto her ripening stomach. "You are not going to make our baby an orphan before it is even born!"

Dryados's physician looked up from working on the wound and nudged him sheepishly. "As your healer, I think it would be best if you let her do whatever she thinks is best."

"Always a good idea," Dryados said, nodding his head. He looked up at Alesia. He had never seen her so worried. She had gotten more emotional lately. He thought that was the pregnancy. But this was different. She was really scared of losing him. He smiled up at her again. Her face had gotten so much rounder. "I think you are right. I think it would be good if Cleopas stationed some extra men in the area." He glanced at Cleopas. "Perhaps just not at our doorstep."

"That is a good compromise," Cleopas said, nodding his head in affirmation. "But I would also suggest you strengthen your internal house guard." He looked at Alesia. "And you should make a strong room in case the outer security is breached. That will buy you time for help to arrive. You should also plan and make ready several avenues of escape in the event you have forewarning or opportunity to flee."

"All good ideas," Dryados interjected. "All good ideas." He nodded approvingly to Alesia.

There was a brief moment of silence as the physician continued to work. Cleopas moved toward the door. "Now that you are no longer as pale as a ewe's teeth, your doctor said I could introduce you to the man who saved your life." Cleopas walked over and opened the door. He nodded for the man waiting outside to enter. "This is AkAk."

A small man entered the room. He was like the other Indus people Dryados had seen, but shorter and more stocky. Like the others, his skin was a deep brown and his hair black as coal. "We have learned he is of the high mountain people called the Kham. He is one of the warriors they call Gurkhas. Rome has never battled them, and I pray we never do. For this tiny little man is worth ten of my best."

The visitor seemed to understand that he was being introduced and smiled broadly. Despite his obvious fearsome spirit, he had well-worn creases in his face from the smile he now wore. He had cheerful eyes and seemed to radiate a sense of joy. It was at that moment that Dryados recognized him. He had seen the man many times traveling with the Indus caravan. He always seemed to be in the background and was never really noticeable.

Despite a scolding look from Alesia, Dryados rose and sat on the side of his bed. "Thank you. I can never repay you for what you have done."

The Kham warrior stepped forward. He held up an oddly shaped wrapped gift.

"No." Dryados shook his head. "It is you who should be receiving gifts. I am already forever in your debt."

It was unclear if the man simply didn't understand what Dryados was saying or if he would simply not accept no for an answer. But he continued to stand there smiling and holding out the present. Eventually Dryados succumbed to the tiny man's persistence.

"Again, you have my greatest thanks." Dryados reached over and accepted the odd-shaped gift. It was much heavier than he expected. Dryados unwrapped the present and let the wrappings fall onto the bed. Then he held up the strange gift. It was a hooked knife with a black wooden sheath. The blade itself was shaped liked the flexed elbow of a fighter. It was broad and razor sharp. The back of the blade was flat and much thicker than he had seen in other blades. It gave the blade the weight of a small ax.

"Kukri," the Kham warrior said as he smilingly pointed to the stout weapon.

"I couldn't—"

The small man's face became hardened. He glanced around the room. He walked over to Cleopas. Then he stood in front of the Roman and pronounced, "Napja!" Then he grabbed the sword at Cleopas side and shook it. "Napja!" He walked over to the physician, who wore a small knife in his tunic, and again pointed. "Napja!" He walked over to the door and threw it open. A Roman soldier peered in with his spear. The tiny warrior kept his distance and pointed to the sharp lance. "Napja!" He walked back over to Dryados and stood there with a questioning bewildered look. "Napja?"

Some things must simply be universal, thought Dryados as he looked at the petite menace with the questioning pose. Dryados did not know what *napja* meant. Perhaps it meant weapon? Or prepared? Or something else. He did not know. But he did know the tiny warrior was right. He had no weapon and was not prepared. And that needed to change.

"Thank you." Dryados smiled and held up the sharp blade. He waved it back and forth, watching the glint in the edged blade. He looked questioningly at AkAk. "Kukri?"

AkAk nodded his head quickly up and down. His big smile returned. "Kukri, kukri…"

John was tired. He had heard that Domitian was insane, but his actions yesterday were beyond bizarre. Now a new day had dawned, and the process had begun again.

"Did you enjoy the practice run yesterday, old man?" sneered one of the guards. "Today I heard they are going to cover you in animal entrails and throw you into a box filled with starving rats. Course the animal entrails will be the best part of the meal for rats. Ha-ha-ha-ha…"

"No, I heard they were going to burn you at the stake. Someone said you had complained about being cold. Domitian is just trying to be a good host. Yah-ha-ha…"

And on it went. Finally, it was time.

The route to the Colosseum was different today and was taking much longer. This road too was cobbled, and the wagon clanged and jarred viciously with each gap in the stone. John peered through the bars. They were heading south. They slowed as the crowd on the street became thicker and thicker. Suddenly the masses on the street seemed to recognize him. "Traitor! Blasphemer! Apostate! Deceiver!" People ran beside the wagon, trying to grab him through the bars. John clung to the front of the wagon. Then the wagon stopped. The Romans dismounted and shoved the crowd back. "Betrayer! Highbinder! Lawbreaker!" Rocks pelted against the side of the wagon and crashed against the bars.

"Enough of that!" The centurion shoved his way through the crowd to the back of the wagon. Soldiers on horseback pushed the crowd farther away. The guard unbolted the gate and yanked John out the door. He tried to get his bearings. He was outside. He could see the city wall nearby and a wide gate fashioned into the stone. They were nowhere near the Colosseum. A rock struck John hard in the cheek. He saw stars for just a second as he reeled backward. The soldiers tightened their grip on his thin arms and dragged him into a large plaza. The center of the plaza had already been cleared and a wide perimeter established by the Romans. John could smell the smoke of a fire. *Burned at the stake*, he thought. *Just like Matthew. Or was Matthew killed by a sword?* He couldn't remember anymore.

He stumbled forward. The sound of mocking and jeers filled the plaza. People spat on him and threw rotten eggs and fruit at him. He tried to hold his head down. He wished it were already over. As he glanced up, he spotted a massive cauldron. It was black and well used. *Probably a giant cooking pot used by the Roman legions*, he thought. *You could cook a horse in that.* He saw a low fire burning beneath it.

The centurion yanked John to the center of the crowd and read the charges. John paid little attention. He stared at the great cauldron. The centurion finished his proclamation. John's chains were removed, and he was strapped into a large wooden crane. They hoisted him high in the air and spun the arm over the simmering pot. John looked down to see the contents seething and swirling within it. A light mist of steam enveloped him. It felt warm. They slowly lowered him in. It was thick and slippery. Some of the contents splashed over the side as his body settled in. The fire below leaped high into the air. *Oil*, he thought. Then he smiled. *My last anointing.* The oil was hot but not yet boiling. The centurion jeered, "You will die like a frog, old man! Like a slow-boiled frog!" The crowd burst into cheers.

"Slowly...now add the wood. Let's see how long it takes to cook this old miscreant," the centurion taunted.

The soldiers started adding one piece of cordwood at a time to the fire. Then they would wait. The fire slowly grew.

John was an old shepherd. And like any experienced shepherd, he knew when he had a crowd's undivided attention. So like any good shepherd, he began to preach.

"God so loved the world..."

"Add more wood," ordered the Centurion.

"There is no other name..."

"Come on, men. Be quick," barked the commander.

"Redeemer of the lost. Restorer of broken hearts..."

"Stack it on the sides!" yelled the leader.

"By faith you have been saved..."

"Faster, men! Faster!" raged the centurion at his men.

The cauldron was boiling now. The scalding oil leaped over the sides. Fire erupted with each splash of the gooey liquid. Vesicles of hot oil erupted from the surface like a thousand small volcanoes. The cauldron boomed and popped and hissed. John's preaching did not stop. The soldiers tossed on more and more wood. The cauldron boiled widely. Smoke billowed into the sky. John kept preaching. The soldiers were running frantically, looking for more wood or anything else that would burn. The centurion kept yelling.

John proclaimed loudly, "As it was from the beginning..."

That is when the first great bubble formed. It was completely different from all the rest. It was big, and grew bigger and bigger. It glowed like phosphorescent mother-of-pearl. Then it suddenly burst. A silent concussion of consciousness buckled through the crowd. Suddenly everyone there was transported in their minds to the consciousness of a living child. They were outside playing with their mother and father. Their father was tossing them in the air. Then they were on the ground playing with a toy as their mother kissed them on the cheek.

The crowd's minds bounced back to the plaza. Another bubble exploded. Each was a child spending the night at a friend's house. They played games and ate sweet honey chips. Everyone was laughing at a funny joke.

Even the mind of the angry centurion returned to its body with a smile. Another bubble expanded and broke open. A pack of female lions wrestled on the open grasslands of a distant land. Strange long-necked animals stretched as high as the trees to eat green leaves. Small cubs joined into the playful battle. A mother licked her rambunctious cub clean of some invisible contaminate.

A bubble, a burst, a new flash of consciousness. A mother cried as she watched her sick child die…a man rejoiced with his crew over a great catch of fish…a man struggled in a field working his crops…a cheetah chased a gazelle, but missed…a man married his childhood sweetheart…a great eagle flew high above a smooth-flowing river, watching fish beneath the surface.

The plaza was filled with smoke. John proclaimed, "One hope, one universe, one God. We are all one…redeemed by the mercy of His grace."

A burst, a flash. A burst, a shared awareness. A burst…a father forgave his rebellious son…a judge granted mercy to a repentant criminal…a widow gave a mite to a poor beggar…a soldier acted with honor in a fierce battle.

The consciousness of the living world, of what they knew should be but often was not.

"You *can* be reborn!"

All the minds returned to the crowd. No one spoke. The sermon had ended. Everyone in the plaza stood there as a new creation.

The soldiers extinguished the fire. John was pulled from the cauldron and given a clean tunic. The soldiers took him back to the prison. They brought him a large meal and a warm blanket.

Chapter 24
Beating a Bruise

The two sat alone in the imperial throne room. It was the seat of power for the greatest nation the world had ever known. Its vast hall was filled with riches that bespoke the glories of its makers. Still, the hall echoed in silence. Rows of torches burned along the walls. Still, the room was cold. Emperor Domitian rested his chin in his hand. His eyes were bloodshot and sore. Dawn was still a few hours away. Ivoluntas smoldered within him. Both beings were lost in thought. Both had faced defeat before. Both knew how to deal with it. But after the defeat at the Colosseum, it was like beating a bruise. In front of all of Rome they had been defeated. Impotent to kill one frail, old man. The emperor rose and paced the empty hall. His thoughts were focused. Dealing with a defeat always came down to the same two options. *First, make it look like a victory. Pretend it was part of the plan, something you intended. Make it look like you are still in charge and that your underlings are simple too stupid to understand your hidden brilliance.* After the events here in Rome, that appeared impossible. *Or second, hide it as quickly as possible and move on.*

The emperor and the Prince of the Power of the Earth walked together. No attendants had been called. No Black Voids had been summoned.

"We need to get John out of here." The words echoed off the polished marble and gilded elements of gold.

"Yes, but where?"

"It must be far away. A place where none will go. A place so isolated that whatever happens there is lost to the ears of the rest of the world."

The pacing rhythm of the emperor's shod boots clanged through the great hall. The torches flickered in a stray breeze.

Domitian began to smile. "Patmos! That will do quite nicely."

"Yes," Ivoluntas mused, "a barren rock in the middle of the Aegean. Populated by wild goats and lifeless prisoners working the forsaken mines." Ivoluntas began to laugh. "Yes, let him preach to them. Let the bleating animals and soulless men be his new flock."

The two walked back and sat down on the great throne. In a heartbeat the room was filled with the mindless followers of both.

Chapter 25

Cat and Mouse

"None of this makes sense." Dryados read the letter out loud again to Alesia as they sat outside in the garden. "First, Darius says John is dead. That he was poisoned or burned alive or something. Darius isn't sure. Then he says that he is not dead, but that no one has seen him. His sources tell him John is being moved somewhere, but Darius is not sure where that is." Dryados looked at Alesia with an exaggerated grimace of confusion.

Alesia just smiled as she rubbed her stomach. "He is kicking a lot today. And I think he has flipped upside down."

Dryados walked over and placed his hand on the same spot. "Whoa! *She* is kicking like a mule." He looked comically at Alesia, "I think *she* is going to be a lot like you."

Alesia playfully pushed his hand away from her stomach. "You said like a mule. Mules are stubborn, pigheaded, and ornery. No, that would be more like *his* father." She propped her feet up in the air. "This stuff with John is hugely important to all the Iredenti. You would think news of what is going on would flash through the caravan system like a fire. Haven't you heard anything else among the other merchants? There must be some news or rumor working its way along the trade routes."

"Yes, but it is much the same as what Darius has written. It all seems self-contradictory. But the consistent elements are that several attempts were made to kill John, but somehow he survived. There is talk of miracles and that many have been made Iredenti. It is also said that Domitian has been quick to get John out of Rome. But it is still unclear as to where."

Dryados watched as one of the new house guards passed by the window on the side. "Things are really coming to a head. I think hiring the house guards was a good idea. I am thankful that Cleopas suggested them."

Alesia looked up from her chair. "Well, that's new. You have never said that before. What made you change your mind?"

Dryados quickly changed the subject. "Oh look. I think she's flipped herself right side up again…"

Thyatira

"Jezebel, I told you I need to get going. Sperta will be expecting me, and it is getting late." Ascalon stood and straightened his tunic. "Thank you so much for giving me this opportunity, but…"

"Ascalon, I know the work at your smithy often keeps you there much later than this," Jezebel interrupted. "As prophetess, I must know everything that is happening among our people. I am really going to need your help if there is going to be any chance of me understanding what is going on with you and the Iredenti that you work with."

"I'm sorry. You're right. I did not mean to be disrespectful," he stammered. "It makes sense for you to be aware of the health of the sheep in the flock. It's just that I usually work more with Jakotrudi." Ascalon settled back into his spot on the floor. Jezebel's home was so large. He had never been invited into this part of the house before. The blankets and furs on the floor were as soft as goose down. The curtains gave them a sense of privacy as the servants scurried about. Ascalon grabbed some more of the smoked lamb and pickled fish. The garnish of dry salted nuts was delicious. "Well, first let me tell you about Procelus. He is one of my new stable hands. We have been sharing with him since he started to work for me. He has a very open mind and has been asking a lot of questions."

Jezebel poured Ascalon some more wine. "That is such a blessing. You and your men are doing so much for our fellowship. Tell me more. How did you first approach Procelus? Did you…"

Ascalon got home sometime later. Lautus was playing on the floor with one of his toys. Somehow he had gotten ahold of some cooking pots from the kitchen and was now making a fort out of them. Sperta gave him some bread to snack on while he played. She and Ascalon sat quietly watching the innocent little boy. Ascalon wasn't hungry. Sperta noticed that he seemed strangely distracted but thought she would just give him some space for a while. Not too long after that, Lautus got frustrated with his efforts with the unstackable pots and began to have a tantrum.

"There, there, Lautus, everything is OK." Sperta got up and gave him some cool water to drink. As she knelt down to hug him, Lautus started screaming and threw the cup of water and the remainder of his bread across the floor. Then he had a total crying fit. "Oh, mama's little man." Sperta scooped him up, kicking and screaming, and whisked him off to bed. After a quick diminishing set of screams, he was fast asleep.

Sperta came back out and started to mop the white tile floor. She swung the mop back and forth in a relaxing rhythm. "So why are you so quiet tonight?" she asked.

Ascalon sat unmoving in his chair.

Sperta wrung the mop out and then dipped it back into the vinegar water. She casually continued her work. She was sure he had heard her question, but she assumed he was lost in thought.

"The guild will always be upset about something," she added. "Try not to let them wear you down." She shoved the mop into a corner and worked it back and forth as she scrubbed some congealed bread up off the white tile.

"It's not the guild," he answered stoically.

Ascalon's voice sounded...lost. Sperta put the mob back in the bucket and skirted around the wet floor closer to her husband. "Then what is it?" Her face betrayed her worry. She stood directly in front of her husband. "Is it the Romans? Do they suspect you are Iredenti? Have they been asking questions or acting suspiciously?"

His eyes seemed to look right through her. Then he glanced up. His eyes were red. "We need to talk..."

A hundred different scenarios ran through Sperta's mind. All of them came down to either the Romans taking someone they knew or the guild finally deciding to shut Ascalon's business down and leave them destitute. She thought the latter would have caused Ascalon to be more outraged and vocal. His silent anguish was more suggestive that someone had died.

"I don't know how to tell you this." Ascalon stared up at Sperta.

"The Romans...who did they take. Have you heard what they are planning? Was it just one or an entire family? Do we need to flee?" The questions began to fly like frightened chickens from a coop.

Ascalon sat there, still unmoving. His silence was more frightening than the horrible scenarios she had already pictured in her mind. Sperta stood in front of him as a terrifying chill ran up her spine. She wrapped her arms around herself, squeezing tightly as if she were cold.

"It's not the Romans," Ascalon said blankly.

"Then it's the guild!" Sperta's face flushed in anger. "They have been hounding you for over a year. This is ridiculous." She paced to the other side of the room. "Are they demanding more money? Or have they finally got around to just shutting us down and being done with it? This is ridiculous. Greedy, power hungry—"

"No, it was not the guild." His voice was heavy and forlorn.

Sperta looked questioningly at her husband. "Then what?"

"I wasn't at the smithy working late…and I wasn't meeting with the guild or with the Romans." Ascalon still stared blankly ahead.

"Then where have you been?" Her face filled with scared confusion.

"I've been with Jezebel." Ascalon looked up silently at his wife.

The words whirled around in Sperta's head like some incomprehensible foreign tongue. But the look on Ascalon's face…that she understood. "Nooo!" She was crying before the last of that single word had left her lips. "Ascalon, no!" She sank to the ground as her legs folded up beneath her.

Ascalon put both his hands to his forehead as if the memory was too painful to bear. "She invited me over to her house. She said it was about the fellowship. That she needed to hear about those in the fellowship that I looked over. It all sounded very reasonable. I really didn't expect anything beyond that. Honestly, Sperta, I really didn't."

Sperta sat crying on the floor.

"We talked for a while about the fellowship just like she said. It was late, and she offered me something to eat. Before I knew it, I had several glasses of wine and—"

"That doesn't excuse anything! You are a grown man!" She wept as tears poured down her face.

"Yes, Sperta, I am. I am not making any excuses. I don't know what happened. I was just sitting there. She was very alluring…"

"How can you say that! How can you just come right out and say that!" Sperta rose and stormed out of the room.

"Sperta, no, let me finish!" Ascalon shot to his feet and raced after her. He caught up with her in the kitchen and held her.

"Let me go! Let me go! You can never touch me again!" She thrashed and wiggled out of his arms.

"Sperta, please! Let me finish. Nothing happened. I swear to you…on all we have together…nothing happened!"

"You said you were with Jezebel. You said she was alluring. What do you mean nothing happened?" Sperta's face was red and twisted in confusion.

"Seriously, I don't know what happened. She leaned across me. Then she started kissing me. I started to pull away, and she grabbed my hand and put it…I was half drunk, but I still knew what was going on. I tried to crawl away. But she just kissed me even harder. She reached up and somehow pulled the top of her tunic down. I scrambled back as fast as I could. I finally made it too my feet. I thought I was going to pass out. I didn't realize how much wine I had drunk. I apologized to her several times. And then I just ran out of the house." Ascalon took a deep breath. "Honestly, Sperta, that is all that happened. Those kind of days are long past. I love you and Lautus. I would never do anything to hurt you."

"Then why did you apologize to that whore?" Her face was still wet, but now filled with rage.

"I don't know…I just did. I was trying to get out of there. Maybe she thought I was interested in her or something. I don't know. I just ran."

Sperta stormed closer. "I have heard rumors from some of the other woman about their husbands acting funny. None of them know exactly what's going on. But several of the wives have suspected the same thing. And they all blame it on Jezebel. I have tried not to pay any attention it. I thought it was just gossip, and I didn't want any part of it. But this is exactly what the other women have been suggesting."

Ascalon tried to calm her down. "I don't think there is anything going on—"

"She just tried to have sex with you! What do you mean you don't think there is anything going on! I am going to make sure everyone knows what kind of woman she is. I'm going to—"

"Sperta, no. That is not the way to handle this. We need to be wise and figure out what to do."

"I know exactly what to do! I'm—" She started to rage toward the door.

Ascalon raced behind her and put his hand gently on her shoulder. "No. Let me talk to Jakotrudi and the other elders. Give us some time to figure this out."

Sperta stopped and spun. "Fine, you and the elders figure it out. But if you don't figure it out quickly, then the other wives and I will figure it out for you."

"I'm sorry, my love. I'm really tired. My head is killing me…" Ascalon looked at her pleadingly.

"Great. You deserve it!" Sperta stormed off to bed. "And you can sleep out here, for all I care."

"But it wasn't my fault." Ascalon raised his hand in the air.

"I don't care!" The bedroom door slammed shut like a clap of thunder.

Smyrna

Suistus read the letter out loud in a mocking tone. "Everything is fine. I am continuing to gather information and build up the needed resources. I will let you know when things are ready." Then he groaned. It was the same report he was given every week.

"He will let me know…paa! He will let me know when the sun falls from the sky!" Suistus sat at the table and continued to eat his meal. "Parceida has taken the money and spent it all on his wild lifestyle!" He washed down the last of his meal with several large gulps of wine. "I will go and see him this very evening. I will get the truth of what he has been doing. Does he truly have what it takes for ridding us of this…Dryados? Or has he just been squandering our money?"

Suistus grabbed his finest tunic and summoned several servants to act as his entourage. They crossed the city using one of the wagons owned by the synagogue. Suistus's rage only grew as they crossed the city. "I will show him who is not to be trifled with. He will face the wrath of the entire synagogue if he tries to play us for fools. I will speak to the governor personally..." Suistus stopped in the middle of his tirade as the wagon pulled up to Parceida's villa. Suistus's mouth gaped silently open. Mounted horsemen swept past him with murderous eyes. There were heavily armed house guards everywhere. Every eye was on him and those in the wagon. Swords were being slowly drawn from their scabbards. "Perhaps it might be best if we turned around and went home," he said softly to the driver.

One of the house guards approached the wagon and brought it to a halt. "Lord Suistus, we were not informed that he was expecting you. I will send word that you have arrived. Please come in. I will escort you to his receiving room." The wagon was quickly surrounded by several of the house guards. "If you will all follow me." Suistus was not given an opportunity to answer.

The guards led the group through the luxurious manor but did not speak further. They stopped in an exquisite antechamber by a garden. "Lord Suistus, I will have your entourage wait here. Lord Parceida likes to meet with his guest in private. Please, follow me." Lord Suistus nodded and continued on alone, wringing his hands as he walked.

They continued down the long corridor and then exited outside through the garden. The house guard stopped on the manicured path. "Right this way." He waved Suistus straight ahead toward a magnificent outbuilding nestled among the flowering trees. The round monument stood over two stories tall, with a gleaming dome roof supported by two rows of thick marble colonnades. Each stone pillar was polished white, with a Corinthian top. Flowering vines clung to each of the colonnades and seemed to blend the building into the surrounding garden. Suistus stopped beside the house guard for an instant to admire the perfection of the architecture and then entered the building alone. In the center of the structure he found an area segregated off by a much smaller set of decorative columns paralleling those on the outer perimeter. It too was round and was laid out with several chairs and a larger settee in the front. He assumed this was the appropriate spot to wait, seated himself, and began to admire the decorative gardens outside.

Moments later an attendant arrived with some refreshments. "Lord Parceida will be with you in a few moments. He is just finishing up with some other obligations." The attendant placed the tray of fresh fruit and honey candy on one of the tables. "Lord Parceida sends his compliments." The attendant handed him a sculpted silver goblet filled with scarlet juice. He swirled the juice around inside the cup. It was too thin to be wine. He held the cup up to his nose to check the aroma. The fragrance was light and fruity, yet familiar and pleasant. He took a sip. It was as cold as the snows on the mountains. Yet it was the embodiment of summer. Suistus smiled. It was pomegranate juice. His favorite.

Suistus stood and started to stroll the gardens. He stayed close by, keeping a watchful eye for the arrival of his host. After what seemed a long stroll, Suistus returned and resumed his same seat in the segregated cloister. A few moments later his host arrived. Several guards accompanied him but remained outside the monument along its perimeter.

"Lord Suistus, you honor me with your presence." Lord Parceida lumbered his large frame into the quiet retreat.

"Lord Parceida, please excuse my unannounced arrival, but I was hoping—"

"Yes, yes, but first tell me, how is your family?"

"My wife and children are all fine. But I would really like to get a more thorough update on—"

"Yes, yes, and that old dog of your, Brutus? Is he still sneaking in under the table to snatch stray morsels off the floor? You know, I love dogs." Parceida strolled closer and placed a heavy hand on Suistus's shoulder.

"The dog is fine—"

"You know your daughter Captiosus feeds him under the table when you are not looking," Parceida said with a mischievous grin.

"No, she doesn't. I told her to stop that—"

"Yes, yes, children, they never seem to listen. But they are still such a blessing. I love to watch them play, so innocent. Your son Praecinctor, does he still play with that boy down the street? Oh, what is his name…" Parceida seemed to gaze blankly at the floor for a moment. "Niequior…yes, that's it. Are they still as close as they were a few years ago?" Parceida looked smilingly at Suistus, waiting for a reply.

Suistus's heart slowed…way…down. Each beat was like the death cadence at a funeral. Praecinctor and Niequior had been best friends since before the time they could walk. They still played together but usually down at Niequior's house. "Yes…they are." The words crept out of Suistus's mouth like cold molasses.

"I had a son once. He was killed in battle. Very sad. But life goes on for the rest of us. More juice?" Parceida raised a hand to signal one of the servants.

"No, that is quiet all right. I was just—"

"And how is Lorem?"

Suistus's heart…stopped. He couldn't breathe. It was hard to even force the words out. "I'm not sure—"

"I know you haven't seen her since the beginning of the month, but how was she doing then?" Parceida leaned forward and grabbed a piece of fruit off the tray and tossed it at Suistus. "Here, try an apple."

The apple landed in Suistus's lap. Still he did not move. He just looked straight ahead. It was as if he had just died. Lorem was his secret mistress. She lived outside the city. He would steal away from the synagogue to see her. No one ever questioned where he was going, as he had business all over the city. No one knew. Not even his most trusted aides. His wife had never even remotely suspected him.

"She is several years younger than you. I hear she is a good mother. And her son, Ishmael, looks just like you."

The boy's real name was Kalnia, but it was clear that Parceida was already well aware of that. Suistus also understood the implications of his host's allusion. Ishmael was the son of a righteous man who took matters into his own hands, and Ishmael caused nothing but trouble for the righteous man from then on. Suistus sat there motionless. His heart felt like it would never beat again. He did not speak.

Parceida grabbed a large ripe apple off the tray and took a big bite. Juice dripped down the sides of his face. He chewed it like a cow chewing its cud. He looked out into the garden. "Mr. Dryados is close friends to the Romans in Philadelphia. He is raising an army of secret followers. We are not sure of how many fighters he has, as we have been unable to infiltrate their gathering. He has also been hiring men to build up his personal guard. We know he lives in the Acropolis overlooking the city, but we have been unable to follow him to the exact home. Because he has been so aggressive in establishing his forces, I have been forced to respond in kind. I have raised my own army. We will storm the city and kill them all, if that is what it takes." He looked at Suistus with murderous eyes. "Just be sure you pay my final bill quickly when it comes." Parceida took another savage bite out of the apple. "Was there anything else?"

Suistus sat unspeaking for several seconds. "No. No, that will be all. Thank you for your kind update." Suistus rose slowly. "I can show myself out."

"No, I could never have that." Parceida laughed. "My men will take you home."

As if given a silent cue, four heavily armed men trotted over with their swords drawn. The clatter of their riveted leather and shod feet sounded out of place in the quiet of the garden retreat. Suistus did not move or even breathe. The four soldiers formed a tight box around the chief priest and then suddenly stopped. A fifth soldier arrived a moment later at a much more relaxed paced. "You will follow me," he sneered. Suistus's heart was racing as the five mercenaries escorted him directly to the front of the villa. He still was not sure he was going to make it out alive. His entourage was already there waiting in the wagon when he arrived. Their faces were white with fear. The wagon was surrounded by at least two dozen men on horseback. No one in his entourage spoke. The dragoons around them all appeared angry.

Suistus nodded politely to the squad leader. "Please give Lord Parceida my thanks." He scurried into the wagon and sat silently with the others.

The wagon driver glanced at all the soldiers and then snapped the horse's reins. "Off we go there." The horses jarred suddenly forward. The leader of the dragoons kicked his stallion in the flanks, and the entire company moved forward in one smooth motion. In a single heartbeat the wagon was surrounded with angry horsemen. Suistus began to silently pray that they would just make it home alive.

Philadelphia

"They are still there, Master Dryados," whispered Jo-El. He closed the door silently behind him.

"That makes it over nine days in a row. This is getting ridiculous. Who are these men?" Dryados rose from behind his desk. The export inventory for the next caravan shipment east was almost completed. They just needed a few more things shipped in from Darius in Smyrna, and they could send everything out.

"I don't know, but it's pretty clear they mean to do you harm," Jo-El said with worried concern.

"I am a merchant. Who would want to hurt me? This is just business. We buy and sell merchandise. We don't hurt or offend anybody."

"Obviously there is someone out there who disagrees with you. And…they disagree with you enough to want you dead."

Dryados shook his head. Jo-El was never one to mince words, and he knew his assistant's words were probably right. He walked nervously back over to his desk and slipped the last piece of the inventory list back into a drawer. "So do we switch at the tea shop or the bakery?"

"I told Darmock we were going to mix it up today and switch at the tunic shop on the other corner. He is there already waiting."

"I know the one." Dryados sighed. "This is just getting ridiculous." He grabbed his blue cape off the nail in the wall and threw it on. Then he shoved the broad brown work hat next to it underneath his tunic. He walked anxiously back toward the door and stopped. "OK, after you." He waved smilingly for Jo-El to go first.

Jo-El chuckled and grabbed the handle. "OK, time for today's performance." He slowly opened the door and stepped cautiously outside. The two strangers were still there pretending to eat some street food. Jo-El pretended not to notice them but looked suspiciously around the rest of the street. Then he turned and furtively motioned for Dryados to come out.

Dryados exited his office and did a mock scan of the street for any hidden assassins. Then he turned and followed Jo-El up the road. As he did, he pulled the blue cape up over his head, pretending to conceal his identity.

"I think they took the bait." Dryados turned to look behind him. The two were following a little ways back. He made sure they saw his face. He and Jo-El weaved quickly through the crowd. They were almost there.

"OK, right as we go around the corner," Jo-El ordered. "Ready…now!"

As they rounded the corner, Dryados spun in the side door of the tunic shop. He threw his blue cape on his friend Darmock, who quickly pulled the hood over his head and stepped back out onto the street beside Jo-El. No one even had to break stride. It was perfect.

Inside the tunic shop, Dryados pulled out the broad work hat and put it on. The two spies had just walked past, frantically trying to get around the corner and get an eye back on their prey. As they passed, Dryados walked out the front door with Sussana, Darmock's wife.

"Sussana, I cannot thank you enough. And please, do not tell Alesia." Dryados put his arm around Sussana.

"Dryados, that is not fair to her. She deserves to know." Sussana smiled, and the two walked down the road like a happy couple.

"Yes, she does. But I don't want to worry her. After the baby is born and everything settles back down, I promise I will make sure she is aware of everything that is happening. I just can't tell her right now." Dryados continued to search the street ahead as they walked.

Sussana shook her head with a frown. "Keeping things from your wife is always a mistake."

"I know." Dryados nodded, but his eyes were fixed straight ahead.

"And if she finds out, she will kill you worse than those strangers would." She glared at him with womanly eyes.

Dryados nodded in strong affirmation. "I know." They continued to walk determinedly up the street. "Where are my personal guard?"

"Two were across the street from the tunic shop and one was just at the store next door. We walked right past him as we exited the shop. Let me check." Sussana slowed and then stopped. "Oh, Darmock, that was the nicest thing…" She leaned over and gave him a hug. As she did, she glanced behind them. She whispered, "The one guard is just two paces behind us. The other two are quickly making their way through the crowd. They will catch up in just a few moments." The street was crowded, but there did not appear to be anyone else following them. An instant later the one guard walked past them and assumed a position several paces in front of them. Dryados recognized him and immediately relaxed.

Dryados and Sussana took the next turn heading up to the Acropolis. The crowds slowly thinned but were still dense. "Oh, and make sure you take off that silly hat before anyone else sees you," she said with a small grin.

"Thank you again, Sussana." Dryados took off the broad work hat. Sussana turned at the next intersection and headed home. People on the street started to address him by name.

The three guards stayed close but tried to be as inconspicuous as possible.

Chapter 26

Patmos

When they had finally reached shore, and John stopped vomiting, he had thought it was a great blessing. Now he wasn't sure. He had been in the River many times. He recognized it immediately. Whether he was awake or asleep, it did not matter. He could feel the presence of God. Still, being on Patmos, it was different. There was a palpable tension in the Great Waters. It was like floating along a peaceful stream and seeing great cataracts and waterfalls ahead. The River was still the River. The stream below the waterfall was still the same stream as the one above. The waterfall did not change it. It simply added to the River's complexity and beauty. But he could feel the water was very close now. The River around him was energized like the warm sea before an approaching typhoon. It made him feel like he was a child leaving the playground and suddenly discovering…that the world was so much more. And that some of it was terrifying.

Today he and Prochorus were going for a walk. Prochorus poked the last goat gently in the hindquarter. "Come on there…there's a good goat." The tardy animal sprinted a few feet forward, passing some of the other goats in the herd. Then it quickly slowed back down, resuming its previous pace. It seemed to know that as long as it wasn't the last goat in the group, it wouldn't get goaded. "Come on…there's a good goat." Prochorus poked a goat off to the left that was munching on a stray weed growing between the barren rocks. They walked slowly as they worked their way higher up the mountain. John set the pace, not the goats. And at John's pace, the goats got plenty to eat along the way.

"For a scribe, you make an excellent goat herder," John mused. Prochorus was more than John's attendant. He was like a best friend, scribe, and caring nurse all wrapped up into one.

"Well, it is just research for the book I'm writing. It will be about getting back to a simpler lifestyle. Being outdoors and in the sun. That sort of thing," Prochorus said, smiling. "There's a good goat." He poked a stalled animal in the leg. It was actually the same one he had poked earlier.

The wind was starting to pick up, and they felt the occasional drop of rain. It was of little concern. It rained rarely on the island, and when it did, it was usually light and blew over quickly. The goats seemed to pay little attention and continued to munch their way slowly up the hill. The sun was still out. John looked up at the darkening sky. The clouds overhead were starting to congeal into a black swirling mass. The wind began blowing harder. Soon John's tunic was flapping about like a fresh-caught fish brought into a boat. Despite the strong winds, the spinning mass of clouds overhead did not seem to be moving away but hung directly overhead.

Then the downpour began. Both men heard distant thunder. "John, this way!" Prochorus started waving his stick and hitting the rocks beside the goats. "Come on, quickly now…good goats…be quick…good goats…" The trail they followed was well traveled but still rocky. Even with his cane, John could not keep up. Prochorus noticed him falling behind. "John, just this way…just stay on the trail. I will be right back." Prochorus continued to bang his stick on the rocks, "Come goats. Come…" The sounds of the bells around the goats' necks faded quickly as Prochorus and the goats disappeared among the rocks. John fumbled along the trail. With his failing sight and the rain, he could barely see the path in front of him. When he finally rounded the next turn, Prochorus and the goats had disappeared.

"John! John! Just here!" John looked over to see Prochorus's blurred head sticking out above the stones and his waving arm. In a moment, Prochorus was by his side. "It is just there…around the corner. Just there…" Prochorus grabbed John's free arm. Using both Prochorus and his cane for balance, John edged himself forward on the loose wet gravel of the trail. The rain had now become a storm. He could no longer see anything. They shuffled down a slight embankment.

"Here, it is an old shepherd's cave. I have pinned the goats in here many times. It will keep us dry and out of the wind."

The blasting wind raged louder as John and Prochorus entered the mouth of the cave. "Watch your head," he warned. "Some of the areas are lower than others." John let go of Prochorus's hand and reached up. The roof of the cave was just inches from his head. It was rough and irregular. But the stone was warm. "Here, Master, sit here." Prochorus led John to a ledge honed out of the stone. As John seated himself on the ledge, Prochorus hurried about inside the cavern. A moment later John felt the weight of a heavy blanket. "Here, keep this on. I will have a fire going in a few minutes."

True to his word, in a few minutes John could hear the crackle of the burgeoning fire. Prochorus also lit some small oil lamps that had been stationed in the cave. Despite the glow of the lamps, John could barely see. His eyes had gotten steadily worse. At this point he was nearly blind. He could make out anything in the distance. And what he could see inside of ten feet was limited to varying blurs and smudges in a field of twilight.

As warmth gathered in the stone hall, John let the blanket fall onto his lap. He ran his hand across the stone of the ledge beside him. It was warm. It felt... John got up to explore the rest of cave. He could smell the age in the stone surrounding him. He ran his hands across the rough rock as he clung to the walls. They were warm and so...familiar. "I know this place," John said. He glanced at the formless mass of Prochorus's figure. He could not see his face, so he had no idea how Prochorus was reacting to his proclamation. "The stone is as familiar as the walls of my home back in Ephesus. Over there is another ledge. And just above it there to the left is a painted figure of a man tending his herd." John's hand pointed about in the darkness.

"How did you know that?" Prochorus rose to his feet.

"I don't know how. But I know this place. I know the strange warmth of the cold stone. I have been here many times...though never to this specific place." John's eyes probed the darkness of the cavern. "And still there is an uneasiness here. Like the knock at the door by a Roman soldier." John started to smile. "Though that may sound strange to young ears, I assure you I am not demented."

"No, Master. I would never—"

"Please, Prochorus, over there under that pile of rags and tools is an old chair. Please bring it here, that I might sit closer to the fire."

Prochorus rummaged through the pile. True to John's statement, he found an old chair buried in the pile and brought it closer for his master. John continued to cling to the stone of the cave wall. He stood with his forehead pressed to the stone in front of him and both arms stretched out wide. He looked odd, as though the stone were a long-lost friend that he was greeting with a long embrace. "Did you hear that?" John whispered. "Did you see the great..." John pulled his head from the stone and looked at Prochorus. Though John could not make out his face, he fully understood the implications of Prochorus's persistent silence. "Never mind." John pulled himself away from the invigorating heat of the stone and sat down by their meager fire. "Tell me everything you know about this cave..."

John fidgeted to find his spoon on the table. Then began to eat the hot fish stew. "I loved Him. He was like my father and my brother and my best friend all rolled up into one." He looked up at the others and chuckled. "Sometimes I am not the easiest person to get along with, you know."

"I can attest to that," Prochorus interjected.

"No, it is true. We are all...difficult at times. Some more than others. Because we are all fallen. And still, knowing all my faults and my fallen nature, to learn that he was God and that He loved me. It was incomprehensible." John broke some bread and dipped it in his soup. "I do this now whenever I eat bread…to remember."

Elias and Cora sat listening. They had rented the small shack on their property to John and Prochorus as soon as the men had arrived there in exile. Over the last several months, the couple had heard the good news and become Iredenti. They had since taken John and Prochorus under their wing. Now they were all very much a family. They ate dinner together most nights. So they talked a lot.

"But now you say that has changed?" Cora rose and got more of the fish stew and refilled John's bowl. She also brought over some more bread. She placed John's hand upon the bread so he knew where it was. She and Elias were both natives to the island. Their families had come here ages ago. They lived in the small fishing village and sold fish to the small Roman garrison stationed there.

"No, it's not that. I wouldn't say it has changed, because everything that was has remained as it has always been. Now there is just more. And it is different. I can't explain it." John took a sip of water and slurped down some of the broth from his soup. "Do you remember months ago when I taught you about Moses?"

Everyone nodded their heads.

"To tell you the truth, I never quite understood why Moses fell to his face. Or why he later hid in the cleft of the rock. For me…I love God. I know He loves me. There is a relationship there that He has gone out of His way to restore. So I am confident in that. But now…" John had moved his hand and was now fumbling to find the bread again. After he found the loaf, he broke off another piece. "Now I realize He is still *on* His throne. Those instances in the cave last week, they touched my soul with the power of God's might. It was barely a trickle of awareness…but still, it was frightening. I clung to the stone to take it in, and to hide from it at the same time."

Elias stood up and took his plate into the kitchen. "You have taught us about the nature of the one true God. That there is nothing outside of Him and that everything comes from Him."

"Exactly. I could not have said it better myself. But there is a difference between knowing that in your mind and actually standing in His presence. To feel the power…of everything…emanating from Him like a tide. To know that all of it, the entire universe, could just as easily flow back into Him like the turning of the same tide." John stopped eating and sat in his chair. He looked up at Elias towering above him. "To truly understand that the existence of everything hangs on the knife edge of His will, and His will alone. To grasp the fearsome reality that it is only His momentary thought that separates everything…from nothing. It is beyond terrifying."

"What happened in that cave that you are not telling us?" Elias put his dish in the kitchen and sat back down.

"Yes," Cora seconded. "Please, we hate to see you so troubled."

"I'm not troubled," John said as he broke off more bread. "I'm just, just trying to figure out what to do." John pushed his chair away from the table. "God can go anywhere. He can be anywhere. But I think he wants me to go back to that cave." John sat there quietly looking at the others. "He told Noah to enter the ark. He called Abraham to go to the land beyond the Jordan, and He told Mary and Joseph to flee to Egypt. Now He calls me to go back to that cave."

"Teacher, then why do you wait?" Prochorus asked, confused.

John looked slowly up at the others. "Because I am afraid."

There were no goats on the hike today, just two men. Both were curious and excited. One was still afraid. Neither man spoke. They made slow progress up the rocky trail. The wind blew steadily across the large, barren stones of the hillside. The sun was up, but the steady breeze left each man feeling chilled. Prochorus walked beside John with one hand wrapped around his shoulder and the other holding his hand. John shuffled forward with his cane in the other hand.

"I have walked this trail before."

"I know, Master. I am just trying to steady you. The path is very difficult."

"Thank you, Prochorus, but I can do it." Prochorus let go of John's hand but kept his arm wrapped loosely around him.

"Master, I have been thinking. There are some things that I don't understand. Why here on Patmos? Why the cave?" Prochorus continued to monitor the trail for loose stones.

John huffed and puffed his way up the trail. "Why Jerusalem? Why Mount Ararat? Why Bethlehem or Nazareth?" he asked confidently.

Prochorus nodded as if he understood. John moved his cane back and forth in front of him, trying to feel the contour of the trail. His footing slipped on some loose gravel. He lost his balance for just a second. Prochorus tightened his grip around him. John regained his footing and stopped. "Let us sit for just a moment. This is not a sprint." John sighed.

The two men sat down together on some large rocks. There were many to choose from. "I think I would like some of that honey bread Cora has made for lunch. I know it is early, but I don't think she would mind us having a snack."

Prochorus rummaged through his pack until he found their hidden lunch. He handed John the small loaf. John broke off a piece from the end and put it in his mouth. He still had all his teeth but seemed to be holding it in his mouth, enjoying the sweetness of the honey-soaked morsel. He handed the loaf back to Prochorus, who also broke off a small piece. The two sat enjoying the brief respite.

"Master, why now? If this is as important as you suspect, why did He not share it sooner?"

"I don't know." John broke off another piece of bread.

"Why did He not do this when all of you were still alive?"

"You mean the other apostles?"

"Yes."

"I don't know." John shook his head and drank some water from the goatskin.

"But you knew Him. If you don't know…how are the rest of us supposed to figure it out?"

"First, you speak as if it were in the past. It is not that I knew Him then. It is that I know Him now. As for the rest of it…that is where the joy is found. It is like going on that second date with the one you love. You know you are in love, and still there is the expectation that there is still so much more to come. That is how it should be every day as Iredenti." John smiled at Prochorus. "That is how it will be every day for all of eternity. Not knowing…that is part of the good stuff. That is part of the excitement of loving Him." John fumbled to his feet. "Now let's get going. I have a date, and I have no intention of being late."

Prochorus looked up, smiling. "So, old man, you are going on a date?"

"Yes." John's old eyes said the rest. Prochorus got up and again wrapped a steadying hand around his excited master.

"It is there…just around that next curve." Prochorus pointed reassuringly.

John hunched down as they entered the mouth of the cavern. Prochorus guided him over to the chair they had found on their last visit. John sat down as Prochorus sorted through the supplies. He added fresh oil to the many small oil lamps scattered about the cave. Then he went over and quickly started their small fire. The oil lamps were quickly lit, and the cave started to warm up. Prochorus placed a clean blanket he had brought across John's lap to keep him warm.

"Now what?" Prochorus asked.

"I don't know. Tell me a joke."

"What?"

Even half blind and in the dark, John could make out the shocked look on Prochorus's face. John started to chuckle. "See, that's the good stuff. Not knowing. The unexpected. It is the joy and the terror of the journey all wrapped up in one." John pulled the blanket up to his chest. He glanced around the cave. He could feel the flow of the River in the stone. He looked back at his younger friend. "Perhaps we should pray." Prochorus edged closer to his master.

John closed his eyes…

It was like the blast of a mighty trumpet right behind him. John spun, jumping to his feet. He stood suspended in the vast emptiness of the created heavens. Words flooded his mind. They were the summation of the whole universe. The answer to every question and conclusion of every journey. *I am Alpha and Omega, the first and the last.* John found himself surrounded by an endless sea of galaxies and stars. Floating in their midst were seven great points of light suspended in golden splendor—lampstands shining in a sea of speckled blackness. And walking there among the lampstands was someone like the Son of Man. He was wearing a long robe that extended down to his feet, with a golden sash girded around his chest. And His voice was like the sound of mighty waters. He drew closer. As He did, John could feel it...the power emanating from Him started to burn the very fabric of existence. The universe was as fragile as his old body. It could be remolded, reshaped into anything or nothing at the will of Him who came. He was Judge and Advocate, salvation and doom. John sought for something that could shield him from the gaze of Him who saw all things. There was nothing. He tried to run. There was no place to go. John froze.

As He approached, John could feel the dark rents in his soul being exposed to his approaching God. In His right hand He held seven stars, and out of His mouth came a sharp two-edged sword. His face was like the sun shining in all its brilliance.

John fell at His Creator's feet like a dead man.

The God of the universe placed His right hand on John's shoulder and spoke softly. It was a voice John recognized from when he traveled with the other eleven. It was the voice of the One who loved him. "Do not be afraid. I am the first and the last. I am He that is the Living One. I was dead, and now look and see, I am alive forevermore. And I hold the keys to death and hades. Therefore write the things that you have seen, and the things which are now, and the things which are to happen..."

"Master, are you OK?" John awoke. He was now lying in the narrow ledge in the cave. Prochorus kneeled beside him.

"What happened?"

"You started to pray. Then suddenly you flung forward." Prochorus shook his head. "I almost didn't catch you. Then I carried you here. Your body remained, but it was clear your spirit had departed. You were as a dead man, for you did not breathe, and there was no beating of your heart within your chest. Still, I knew you were alive. It was as though your body had paused, suspended between two heartbeats."

"Yes, it is as you say," John stammered. "For I was only there for just a moment...less than a heartbeat."

"No, Master. You have rested here for more than three hours."

"No, it cannot be. I just closed my eyes a second ago." John looked at the blurred look of affirmation on Prochorus's face. "Three hours?"

"Yes, Master."

John sat quietly, drinking his warm tea. Finally he shook his head. "Time is such a confusing thing. We have it all jumbled up. Young, old, one hour, one millennia...to God, it is all the same. It is truly all just the space between two heartbeats. But listen, for I have received a revelation that God has prepared for me to write down more of His Word. But my eyes have failed me. So I know it is His plan that you should write down that which I see. I will speak the words as He gives them to me. It shall be done here in the cave. For this is the place He has chosen."

"Master, it is a refuge for goats."

"Yes, and I am an old goat. And you are a young one. So isn't it amazing how that has worked out so well." John laughed and patted Prochorus on the shoulder. "There is much to do."

Prochorus sat there on the cold stone beside his master. John had lain on the ledge for three days. John had not eaten or drank anything since his spirit had left him. He had not breathed. His heart had not beat. Prochorus put some more wood on the small fire. It kept the cave from getting too cold. Elias had been up once a day with new supplies. Prochorus started to snack on some dried meat. He heard John moan and start to cry again. The tears rolled down his unmoving face. He often cried when he was in the Spirit. It would be worse when he awoke. Prochorus returned to his master's side. Then John began to speak...

"There was a great earthquake. The sun turned black as sackcloth made of goat's hair, the whole moon turned blood red, and the stars in the sky fell to the earth as figs drop from a fig tree when shaken by a strong wind. The heavens receded like a scroll being rolled up, and every mountain and island was removed from its place. Then the kings of the earth, the princes, the generals, the rich, the mighty, and everyone else, both slave and free, hid in caves and among the rocks of the mountains. They called to the mountains and the rocks, 'Fall on us and hide us from the face of Him who sits on the throne and from the wrath of the Lamb! For the great day of their wrath has come...'"

Prochorus wrote down each word as it was spoken. He too could now feel the warmth of the stone around them. He could sense the red hues in the rock shift to fire as the words were spoken. As he wrote down the words, the implications for all humanity hit him. There would be one final path to redemption for a fallen race. A path openly proclaimed that could not be denied by any soul, that He alone was God. For those who could not see His majesty in His grace, they would be given one final chance to come to Him in His wrath. They would be shown a tiny tendril of His power and a hint of His fearsome judgment to come. A final chance to say "Yes." He pictured it in his mind's eyes. He had seen catastrophe, famine, and death around him his whole life. He knew them all very well. It seemed those in generations to come were strangers to such events. Yet they would be visited upon them as well. Prochorus too began to cry. His moans and tears filled in the silent spaces between John's voicing of the Word. The cave was cold indeed. Then a forgotten noise returned to the cave. A loud *whooooo* as John finally exhaled. Then there was an even louder *h-h-huuu* as John's lungs rose again, filling with air.

"Master?" Prochorus took John's hand. John sat motionless for a moment, and then his eyes slowly opened. A smile crept onto his face. Then he nodded. "Yes."

Prochorus got up. "I will get you some warm tea."

John sat up on the ledge and stretched his neck. "How long this time?"

"You have been gone three days."

"Three days!? Oh, Prochorus, I am so sorry. Are you OK?"

"Yes, Master. Elias has come here daily with new supplies, and Cora is a good cook. But your words have been very troubling."

John did not speak for some time. He seemed lost in thought. Prochorus started putting their things in his pack. "It is so odd for me to see you pack. For me it is as though we just arrived moments ago."

"Master, I am very tired." Prochorus sighed.

"No, no. I didn't mean it that way. Of course you are. We will leave as soon as you are packed, and get you to a real bed." The two drank the last of the tea. Prochorus put some dirt over the fire to try to preserve the coals. He left most of their supplies there. Few used the cave this time of year, and they would be returning soon enough.

Prochorus got his pack on and moved closer to John. "Master..." John fumbled his hand out and grabbed Prochorus's arm. The two shuffled out the mouth of the cave. John leaned on Prochorus's arm and poked his cane ahead of him as they went down the mountain.

Cora was cooking bacon in her kitchen next door. The two homes were close. Close enough that the aroma of that sweet delicacy would fill John and Prochorus's small cottage. Cora set the table. She knew the Roman soldiers used trumpets to announce the times for meals. But she had found that a good meal did that all on its own. She assumed the soldiers at the garrison simply didn't eat well. She continued to lay the plates and utensils out on the small table. True to her prediction, the enticing fragrance woke even Prochorus up out of bed. Soon he had let himself in and was dodging around the kitchen, trying to sneak some of the crispy morsels. As always, Cora politely let her guard down just long enough for him to steal a few of the crispy treats and flee out of the range of the fearsome wooden spoon she held. Then she nodded and pointed him to the back of the house. John had arrived much earlier and was sitting outside behind the house—crying.

John sat in a chair staring at the large smudge he knew to be the rocky hills surrounding the bay. Silent tears rolled down his face. He wiped them away with the sleeve of his tunic. Prochorus pulled up a chair beside him.

"It is worse in person, you know," John said. He still looked blankly at the rocky slopes. "To witness destruction on a planetary scale. To be at one instant in the heavens watching millions perishing. And then in the next to be on the ground beside them. Watching them die needlessly. Invisible to their senses, but screaming with all your might, 'He is here! He loves you! He has made a way! Just say yes!'" John wept bitterly. "The veil is torn. But men choose to build new ones with the towers of their pride."

Prochorus sat silently by his master, listening. John stared at the barren hills. "I have seen the greatness of man's achievements in the days to come. And I have seen each one become tainted by the fallenness of his soul. The world will change, but the spirit of man will not. Every great discovery for good will be twisted by others for evil. Every step forward will come at great cost. And with each advancement, the vanity of man will grow. But it will be the last days. And what man has not learned, in mercy I pray he would yet learn in the days of wrath. For even in those days it will not be too late. But then even the days of wrath will end. And then will come the more terrible days of judgment. For those days will be eternal." John's face contorted in agony. His groans were like the pains of childbirth for a new mother. Prochorus held his master as he wept. He knew not what to say.

The food was long cold when John's weeping stopped. Elias had left and gone down to his boat. Cora had gone to the well to do laundry. Prochorus stoked the fire back to life and reheated the bacon. He knew the kitchen well and in quick order had bread and cheeses added to the meal. "Today I think we will go to the village. It will do us both good. It will give you a chance to be in fellowship with those who have been made Iredenti here on the island."

"No, there is much to do. We must return to the cave." John shook his head as he munched on some crispy bacon.

"That is a great idea, but as I will be in the village, I don't see that happening. You cannot make it up the mountain without your guide..." Prochorus sucked on some dried cheese. "And I am your guide."

John turned, looking confused. "What?"

"We are going to the village today," Prochorus said loudly. "So eat your meal."

The walls in the cave were now a swirling tempest. Bolts of lightning cracked across the grain of the stone. A raging whirlwind stripped the walls of everything. Even the rock itself at times would peel away in sheets and be lost in the cyclone. In the center of the storm laid an old man on a thin stone ledge. Next to him knelt an exhausted scribe with blood-stained eyes. Only the flickering of the clay lamp next to them seemed to anchor them in the world of substance. Three days was now the standard time that John would be in the Spirit. Sometimes he would speak at length. Other times he might utter only a sentence or two.

John had seen the seven seals broken. After each seal, they had rested for a day.

He had seen and heard the seven trumpets. After each of those, they had rested for several days.

The woman, the wars, and the beasts of sea and earth had caused them to rest a week for each.

With every bowl judgment, it had been a fortnight.

The great harlot and the destruction of Babylon resulted in a month.

Now invisible lightning filled the cave. John was in the spirit. Prochorus kneeled alone on the floor, writing the words. He did not see or hear what John did. Yet the echoes of John's words lingered in the cavern around him. Silent tears fell down John's face again. Prochorus clung to the stones and the words coming from John's mouth. He could only imagine the scene where John now stood...

John walked invisible on the battlefield. There was no sound of trumpets calling the warriors to the site of engagement. No banners waved in the wind. No war drums sounded the cadence. The battle itself had been incredibly quick. Fat ravens now left the bloated corpses. Thinner ravens rushed to their spots at the banquet table. The pride and glory of man tasted as good to the ravens in death as it had to these arrogant dead when they were alive. John walked for what seemed days. The scene did not change. The sons and daughters of humanity lay sacrificed on the altars of pride they had built to themselves. John wept and wept. He knew that loss was only tragic when it was preventable. And this banquet was the greatest tragedy in all of human history.

John gasped back to life. The storm upon the earth had passed. There was a long silence as both men took in the events they had just become a part of. Prochorus lit more oil lamps. They packed up their empty supply containers. There was the occasional "I think we can leave this here." And the intermittent realization "Oh, we need more lamp oil...more wood for the fire...more smoked goat meat." But there was no discussion of what had been revealed for Prochorus to write. They simply packed up and left. Prochorus could barely walk. The hike back home was as silent as the lifeless battlefield John had just witnessed.

Arriving at home, Prochorus threw his pack on the floor and collapsed into bed. John walked through the house to his chair on the porch and stared as the lifeless stone hills. The tears arrived, as did the sun. The days passed.

"Prochorus, you said you had a question."

"Yes, Master. It has been really bothering me."

"What's that?"

Prochorus sat at his writing desk with nine stacks of written parchment. He grabbed one of the stacks and started rummaging through the pages. "Here, Master. You said, 'And I saw heaven open, and behold, a white horse, and He who sat upon it is called Faithful and True.'"

"Yes?"

"And then you go on to say, 'And He is clothed with a robe dipped in blood, and His name is called The Word of God.' Then just a bit later, 'And on His robe and on His thigh He has a name written, "The King of Kings, and Lord of Lords."' The Word of God tells us He has many other names, 'Rock of my Salvation, Cornerstone that the builders rejected, Lilly of the Valley, Rose of Sharon, the True Compass, Christ, the Lamb, Savior, Redeemer, Friend, Root of David, the Resurrected One, Emmanuel—God with Us, the Visible Image of the Invisible God.' And on and on."

"Yes, He has many names," John reaffirmed. "Each one captures a piece of who He is. He is called—"

"No, Master. It is not the many names of the Select Arrow that raises my question."

"Then what?"

Prochorus fumbled in his chair. "Well…what I'm really trying to find out is… ah…well…" He looked up cautiously at his master. "What's the name of that horse?"

John looked surprised.

"No, Master, wait." Prochorus sat up with animated vigor to defend himself. "I'm serious. You know that fast horse at the hippodrome back in Ephesus. That owner named it after his assistant—"

"Yes, Receptionist, very fast horse."

"And that sailing merchant whose horse won the last race. His horse's name was—"

"Ocean Cake."

"And that famous masked vigilante west of Laodicea. What was his horse's name?"

"Gold."

"Yes, exactly," Prochorus said eagerly.

"So what is your point?" John asked, half confused and half smiling.

"Well, I have been thinking. If the King of Kings and Lord of Lords is coming back riding a horse, it must be some spectacular horse." He looked at John, waiting for him to say something. John motioned for him to continue. "Well, we know the names of all these other famous horses. So, what's the name of that horse?"

"What's the name of the horse?" John repeated, half laughing. Then he shook his head and walked closer. "Prochorus, you may not realize it, but that simple question may have some of the greatest theological implications of our age."

Prochorus slumped in his chair. "Now you are just making fun of me. I'm serious. I have searched the scriptures, and the name of that horse is nowhere to be found." He was starting to feel very embarrassed.

"I am not making fun of you. And you are right, Prochorus." John pulled up a chair by the desk and sat down. "There are so many amazing passages in the written Word. They are important for what they say. This passage is important for what it does not say." John shuffled through one of the stacks of parchment. He stopped and smiled as he read the passages. "You are right. We never know the name of the horse in this passage." He smiled at Prochorus. "So why do you think that is?"

"I'm not really sure. We know all those other names, so I was just thinking…" John sat silently next to him, waiting for him to continue. "Well, I suppose because the passage is not about the horse."

"Exactly, Prochorus! Exactly! The text is not about the horse. It is all about the Rider." John rose to his feet, grabbed his cane, and paced around the room. "What is the horse's job in context to this King?"

Prochorus sat back in his chair. "The horse is to obey the commands of the Rider."

"Yes, that is true," John said excitedly. "But more specifically, what is the horse supposed to do?"

Prochorus waved his hands to his side as if stating the obvious. "Take the Rider where He wants to go."

"Yes! Now you see, don't you?" John seemed ready to burst.

"Well, I'm not really sure…"

"Is it the horse's job to fight great battles and defeat mighty armies?"

"No, of course not." Prochorus chuckled. "That's the Rider's job."

"Exactly! Exactly! And is it the horse's job to save your marriage? Or help your kids? Or help you deal with your boss at work? No, of course not." John shuffled around the room. "That's the Rider's job too! The reason this passage is so important is because so many times in life, people forget they are not the Rider. They are just the horse." John stopped, looked at his assistant, and then raised a finger. "You, Prochorus, you…are the horse." Prochorus nodded.

John sat down. "So many people in the ages to come will lose heart in doing good. They will grow weary because they will think it is their job to fix things. That all this stuff is their responsibility. They will miss the harvest because they do not understand their role in the battle."

"And what is that, Master?"

"It is the same job unspoken in this passage, to bring the Rider. You have problems in your life, bring the Rider. There are problems in Macedonia, Corinth, Rome, and in all the four corners of the world, bring the Rider. Now, to loosely paraphrase *all* the commandments of God in your life into one sentence, it would be this: 'Gitty up!'"

John got back up and walked toward the door. "Now after such a rousing speech, I'm going to back to bed."

After witnessing the wedding supper of the Lamb, it would be a full month before they would return to the cave.

"And I saw a new heaven and a new earth, and the first heaven and the first earth passed away, and there is no longer any sea...

"And he showed me a river of the water of life, clear and crystal, coming from the throne of God and of the Lamb...

"And there shall no longer be any curse...

"Behold, I am coming quickly...I am the Alpha and the Omega, the first and the last, the beginning and the end.

"Yes, I am coming quickly.

"Amen." Tears rolled down John's face like so many before. Yet Prochorus could tell in his tone, these were tears of joy.

John's face was serene. "Come, Lord Jesus."

The confines of the cave seemed to calm. It was just a cave again. John gasped in a deep breath. He leaned over to his side and sat up on the stone ledge. A long-forgotten smile returned to his face, beaming with joy. He looked over at the exhausted scribe. "He is coming again!"

Prochorus had decided on nine copies to start. One for each of the seven churches. One for him and one for John. The compiling went quickly. Months had passed since the process had begun. They were both changed men. Both older. Both filled with joy and sorrow. Men of passion. God was on His throne, and that would never change. But likewise, never would the fallen heart of man. Some would be saved. So many would be lost. Yet John had taught the lesson well. They were just the horses carrying the Rider.

Chapter 27
The Final Word

Ivoluntas seethed inside his human host. Surrounded by the greatest wealth humanity had to offer and dwelling inside the body of its most powerful leader brought him no solace at all. In fact, his very surroundings seemed to mock him for who his host was, rather than serve as a testimony to him. He read through the parchments. "So this is the final word. He has already polluted the entire universe with the signature of His glory. Now He has to put it in writing! His glory and eternal plan for every human soul. It makes me sick." He read through the writings over and over. He had been with the Word for eons. Walked with Him. Spoken with Him. Yet all these words were completely unknown. "And the most wrenching detail of His eternal plan…He's coming back! Aahhhhh!" He turned, facing his minions. "This is catastrophic!"

He sat on the throne of the greatest empire the world had ever known. Dozens of Black Voids floated silently beside him. "Every battle strategy I have worked on for millennia has been spelled out for all the world to see. The element of surprise is lost." He was ready to vomit. He stood and paced around Domitian's throne room. His boots clicked on the marble floor. His mind raced. Then he stopped. "No, people are stupid," he thought. "Few will bother to read the Word or listen. And even fewer will take heed." His smile grew as he reread the words. The words told the future of his own success. Some of his plans would work out, if only for a little while. He looked proudly out at the floating masses of his compatriots. "I will grow strong!" he proclaimed loudly. Joyous elation filled his spirit. "He has given time for all the children of the earth to be born. He has given time for every soul to choose." Ivoluntas chuckled. His laugh grew louder and louder. It was almost manic. "He has given time for pride in achievement to be worshiped. Pride in independence to be made a sacrament. Pride in wealth to become a virtue. He has given time, for me to work." His laugh echoed down the empty chamber. "Surprise has not been forfeited," he mused. "It has simply been rendered unnecessary." Bliss welled up within him. "Still, the clock is ticking. We must find a weakness somewhere in His final plan."

He closed his eyes and summoned his legions from across the great expanse. Black Voids popped into existence all around him. Thousands upon thousands hovered in the air beside him like a myriad of small thunderheads. "Every plan is contingent on a few key elements. We must search through this final Revelation He has given and merely find one such pillar that can yet topple."

Ivoluntas raised his hand, and the inscribed pieces of parchment floated in the air among the host. Myriads upon myriads of Black Voids read the words, searching for an answer. The Star of Morning stood in their center. The Qui Malaam scoured through the substance of every word. They tortured and twisted every sentence. There had to be a way. Hours passed, and then days.

Ivoluntas had read and reread the text thousands of times. Suddenly, the speed of his intellect crashed to a stop. There it was again—the text about the fifth trumpet. He reread the passage again. "And I saw a star fallen from heaven to the earth. To him was given the key to…" Ivoluntas looked up and let his thoughts drift back to that strange day so long ago in the Room of Keys. He reached up and held the key around his neck. He felt the inscribed word on its surface with the tips of his human fingers, "Otvoriti." The word stuck in his mind like a splinter in his eye—to open. He wondered. Bewilderment and great sadness filled his soul. *How did He know*, he thought. "Even then, how did He know?" It was ages before Ivoluntas had considered his fallen scheme. Ages before the rebellion. Ages before the fall of man. *Still, even then, He knew.* Sadness gripped him. God had loved him even then, knowing what he would do. *How…*

"Master, here, I think I have found it!" One of the Black Voids floated formlessly above the rest. His voice was full of victory. "Here in the letter directed to Thyatira."

The written page of parchment snapped through the air and floated before Ivoluntas. The Black Void scurried frantically to catch up. "Here, Master. Here in the text to Thyatira it proclaims, 'To him I will give authority over the nations, and He shall rule them with a rod of iron, as the vessels of the potter are broken to pieces.'"

Ivoluntas reread the passage.

"Master, that does not make any sense," voiced one of the other host. "There are so many other things that must happen first. The scattered seed must return to its root. All the words spoken by the prophets of old must come to pass. And here in this Revelation, there are—"

Ivoluntas's face filled with rage. "Silence!" The shouted order blasted through the great hall. It was not the frail voice of a human emperor. It was the battle cry of the Son of the Dawn. Ivoluntas moved to the center of the room. Slowly he released his essence from the confines of his human host. The flesh surrounding him wavered and buckled, yet it held intact. As the emperor's arms slumped to his side, great iridescent wings unfolded across the span of the chamber. Rainbows upon rainbows of color danced before the entirety of the fallen legions, each color as bright as the sun. Even lacking eyes, they could perceive the beauty of their ancient leader. "The Old Farmer never makes sense. He never does what He says He will do. Look at us. He betrayed us. His words are as a flimsy as the parchment they are written on."

Silence and fear filled the room.

The fallen angel walked around the hall. "This all began with John and that… that blasphemy at the Porta Latina." Ivoluntas's angelic form pulsed with seething power. The beautiful iridescent rainbows of light emanating from his presence shifted into a beacon of black ink. The room around them was suddenly flooded with raven-black shadow. The Black Voids shuddered. Even they could not see in the depths of Ivoluntas's anger. Blackness consumed everything. Ivoluntas stood motionless and breathed in slowly, calming his soul. Small streaks of light slowly began to penetrate the obsidian world around them. The sun was rising in the east. Ivoluntas spoke slowly. "In my mercy I spared John's life. And that mercy has been turned against me. How long has it been?"

"Over a year, Master, since he was exiled to the island of Patmos," uttered one of the faceless shadows.

"Yes. Then we shall consider that the starting point. Clearly this plan to seize our power has been underway for at least that long. And if Thyatira is the place, then that is where we shall focus our wrath." Ivoluntas stopped abruptly in the corridor. "There is one thing we can say about the Old Farmer—He is consistent. If He came as an innocent child before, He will come as one again. So we will—"

"But, Master, it says He will come as an adult in all His glory, riding—"

"Silence!" A web of twisted lightning exploded around the room. Charred streaks of black appeared instantly on the walls. Many of the great pieces of art stationed there were smoking or burned. Dust drifted down from the shaken ceiling. "*There will be silence!*" Ivoluntas roared each word individually like a warning of death. "Nothing will interfere with my plans. Nothing will alter what we must do." The Black Voids shifted slowly away from the gathering thunderhead of their master's fury. "Nothing can save those whom we are about to kill."

Calm seemed to wash over their great chieftain. "Come…" The angelic form of Ivoluntas turned and stepped across the fabric of the world to the Great Altar in Pergama. The host of the Qui Malaam followed through the same gate in the fabric. "First, let us make sacrifices to our own greatness. We shall bask in the brilliance of our own majesty. Then, then we will destroy this flawed plan of eternity."

Suistus's villa, Smyrna

"Suistus! Are you listening?"

Suistus's mind popped back to the breakfast table. "Yes, dear, of course." He reached over and slowly started to sip on his pomegranate juice.

"Then what was I saying?" His wife, Vanus, folded her arms in front her and stared at him angrily.

Suistus thought he had heard her say something about plants. "My love, you were talking about gardening?" It was a gamble.

"I was talking about expanding the whole rose section. This…"

Vanus droned on. Suistus's mind raced with a more pressing problem. *Why does Parceida want to meet with me today?* Suistus had no idea what to do. *If I don't go, Parceida might very well have me killed. If I do go, Parceida might very well have me killed.* He was stuck. "Yes, dear, I think that is a wonderful plan. As always, I leave the garden to your impeccable sense of taste and elegance." Suistus rose to his feet, sipped down the last of the pomegranate juice, and laid his goblet on the table.

Vanus looked up at him, smiling. "Oh, I know you are just going to love it. I promise." Her face glowed like a child getting ready to open the biggest present at her birthday party.

Suistus bent over, giving his wife a kiss on the forehead. "I may be home a little late today. I have an important meeting, and I am not sure how long it is going to last." Then he turned and departed.

The rest of his day was much like breakfast. People rambled on, but he heard none of it. *Parceida says he has news. What does that mean?* His thoughts continued to loop in his head. *The fortune we have paid him is not enough? The army he has raised is still not big enough? The mission is impossible?* Fear edged its way forward in his thoughts. *Or perhaps he has betrayed me to the Romans?*

His heart seemed to beat faster and faster as the day went on. It was getting to be time to leave for Parceida's villa. Now he was starting to sweat. *Would it be safer to bring a large force?* he thought. *No, Parceida might kill them just to show that he could.* He got up and walked around his desk. *No, I shall go alone.* He paused for a moment. *No, then he can kill me and deny I ever even arrived for the meeting.* He paced faster. *No, I shall take a single aide with me.* He put on his cape. He was getting cold. *Easy meat for the butcher,* he thought. He stood back up. He reached over to the small summoning bell sitting across the desk and gave it several shakes.

"Yes, Lord Suistus?"

"You and I will be leaving in just a moment for a meeting across town. Tell the entire staff we are going to meet with Lord Parceida so they know where we are. That is, so they can contact us in the event of an emergency."

"Yes, Lord Suistus."

His attendant closed the door. Suistus resumed his pacing. *He is a rational man.*

There is nothing to be gained by killing me—

"Lord Suistus, the wagon is ready."

"Yes, of course." Suistus walked silently down the hall and out of the synagogue. He did not say a word as they climbed into the wagon nor as they drove across town. He nodded silently when his attendant announced him to the string of guards at the gate. All he could think about was not dying. Now he sat in the receiving room silently regretting his decision to come. His attendant clearly recognized the extent of his apprehension and stood a few paces away, hyperventilating. The waiting dragged on.

The door opened. "Lord Parceida sends his regrets and will be with you momentarily."

Suistus politely nodded. "Why, of course." He glanced to his attendant, who looked like he was about to pass out.

The room was quiet as they waited. He entertained himself by admiring the valuable treasures displayed around the room.

The door opened. "Lord Parceida truly regrets his continued delay. Please enjoy some wine and refreshments." A squad of attendants quickly entered the room with an extravagance of food and several bottles of wine. Then in a heartbeat, the attendants were gone, and the two again waited alone.

An hour passed. Then another.

The door opened, and again the servant entered. "Lord Parceida—"

Suistus jumped furiously to his feet. "This is getting to be redic—"

Lord Parceida entered the room with a big smile and several armed men. "Lord Suistus, it is always such a pleasure to meet with you." His host came over, giving him a warm and powerful embrace. More of Parceida's men flooded in behind him. "And who is this other fellow you have brought with you?" Lord Parceida walked over gave the aide an equally warm and powerful hug. "A pleasure to meet you. Yes, any associate of Lord Suistus is always welcome in my humble home." Then he looked over at the chief priest, his countenance far more serious. "But I assumed our business here today was for our ears alone."

Suistus glanced up at Parceida. "He is my most trusted…" He looked at Parceida's unblinking snakelike eyes. "My servant was just leaving."

"A great pleasure, Lord Parceida." Suistus's attendant looked physically ill but bowed politely and was escorted out.

Parceida and the others stood quietly, waiting until the attendant was out of the room. "Good." Parceida sat down opposite Suistus in an almost throne-like chair and poured himself some wine. "I have received the final word from my associates. We have successfully recruited all the mercenaries we need, and our army is now ready to go. There are some final arrangements that need to be solidified, and the date of the attack to be settled, but beyond that, everything is set."

"How exactly is this going to work?" Suistus asked politely.

"The mercenaries will approach the city of Philadelphia as any other caravan. When they arrive at the gate, the Romans will begin their routine inspection. When they do, the mercenaries will attack, and the gate will be breached. As soon as the battle is engaged, an alarm will sound throughout the city. All available Romans will be called to the gate as reinforcements. It will be standard Roman protocol for all other units to be mustered. They will be sent to the other gates and walls in anticipation of a larger assault on the city. This will leave the residential areas inside the city unguarded. That is when we will kill Dryados. With my assassins already there, and the Romans otherwise occupied, it will also give me an opportunity to kill several of my personal enemies." Parceida poured himself some more wine and then continued on smugly. "Opportunities like this are like young, eager women—they should always be exploited as much as humanly possible…bahaahaahaaaa!" He threw his head back and roared in sensuous laughter. The soldiers nearby joined in with their leader's mirth.

"Yes, of course." Suistus tried to smile in agreement, but all he could manage was a snarled grin. "And what should happen if one of these mercenaries is taken alive? Whose name are they going to surrender to the torturer as the instigator of this little insurrection?"

Parceida laughed again. "Not yours and certainly not mine. We have given the mercenary commanders the impression that this is secretly being funded by Philadelphia's rivals in nearby Laodicea. With the great wealth that Laodicea has at its disposal and the recent prosperity of Philadelphia, it seems reasonable that a conflict would eventually arise."

"Yes, but clearly the mercenaries understand they have no hope of victory?" Suistus asked, bewildered.

Parceida leaned forward like he was going to tell Suistus a secret. He chuckled as the words left his lips, "No, none at all. In fact, I am sure all those attacking the gate will ultimately be slaughtered. But I think they will make it partially into the city first." He turned, facing one of his men. "In fact, my commander here and I have a small wager going on that—"

"Why would they possibly go on a suicide mission? That doesn't make sense, even for mercenaries."

"Well actually, they have somehow gotten the impression—and trust me, it is not my fault—that there will be several other groups simultaneously attacking the other gates." Parceida leaned back in his chair. "I'm afraid they have gotten some very bad intelligence on that. Tragedy."

"Then who will kill Dryados? That was the whole goal behind this entire undertaking. That's what I have been paying you for." Suistus sat with his mouth agape.

"Yes, yes, yes, of course. How thoughtless of me. I have also sent in several squads of men, one or two at a time, into the city. When the Romans garrisoned in the city have been dispatched to their positions, my men will assault the Acropolis. They have narrowed Dryados's location down to a specific neighborhood. They will kill everyone on those streets just to be sure." Parceida grabbed some more grapes.

Harsh reality spun in Suistus's mind. He fidgeted in his chair, crossing and uncrossing his ankles. *This man is going to kill his own mercenaries without batting an eye. He's willing to kill streets of innocent people just to kill one man.* It was time to leave. "Well, it sounds like you have everything completely under control. I really don't think I need to inconvenience you any further with my presence. Thank you so much for your time." Suistus smiled and rose to his feet. "Good—"

"Sit down!" Parceida's face lost all of its jovial shine.

Suistus slowly sat back down, forcing a smile. His heart pounded even faster in his chest. He glanced around the room filled with armed men. There was no route of escape. Still, no one was making any overtly hostile moves. He sat up and politely folded his hands in front of him.

Parceida leaned back in his chair and continued to munch on some grapes and drink his wine. He spoke casually as he enjoyed the food. "Since I promised the mercenaries half their pay when the job was completed, the fact that they are all dead will save me a lot of money. I will of course pocket the savings for myself. You, on the other hand, will still pay the agreed-upon price and act none the wiser." He held up a single grape and admired it like a valuable jewel. "These grapes are truly amazing." Then he popped it into his mouth. "You will make the final payment tomorrow." He stopped and looked Suistus in the eyes. "Tomorrow," he reiterated firmly. Then he noted, "Oh, and you will pay an additional quarter talent of silver for my inconvenience." He stopped eating and stared blankly at Suistus.

Suistus took a deep breath. "Why, of course. I think this project has turned out to be far more complicated than anyone could have possibly anticipated. I apologize it has taken up so much of your valuable time."

"Good!" Parceida's face instantly regained its look of jovial happiness. Suistus had no idea which of the faces that Parceida wore was the real one. Nor did he care to find out. He simply sat there smiling in return. Parceida slowly rose to his feet. "Oh, I do suppose we should select a date." Parceida rummaged through his tunic and pulled out a pair of old dice and started to shake them. He smiled as he looked over at Suistus. "Divine providence—always best to leave some things up to the gods." He threw the dice on the table.

The Great Altar of Pergama

Killing the old tiger was proving to be far more difficult than they had anticipated. Several dead priests now lay at the base of the Great Altar. The big cat stood over one of its fallen victims, guarding its gruesome prize. The other priest stood shaking in fear several yards away, trying to figure out what to do next. After a moment, the hungry tiger ripped into the midsection of the fat dead priest and started to gorge itself.

"This is ridiculous." Ivoluntas motioned to one of his servants. A moment later the servant returned with his bow. The governor strolled near the fire, with his great master filling his frame, and pulled back the bow. The angelic missile flew through the air and sliced through the hungry predator without the slightest loss of speed. By the time the big cat dropped dead, the arrow had vanished into the distance across the valley below. "Done! Now slit its throat and throw it on the altar." Ivoluntas rose to his feet and threw the bow back to his servant. "Do the same to the priests for ruining my mood."

"The live ones or just the dead ones?" asked one of the soldiers.

Ivoluntas did not speak. He merely looked at the soldier with an expression of disappointment.

The gathered horde of soldiers did not hesitate and drew their swords. Ivoluntas's priests froze in disbelief. In a dozen heartbeats, they were all dead. The last few of those beats were used to drain their scarlet blood onto the altar. Ivoluntas motioned to his soldiers. "Don't forget the dead ones." He looked at the scattered bodies at the base of the altar and added, "I hate to be wasteful." Then he smiled. "They all had served me so well. I am sure they would want it this way." The bodies of the dead priest were thrown into the fire on top of all the others. Ivoluntas relaxed on his throne. Human soldiers and Black Voids mixed together in his worship like waters from two merging streams. Fire exploded from the Great Altar high in the sky above Pergama. Some of the dead bodies moved in the blaze as their tendons and muscles contracted in the heat. "Oh, so much better." Ivoluntas snuggled up in his majestic chair. The wine he drank was as thick and as sweet as the blood now being sacrificed to his name.

The Black Voids filling the courtyard began to sing. It was an old song from back when they were in heaven. They sang the verses with joy and pride. They had changed the name to whom they sang it and had rewritten several of the verses entirely. But still, they sang it with exuberance.

Hours of blissful worship passed.

As the fire died down and the songs began to fade, Ivoluntas summoned the demon commanders of his fallen ranks. He rose to his feet.

"He has proclaimed that He will be born again at Thyatira. The date of His birth is already come. Like a plague upon the earth, He has struck again without warning." Ivoluntas strutted along the edges of the Great Altar with the smoke of the sacrifices still rising behind him. A cyclone of Black Voids circled him like a silent tornado. "And as He has done to us, so we shall now do to Him. We shall strike without warning." Mouthless cheers rose from the Qui Malaam. "We shall unleash our wrath on the hatchling eagle before it has grown to soar. Though He may think it safely hidden with the other hatchlings still in the nest, we shall not be hindered. We shall kill the youngest children within the city of Thyatira. We shall destroy His plans as He has destroyed ours."

One of the commanders floated out of the circling mass. "How will we know which children to kill?"

"John has been on the island of Patmos for over a year. We will use that as a rough start date. So you shall kill any child two and under. You may kill more if you choose."

Another one of the commanders rose from the surface of the torrent. "And what tools shall we use to achieve our mission, Great Son of the Dawn?"

A broad smile spread across Ivoluntas's human face. "As you can see, the governor of Pergama is my own possession, willing and devoted. We shall use the forces we already have here at our disposal. We shall use the Romans."

"And what of the Roman soldiers stationed in Thyatira?" asked the same dark lord.

"We shall recruit those loyal to me to our purpose as well. But it has been my experience that local troops are sometimes too restrained for such purposes as I have in mind. So those not in our possession we will have dispatched from the city prior to our arrival." The governor walked along the smoldering edge of the sacrificial fire. The severed limb of one of the priests laid half charred on the marble edge. He took his shod boot and kicked the stump into the remaining hot coals. "We will move quickly, and we will let none escape."

"But, Master, did we not try the same tactic the first time He came?" Another one of the black commanders floated up out of the masses. "Was his family not warned to escape?"

"Yes, I am well aware of that…"

Another shadowy figure ascended among the warrior throng. "Great One, are there not other prophesies that must first be fulfilled? The scattered seed must return. The—"

"Enough!" Ivoluntas roared. "The matter is already settled." His face grew placid and determined. "You will take possession of our minions here in the city. We will use only those units of the most ruthless composition. I do not want squeamish men slowing us down." The governor turned and started to walk back toward the palace. "Tomorrow you will announce to your men that they will be needed for combat. Prepare them. We will not tell them of their target until they stand outside the city gate of Thyatira." He walked determinedly back to his throne room. Several young maidens were already there waiting. It was time to continue the celebration…less formally.

The night passed quickly. Ivoluntas ran his host's hand across the soft rump of the girl lying to his right. The governor's body was completely spent. Still, it was not the same. It was not his own body that relished in the pleasure. Now, he was more like a voyeur, pretending. He remembered the days in the past when such finite limits had not been placed on his physical pleasure. He thought of the countless acts of sexual debauchery he had committed with the humans. He remembered the Nephilim, the human children that had been born to him. Then a great sadness overcame his sprit. He looked at the arms and legs that now encased him…they were not his. It was these acts of sexual abomination that had brought God's judgment to stripp him and others of their physical beings.

One of the governor's Roman generals entered the room. Ivoluntas got up and walked naked across the room. The governor had a fine human body, and Ivoluntas was proud of its physique. Slowly he put on his clothing. "How can I help you, General?" He slid on his magnificent Opus Angelorum armor.

"The troops have been prepared." The general spoke confidently. "Now we just need a sense of when this attack will be launched and how far we must travel to get there."

Ivoluntas stopped and gazed intently at the officer. The general had given the requisite bow before he spoke. Granted it was little more than a nod, but he had made some effort. Ivoluntas really couldn't fault the man for his pride. The man was a general, so he did have a right. But still…

"Are you a gambling man, General?" Ivoluntas asked enthusiastically.

"Why, yes I am." A big grin crossed the worn soldier's face. Several teeth were missing, so his smile was almost comical.

"Good. So am I. Do you have any dice?"

"Yes, of course. Carry them right here, just in case. Never know when you'll have a chance to win some coin." He rummaged through his armored chest piece and pulled out a set of dice he had stashed behind it. Then he walked over and handed them politely to the governor.

"I am thinking this Friday. Let's see what the dice say. If I am wrong, I kill will you where you stand. If I am right, you live to fight and die in my service on another day. Either way, you will die for me, so you can't possibly lose." The governor smiled happily at the general.

The general's face went white.

The governor nodded and threw the dice on a nearby marble table. "Which month…" The governor cast the dice several times. "Adar! That's March. That's this month. Fabulous! Now let's see which date." He shook the dice around in his closed hands and gave the dice another toss. The dice landed. "That would be toward the middle of the month…good. And that…" He threw the dice again. "That would be Friday!" A giant smile crossed the governor's face. "I am right again!" The governor placed his hand on the general's shoulder. "I am sorry you will not be able to die in my service today. But perhaps in the battle you will have better luck." The governor smiled and nodded happily.

The general's face was still blank. "Perhaps."

"Good. And you will only be going as far as Thyatira, so that is very good."

"Yes, that is excellent." The general's eyes, however, filled with concern. "Still, we will need to leave the day after tomorrow if we are to engage them on Friday."

"Yes, Friday you will fight. I will give you your final instructions the morning of your departure."

Snyrna, Lord Parceida's Villa

Suistus watched as Parceida shook the dice to determine the day of the assault on Philadelphia. After one more quick shake, he threw the dice and let them tumble on the carved mahogany table. The two cubes finally came to a stop. Suistus stared at the final throw of the dice. "That would be this Friday."

"Yes, so it is. Just as I have already instructed our mercenary friends." Parceida smiled. "Friday always seems to be a good day to die."

"Friday is Purim," Suistus said, half questioningly.

"What does that mean?"

"It is Hebrew. It means—"

"Yes, I love these dice. I have used them countless times." He leaned forward again with his secretive smile. "You know I can throw them to land on whatever I want. Seems to be most helpful in a game of chance. Eliminating the chance part, I mean."

"Yes, or course. Much more convenient, I would think." Suistus nodded.

"Yes, it is." Parceida leaned back in his chair. The Black Voids that filled his frame had grown so accustomed to their home there they could guide his hand to throw anything. "We will see you tomorrow then with the final payment. My men will escort you out."

Suistus rose and bowed deeply to his host. "Again, it has been my greatest pleasure."

Chapter 28
Interrupted

Philadelphia

*B*ang! *Bang! Bang!* Dryados stood in the emptiness of the black landscape. His dream had finally returned. He sprinted across the vacant
blackness to the forge he knew awaited him. *Bang! Bang! Bang!* His
dream jerked forward. Everything seemed to be dumped into his consciousness
in one giant mass of sensory overload. The hot smell of the forge, the pounding
of the hammer, a hooded angel with eyes of fire, a key! Then the dream slowed.
The angel at the forge worked delicately now. His hands moved with the grace-
ful precision of a dove landing on a branch. The pulsing white key was being
reshaped. The pounding of the hammer became a tapping, then the tapping
became a scraping, the scraping became the soft rubbing of a final polish. The
glowing key became the shape of…

Thyatira

Bang! Bang! Bang! Ascalon stood alone in a field of blackness. This world was
devoid of every sensory input except the sound of the hammer. The beating of
the hammer was quick, as though the one at the forge was in a hurry. The sound
was so familiar. He ran with speed beyond his human strength. Instantly he was at
the forge. A great hooded smith stood working some glowing metal. *Bang! Bang!
Bang!* The heated melted became a key of white purity. The hooded figure smiled.
Then *Bang! Bang! Bang!* The great hammer fell over and over again, slower and
slower. Then more and more delicately, the smith worked his trade. Then silence.
The hooded figure held up the retooled key. Now it looked like…

Dryados and Ascalon stood opposite each other watching the same dream unfold. The angel at the forge shook his hood loose from about his face. But the hood did not fall to his shoulders. Instead, the hood split in half and folded upward, behind, and above the angel's head. Wings of florescent gold ruffled in the stillness like the leaves of an ancient oak. The light forced the darkness to retreat. Dryados smiled. He had heard of the seraphim but had never seen one. Ascalon stood in awe. The seraphim held up the object of his labor. To Dryados, the key was now the exact likeness of Ascalon. To Ascalon, it was the exact likeness of Dryados. The seraphim nodded and smiled, holding the object up for both of them to see. Then he started to point...

Crash! Bang! Whoosh! Pow! The fabric of the dream shimmered. A flash of surprise crossed the seraphim's face. "Ivoluntas!" The seraphim clenched his jaw. The walls of the dream surrounding the men started to buckle. "To Sardis! Now! Both of you!" Ascalon and Dryados could feel the covers of their beds pressing against them. Pulling them out of the dream. *Crash! Bang! Pow!* The image of the Seraphim wobbled like the reflection of man on a pond. "To Sardis now, quickly, you are both..."

A large rat scurried across the shelves in Ascalon's bedroom, knocking things to the floor. Ascalon jumped to his feet. In a second his mind was clear enough to run and grab the broom. Sperta sat up in bed. "Ascalon, what's all the commotion? You're going to wake Lautus."

"It's was monster rat! Right here in our room!" Ascalon returned with the broom and searched the room. He thought he caught a glimpse of the monster and took a swipe at it. Several more things fell down from the shelf, but no rat.

"Ascalon, get back in bed. It's the middle of the night." Sperta plopped back down in the bed and drew the covers up over her head.

"Stupid rats! First thing in the morning I'm putting out some traps," Ascalon gibed.

"You just be sure you put them somewhere where Lautus can't get into them." Sperta moaned groggily.

"I hate rats! Disgusting things." In a moment, Ascalon was fast asleep. The rest of the night was filled with odd noises and similarly strange occurrences, which seemed to wake him whenever he started to dream.

In the morning he woke up tired but remembered the bizarre dream about the key. *It clearly meant something,* he thought. *But what?* His mind circled around the cryptic images. *The key seemed filled with power. But power to do what? And what did it mean that it looked like Dryados?* He lay in bed for some time thinking. But the more he thought about it, the more confused he became. *I will need to talk to the elders about it at the next fellowship meeting,* he thought. *They will know what it means and what to do.* He rolled quietly out of bed to go to the toilet. Then he grabbed his arm brace off the shelf and started the process of strapping it on.

The wind whipped the curtain straight out from the rod. *Whoosh! Snap! Snap! Shooo!* The fabric danced horizontal in Dryados's bedroom. The tail of the curtain lashed out, slapping a small figurine off Alesia's nightstand, hurling it across the room. *Crash!* It broke into a hundred pieces on the bedroom floor. Dryados jumped to his feet. He grabbed the kukri from its spot on top of the nightstand. He stood panting, with the curved blade held high and ready to strike. "Dryados, it's just the wind." Alesia put her hands to her enormous stomach and rolled over in the bed. "I've been up for hours." She rolled to her side and sat up. "I have to go pee an—"

"Don't move. There is broken pottery all over the floor. Let me go get the broom." Dryados put the heavy metal blade back to rest on the nightstand and tiptoed out to get the broom.

He returned a few moments later. "Alesia…where are you?"

"I'm in the bathroom. Our baby has been up all night kicking my bladder."

"Stay there for a minute, and I'll get this all cleaned up."

Alesia waddled out a few minutes later. "I hope today is the day. I am so ready to have this baby."

"Ha-ha." Dryados chuckled. "Well in another two months, you will get your wish."

Alesia plopped back into the bed. "Can you just rub my back?"

Dryados gave her a small kiss on her neck and then gently began rubbing her back. He would tell her about the dream in the morning. In a few moments they both drifted back to sleep.

Chapter 29

Cherries on Snow

Parceida's mercenary army, the forests outside of Philadelphia

"Can't sleep?"
There were about a dozen men gathered around the fire. Two or three sharpened their swords. Others drank tea or snacked on things from the supply wagon. One stared blankly into the red coals at the base of the campfire. They all rose to their feet to greet their leader.

"No, no. Sit down. I have a hard time sleeping the night before a big battle as well." He flung a large wineskin toward the men. "That will help you sleep." One of the men caught the wineskin in the air. He popped the top off and took a swig. "No, not like that," the leader scoffed. "At least make a show of it." Sargon walked over, retrieving the wineskin he had just tossed to the men. "Now let's see who can get the best distance." He held the wineskin in the air and shot a stream into his mouth. Then he slowly backed the wineskin away. Farther and farther until at last it was a full arm's length away. His men rose to their feet. Wine dribbled off Sargon's face as he tried to drink down the rapid flow of wine. "Aaaahhh!" Sargon held the wineskin up like a well-earned trophy. "There boys—like that!"

He tossed the wineskin back to a stout man with a scraggly black beard. Muffled cheers rose from the others by the fire. The man shot a similar stream into his mouth and quickly extended his arms, repeating his commander's feat. "That's the way, man! That's the way!" Sargon took a seat on one of the logs near the fire. "Today is going to be a glorious day. By this time tomorrow, we will have killed a lot of Romans and become filthy rich in the process."

The man who had been staring into the fire now held the wineskin. He held it like a lost boy holding on to his favorite blanket and drank from it a great length. Sargon had seen that look many times.

"And the Laodiceans…what fools. 'Take fifty,' they said. 'Rely on the other forces,' they said. Now that is a good way to get yourself killed." Sargon leaned back by the fire. "Here is a lesson, boys. Do not rely on anyone but your own army and its sharp swords. Trust in the fury of the men you know and the heartlessness of their souls. That is how to achieve victory in every battle we fight. And that is why we have gathered an army of over nine hundred cruel men like yourselves." The small glimmer of a smile started to form on his face. "Perhaps the Laodiceans are right. But 'perhaps' is not how we fight. If the Laodiceans are correct and all the other forces they have promised arrive, then we might very well take the city. If not, then we will sure as heck make a big dent in it." Sargon had an infectious grin, and the men's faces soon reflected his victorious glow. "And no matter what, we are going to kill a lot of those scum Romans and carry off half the wealth of the city." The men at the fire beamed with confidence. The wineskin was being passed around like a drunken bar maid. Sargon rose to his feet. "Try to sleep, men, if you can. We will have a lot of spoil to carry away tomorrow, and you will need to be rested."

Sargon went back to the quartermaster's stores and got another wineskin. There were still many more campfires he needed to visit before dawn arrived.

Dryados's villa at the Acropolis of Philadelphia

Dryados woke up and snuck out of bed. Alesia had been up most of the night again. Now she lay deeply asleep. He crept quietly down to the kitchen. The cooking staff were already busily at work. "I want a lovely breakfast of fruit, bread, and some cheeses taken up to her as soon as you hear her stirring. Have some of those honey chips on the side, and some flowers. Let have her breakfast in bed." Dryados looked around the kitchen. "And make some of that sweet tea out of those…flower things…you know the ones she likes. Maybe that will help her back."

"Yes, Master Dryados. The chamomile tea is her favorite," answered a motherly cook.

Dryados wolfed down some bread and cheese and then walked into the backyard. He grabbed his small pruning knife and picked up trimming the grape bushes right where he had left off. He had come to love the simple peace he found in working the garden. He looked over at his ever-present companions, the ceramic fox, hound, and baby fox. *I really hope it is a girl*, he thought. The morning was still cool. He could see the outline of the road approaching the city. No caravans would be arriving this early. It would be midafternoon at the earliest. He looked down to see the first caravan starting to leave the caravanserai. It had a long stream of heavily loaded camels. *Probably Persians from Susa*, he thought. He worked in the garden for another hour as Alesia slept in. He heard the scurrying of the servants that announced she was awake. He put his tools down and raced to the bedroom to help her up. She was still there when he arrived. He reached over to give her a helpful tug out of bed. There were some grunts and groans as she rolled onto her side and flung her feet out the side onto the floor. Dryados waited patiently.

"Whatever I do these days has turned into a process, not an event," she said with a grunt. Once she tottered to her feet, she turned and hurried down the hall to the toilet. Her steps were much more determined these days, but not always successful. She came back a few moments later.

Dryados wrapped his hand around her back to help steady her. "Can I help you back to bed? I told the servants to serve you breakfast up here this morning."

"No. But thank you for letting me sleep in. I was up so much last night. And then there was that whole thing with the wind blowing things around."

"I barely remember any of that," Dryados said, shaking his head. "I was back to sleep in less than a minute."

Alesia looked out at the bright day. "Dryados, I know it is still early, but how about we eat in the backyard."

"Great idea. I had a little bit to eat earlier, but I could use a snack. It'll be fun. I'll have the servants get things ready."

The road from Pergama to Thyatira, past midnight

"By columns of three!" The centurion spun on his horse as he tried to hold his position beside the road. The horse whinnied and stomped at the clamor of the passing army. "Pass the word to the regiments in the back to hold in place. The road has narrowed again."

The centurion heard his command relayed down the long line of soldiers. Finally there was the familiar sound of Roman trumpets far to the rear, sounding the troops there to a halt.

"Torches on columns to the left!" barked the centurion. His horse bucked, trying to escape the close quarters of the marching army.

The torches in the marching columns were passed to the soldiers on the left. The light shifted to better illuminate the deep cliff extending to the river below. The sounds of the cascading waters were completely drowned out by the trudging tumult of the battle-clad soldiers.

"Columns of three to the quick step, and pick up your feet to reduce the dust for the men in the back!" As the company of men narrowed into columns of three across, the men sped up to a slow jog. "Remember what your commanders have instructed you—you will not speak of your orders once you are in the city.

You will not talk among yourselves. You will not speak to the locals. There must be no warning given. We will strike together at noon. Now pick up those feet!" The columns of soldiers jogged by on the quick step.

As one flight of soldiers passed, the centurion nudged his horse up the base of the hill on the right side of the road, hoping to get out of the way and above the growing cloud of dust. He repeated his instructions over and over again as flights of soldiers passed him in endless columns of threes. "Remember what your commanders have instructed you. You will not speak…"

After about an hour of reiterating the same warning, neat rows of mounted cavalry began to pass. The centurion issued the warning to their commander and then sped off to regain his position near the front of the advancing army. Beyond the narrow canyon the road widened quickly. The soldiers returned to columns twelve across and slowed down to a normal long-march pace.

The centurion rode up to join his general's retinue at the front. "All the soldiers have been instructed again on the need for secrecy when we arrive. I have issued the warning personally."

"Well done. Well done. I have sent riders ahead to inform the guards at the gate of Thyatira of our impending arrival. We will time our arrival to occur precisely at sunrise, when the gate is opened. As we enter, the men will disperse throughout the city. They will ask their questions. They will congregate near their targets. They will stand a post as if doing guard duty. Then at the sounding of the second watch, we will strike. While the men disperse across the town, I will seek to recruit the local units. Only when they have joined us will they be informed of our objectives. The governor wants no mistakes. We will burn any inconvenient evidence before we depart back to Pergama."

Main gate of Thyatira

The city gate of Thyatira opened as it did every morning, right at sunrise. As the gate flung open, a gallantly clad general and his entourage of commanders entered the city. They spoke quickly to the gate officer. They showed him copies of their orders with the governor's seal. They specifically pointed out the written instructions for absolute silence, discretion, and calm. The officer spoke quietly to his men. As he did, he looked out the gate to the open field in front of the city. A large column of soldiers marched quietly in. There were no trumpets. No drums of war. Not even the sound of centurions barking orders. Just the subtle thumping of thousands of clad boots. Some of the soldiers had wrapped rags around their spears to prevent them from making noise against their shields. Unless someone stood on the wall looking out, it was just another ordinary day for the city.

The general in charge of the city's troops arrived quickly at the gate to review the orders personally. "No, some of my units could not be counted on to participate in this undertaking. Even if I threatened to decimate them myself." The city's commander studied the orders. "They are Roman soldiers, but I can see conflict arising within the ranks from such an order. All the units recruited from here in the city will need to be dispatched out of the area immediately. We can call it a training exercise. I will only keep those troops transferred here from outside the area. I will make the arrangements immediately." The general was quickly back on his horse and galloping back to the barracks. The sound of the horse racing up the cobbled streets was the loudest noise in the city.

The entry of the army into Thyatira appeared well rehearsed. As each unit entered, the commanding centurion made hand signals directing the soldiers down the appropriate street. The city's roads were assigned sequentially. No one said a word. No verbal commands were ever issued. The soldiers peeled off in different directions. None of the roads appeared inundated. By the time it came for the next unit to proceed down a particular road, the one in front of it was already out of sight. Their deployment was perfect.

Ascalon's home on the outskirts of Thyatira

Sperta got out her mop. Lautus had spilled half of his breakfast all over the white tile floor. The other half was smeared all over his face and clothes. "I have no idea how this child survives. None of his food ever seems to find its way into his mouth." Sperta reached over and gave Lautus a kiss. "Still, he is mommy's little man." She rung out the mop and cleaned the last bits of mush off the white tile floor. Some of it was already congealed, and she had to get down on her knees and give it a good scrub. "There we go. Clean enough to eat off…and you, my little man, often do, don't you? You little cutie pie." Sperta looked up at Lautus's smiling face, got up, and gave him another kiss. Then she started to clean off his face. "Ascalon, can you help change his clothes before you go?"

Ascalon came around the corner. He already had his work clothes on and his forked arm brace lashed in place. "Of course. Besides, it will give me a chance to practice with my new brace. I have been forging the tips finer and finer as my co-ordination improves. Here, you can even time me this time as I change his diaper." Ascalon pulled Lautus out of his chair and took him to the back room to change the diaper. "OK, when I say go, you start counting." Ascalon placed Lautus in the center of the counter. He got everything he needed and positioned it all so he could get to it quickly. "OK, ready…go!"

Sperta stood in the living room, smiling. "One…two…three… You know, my mother changes his diaper faster than you."

"Yes, she does, but she raised eleven children. This is my first. Just keep counting..."

"Thirty-seven, thir—"

"Thirty-seven! What do you mean, thirty-seven?"

Sperta laughed. "OK, where was I? One...two..."

"No, don't start over. I'm serious. I want you to time me." Ascalon's hand worked as fast as he could. The one point on his brace was now sharp enough to catch the fabric and pull it over to the other side. Fastening the pin was still the hard part. He had to be very, very careful not to let the cloth slip off the tip of the sharpened brace. "Almost...almost," he whispered softly as he made a funny face at Lautus. Then he screamed, "Done!"

Sperta came running in. She looked at the changed diaper. Lautus stood up on the counter. The diaper held. She reached over and gave Ascalon a deep, passionate kiss. "The doctors said you would never be able to do something like that." She ran her hand through his hair. "I will have a special reward for you later tonight after Lautus goes to bed."

Ascalon swept Lautus up in his good arm and held him up proudly. Then he shook his head. "I don't know...he looks really wide awake. I think today would be a great day for him to skip his nap." Ascalon wore a boyish grin.

Sperta groaned and grabbed her son. "That's terrible. I think you need to be getting off to work. And we will just see what happens tonight." She turned away, bouncing her young boy up and down as she carried him down the hall. "No nap? What was he thinking? Look at mommy's little man..."

Ascalon packed some dried meat and cheese for his lunch. He threw in a couple of cake rolls that had been sitting in the cooking area, and some fruit. He was going in much later than usual. He walked to work along the same route he took every day. The sun was getting high in the sky. It was a beautiful day.

Parceida's mercenary army on the road just outside of Philadelphia

"We need to look like merchants. No weapons. No Armor. Only the men riding on the perimeter can have any weapons out in the open." Sargon rode up and down the makeshift caravan. "Once we have Philadelphia's gate secured, horsemen can race into the city from the nearby forest. Until then, I don't want one fighter or horse seen on the roads. Horsemen will stay in the forest." Sargon inspected one of the wagons. "Tie more cooking pots to the sides. And for crying out loud, get some smaller men to drive in front. You men are too big to be merchants. Get in the back with all the others."

The two large men chuckled at each other. "We don't fit. It's packed like fish in a barrel back there."

"That may be true, but the two of you are much too frightening to be seen by some timid Roman soldiers before the fighting breaks out. After that, you can scare them to death." Sargon flashed his victorious smile. "How you do that is up to you. But until then, in the back you go." The men shuffled out of the front of the wagon and into the back. A few moments later two men of far more modest frames shuffled into the front to take their place.

"We be the tiniest men back there, Lord Sargon. So they sent us up to drive."

"You two will do nicely. Just act like you're on your way to sell some pretty dresses, and everything will be fine." The men climbed into the wagon and slid their swords beneath the bench.

Sargon rode back up to the front of the long line of wagons. There were several strings of loaded mules scattered among the caravan to enhance its realistic appearance. He brought his horse to a stop alongside the first few wagons. Then he spoke with the same inspiring tone he had used when he was a general in the Roman legions. "You men in the front are the tip of the spear. You will be the ones who determine if we are successful today or not. Kill anyone in your way. Get to the gates and portico winches, and hold them. If the gates close, you will be alone and you will die. If the gates stay open, you will live and we will take the day." He rode a little farther back. "The rest of you men, the initial goals are simple. You will kill anyone you see. Anyone. Old, young, women out shopping, or children playing. It doesn't matter. Do not try to sort it out. It will just slow you down and leave people alive who will ultimately get in the way. Kill anything that walks on two feet. You will get no quarter from the Romans, so give none to her people." Sargon pulled back hard on the horse's reins and kicked it forward at the same time. The horse flew back on its hind legs, kicking in the air. It had the dramatic effect he sought. "We will take spoil and load the wagons to the cover tops once we have secured the area. If any man stops to rape or take plunder before that, I will kill him myself." Loud raucous cheers rose from his men. Sargon turned and rode to the first wagon in the lineup. "Drivers, kill the first ones with your knives. Then get the wagon through the gate. You men in the back of the wagon, once inside, take the gate and the winches. That is your only job. Take the gate! I will be right beside you." Sargon rode to the back of the first wagon, took off all his battle armor, and threw on a loose-fitting old cloak. He had two old swords attached to the saddle in plain view, like one would expect for any caravan warder. He secured his horse bow and quiver of arrows on the rump of the stallion right behind him and then rode several yards off to the left. He glanced up and down the long row of wagons. Everything looked right. Then he nodded confidently at the first driver. The inexperienced teamster whipped the horses harshly. The horses brayed and kicked and then lurched chaotically forward. The rest of the caravan jerked forward in succession. The wagons were old and worn, the heavily used look one would expect from wagons that had just completed the same arduous journey. And as it were, these had. They were all part of the same caravan the mercenaries had taken two months earlier. They had killed its previous occupants and stolen everything, including the clothes off the dead bodies. Sargon had used the coin from the sales of all the merchandise to help recruit and arm his current larger army. Except for a few large blood stains on their tunics, everyone looked their part.

Dryados's garden inside Philadelphia

"OK, 'Talmun' is a given if it is a boy. But what if it is a girl? What would you like to name her? I feel bad about hogging the boy name." Dryados rubbed some cheese on the hot bread and took a quick bite.

"You are not hogging the boy name. 'Talmun' is the name we both want. Talmun is your brother and will always be a part of our family." Alesia leaned back in her chair and let the sun shine on her face, thankful to just sit in their backyard. She slowly rubbed the sides of her stomach. After a moment, she looked back hesitantly at her husband. "If it is a girl, I would like the name to be 'Justinia' after my cousin. She is the sweetest and most gentle person I know."

Dryados rolled his eyes. "Yes, she is very nice. But have you ever gotten into an argument with her or debated an issue with her? I remember her from the wedding. She is one of the most pigheaded people I have ever met. Very thoughtful. But she will not concede a point if her life depends on it."

"She is not pigheaded. She is determined and decisive." Alesia leaned forward and drank some of the cool cherry juice the servants had just laid on the table. "In fact, she reminds me a lot of you. That is why I thought it would be such a perfect name."

Dryados smiled. "I actually enjoyed our debate. And seriously, she is just like you—too smart for her own good." Dryados walked over and gave Alesia a small kiss on the top of her head. "Besides, I also know a Justinia here in town who makes great roasted chicken, so I love the name." He smirked.

Alesia looked up. "So Justinia it is?"

Dryados smiled down at his wife. "So Justinia it is." He walked slowly to the back wall of the garden and looked out over the city and the cultivated plains. The late morning sun was well into the sky. He sipped on his cool cherry juice like it was an expensive wine. He always enjoyed the view. Then he stopped. "That's strange."

"What's that?" Alesia continued to lie in her chair, enjoying the warmth of the sun shining on her face.

"There is a caravan approaching the city." Dryados sounded confused.

"So what's so unusual about that? There are always caravans coming and going from the city."

"No, there aren't," Dryados said firmly. He laid his cherry juice down and leaned over the garden wall, trying to get a better look. "The caravans leave in the morning and arrive in the late afternoon. In order for that caravan to arrive now, it would've had to spend the night out in the open. No caravan master would do that. They would force their caravan forward to the protection of the city and the caravanserai no matter what. Something is terribly wrong."

Alesia continued to relax at the table with the sun on her face. The servants shuffled the dirty dishes off the table. Dryados stayed by the wall, watching the approaching caravan. It was still about two hundred yards from the city gate. "There!" Dryados spun around, trying to get Alesia's attention. "The caravanserai has raised its orange flag!"

"What orange flag?" Alesia started to rub her stomach but otherwise made no effort to leave her comfortable spot.

"The orange closure flag. They raise it every evening fifteen minutes before they close the caravanserai for the night." Dryados turned back, looking out over the wall. "They are going to close the caravanserai! They know something is wrong, and they are not going to take any chances."

Alesia slowly forced herself up out of her chair and waddled over to the back wall.

"Look!" Dryados raised his hand, pointing at the caravanserai in the distance. "You can just barely see the people scurrying to get in before the caravanserai closes the gates."

The caravan continued to head straight toward the main entrance to the city. The caravan was less than one hundred yards from the city. The orange flag above the caravanserai was quickly lowered and a red one raised up in its place. Other red flags started to be hoisted from the other caravanserai towers. Dryados frantically pointed to the caravanserai in the distance. "They've locked it down! They've locked it down! No one is going in or out." The caravan continued slowly forward.

"There!" Dryados shouted. "Look at the caravanserai watchtowers. See the movement there and along the catwalks? They are posting their archers." Dryados shook his head. "They are taking this very seriously."

Several long silent moments passed as the two continued to watch. The caravan was now less than fifty yards to the city. Dryados started to shake his head. "Something is very wrong. That caravan should have made its turn to the caravanserai long before now."

"Maybe they have seen the red flags and decided to just go directly to the city?" Alesia said questioningly.

"No, that is not how it is done. Even if the red flags are up, the caravan is to proceed to the caravanserai to be inspected and then cleared to enter. You can't have giant caravans plugging every road in the city." Dryados glanced over to Alesia. "These protocols have been in place for centuries. They were established by the Persians when the first caravanserai systems were built. Every merchant who has ever been on a caravan knows all of that." His eyes darted back out to the approaching caravan. It was less than twenty yards from the city gate. He glanced back at the caravanserai. "Look! Look! See there…the black smoke coming from the top of the walls of the caravanserai?"

Alesia looked up in shocked confusion. "Is the place on fire?"

Dryados raced to the far corner of the garden to get a better look. "No, no… they have lit their oil and tar kettles. This is not a drill or practice run or just being cautious. They are getting ready to fight!" Then he shot back to where he was standing before. He pointed frantically to the city gate. "The Romans don't see it! They don't see it!" The front wagon of the caravan was less than ten yards from the main gate. Dryados watched in terror. The caravan's perimeter horse guards were now trotting toward the front wagons. "No! No! The horse guard stays in place until the last wagon is secured! This is a trap. They're going to attack!"

The attacking mercenary wagons, Philadelphia

Sargon rode alongside the front wagon. "Now when we come around this corner, the caravan will be visible to the watchmen in the city towers. I will return to my post there, off to your left. Remember, get your wagon in as fast as you can to clear the path behind you so the others can storm in. Then take the gate. Just keep saying that over and over and you will do fine. 'Clear the path. Take the gate. Clear the path…take the gate…'" Sargon nodded to the drivers.

"You men in the back got that?"

A loud "Clear the path…take the gate" resounded from the troops hidden in the back.

"Good. And just remember, this is a rich city. When we are done, we will all be kings and lords." Sargon kicked his horse and rode to the perimeter. He made sure his swords were loose and ready. He threw a loose blanket over the horse bow behind him. Now all he could do was wait.

The caravan moved slowly forward. Sargon could see the driver of the first wagon continue to glance toward him, but he ignored him. The slow pace they were going was perfect.

Sargon tried to smile. If anyone on the distance caught a hint of his face, they would see the joy of a man arriving at his destination. And if his own men saw him, they would see he was happy and that everything was going according to plan.

About two hundred yards out, orange flags shot up the towers of the caravanserai. He gritted his teeth. He had no idea what it meant. But it meant something. And whatever it was, it was bad. Still, there was nothing he could do. He rode on at the same slow, steady pace.

The driver of the first wagon looked over at him in panic. Sargon smiled and nodded. *All part of the plan*, he thought. *All part of the plan*. Obviously it was not. But the dice were cast. All he could do now was act as confidently as he could and pretend to be in absolute control. *Slowly, slowly…*

At a hundred yards, red flags replaced the orange ones. He clenched his jaw. Whatever it was, it was more bad news. He had seen the people scurrying around the entrance to the caravanserai. Now those outside seemed to be fleeing toward the city. The caravanserai was obviously locked down. The front wagons would get to the city gate before any of the people did, so that would be OK. But two hundred of the soldiers in the back had been assigned to take the caravanserai by surprise. That clearly was not going to happen. Hopefully the commander of those units would realize it was a lost cause and bring his forces to join in on the assault of the city. He glanced at the city gate. There was still no response from the Romans. Either they had not seen the activities at the caravanserai, or they were like him and had no idea what they meant. In either case, they were still completely unprepared.

Twenty yards. Smoke started to billow up from the towers of the caravanserai. The Romans took notice. Several of the city guards walked outside to look at the billowing smoke.

Ten yards. The people from the caravanserai were rushing toward the city guard. The Romans signaled for the people to slow down and not to rush the gate. One of the soldiers pulled his sword and began signaling for the people to stop.

Five yards. A fight broke out as the frightened people tried to enter the city. Several of the Roman guards rushed out to help their outnumbered comrades. No one paid any attention to the caravan. Sargon smiled and started to ride toward the wagons. *Perhaps we will get lucky*, he thought. The old caravan plodded to a stop.

One of the drivers slowly climbed down and waited for the Roman soldiers to approach him.

The two guards remaining at the gate continued to watch the small melee as the other Romans formed a line holding back the frightened people fleeing from the caravanserai. Most were foreign and spoke no Greek or Roman tongue. After a moment, the two guards walked over to the dismounted driver. One of them held out a calloused hand. "Papers!"

"Of course." The driver turned, smiling at his friend in the front of the wagon. He calmly slid his hand under the buckboard in front, grabbed his sword, and gave a slight nod to his partner. The other mercenary pulled his knife from his sleeve and smilingly nodded back. The driver took a deep breath…and then spun. His sword hit the Roman low in the gut, just beneath his armored chest plate. The impaled Roman reached for his belly. The driver jerked up hard on the blade and drove forward with his shoulder. At the same instant, the other mercenary leaped from the wagon. His knife blade stabbed deep into the side of the second Roman's neck while he was still looking at the small melee outside the city wall. The slender blade rose and fell mercilessly on the Roman's throat.

The sounds of the fight signaled the men in the back to join the attack. They flung the tarp off the wagon and jumped to their feet. Their bows were already nocked with arrows. The first volley fell on the Romans on the ground trying to hold back those fleeing the caravanserai. Some of the arrows struck the Romans. Some hit the people. It didn't matter. Before any of them had fallen to the ground, another volley hit their ranks.

The driver spun, tugging his sword from the dead Roman, and scrabbled back up into the wagon. "Hhyaahh! Hhyaahh!" He lashed wildly at the now frantic horses. Chaos exploded all around. The wagon shot into the city. Some of the men in the back were jumping from the wagon, while others clung on for dear life. A handful of men on the ground raced toward the wounded Romans outside the wall. The drivers of the other wagons slammed the reins on their horses. Frenzied mercenaries leaped from the line of wagons and poured wildly into the city. Sargon raced to the courtyard inside the gate. He grabbed his small horse bow from under the blanket and began to unleash a stream of arrows. Bolt after bolt slammed into unprepared flesh. The horse bow did not have great range, but it was deadly accurate in the closer quarters of a heated battle. People fell before him like wheat. Scared civilians running for their lives or brave Romans stupid enough to stand and face him. It didn't matter. Sargon was soon nearly out of arrows. He saw a young lad quivering in fear in one of the alleys, trying to hide behind a small pushcart. He used the last arrow to kill the quaking youth. The last of the wagons sped inside through the now billowing dust, smoke, and turmoil. Volley after volley of arrows rose from the speeding wagons and mercenaries on the ground to kill the Romans still on the parapets.

Blood quickly filled the courtyard. The mercenaries followed their orders to the letter. They killed anything on two legs. No quarter was given. The children who had been playing in the courtyard were as dead as their mothers who were out shopping nearby. All were slaughtered without hesitation. The gate was quickly secured.

Sargon's experienced eye appraisingly scanned the mayhem from atop his horse as his men quickly regrouped. He raised his blood-drenched sword as he barked his commands. "I want fifty men down that street to the south. Kill anything that moves." His horse snorted and spun nervously from the raucous noise and pungent scent of fresh blood. He jerked hard on the animal's reins to bring it back to a halt. "And I want fires! Lots and lots of fires! That will distract the Romans, panic the populous, and give them all something else to fight other than us. Burn it down! Burn it all down!"

Sargon kicked his horse and raced to one of his commanders just outside the gate. Sweat was already pouring from his brow. "Tell the men outside to abandon any assault on the caravanserai. They are to join the fight inside the city. I want at least two hundred men kept at this gate at all times. This gate is our exit point from the city. Archers to the rooftops and parapets. When the Romans arrive, I want them to know they are fighting one of their own."

He looked up for a moment, glancing at the horizon. "It is clear the Laodiceans have betrayed us. There are clearly no other forces attacking the city as we had been promised." His horse whinnied and kicked at the dirt. "This was all probably a ploy to get vengeance on me for slaughtering all their troops on the plain of Decapolis all those years ago." Sargon smiled and gave a little chuckle. "Still, we will make the best of it. And maybe we can get the Laodiceans off my back in the process." He looked west. "I want four hundred men with me. We will attack the Acropolis, kill their aristocracy, and rob the treasury!" He looked sternly at his commander. "I want to be out of the city in three hours, four at the absolute most."

Inside the city of Philadelphia, at the Acropolis

Parceida's men walked casually to the agora one or two at a time. It was early morning. They blended in with the crowds. None wore armor. None carried swords. They all had several knives tucked into their tunics. Their initial plan was to bring their swords concealed in blankets thrown over their shoulders. But since their arrival in the city, they had devised a far less risky plan. As the sun rose slowly in the cool morning sky, they gathered near a familiar sword-maker's shop near the center of the agora. He was exceptionally well skilled at his craft. His swords were known as the best blades in the region. Very expensive. The men had been there several times before and had each picked out the blade they desired.

Now they waited. Some milled about looking at the amazing array of merchandise. A few made sport by arguing with the merchants over the price of some article they knew they would never buy. Some sat, eating street food. They all acted surprised when the first alarms were raised. Trumpets began sounding throughout the city. At first the melody was the same throughout Philadelphia, a general alarm. Then the melody changed. It was a specific alarm announcing where in the city the attack was occurring. The men acted as frightened as the people around them. They pointed with looks of terror at the smoke rising to the east in the lower city. They gawked and muttered like everyone else as the Roman cohort from the garrison at the Acropolis marched passed in full battle array toward the main gate. Unlike the rest of the crowd, however, they did not flee back to their homes.

Soon the Agora was nearly empty. The fearful merchants quickly packed to leave. Parceida's men scanned the area. The Romans were all gone. It was time.

"Here, let me take a look at that." The sword merchant looked puzzled as the mercenary grabbed the fine blade and then held it up as if inspecting it.

"You can come back and look at it tomorrow," stammered the frightened merchant. He reached anxiously to retrieve the elegant blade so he could flee with the others. "I will be happy to…"

"*Aahhh!*" The mercenary lunged forward and ran the blade deep into the merchant's chest. The shopkeeper's eyes widened as he grabbed at the blade, moaning. The mercenary charged forward, shoving the dying man across his shop toward the stone wall in the back. A flurry of other blades rose into the air as the other mercenaries grabbed their selected blades. There were two other workers and one stray shopper still in the booth. Their looks of stunned confusion were met by the *swish* of long blades slicing through the air. The looks of confusion were still on their faces as their bodies careened to ground and four large pools of blood formed on the shop floor.

The other mercenaries outside quickly raced into the shop, grabbing their selected weapons. Their leader divided them into their four predetermined squads of six men each. A fifth squad was also supposed to be there, but the men were all missing. Their leader spoke rapidly. "We have one mission and one mission alone. We are here to kill this Master Dryados. We do not know exactly which house is his. But it is in this neighborhood here." Their leader pointed his sword at the expensive row of houses and villas behind them. "It is simple—kill everyone in the block. Once we have cleared the houses, we will join together on the other side. Then we will sweep back and loot everything we can carry. Do not slow down to grab a prize until we have completed the slaughter, or I will kill you myself. We have one objective. Butcher this Dryados fellow and get out alive. Anything beyond that is a bonus."

Dryados's villa at the Acropolis, near the agora

Dryados and Alesia stood at the back wall of the garden in stunned horror. The battle for the gate was already over. They were both dumbfounded by how quickly it had fallen. Now they stood and watched as more of the invaders poured in. Raiders sprinted across the field in front of the city from behind the hill on the other side. Horsemen galloped out from their concealment in the tree line.

"There are hundreds of them!" Alesia muttered in absolute disbelief.

"This is some foreign army…attacking the city!" Dryados stammered. "But who? Who would dare attack the might of Rome?"

"This is no foreign army, Dryados. This is a horde of ex-military, mercenaries, and bandits." Alesia moved a little over to the left. "Look there. The second group of horseman crossing the field. Look at the order and how they hold their weapons and shields. Every one of those men has been trained in the Roman cavalry." She stepped back away from the wall. "And whoever is running this assault was either a Roman commander or some sort of general." She looked out at the burning city. "We need to get to the strong room."

"No!" Dryados reached over to hold her hand. "We are at the Acropolis. No foreign army has made it this far into the city in over a hundred years. We are totally safe. We can just watch the fighting from here. The Romans have surely dispatched soldiers by now. This is going to be incredible to see."

"The city is under attack by an unknown force," Alesia said firmly. "They have come in significant numbers and are obviously well led. We need to arm our security forces and get to the strong room until this is over." Then she turned and started to walk determinedly into the house.

Dryados jogged over to catch up with her. "You have got to be kidding me! This is the chance of a lifetime. This has got to be one of the biggest attacks in the history of the city of Philadelphia. We have front-row seats…" Dryados pointed back at the view of the city below. "And we are well away from the fighting. It is perfectly safe. Come on—this is going to be great."

"No," Alesia scolded. She continued to walk quickly into the house.

Dryados ran in front of her and came to a stop, blocking her path. "OK, fine. Let's alert the house guard and have them go to arms. But we can still watch the battle from the garden." He looked at her imploringly with a growing smile. "If anything changes, then we can scurry into the strong room like good little mice."

Alesia stood there shaking her head. "Fine. But if they even get near the Acropolis, we go to the strong room and seal ourselves in. That is why we had the thing built, isn't it?"

"Yes, my love. Of course, and I will go alert the guards. You go back and tell me what I miss. Everything is going to be fine." Moments later Dryados returned. "The guards are alerted, and the house is secure. So what did I miss?" Dryados looked out at the smoke now rising in clumps farther to the south. His eyes grew wide. "They are burning the city…" His voice was full of dread. "That could spread quickly in this heat. We haven't had any real rain in weeks."

Alesia stood there straining to hear the Roman trumpets. "My father trained me to listen to the calls of the Roman bugles." She paused again as the horns blew in the distance. The wind blew her hair lightly as she concentrated on the melodies. "The main gate is fallen. So has the southern agora, the courtyard of Backus, and the bridge gate." Tears formed in her eyes.

Dryados stepped forward, wrapping his arms around her. "We are safe. The Romans will fend off the attack. Soon those trumpets will be sounding in victory." They both stared out at the rising smoke.

Suddenly the muffled sounds of distant battle grew instantly louder. The two could hear yells and screams coming from the street in front of the house. One of the servants dashed out the back door. "They are here! The raiders are here! On our street!" The servant raced back into the house. The small house bell began banging like an alarm. *CLANG…CLANG…CLANG…*

"Stay here! I'll be right back." Dryados gave her a kiss on the cheek. And nudged her back away from the house. "Stay here. You're safe."

"No…" Alesia reached to grab his arm.

It was too late. Dryados ran into the house. Alesia edged toward the back wall of the garden. There was a raucous clamor at the front of the house. The servants were screaming. She took a few steps toward the house. She could see people running inside. Everyone was yelling. Then suddenly, *CRASH! BANG!* Instinctively she jumped backward. She could tell the front door had been battered in. "Stop them! Stop them!" It was Dryados's voice. She wanted to run into the house. She thought of the baby she carried inside her. She started crying. She edged toward the back wall. She glanced around. There was no real place to hide. The house in front of her was now filled with the sounds of swords and men dying. She grabbed the curved pruning knife Dryados had just been using to prune the grapes. She stood there waiting to defend the baby inside her with her last breath. She could see the fighting inside being pushed closer and closer.

Dryados stumbled out of the house. He was covered in blood. He held his stout kukri in his hand. Alesia could see it too was covered with red. "Run!" he screamed. "Run!" But there was no place to go.

Everything seemed to suddenly slow. Dryados saw Alesia start to raise her finger, pointing behind him. He pivoted, clenching his blade. "Behind you! Behind you!" As he turned, he could see the raider just a few steps away. His sword was raised high above him. He saw movement as the blade dropped toward him. Dryados dove at the attacker's knees. It was a move AkAk had taught him. The assailant lashed out with his blade. But it was too late. His right knee broke backward as Dryados plowed his shoulder into the extremity. The swinging sword ripped through Dryados's tunic but met no flesh. The attacker toppled over Dryados and crashed to the ground face first, screaming. Dryados lay on the ground by the man's feet. The attacker fumbled for his sword. Dryados slammed his kukri into the man's nearest leg. He felt the crunch as the blade bit into the bone. The man screamed. Dryados raised the kukri again. He saw the glint of the man's raised sword.

Alesia did not hesitant. She had a weapon. The man crashed over her husband to the ground in front of her. She lunged. The man screamed. She saw the sword arch upward. She slashed the sharp pruning knife deep into the side of the man's neck. A large gaping hole ripped open. Blood sprayed across the fine white marble of the garden patio. The attacker's sword wilted in the air. She watched as Dryados leaped over the man's body and slammed his kukri deep into the man's chest. The attacker's body went limp.

Alesia crawled backward away from the corpse. She could see Dryados. He seemed frozen on top of the man's body. She watched as her husband pulled the dead man's head from off the ground and stared at his lifeless face. "*Aaahhhh!*" Dryados screamed, shaking the dead man's head. "What do you want! What did I ever do to you!" Then he let the raider's head fall back to the ground.

He looked over to Alesia. "They knew my name, Alesia. They were asking for me!"

There was a renewed burst of fighting from inside the house. There were more screams of death. Then an instant of silence. Dryados and Alesia froze.

"Barricade the door and the front windows!" They both recognized the voice.

"Stay here." Dryados started to move toward the house.

A large, bloodied Roman soldier stood in the back doorway. "Dryados…thank God." He walked out into the back garden. Fresh blood was splattered all over his armor. "I didn't think we would get here in time. Thank God."

"Cleopas?" Dryados let out a deep breath. "Thank God for you and your men." Dryados limped forward. Blood seeped from his left hip. "Thank you. I will be eternally grateful for—"

"The fighting is not over." Cleopas stepped forward, quickly examining Dryados's injury. "There are at least another dozen men out there on the road. I could only spare a squad of ten to try and mount a rescue. Now we are down to four."

"But how did you know? How did you know they were after me?"

"We intercepted a group of men headed for the agora. They looked out of place. My men arrested them and found them carrying a great stash of concealed weaponry. When they were brought to me, I questioned them. When I told their leader I was going to cut his head off, he just laughed. Once I had him strapped down to a chopping block and pulled my sword, he sang like a morning dove."

"You would not have cut the man's head off for looking out of place, would you?"

Cleopas looked blankly at Dryados. "He said they had been sent to kill you and that they had one other squad of six as backup. The city was under siege. I thought ten would be enough. Obviously the man lied."

Alesia interrupted, still panting to catch her breath. "What about the safe room? Can we make it there during the respite? It's on the far side of the house." She looked at Cleopas, still holding the pruning knife tightly in her hand.

"No, they will just burn you out. They are here to kill Dryados." He looked soberly at his friend. "You need to escape. I told you to make several other escape routes. Did you do as I suggested?"

Dryados shook his head. "Yes, but I don't think it will work now with Alesia pregnant." Dryados walked over and pulled a long, heavy, knotted rope from the small shed. He jogged over to the back wall. "Below is the park by the city's theater. We can hide there. But I don't think Alesia could climb down in her condition. And I'm not leaving her."

"You will leave or you will die." Cleopas took the rope from his hand and secured it to one of the stout pillars they had erected in the garden. Then he threw his weight against it. He looked up with a nod. "It will hold. I will cut the rope and toss it down to you when you are at the bottom." He looked at Alesia. He deliberately stared at her stomach for a moment and then looked up at her with imploring eyes. "For your child...*now!*"

Alesia grabbed the rope. "I can do it. Just help me to get started...here..."

Dryados grabbed her arm and helped steady her as she started over the back wall. *Bang! Bang! Bang!* The clamor of battle resumed at the front of the house. Cleopas glanced back inside. "The door will not hold them long. Dryados, you must jump as soon as you get close to the bottom."

"Let me stay...I can help you fight..."

"No, Dryados, you will only die with the rest of us. The men we have here will never hold them off. Now, go quickly." He waved Dryados toward the back wall.

Alesia rolled as she tripped off the rope at the bottom.

Dryados shot over to the wall. Cleopas grabbed him by the arm and looked him in the face, smiling. "Few men get to pick where they will die. I always loved this garden..." His smile widened more broadly. "And your friends in the corner." He nodded at the ceramic fox, hound, and their shy baby. "I will die well... go quickly now." Dryados raced down the knotted rope. Cleopas ran over and grabbed the baby fox ceramic. He ran back just as Dryados got to the bottom. "Here..." He tossed the ceramic companion. "Now run!" Cleopas spun, cutting the rope, and tossed it over the side in a single fluid motion.

Dryados caught the baby fox. From above them in the garden, they heard a violent *Rraaahhhh!* and then the crash of armor and swords. Dryados grabbed Alesia's hand, and they vanished into the woods.

Inside the city of Thyatira

It was a beautiful day. He was going in late, so there were a lot more people on the street than he was accustomed to. Ascalon smiled and nodded happily to the strangers he passed as he walked the familiar road to the smithy. He even found himself humming a praise song from the fellowship. He came around the next corner and stopped. Romans. A lot of them. His heart fluttered. He thought of turning and going the other way but decided it would look too suspicious. He took a deep breath and kept walking. *I am just a smith on my way to work. I have done nothing wrong. Just try to ignore them,* he thought. He walked past the gathered soldiers without incident. *Just keep walking…just keep walking…* He tried to calm his mind. His heart was still pounding when he rounded the final corner to the smithy. A dozen Roman soldiers stood guard in the alley. He continued forward slowly. Ascalon scanned the area where the soldiers stood. There was nothing of any importance anywhere around them. There was nothing to guard. *What are they doing?* It was strange. He picked up his pace and went straight into the smithy.

Ascalon put on his apron and stoked the forge. He kept a furtive eye on the Romans. The billows *whooshed.* The embers quickly jumped to life. He threw more wood on the fire. The squad of soldiers stood unmoving in the alley. He grabbed his hammer and pulled a metal rod from the stack along the wall. He shoved the rod deep into the coals and continued pulling up and down on the billows. With each blast, the furnace grew hotter. Soon the metal was red and malleable. He slammed his hammer hard into the glowing rod. *Bang, bang, bang.* A Roman short sword quickly took shape. He and his apprentice glanced nervously at each other as they watched squad after squad of Romans cross the square. "There has to be scores of them," Ascalon whispered. The apprentice nodded but was too nervous to speak. They watched as the Romans stopped and questioned everyone in the square…but did not detain any of them.

One of the women stopped by the Romans walked close to the smithy. Ascalon questioned her. "What did they want? Why are they stopping everyone?"

The woman shook her head in confusion. "They said they were doing a census. They asked if I was married, did I have any children, how old were the children, who took care of the children, where were the children now, and on and on. It was mostly about the young ones. Very strange." She looked over her shoulder cautiously at the increasing number of Romans in the square. "And another thing…I didn't recognize any of them. It's not that I pay any attention to the Romans, but after a while you do start to recognize some faces. I didn't recognize any of them. Then, when I told them of a woman I know who watches over a large number of children for the other mothers, I had to give them the directions several times. They had no idea of how the city was laid out." She glanced over her shoulder at the Romans, shaking her head. "It was all very odd. I'm going home." The woman turned and hurried away.

Ascalon doused the unfinished blade in the cooling bath and tossed it back in the pile. "I think I am heading home for an early lunch," he said to his men.

One of his workers chuckled. "Sounds like you have finally figured out this whole 'being the boss' thing."

Ascalon smiled at his fellow smiths and then went over and grabbed a carry-box of tools and his hammer.

"What's that for? I thought you said you were going home?" asked an apprentice.

"I am." He nodded at the workbox and hammer. "This is for the Romans, in case I'm stopped. This way I can just tell them I'm headed across town to fix a horse that's thrown a shoe. Nothing suspicious about that." Ascalon put a couple extra horseshoe rims in the wooden workbox. "After I leave, you men might want to take an early lunch as well. The Romans will see me leave. Workers taking an early lunch when the boss is gone will not raise their suspicion." Ascalon glanced over at the streams of Romans walking through square. "None of them seem to be in a hurry. That in and of itself is strange enough to get me worried. They are up to something. I strongly suggest you men leave as soon as I am out of sight." Ascalon grabbed the workbox and headed out. "Wish me luck."

He walked determinedly out of the square. The farther he went away from the business areas, the more frightened he became. His heart was pounding. Yes, there were extra Romans downtown, but they had actually amassed themselves in the residential areas. He tried to act inconspicuous, but no one else was stupid enough to be on the street at this point. He felt like a parakeet at a cat convention. Squads of Romans in groups of four or five dotted the roads. They seemed to stand nonchalantly in small formations, like they were guarding a section of dirt.

He watched as a crier walked casually up the street toward his watch post. The Romans dotting the area seemed to suddenly awaken from their stupor. At least one soldier from each Roman squad pointed or nodded at the crier. Hand signals were being made toward some houses nearby. The crier took immediate notice of all the attention that he was suddenly garnering. He stopped on the street and glanced at the scattered troops. He was surrounded. His eyes quickly darted around the street, looking for a route to flee his captors. There were too many. He froze. Still none of the Romans made the slightest move in his direction. The crier stood dumbfounded, clearly not knowing what to do. His eyes continued to race up and down the street at the amassed troops. He edged his way forward. The Romans remained motionless, but all their eyes were fixed on him. He walked slowly and then paused at the bottom of the raised crier's podium. None of the Romans moved. It looked as though they had stopped even breathing. He climbed the short flight of stairs with his eyes on the Romans. Ascalon kept his gaze riveted on the crier, who seemed to stare at the Roman's hands. Ascalon's glance followed the crier's.

He watched the hands of every Roman on the street slide silently to the pommels of their swords.

Ascalon stopped. Casually, he bent down and lowered the workbox to the ground. He grabbed the hammer inside. He saw an unguarded alley off to his right. He clenched his hammer tightly in his hand.

The crier stood atop the podium looking out over the scattered army. *This is bizarre*, Ascalon thought. It was as though the crier were a great general about to address the troops. Every soldier as far as he could see stood at attention with his hand on his sword, his eyes locked upon the crier.

The crier took a deep breath and sounded the noon hour.

The glint of a thousand swords suddenly flashed in the noon sun. Battle cries rang out in every direction. Ascalon sprinted across the street and down the alley. There were no soldiers. He glanced over his shoulder. None of the Romans had followed. Blood-curdling screams rang out all around him. He sprinted down the alley. The sounds of death and terror rang out all around him. Soon his side was starting to ache, and he couldn't breathe. He sank to the ground on the side of the alley behind a pile of refuse. *I am a smith, not a delivery boy*, he thought. He panted, catching his breath. Beyond the sound of the wind sucking into his chest, the air was tainted with living horror. It boiled with a symphony of anguish and loss. The cries around him were not the cries of men dying in battle. There was no clashing of the sword or shouts of charging men. These were the moans of hearts ripped in two by grief beyond measure. It was like being in the heart of death, surrounded by a thousand funerals.

Ascalon got back to his feet and fled down the narrow passage between the buildings. He intersected a road. What his eyes saw smashed into his consciousness. It was like an impenetrable wall. His legs stopped moving. He stood in the middle of the road, empty of all awareness except what his eyes beheld. It was the abomination of sacred innocence made incarnate. The Romans were killing the children.

He did not know how long he stood in the road. It could have been hours or seconds. He did not know. He watched wailing parents claw at the Roman soldiers as they carried the bodies of their children and threw them on a burning pile like yesterday's garbage. He watched as the mothers tried to pull their infants from the fire. Most were already dead. Most...but not all. He watched as the occasional mother or father was killed and thrown on the pile with their little ones. He still held his hammer, but he did not move. The Romans glared at him several times but seemed to sense he was no threat. He fell to his knees on the street. His mouth gaped open.

He kneeled there stupefied and panting. His hand instinctively tightened around the hammer. His mind jerked suddenly awake. "Sperta and Lautus!" He jumped to his feet and dashed down the road, running to his house. He slowed, then he sped up, shifting onto the side roads and in and out of alleys. He did whatever he had to do. He passed several of the burning piles. The foul odor of burning flesh filled his mind. He did not stop. He lived farther out from the center of town. Maybe the Romans hadn't gone out that far. Sperta had said it would be better for their family…

He made it to his own street. The same cries of anguish filled the air. There was a Roman standing at the front door of his home, looking inside. Ascalon crossed the path in the front in two strides. The Roman started to turn at the crashing of Ascalon's footsteps. Too late. Ascalon's hammer slammed down square on the roman's head. The metal of the helmet held. Ascalon thought it may have been one he had made himself. It didn't matter. The soldier's neck was crushed like a loaf of bread under a boulder. He fell where he stood. He uttered no sound. He simply dropped. The *thud* of the body sliding off the porch was drowned out by Sperta's screams coming from inside. Ascalon glanced in. There were three soldiers. He could barely see Sperta holding Lautus in the back of the room. One of the soldiers started to turn. Ascalon stopped and pushed himself back, hiding behind the doorframe. He heard the sound of boots running across the tile floor inside. He pressed himself to the wall, watching the door. The tip of a Roman spear, the shaft, hands, a shoulder… Ascalon pivoted, slamming the sharp tip of his arm brace into the midsection of the Roman exiting the front door. He was too close to swing his hammer. He reached around the Roman's back and tried to shove him to the floor. The Roman was strong. He roared and stood straight up, shrugging Ascalon to the side. The Roman reached to pull the tip of the arm brace from his impaled gut. As he did, Ascalon swung. The hammer slammed into the back of the Roman's left shoulder. The Roman staggered to the right from the impact. Ascalon leaped toward him. He didn't have time to raise the hammer. He slammed the point of the arm brace into the Roman's ribs. They crashed to the ground. They wrestled wildly in a flail of arms, blows, and blood. The Roman caught Ascalon with a blow to the chin. The world went black. In the blackness, he heard a cry from Lautus like he had never heard before. He was on top of the Roman. Lautus went silent. He slammed his fist into the Roman's face. Sperta wailed from inside the house. It was not a cry of injury. It was the wail of a mother whose heart had been torn asunder. It was the wail he had heard earlier on the street. The Roman now laid limp beneath him. Ascalon rolled exhausted off the Roman and grabbed his hammer. Sperta screamed again and again. Then she too went silent.

Ascalon charged. One of the Romans inside was kneeling on the floor over… there was blood everywhere. The other stood behind him. Ascalon's stride did not break. The first Roman turned. Ascalon hurled his hammer. It hit the surprised soldier square in the chest. As the wind was knocked from his lungs, he dropped his sword and stumbled backward. He began to trip over the Roman kneeling behind him. It made no difference. Ascalon crashed into both of them, sending them all tumbling to the ground. The last thing Ascalon did as he collided with the Roman was to grab his enemy's throat. As they fell, he ripped and twisted it with all the strength the years of working hard metal had given him. He felt the cartilage crack and pop before they even hit the ground. He felt the cartilage snap off at the top and the bottom inside the dead man's flesh. He dropped the lifeless body to the ground like a large rag doll.

Ascalon's war cry echoed down the street outside. A squad of soldiers in another home heard his roar. It was not the wail of the injured sheep. It was the roar of a predator come to challenge their claim for blood. Two of the soldiers drew their swords and raced toward the house.

Ascalon saw the glint of the arching sword to his left. He instinctively started to raise his arm. The blade slashed down. The last Roman was still pinned on the ground in the pile. It was a poor swing with little power. Most of the impact was taken by his arm brace, but his upper arm exploded in pain as the blade ripped through the muscle. He had no weapon. Ascalon dove at the wife killer with the veracity of an avenging husband. The only way his arms would halt his attack was with his own death. Ascalon felt his enemy punch him in the face and body. They were meaningless. The child killer would feel the essence of rage. The murderer clawed at Ascalon's face. It was as meaningless as the punches. *It is a terrible thing to fall into the hands of angry father or husband.* His only son had been cut down. His bride had endured the anguish of loss and then butchered. *It is a terrible thing indeed.* Ascalon punched and bit. He ripped and tore and strangled. He finally stopped when he heard yelling out front on the street. He did not know how long the guilty man beneath him had been dead. He really didn't care.

He crawled to his feet. He walked over to the bodies of his wife and son. He looked at the white tile floor Sperta had always tried to keep so clean. Both his wife and son lay there. Their blood had fallen upon it like cherries on snow. The blood of innocence. The blood of the future and hope and love and a thousand other things. All destroyed by men he did not even know. He knelt down, kissing them both. He retrieved his hammer. This is where he would die. He would wait and kill them all. He heard the men out front. They were waiting for reinforcements.

Time around him slowed. The Romans...they were so different from him. Their way was cruel and unjust. None cared for the world around them, or the poor, or weak. They were his enemies. Still, he had helped them. There were so many things they could not do on their own. He had helped them! He had seen their needs. Gone out of his way. Given it his all. Despite all that, they had murdered his son. They had tormented and killed his bride. This was insanity! Who were these men who thought themselves to be god?

Ascalon walked closer to the front door. He could attack now before their reinforcements arrived. He looked at his hammer covered in blood. He flexed his arm. His strength had returned. He could fight. But in the depths of his despair, he knew this was not the time. He wasn't sure why. He just knew it wasn't. The slayers of the innocent would die. It would just not be today.

He walked over and knelt back down by the broken bodies that had been his entire universe. He kissed each one softly on the head. "Good-bye, my loves… good-bye…" He rubbed his cheek softly against Sperta's face. He reached over and closed Lautus's still-open eyes. Tears rolled down his face. Then he fled out the back door, racing down the alley.

Chapter 30
Thorns and Manure

The park next to the theater, by Dryados's villa, Philadelphia

Dryados and Alesia raced through the brush. The sounds of battle raged around them. Roman bugles sounded in the distance. "There! In the thicket!" They paused and then shifted directions. Dryados reached over, shoving branches out of the way to help Alesia through the underbrush. "Here, let me get that…" Alesia stumbled forward through the thick vegetation, holding her stomach. Dryados sped ahead and dropped to his knees at the edge of the thicket. He pulled out his kukri from inside his tunic and frantically began to hack away some of the thorny branches. He pulled the loose debris free and shoved it to the side as he worked his way forward. His muscles were quickly fatigued. He slammed the kukri down again and again. Each exhausted attack at the brambles was accompanied by a louder and louder "Ahh! Ahhh! Ahhh!" His face dripped with sweat and was covered with clinging dirt and leaves. He hacked his way into the heart of the large thicket, making a narrow tunnel. Near the center of the briar, he cleared a wider area where he and Alesia could conceal themselves. "One more minute…" He pulled up the bottom of his tunic and used the kukri to cut off a long segment cloth. He laid the rag down and spread it out. "Here…" Alesia scrambled into the thorny bramble. Dryados took the pile of branches he had hacked off earlier and pulled them over the tunnel, sealing them inside.

Then they froze. Neither breathed. The silence of the serene park was shattered all around them by battle cries in the distance. Those raging at the Acropolis behind them were the loudest. They did not speak. In between war cries, they listened to the leaves shifting in the trees. They heard a small rabbit scamper across the forest floor. The sounds in the distance remained filled with tumult and death. Bugles sounded, mercenaries yelled, dying civilians screamed. The briar around them was thick and dense. They could not see beyond it. But the sky above them was filled with thick plumes of drifting smoke. Some of it came from directly behind them. The Acropolis was on fire. Perhaps it was one of the temples. Perhaps it was their own home. They did not know. Alesia laid her head on Dryados's shoulder and snuggled against him. Dryados quietly pulled the top of his tunic over her as best he could. They both closed their eyes and tried to rest.

Dryados kept the kukri in his hand. He focused all of his attention on listening to the forest around him. Like a man trying to see into a dense fog he knew was full of assassins. He did not move. There was the gentle movement of leaves and the occasional creak of swaying trees. Nothing more.

The blast of distant Roman trumpets jerked him back to the moment. Alesia squeezed him tightly but did not move. "The Romans are taking back the city," she whispered. "The invaders are retreating out the main gate, which they still hold."

Dryados remained motionless. "What are the Romans…"

"The trumpets say no more than that," she answered.

They both stopped talking. Time passed slowly. Roman trumpets occasionally blew in the distance. "The Romans are making progress. They have retaken the south agora," she said blankly. With each sound of the bugles, Alesia would quietly announce what more of the city the Romans had retaken. Then she would stop talking. The sun had gone down enough that they sat totally in the shade. They snuggled closer to fight the chill. Hours passed. It grew darker. Then the trumpets sounded a new tune.

Alesia sat up. "The city is retaken," she announced eagerly. "I think it will be safe for us to return home now." She started to straighten herself up and brush the debris off her clothing.

Dryados did not move. "They knew my name," he said stoically. "They knew where we lived, and they came specifically to kill me." Dryados looked up at her as he still huddled unmoving on the ground. "We should stay here till morning. It will—"

"I'm already getting cold."

Dryados sat up. "I know. I am too…and you are pregnant." He shoved a stray branch of thorns off his shoulder. "These assassins have gone to a great deal of trouble to kill me. If they think I might even remotely be alive, they will wait around and see if I show up. I think going back home right now is a mistake," he said blankly.

Alesia stretched out her leg. "My foot has fallen asleep, and the back of my leg is cramping." She looked at him with eyes of frustration.

"I can rub your feet and your leg. We can snuggle together and sleep here."

The look of frustration on her face did not change. Then she reached over and pushed his foot out of the way. "Fine. But I have to go pee." Alesia struggled back onto her hands and knees and started to crawl around him. "I will sneak out of here for just a minute. And while I'm doing that, you do whatever you can to make this place more comfortable or warmer or something…"

Dryados scooted in front of her and pulled away the stack of briars he had piled over the opening to conceal them. Soundlessly Alesia crossed the forest floor and did her business. Dryados snuck out and quietly garnered up several large piles of leaves and threw them inside the briar. Some he used to line the bottom of their small enclave. The rest they would use to cover themselves up to keep warm. Then he went over to the same tree Alesia had used and did his business. Once they were back inside, Dryados sealed them back in with the thorns.

Thyatira

Ascalon ran down the alley. The sounds of terror filled the streets around him. He had to think. He stopped in the alley near a stack of refuse tree branches and yard waste and hid behind the pile. *The Romans will know that I did it*, he thought. *That I am the one who killed those soldiers.* His life was over. They had killed his family. Now they would kill him. *Think…think…think…I can't go back home…* Ascalon glanced down the alley. Screams still echoed around him. He saw the occasional person dash across a section of the alley, but no one entered. *They will probably be waiting for me back at the smithy…* He glanced again. The alley was clear. *No, the whole city is in total chaos. If I go now…* He rose and started to run. His eyes scoured everything around him. *I have to clean myself up. I have to clean my hammer.* He glanced around as he ran. There was no water. They hadn't had rain in weeks. He came to an intersection. Just down the road was a horse trough. It was too far. There were no Romans. He thought about it…no, the horse trough was too far. He couldn't risk it. He sprinted across the road and down the alley on the other side. Cat and mouse, he worked his way back toward the smithy.

He got to the square and stayed in the narrow alleyway. He snailed his way forward, hiding behind whatever debris was big enough to conceal his large frame. There were Romans scattered around the square. They all had their swords or spears in hand. Across the way was the smithy. Most of his men were still there, corralled together near the main forges. They were under heavy guard. His workers were seated peacefully, chatting. It was clear they had no idea what was happening in the city. Many had families with small children. Ascalon backed slowly away. There was not even the remotest possibility of freeing his men. He quickly made his decision. *I will skirt around to the back of the smithy to the horse corrals. I will get what supplies I can. Then I will flee. Simple.*

Hours passed. Getting to the other side of the square was far more difficult than he had anticipated. *Move-hide-move-hide-wait…wait…wait…move-hide.* He was exhausted. It was already late afternoon.

He raised the old barn latch as quietly as he could. He crept into the barn like a mouse expecting the resident barn owl to swoop down and eat him. He moved slowly to the front. Sunrise, his favorite horse, looked out of its stall at him, waiting for its usual treat. The smell of the hay and darkened twilight of the inside of the barn made him feel much less tense. He reached for the bucket of apples nearby. Suddenly the front door slid open. Ascalon dove into the straw. "I think we can billet the men in here for the night. There's plenty of hay." A handful of Romans entered the barn. They walked slowly around, doing a cursory inspection. "Yes, this will do nicely. It may be a little cramped for all the men—"

"No," another interrupted. "We should reserve this for officers. There is plenty of room and—"

"The officers will commandeer the homes of the local aristocracy or some of the taverns. No, this will work well for the men. It will also be easy to secure. A few guards around the perimeter and this will be perfect. Instruct the men there will be no fires of any kind. Not even torches, for obvious reasons. If they need light, they can just keep the doors open."

The Romans continued their inspection as they milled out the back door. He was trapped. In a matter of hours, there would be troops sleeping on every piece of hay in the place. His heart stopped. The soldiers continued to linger at the back door. *Maybe I can slip out the front…* The mucking stall was on the other side of the barn by the front door. It was overflowing with horse dung. He had been yelling at his men for over a week to get the wagon and hall that stuff out of there.

He heard the soldiers still talking at the back. He dashed across the barn and dove into the manure-filled stall. He scurried through the warm pile of smoldering dung and peeked through the loose planks of the barn wall. The courtyard and smithy were crawling with soldiers. More soldiers were now walking toward the barn. He was out of time. He couldn't get back over to the other side or make it to any of the stacks of hay to hide inside. The soldiers were almost there. He scrambled over the pile of manure to the back side. He scraped into the manure pile and created a small shelf. Quietly, he lay down and then raked the horse dung over him like a thick blanket. He left a small opening facing the back wall so he could get some air to breathe, and settled in. Soon the barn was filled with the raucous noise of encamping soldiers.

Philadelphia

Dryados didn't move. Alesia was snuggled in his arms with her body pressed hard against him, sound asleep. He heard the loud crunching of leaves and breaking of fallen branches as a group of men came noisily up the hill. He held the kukri in his hand. He tried not to even breathe.

"Any place will do. This looks pretty good—at least it's flat," one said hoarsely.

The group stopped about twenty yards down the hill from the briar. Soon Dryados could see light mounting up from a small fire. There were perhaps eight or ten in the group. Behind the impenetrable wall of the thicket he could not make out any more detail than that. Different voices spoke out in the darkness.

"I'm starving. Anybody got any food?"

"Yes, got me a treasure trove right here. Stole it during the attack by them raiders. Even got me some bottles of wine too. Ha-ha-ha."

"Here, let me have some of that…"

Soon a small party broke out in the darkness of the hillside park. Dryados kept his hand wrenched tightly around his kukri. He stared down the hill, catching the occasional glimpse of the group as their small fire flickered in the darkness.

"I wish they would shut up and go to sleep," Alesia snapped quietly.

"Alesia, I'm sorry. I thought you were asleep. I think they are just some of the nameless people of the street. I don't think they will do us any harm. They probably sleep here in the park every night."

Alesia did not respond. They both lay silently, listening to the homeless people in the woods just below them. Soon enough the small party ended, and everyone in the park slept. Including Dryados and Alesia.

Thyatira

Fear kept Ascalon awake. The barn was full of Romans. At least they had no torches, so he was well concealed in the blackness of the manure pile. He could hear the voices of dozens of Romans talking nearby. He could see no faces.

"The men marched all night and spent the day butchering, stoking fires, and beating back or killing lamenting parents. They're starving," complained one soldier. He sounded like a Roman of at least moderate rank.

"Where's the quartermaster? Where are the food stores? I'm hungry myself," echoed another.

"We were dispatched quickly. Apparently there were no orders given to bring supplies. It was felt they would just slow us down, and we are supposed to be leaving tomorrow," spoke a third voice.

"Well, what are we supposed to do between now and when we get back to Pergama?" complained the first one.

"Forage. Our orders are to forage."

"Forage? That is the most %@*&# thing I have ever heard!" Ascalon could hear the soldier kicking the hay on the floor. "Fouled up beyond all recognition. Nothing ever changes. Couldn't bring a couple of wagons for support? This is so @#$&^$# stupid!" The soldier fell silent for a few moments. "Fine, we will forage. See that horse in the stall there. Take it outside. Gut it, and I want it cooked and ready to eat in an hour!"

"Yes, sir."

"And send some squads out to get some real food in case we end up stuck here longer than tomorrow."

"Yes, sir."

"And I want wine. Tell the men if they come back without some wine, I will roast them on the same spit as that spry horse."

"Yes, sir."

"Of all the %$@#*&$&…" The muttering faded as the angry commander walked farther into the barn.

Ascalon listened as Sunrise was taken from her stall. She was a gentle horse and followed along quietly behind the soldiers as she was led away. Silent moments passed. Sunrise was a big horse, strong and healthy. She was no old nag needing to be put down. Sunrise was in her prime.

Suddenly there was the billowing whinny of a horse. Men screamed. Ascalon heard Sunrise snorting and kicking. *Thud, bang!* Her hooves slammed into flesh, and a man crashed into the side of the barn. "Stop her! Stop her!" Her hooves pounded as she ran around the corral. "Archers! Archers, to me!" "Aaahhh!" Men screamed as they were pummeled by hooves of rage. "Where are the archers? Archers to me! Archers to me!" Sunrise galloped around the stall. "Get ropes. Get ropes! You there—use your spear!" Sunrise whinnied in agony. "Break her legs! Break her legs!" There was a final agonal whinny as she fell. He could hear the assault of the soldiers as they hacked her to death with their swords and spears.

Ascalon moaned with silent tears.

He begged just to sleep. To leave this place in his dreams. But sleep was slow to come. The noise in the barn was loud. The soldiers feasted greedily on the fresh meat.

Philadelphia, Sargon's mercenary forces, main gate

Mayhem raged around them as the mercenaries retreated out the gate. The yells of their retreat were as loud as the screams of their assault. The fires they had started had spread closer to their own positions, and now a thick black cloud of soot enveloped the area. Sargon snapped the reins on his horse. "I don't care about the men trapped at the south gate. I said we would leave no later than the fourth hour from our arrival. That hour has passed. We are leaving...*now!*" Sargon turned and roared at the soldiers around him on the ground. "Footmen, we will make one final assault on the Roman positions. As they regroup to launch a counterstrike, we will withdraw out the main gate. Archers will cover your escape." He spun again, facing the other commandeers. "The archers will stay at their positions on the rooftops until the footmen are out. Then they will be pulled out on horseback or in the last wagons. Mounted cavalry will cover the last phases of our withdrawal. Let the men know we will not leave them behind. But when I say withdraw, we withdraw!"

"Yes, Sargon." The words rose like a chorus from his troops and gathered commanders.

"Now, footmen—we attack!" Sargon yanked his horse around and raised his sword. "Yyahhhhhh!" The horse leaped wildly up the street.

The two hundred gathered footmen charged up the road at the oncoming Romans. The Romans' main contingent was trying desperately to form into a phalanx on the debris-strung street. But there was too much clutter in the close quarters of the road. The storming mercenaries drove over them like a great tide at the beach. Their blood-soaked armor lay side by side with the similarly red clothing of the dead citizens.

The footmen withdrew. The treasure wagons departed with them. The archers covered their retreat as ordered. Then, they too raced from the city. The Romans had pulled back and were regrouping just as Sargon had predicted. The cavalry covered the rear as the last of the mercenaries fled. The Roman forces were in a shambles. There were no Romans dispatched to harry their departure.

"That withdrawal was textbook! Absolutely textbook!" Sargon boasted loudly. "And since I'm the one who wrote the book, I would know." He pulled off his helmet and loosened his armor. "It is unfortunate about the soldiers at the south gate. But I had instructed their commander not to go that far. I had warned them we would withdraw without them if they were not back in time." He shifted in his saddle, looking at his commanders surrounding him. "There is a lesson here..." He smiled broadly. "Always listen to Sargon."

His retinue exploded into laughter and chanted his advice. "Always listen to Sargon. Always listen to Sargon..." They looked at the many wagons filled with treasure. Now all they needed to do was figure out a way to keep it.

It was dark before Sargon brought the wagons to a halt again. He had pushed the horses and his men to their limits. He gathered his commanders and as many men around him as could hear his voice. "The Romans have been after me for years. And there is one thing I can tell you—they will not stop. We will divide the spoil here and now. Once you have received your share, I suggest you push on through the night and travel hard all the next day. Carry your loot or hide it some-where along the way. It is up to you. But do not stop. Some of you may choose to stay on the road. You will be ahead of the news and cover more ground. But bad news travels quickly, so do not let it catch up with you. Others of you may choose to travel off the roads. You are less likely to meet up with the Romans, but you will not get as far. I leave those decisions up to you. My men and I will probably do a little of both. Finally, if the Romans take you alive, you will great-ly regret it. So I strongly suggest you spare the torturers their fun and kill as many of those scum as you can before you die. At least that way you deprive the Romans of their last bit of sport at your expense." He spun his horse around. "Great job, men!" He pulled back hard on the horse's reins, forcing the stallion to rise again to its back feet. It was his last flare of drama.

The spoil was quickly divided. They did far better than even he had expect-ed. They had made it to the Acropolis and robbed several temples. They had also made it into the outer holds of the main treasury. They had gold, lots and lots of gold. Some ingots were too big to carry on horses. They needed to keep the wagons. His army had no idea how much they had gotten away with. Still, Sargon could afford to be generous. He might need these men on his next cam-paign.

Sargon and his inner circle had planned their escape well. They had run the road several times in preparation. There was an old cart road just a mile up the way. They would take that and cut east. Then they would double back and head south. If they pressed hard, they might make it past the Hierapolis cutoff before dawn. That would take them well east of Philadelphia. Then they would push south. He had a place…

Philadelphia, the park by the theater

Dryados and Alesia shivered together on the cold ground. The leaves had helped to cushion them from the thorns and rocks beneath them. But between the cold, the restless homeless people, having to go pee inside the briar, and almost nonstop leg cramps, Alesia had hardly slept at all. Dryados had fared better, but not by much. An hour after sunrise, the people in the homeless camp were up and had restarted their small fire. They seemed to devour whatever food they had left as they noisily debated their strategy for the day.

"I tell you, the whole place will be ripe for stealing. The Romans will be focused on protecting the city and chasing down whoever done the attack. They ain't gonna waste any soldiers on purse cutters and quick fingers."

"Well, I'll tell ya this—when times is bad, ain't nobody gonna give nothing to them that is beggin'. When times is tuff is best just go straight to taking what ya need."

Dryados and Alesia remained hidden in their enclave of thorns while the raucous debate raged on. Soon it was decided the group would head into town and steal anything they could lay their hands on. Then they departed en masse.Dryados and Alesia remained hidden for another hour or so to make sure there were no stragglers. The forest park was again silent. Dryados unsealed the entrance, and they both quietly crawled out. They scanned the forest floor around them. They were alone.

Dryados hurried over to the homeless camp and tried to salvage the fire. They had stomped on the coals, but he found two or three small embers with a slight glow. Taking some dry cloth from the inner part of his tunic, he slowly nursed the fire back to life.

Alesia hovered over the burgeoning flames. "We should go past the theater entrance and then up the road to the Acropolis. That will be the easiest way to get back home."

Dryados slowly added larger and larger twigs to the fire. He did not speak for a minute or so. Then he looked at her blankly. "Alesia, I know you are pregnant. We are both tired and hungry. But we can't go home. It's not safe. If they are not up there waiting right now, they will just send someone else later. We must leave Philadelphia."

"Are you out of your mind!?" Her face flushed with anger. "I'm pregnant. Where would we go? Who would help deliver the baby?" She looked at him like he was the village idiot.

"I don't know. I don't know the answers to any of that. But we must flee. Listen to me, Alesia. These people are going to kill us. You know this is not the first time. And with each attempt they have made, they have gotten more and more desperate in what they have tried." He tossed a few more twigs mindlessly on the flames. "Sooner or later we are both going to end up dead."

Alesia had been well aware of the first attempt at the caravanserai. She had heard rumors of others that Dryados had simply not spoken to her about. "How many times have they tried?"

"I have been followed off and on for weeks. But this at least the fifth real attempt to kill me. There may have been others that my security forces have intercepted before I took notice of them. I don't know." He picked up another stick and started poking at the fire. "And I'm not sure, but I think it is the Jews. Don't ask me why—I have no idea. But I think the Jews are trying to kill me. And the most bizarre thing is, I don't think it is the local Jews. I think they're from, well, from someplace else."

"The fifth! This is the fifth time someone has tried to kill you! Why didn't you tell me? Why—"

"It doesn't matter now. None of it matters. What matters now is that we escape, or they will find some other way to have us murdered. Perhaps if we vanish now, they will think they were successful. Perhaps they will leave us alone. I don't know. I just know we need to get out of here while we still can."

Alesia had never seen Dryados so resolute. "Where would we even go?" she asked, still in disbelief.

"First, we will go to the caravanserai."

Dryados hardly needed any disguise. He looked nothing like himself. His clothes had been cut, ripped, fought in, slept in, covered with blood, dirt, and leaves. His face looked much the same as what he wore. He looked no different than any other beggar on the street, except the other beggars might have been a little cleaner. Alesia's identity was similarly well concealed. Her large belly and disheveled appearance made her look like a loose woman, impoverished and in trouble with an unclaimed child. The dark circles around her exhausted eyes gave her the look of desperation that could not be mimicked.

It took them both a while to warm up by the fire. The smell of smoke and moldy odor of sleeping in the leaves just added to the ambiance of their homeless appearance. Alesia walked toward the caravanserai, with Dryados following some distance behind to conceal any relationship.

The streets were more crowded than either of them expected. Smoke still smoldered into the sky from a dozen places about the city. Refuse and dead bodies cluttered the streets. Teams of workers tried to clear the roads. As they did, they pulled out the dead bodies and lined them up on the walkways for loved ones to identify. Wails and laments filled the air as people searched the streets for those they were missing. Their cries were always worse when they found them. Still, merchants pulled out their displays of goods for sale as they worked frantically to repair their shops. Those people who did walk the streets all seemed to be in a daze as they tried to press on with the mundane tasks of daily living. Despite the hopes of the homeless that had camped by them, the Romans had not abandoned the city to chase the attackers and were out in force on the streets. Despite the attack, they had no intention of allowing anything else to disturb the peace of Rome.

Dryados and Alesia kept their guards up. They slowed as they approached the caravanserai. Dryados scanned the street. That was when he saw him. A man with grizzled features scanning through the crowds much as Dryados was. His eyes looked stern. He carried an array of visible weaponry. He looked the type who would kill someone and assume no one would bother to hinder him from escaping.

Dryados casually closed the distance between him and Alesia. As soon as he was close enough—"Stop." It was more than a whisper but went completely unnoticed by others amid the chaos on the streets. Alesia immediately paused at the shop next to her and started to look at the merchandise. Dryados's mind raced. *We should go back to the house. Alesia was right...* Then his mind slowed. *No, if one of them is here, clearly others will be lying in wait at the house as well.* He looked at the caravanserai. *There is nowhere else to go...* Dryados glanced at Alesia. He barely recognized her. *I doubt this man has ever seen me...* Dryados thought. *He is probably looking for a wealthy man. Maybe he knows about Alesia. Maybe he doesn't. If he does, he will be looking for a sophisticated woman of wealth and heritage.*

At that moment Alesia was shooed away by the shop's merchant, who took her for a beggar. She looked questioningly back at Dryados.

Dryados nodded for her to proceed forward. He gave her no warning. *It's probably better if she doesn't know,* he thought. Dryados started to beg from the nearby people on the street. He moved slowly but determinedly toward the caravanserai. He had been approached countless times before by beggars on the street. He knew exactly what to say. "Kind sir..."

Alesia heard Dryados's begging pleas behind her. She quickly followed suit. "Please, sir, the baby..."

The two worked their way through the crowd. Alesia seemed far more successful than Dryados. He walked past her as she pleaded with a merchant Dryados had worked with several times. The man did not recognize either of them. Dryados had always thought the man stingy. But there he was, pulling out some coin to help a poor street floozy. Dryados shook his head, realizing he misjudged the man. He moved forward. He never bothered to check on the man with stern eyes. What was the point? They were out of options.

Dryados did not drop his guard nor his act, when he finally reached the caravanserai security check. "Yes, it's me—don't ask. My wife is just behind me. Just act like we are beggars, and let us pass."

"Beggars are not allowed into the caravanserai," the guard said bluntly as he continued eyeballing Dryados up and down.

"I know that!" Dryados scolded. "But I doubt the people watching us do. Just let us in, and let me get to my office and my storage areas."

The guard shrugged. "You look—"

"It doesn't matter. Just let us pass," Dryados interrupted. "My wife is just behind me. Just let her pass quickly so none will notice."

"One day you will have to share the story of this with me..." Then he motioned. "Enter."

Both Dryados and Alesia were soon inside. Despite his slovenly appearance, his private guards instantly recognized him. He and Alesia were quickly ushered back to the private storage room Dryados had rented since his arrival in the city, and kept out of sight. The storage room also served as his office and was filled with some of his most expensive merchandise and a small hoard of coin.

While he and Alesia kept hidden in the small room, Dryados dispersed his men among the many caravans. "We will need two horses for Alesia and I, as well as one stout mule. Everything we will need must fit on those three animals. More than that and we may appear as too tempting of a target as we travel. Tell no one of our presence. If anyone asks, tell them you have not seen us since before the city was attacked and you fear we may have been killed." While his men scoured the caravanserai for the needed supplies, the two wolfed down some food. As soon as the men returned with new clothing, the two bathed and got out of their now filthy rags. The men returned intermittently as new supplies were obtained. They purchased additional travel clothing, food, blankets, and shelter material. They bought horses and saddle packs. The list grew as Dryados thought of more and more scenarios they might encounter.

"It would make it a lot easier to purchase what we need if we knew what the plan was," Alesia sniped.

"That is true, but since we don't have a plan, we should just prepare for about anything under the sun!" he snapped sarcastically.

"You had better—"

"Look, Alesia. I'm sorry." He reached over, giving her a small kiss on the cheek. "We are both exhausted, and I still need to get some more to eat. I really don't have a plan. We need to get out of here—that is all the plan we have. I have thought of going directly to Ephesus and booking passage to one of Talmun's estates in the Greek lands. But I don't know. We could do the same from Smyrna and use the *Rose Fox*. But that is further away. And if the Jews are behind all this, that would take us too close to their Central Synagogue. I have also thought of going directly to Thyatira to meet up with Ascalon. But that seems a bad idea, as I am sure my enemies know of my business association with him."

"So what are we doing?"

"The men have made arrangements with a caravan going to Thyatira. If anyone finds out, it will make sense to them that I would go there. But we will leave the caravan when it stops in Sardis. I have a friend there and a place we can camp for a few days. That will get us out of here and give us time to think."

"You've never really said much about Sardis other than stopping there on the way to Thyatira. I didn't know you had friends there."

"Well, I think when you meet him, you'll understand."

Alesia gave him a quizzical look. "Fine. At this point, I don't really care. We have a plan. That's good enough. Now I'm going to bed."

Dryados continue to dispatch his men for new supplies. Soon, however, he fell asleep, exhausted. They hid in one of the wagons when the caravan to Thyatira departed. Some of the caravan's soldiers rode their horses. Unburdened horses in a caravan might look suspicious to someone watching. They tried to sleep as much as they could. But the inside of the wagon was cramped and the road north to Sardis bumpy and filled with potholes.

Thyatira, the day after

The Romans packed up beginning at dawn and marched away in the same disciplined columns they had arrived in. They took no spoil. They raided no temple. They robbed no citizen of anything beyond food. Unless one considered the murder of children robbery. Ascalon waited until the last Roman had long left the city. He stayed buried in the manure pile until he heard one of his workers wander in. Then slowly he dug himself out.

He wandered outside to see his men still huddled together in the work area around the main forge. They seemed too scared to move. None wailed or cried. It was clear they still did not know.

Ascalon did not speak. He could feel their curious eyes on him, wondering where he had come from. It didn't matter. He went over to the horse trough and stripped off his clothes. He bathed naked in front of his men. It didn't matter. Then he walked naked across the smithy to his office. He pulled on a clean tunic he kept there and all the coin he had hidden under the planks beneath one of the spare work anvils. He picked the best horse in the stalls and rode off. The smithy, his men, the city…none of it mattered.

He wasn't even sure where he was going. The Romans were headed north to Pergama, so he headed south. Dryados had told him of a quiet place by a river just north of Sardis. He could press the horse and be there by nightfall. He could go there and think things out. Maybe he would go farther south and meet Dryados in Philadelphia. He didn't know. It didn't really matter.

Chapter 31
Intersection

The old leper limped farther up the hill. "I see riders coming from both the north and the south! Riders are coming!" His clothes were ragged. His body withered. But he had the best eyes in the colony. "Decima? Decima?"

Decima walked out from behind a stack of boulders. "Just here, Samuel."

"There are riders coming from both north and south."

"How many?"

"Two from the south. One from the north."

"That is fine. I have been expecting them." Decima began his descent off the hilltop. "Thank you, Samuel. I do not anticipate there will be any others. If you see anyone else, please let me know immediately." Decima had spent his morning in the River and was fully rested for what lay ahead. The other river by the road was not far. He knew both sets of riders were headed to the small glade there to camp. He would meet them there.

Ascalon saw the pair of riders coming from the south. It looked like a man and a woman. They had a third horse loaded down with supplies behind them. Still, he didn't think anyone ever stopped by this section of the river. He was sure they would pass.

Dryados and Alesia watch the single rider approaching from the north. He was alone, which was unusual. Still, they were just north of the city. Clearly he was heading there. No one ever stopped by this section of the river.

Ascalon grabbed his hammer. There was no sense in taking any chances.

Dryados saw the man reach for something. Clearly he was going for a weapon. That made sense. The man was alone and was probably just being careful. Still,

Dryados grabbed his kukri from inside his tunic.

Hands tightened around their weapons as the two groups of riders approached each other. Each traveler focused his eyes on the approaching rider's weapon hand. It took a moment for them to even notice each other's faces.

"Ascalon?"

"Dryados? And is that…Alesia?" The surprise encounter brought a smile to Ascalon's face. He glanced up to heaven, "Oh God, thank You. Thank You." His eyes began to water.

"What in the world brings you here? And alone," Dryados asked with a smile. "And is that your work hammer?"

"It is a tale too horrible to even conceive. It is beyond imagining. Everything… just everything…" Ascalon wept bitterly.

Alesia looked over at her husband. "Dryados, perhaps we should make camp. You said it was right around here…"

"Just there beneath those trees." Dryados pointed to his familiar camping site less than a hundred yards off the road.

"Let us first make camp. Then we shall each share the losses we have suffered." Alesia nodded compassionately at the distraught smithy. She had never met Ascalon but had heard much about him over the last year. From what she had heard, he did not strike her as a man easily brought to tears. "I am sorry, Ascalon. You look so exhausted. Please, come join us. We all need rest and some hot food. Then we can share the troubles of the days we have lived."

Ascalon nodded.

They quickly made camp. Dryados had brought plenty of food and supplies. A large fire was soon blazing and a meal prepared.

Ascalon wept. "They slaughtered them like sheep. Their blood…oh God! I…I…" His wailing cries echoed down the river—the agony of a shattered world wrapped in the cries of one man. He told them of the burning piles of children, parents dying to save them, and the men he had killed too late to make a difference. Alesia walked over and sat beside him. "I am so sorry…"

The dam holding back his tears had burst, and the torrent could not be restrained. He put his head down in his hands and sobbed bitterly. Alesia wrapped her arms around him. He simply wept.

Dryados sat silently, waiting. Several minutes passed. Alesia smiled back at Dryados as Ascalon wept upon her. Perhaps it was her pregnancy and the growing motherly instinct within her. She knew she needed to just sit and wait. The flow from his lake of tears eventually slowed and then stopped.

They ate their meal. Some words were shared about how good the food was. But no one was ready to test the freshness of their wounds just yet.

Finally, Ascalon spoke. "And what of you? Clearly this trip was not planned.

You would never be out here on the road just the two of you." Ascalon sniffled and wiped away silent tears as he spoke.

Dryados and Alesia told of the attack on Philadelphia and their escape via the caravanserai. Once to city of Sardis, they had gathered their supplies and departed from the caravan. They had planned to camp here, but Dryados still could not explain why. Ascalon's wide and unblinking eyes betrayed his shock as he listened to their tale. He started to speak, when—

"Unclean! Unclean!" The shout shattered the moment of conjoined despair. "Unclean! Unclean!" There was rustling in the trees just beyond them. Ascalon and Alesia shot to their feet.

"It's OK. It's OK." Dryados chuckled. He rose to his feet and tried to calm them. "It's just a friend of mine."

"A friend of yours?" Ascalon asked harshly. "That's not funny."

"It's no joke. He's a friend of mine." Dryados looked at Ascalon and Alesia. "And he is a leper."

They all stared into the dwindling evening light.

"Dryados, if it is OK with you, I think I shall remain here and assume my usual perch on my favorite rock," Decima shouted from inside the tree line.

"That will be fine," Dryados yelled. "Actually, that is a very good idea. I have some friends with me that I would like to introduce to you, and they are a little nervous."

Dryados looked at his shocked companions. "His name is Decima Pratti. He is the leader of the local colony of lepers. I have been dropping off supplies to them in the hollow of that log over there for the last two years." Dryados pointed to the log. "In fact, I stop here every time I go back and forth between Philadelphia and Thyatira." Dryados looked at his disbelieving friend and at his wife. "Honestly, he is a good man. And he is very safe. He will keep his distance."

Alesia looked at him with fury. "I am pregnant, Dryados! I am not going anywhere near that man. He is a leper. He needs to stay away!" She stood, nervously rubbing her belly.

Dryados raised his hands as if to surrender, hoping to bring some calm. "That's fine. That's fine. You can stay here. Or you can come as close as you would like. I know you are pregnant"—Dryados backed slowly away toward the tree line—"and I am telling you, it will be OK. I would never take a chance with our child."

"I'm staying right here!" Alesia said firmly.

"That's fine. I totally understand." Dryados shrugged. "You can both stay here if you like. Seriously, I completely understand. But he is a friend of mine, and I am going over to speak with him. And trust me, I'm not going anywhere near him either."

Alesia sat back down on her log by the fire. "And if you come back as a leper…I'm going to kill you."

"Totally understandable…totally understandable…" Dryados backed away, still holding his hands in front of him.

Ascalon looked at him stoically. "I suppose I will meet him, if he is a friend of yours. Honestly, my life could be no worse."

"No, Ascalon…honestly, it's going to be fine. I promise you. You will see."

The two of them made their way through the underbrush. Dryados stopped a few moments later and pointed out the leper sitting in the distance, high on a rock. "See, he is just there. You can stay here or come as close as you like. I usually stop right over there." Dryados pointed to his usual spot on a nearby tree stump and then moved forward and took his seat. Ascalon hesitated for a moment as he judged the distance and then came and sat down beside Dryados.

"A brave man," Decima announced from his perch. "And looking at that hammer and the size of your arms, I would say you are probably a smithy."

Dryados had noticed the hammer as well. Ascalon had not let it get two feet away from him, even when he was eating.

Several long uncomfortable moments of silence passed as the two men stared at the hooded leper.

"So you are a smithy then?" Decima reiterated.

"Yes, I have been a smithy since I was a boy." Ascalon spoke of his life around heated metal and blazing forges. He talked about the first horseshoe he had ever seen and how he thought the idea of shoes on horses was stupid. "But go figure—they actually make a huge difference for the horse," he said, shaking his head.

"Yes, I suppose they would. Like shoes for men," the leper interjected.

"Exactly. But I am no cobbler. Working leather is nothing like working iron and copper. Metal is far more stubborn and needs a lot more convincing to do what you want it to do." He spoke about his business and how it had expanded over the years. The leper seemed enthralled and listened attentively to him. Ascalon told of his relationship with Dryados and their contracts with the Romans. "It is a wonderful life, making things, being outside, putting your body to the task." He held up his heavy hammer. "This old hammer belonged to my father. One day I will pass it on to my…" His voice faded into silence. Tears again overwhelmed his face.

The hooded leper let the silence linger. He quickly put together the pieces of their solitary travel and broken spirits. "Clearly some great calamity has befallen you both. I am so sorry. Please share with me what has happened."

In the growing darkness, two stories of disaster were shared. The men seemed eager to speak. Alesia kept her distance. She kept the fire going. The flicker of the flames through the trees kept the shadows around the three men in constant motion. The figure of the leper on the rock seemed to shift in and out of phase as the shadows danced around him. The two men spoke freely. The flow of their words seemed to help drain the sorrow from their souls. One had lost everything he had worked for. The other had lost everything worth living for.

The leper's attention never seemed to drift. He listened. He nodded. He gave the occasional affirming "Oh" or "Yes" or "No."

"And so there is nowhere we can go," Dryados explained. "For Ascalon, it is the Romans. They will have him executed. And for me...I don't even know who my enemies are. But whoever they are, they are clearly willing to go to great expense to get me killed."

The leper remained motionless. "You could hide with us here...I guarantee no one will look for you among our colony."

Ascalon and Dryados shifted uncomfortably. "No, I think..."

Decima started to roar with laughter and then slid off his rock, chuckling. "But then there is the whole thing about us being lepers...and you not wanting to die horrible deaths..." He stopped, momentarily fading into the darkness behind him...and then faded back into their sight again. "You need a secret place. A place of refuge where you can rest. Where you are not alone...yet where you will not be found. A safe and healthy place for you and the child who will soon join you."

"Yes, but where? The Romans are everywhere," Ascalon said loudly.

"There have always been places they have sought but never found. Places of hiding used by their enemies. Such places have been used for generations, before there was even a Roman Empire to worry about."

"Such a place could not exist," Dryados scoffed. "I am a Roman citizen. I have studied her history and all her sciences. Nothing escapes her eyes."

"Rome is a blind dog with a good sense of smell." Decima laughed. "As a ruling power, its sees nothing. It sees no suffering. It sees no poverty. It sees no injustice. It sees nothing of the lives of the people it rules." Decima paused for a moment as he struggled with his loose garments and climbed back up on his rock. Once atop again and resituated, he continued. "On the other hand, it is quick to sniff out insurrection. It is fast to catch the scent of those seeking to believe in what they choose. The odor of compassion is a stench it cannot tolerate. The fragrance of love for one another an abomination to its senses. No, Rome is blind and its sense of smell set keenly against its peoples. Still, there are places that have long evaded her nose."

"Beyond living with lepers, where could we go to escape Rome and enemies whose names we do not even know," moaned Dryados. "It's hopeless. Perhaps we should go to Ephesus and book passage to the Greek lands—"

"No, Dryados," Decima interrupted. "The place you seek is called Derinkuyu. Kamakalay would also work nicely. But it is too far. As pregnant as Alesia is, you would never make it there in time."

"I have heard of these places," Alesia chimed in. She had walked closer and now stood several paces behind the two men. "My father has spoken of them. The Romans have searched for them for centuries. They are nothing but a myth." She crept closer and then stood silently beside Dryados.

"Alesia, it is a great pleasure to meet you," Decima said excitedly. He shuffled awkwardly atop his rock. "By the way, Dryados is hoping for a girl. And Justinia is a wonderful name...lovely young woman, Justinia. But I can tell you, I think it is going to be a boy. And I am usually pretty good about such things."

Alesia was embarrassed to be suddenly talking about the sex of her unborn child. "Thank you...I'm...I'm..."

"No, the pleasure is all mine. Normally I would shake your hand or give you a hug or something, but given the circumstances, well, I think you can understand," Decima said quickly.

"No, I completely..." Alesia's voice trailed off. Now she was even more confused. She threw her hands in the air. "What are we even talking about?"

Dryados smiled. Decima was always completely full of joy and at the same time seemed totally unfamiliar with social norms. Either that or he had an unusually odd sense of humor. Dryados never knew exactly which, but it was one of the reasons Dryados had always enjoyed their conversations. "I think Decima believes we need to be more focused on boy names..."

"What?" Alesia's face filled with confusion.

"Actually, Alesia, they are not myths," Decima said. "I have been there many times myself. They are just impossible to find. And those who know of their locations have given their lives over and over again to keep their locations secret."

"Decima, surely you are joking." Dryados rose to his feet, shaking his head. "I too have heard of these places. Surely they are a myth. How can you hide an entire city in today's world? There are so many people. These areas have been populated for hundreds of years. How could you keep an entire city a secret all that time?"

Decima started laughing. His hood bobbed up and down. Dryados really would have loved to see his face. "Sometimes the answer is not complicated. It might be right under our feet, and you would never know. Or maybe...we look and we just don't see." He seemed to be looking right at Dryados. "Still, it has been done." Decima fidgeted, making himself more comfortable on his rock. "I know a woman. Her mother was a Canaanite. I have known her since she was a child. Her mother was a woman of great faith. Even when her mother was ignored, rejected, and embarrassed, her faith did not falter. She only sought crumbs of blessings. Because of the enduring faith of her mother, this young girl was healed of a cruel demon. She is a little older now. I have not seen her recently. But she is Iredenti. And she will take you to the secret places where you must go."

Decima repeated the directions several times. They wrote nothing down. They would try to seek refuge in the hidden city of Derinkuyu. He said it was roughly in the direction of the village of Nevasehiria. They could take the Royal Road directly out of Sardis. It would be fast and the most traveled route. But Decima advised against it. Instead, Decima encouraged them to take the southern route toward Tarsus. From there they would cut due north. Decima did not give the location of Derinkuyu. He instructed them they would first need to meet up with the Canaanite girl in the village of Nigidia. Decima said her name was Kayseri.

Chapter 32
Boxes

Thyatira

The boxes came in all shapes and sizes, but most were fairly small. Some were made of stone, others wood or wicker. The smallest seemed barely large enough to hold a loaf of bread. Others were carried by many hands. But no matter what the size, each concealed a great treasure. And those that carried them wailed and cried from their losses. A macabre parade of boxes made its way down the main street of Thyatira. Those lining the streets wailed as loudly as those in the parade. No one in the city had been spared from the loss of the attack. Sons and daughters, grandchildren, nieces and nephews, as well as many of their parents…all killed in the Roman slaughter. The street grew wet with tears. And though every ear in the city was exhausted from the wails of sorrow, the sounds of mourning did not cease. For many, it was their tradition to cremate the bodies of the ones they had lost, but with the abomination the Romans had committed, it seemed strangely inappropriate. The remaining bodies, and the boxes now holding them, would be buried.

The local Roman garrison returned to their station two days later. Many had been born and grown up in the city. Many had younger relatives. Some had joined the Romans freely, while others had been conscripted. They too felt the loss. Many shared their feelings in private conversations around the city and told of their desire to quit—but none dared. For the Romans would kill them just as easily as they did the children. The city mourned.

Despite all the losses, or perhaps because of them, the fellowship meeting at Jezebel's villa later that week was packed. The smell of spit-cooked goat and rosemary dove filled the air. The soft music complemented the gentle flavors of the new wine. It was noisy, but less so tonight than usual. Jakotrudi tried to greet as many as he could. The moments he had between consoling his sheep, he prayed silently to himself. *Oh God, I have nothing to offer these people. I have no words. Please fill my mouth with Your voice.* Some of the families had little or nothing to say—they just cried. Jakotrudi held each of them tightly and cried with them. Others shared their memories, brief as they might be. The color of their babies' eyes, their strong grips, sitting up, standing, walking, or a hundred other tiny things that were each a miracle. The angry ones were the hardest, for their anger was righteous and just. There was no argument to justify what was done. No argument as to the death penalty the perpetrators deserved. But now was not the time to talk about what was right. Now was the time to let the storm rage and lower the sails. As long as the boat did not crash against the rocks or sink, he would gently guide it later to better seas. He had learned that teaching how to understand a great storm was rarely successful in the pain of its highest waves and lashing winds. By the time it was time for him to speak, Jakotrudi was spent.

He made his way through the mourning throng. He looked out at the tear-filled faces. In that instant he was taken back to the storms of his own life. He stood rather than sat on the dais. "When my father and mother died, I cried much as you do now. I was younger then, and they were all I had. They were the well of love that had filled my life. My father taught me his trade and took me to fish at the river. My mother made me honey chips and healed every scrape and cut I ever had. When I got older and had children of my own, I tried to be the parent they had taught me to be. Then my oldest son was killed. My heart was ripped in two again. So many thoughts of love…and failure. I had not been there, not protected him, not…done a thousand other things. And I remembered when he first learned to walk and how angry my wife was as he played in the kitchen with her pots." His eyes filled with tears, as if the sting of death had just touched his frame. "I am older now, and I share with you a lesson life will teach you in its own cruelty. A lesson we all share today…" He looked out at the crying faces. He saw in the crowd the faces of his own mother and father and son and many others he had lost. His own cries blended with those from the gathered fellowship. "Death is an enemy!" He looked out at the faces that were so much like his own. "It stalks us now, from the day were are born until the day we die. And it is not alone. For by its side walks hardship, and sorrow, and loneliness, and disease, and…" He shook his head. "But it was never meant to be this way. Not for the ones we have lost, or even for ourselves. It was not this way in the beginning, and it will not remain this way. The enemy that stalks us, that has stolen from each of us, has already been defeated! The Long Expected One has come!" Then he shared the story of his own life and becoming Iredenti. He shared a message of redemption and life eternal. "For the Iredenti, the only one that stays in the grave…is death!"

"So true, so true," Jezebel interrupted. "And that is a message for all of us." She walked through the crowd and joined Jakotrudi on the raised dais. "And it is a lesson to be lived every day. Each one of us should therefore ask, 'How then shall we live?'" She paused as she too looked out at those gathered. "With such an enemy biting at our heels, we need to live every day as if it were our last. For God and His kingdom"—she paused and nodded consolingly to the crowd—"as well as for those we love and for ourselves." A large smile grew on her face. "The best way to defeat sorrow is with joy. The best way to defeat death is to revel in the life we have been given." She walked closer to Jakotrudi. "Like Jakotrudi has shared. To go fishing with the ones we love, or other things that bring us bliss." She walked more quickly across the stage. "Snatch defeat from the jaws of death itself. Turn this day of sorrow into a celebration of life. Tomorrow, death may come to each of us. So while we live, let us honor those who have died by living life to its utter fullest!" She held her hand high above her head victoriously. "I will not let death have dominion over me! I will live my life as a celebration, without pause, hindrance, or regret!" Her words were followed by several hearty cries of "Amen!"

As was their custom after the lesson, both Jakotrudi and Jezebel mingled with the members of the fellowship until it was time to leave. Jakotrudi comforted several more distraught families. Despite the somber mood, Jezebel was particularly blissful. She made sure the wine flowed in even greater abundance than usual. Slowly the crowd started to thin out. Jakotrudi noticed several of the men and a smaller entourage of women still lingering around to talk to Jezebel. That had become the standard over the last several months. Normally he would have stayed as well, but with all that had happened the last few days, he was exhausted. He was never invited to go downstairs with the others to continue the discussions with Jezebel anyway. He had decided she was trying to develop a separate group of members and elders and was planning to spin off into her own fellowship at some point. In either case, he took each day as it came. Each seemed to have enough worries of its own. And for him, this one was over. He made his way over to Jezebel and the others. "Thank you so much for your amazing hospitality and generosity. I would love to stay and join you with your continued discussions, but tonight I must be leaving a little early." He hoped by excusing himself it would spare Jezebel the trouble of having to lie to him again.

"Oh, I am so sorry to see you leave, but it has been a trying time for the entire city. I am sure as its spiritual leader you are exhausted." She reached over and softly touched his hand. "I will pray for you." She nodded, and then she turned and continued her discussions with the others.

As soon as Jakotrudi departed out the back, she turned and spoke loudly to the gathered men and eager women. "I thought he would never leave! I am so tired of his narrow vision and limited understanding of truth. Besides, we have been planning this night for some time. And despite the recent tragedy that has befallen our city, we have several new arrivals already waiting downstairs." Gleeful smiles sprang on the faces of her followers. "There are deeper things of our faith that cannot be taught with mere words but must be experienced to be fully appreciated. The same is true outside these halls as well. What we learn and experience here is meant to be shared with the world around us. To bring the world joy."

The entire group shuffled quickly down the stairs. The large guard at the bottom unbolted the door and quickly rebolted it as they passed.

Demas's heart pounded harder and harder with each step down the wide hall. He glanced at the faces around him. He could see the growing anticipation in each person's countenance. Eyes glistened. Wry smiles blossomed. Some of the women's cheeks reddened. Everyone breathed faster. Demas instinctively loosened his tunic. Others quickly followed suit.

Jezebel stopped at the now familiar door. Demas's heart raced. "You have been called to run the race set before you," she said, smiling. "But remember, this is a marathon, not a sprint. I will be very disappointed if you finish too quickly." She looked over at Jehoram and smiled. "You are with me tonight, at least to start." She waited for the expected smile that blossomed quickly on his face. "The rest of you should explore as much as you can…" She leaned forward and slowly opened the next door.

Thyatira, Ascalon's smithy

Cellarius looked over at the cold forge. He stoked the bellows over and over. The loud *whosssh* that followed each cycle of his arm was met by—nothing. In all his years as a foreman, he had never seen a forge that was so dead cold. He looked around the rest of the smithy. It had been almost a week since the Day of Sorrow and Ascalon's departure. They had plenty of orders to fill, but somehow, the spirit of the smithy seemed to have died with the murder of the city's children and loss of the smithy's leader. Cellarius looked around at the slow-moving men. Boxes of raw sword forms stood stacked by several of the forges.

"This is just getting ridiculous," he moaned to himself. "That's it!" He let loose of the bellows' handle and stormed into the center of the work area. "Everybody listen up!" he roared. "I want your sorry butts over here right now! That's everybody! I don't care what you're doing!"

The vacant-eyed men each looked up, their faces drawn and empty. It was as though none even knew where they were. Tools were slowly lowered. Horses lethargically led into the coral. The stupor of midnight seemed to grip everyone there.

"Come on! Move along, all of you. We don't have all day."

The men seemed to minutely increase their speed as they shuffled across the work area. But their eyes remained as empty as the boxes waiting to be filled with new forged products.

As his men gathered around him, Cellarius's heart softened a bit. "We have all been through a terrible thing. And the memories of what has happened will haunt each of us for years to come." He looked around at the sunken eyes that had cried rivers of tears. He mustered a smile and nodded. "That is how it should be." He nodded again. "Yet, our lives are best lived by serving the living. And the best way to honor the love we have lost is by rekindling it anew in the world in which we live, and by making sure those we love, that are still here with us, know beyond anything else how much we love them. Part of that is also being faithful in the work that has been set before us. Ascalon has granted a way for each of us to make a living. And in his absence, we need to be about his business. He has laid out what needs to be done. We have plenty of orders to fill. And if we continue to do things his way, this smithy will be even bigger when he returns." Cellarius could see a small glimmer of life being rekindled in the eyes around him. One or two even nodded his head. "Now, I want you four men on forge number three. I want that thing up, running, and hot in less than an hour. You boys there..." Celly barked his orders. Soon the smithy was filled with the shouts of busy men. The *whossh* of each of the five bellows was now immediately answered by the loud roar of flames and the clanging sound of cold, hard hammers slamming against soft, hot metal. *Whossh*...clang, clang, clang...*whossh*...clang, clang, clang... The symphony of daily life had returned. Cellarius felt like singing. "You men, there, what in blazes are you doing? That needs to be..."

Some of Sargon's fleeing men, hill country outside of Colossae

The horse's mouth was frothing. They had stumbled upon a small family traveling on the road and killed them all. The family had little coin, so the horse was their only real prize. Sargon's men didn't even have time to ravage the woman. "That was a terrible waste back there," Menahem yelled.

"No, it was the cost for our own survival. We didn't have time," Nahash sneered. He put his hand up to the bandage over his right eye. The eye had been ripped out of its socket during the battle in Philadelphia. At least the bleeding had stopped. Still, he felt dizzy as he tried to keep up with the others.

"I say we stop in Colossae, get some food, get drunk, and have some women. What's the point of having all this gold if we can't live like kings?" Menahem complained. He was a big man. He liked to kill his enemies with his bare hands. He looked questioningly over at Jeraboam. "We've already left two of our own men on the trail to die as it is."

"Yeah, and I don't want to be the third," Nahash snapped.

Jeraboam brought the group to a stop. The sun was hot and high in the sky. He was one of Sargon's undercommanders, and these were his choice men. "We have stayed in the hills on the side roads and trails. We have moved with speed, but the Romans could have gotten ahead of us on the main roads. Still, you are right. Gold is of no use if we are dead." He looked down at the big gash in his leg. "And I want to find a healer to tend my wound before it goes purulent." He looked around at the other exhausted faces. His men had run a day, fought a battle, and then run for three more days. Each was completely spent. He knew he had lost a lot of blood. He felt dizzy all the time now. He glanced over at their only horse. It looked like it was going to drop over dead any minute. "We go into town. Each of you can do as he wills. But we leave at daybreak. If you are too drunk to run, or oversleep, we leave you behind. Understood?"

No one spoke. They all answered with exhausted nods.

Despite his fatigue, Menahem knew the first place he would visit was the brothel. "When do we get our cut of the spoil?" he asked. His voice always seemed laced with anger.

"You can collect your spoil here in Colossae if you like. Otherwise, we will spilt it up when we get closer to Sargon's. In any case, the horse stays with those of us going east." Jeraboam looked at Menahem's half-snarled face. "Or I can give you enough of your share when we are in the city to live like a king for the night, get a good drunk, and have all the women you want. Odds are, if you take all your spoil, you're going to wake up with a knife in your belly anyway. But it's up to you. It's your loot."

Menahem nodded gruffly. "Yes, that'll do. When it's time, give me enough coin for the night, and I will meet back up with you at dawn."

"As with me."

"And me," voiced some others.

Jeraboam nodded. "Agreed, as soon as we find a place to sleep." Then the exhausted squad hurried on. The sun sucked more and more life out of them with each step they took. Their lone horse stopped with rapidly increasing frequency. Shimei had found a stout switch and beat it mercilessly whenever it paused. Still, it took more and more to get it to move. Now deep bleeding slashes covered its rump. It stopped again. A red spray of blood flew in the air as Shimei lashed out at the animal. Still, the beast did not move. As exhausted as the men were, they knew they were in no shape to try to carry the spoil on themselves. After some heated arguing, the men agreed to pitch in the last of their water for the horse to drink. It seemed enough to keep the horse going just a bit longer. A mile or two outside of Colossae, the heavily loaded horse started to buck and then collapsed.

Shimei screamed at the fallen animal and tugged at its halter. The collapsed horse sputtered and began to cough up specks of blood. Shimei moved behind the heavy burdened animal and kicked it viciously in the rump over and over. "The %#^*$& stupid beast! Dump! Worthless!" He moved back to the horse's head and tugged angrily at the halter. There was no response. "Aahhhaa!" He kicked the horse mightily in the head. "The &*$#@*% piece of $%%*& animal!" He was as red as the blood now pouring from the horse's panting mouth.

"Enough!" Jeraboam roared. He limped over, drawing his short sword as he moved. Without another word, he slammed the blade deep into the horse's chest. The horse whinnied and bucked its legs. Its hooves flailed wildly in the air, but it remained collapsed in the dirt. Jeraboam flicked the sword back and forth in the animal's chest. The exhausted horse's head crashed to the ground. Shimei, who was still standing there holding the halter, dropped the leather reins to the ground. The rest of the squad fell silent. Jeraboam wiped the blood from his blade onto his already grimy and blood-stained fighting tunic. "We are too exposed to camp here, and the spoil is too heavy for us to carry." He turned, pointing his now clean sword at three of the men. "Shimei, Pashhur, and Doeg, I want the three of you to get to town as quickly as you can. Get us a wagon if possible and some horses. Do nothing to arouse suspicion." Jeraboam looked sternly at Doeg and held his blade near the Edomite's face. "Do not kill anyone! That well-used sword of yours will only bring trouble upon us. We will get in, have our celebration, and leave… understood?"

The Edomite begrudgingly nodded. "Yes."

Jeraboam moved to the side of the horse and pulled a small bag of coin from one of the bags of spoil and tossed it to Shimei. "And in the name of all the gods, get us some water!" He turned and started to walk toward a small scrub tree. "Menahem, stand guard. The rest of you, find some shade." Jehoiakim collapsed were he stood. Jeraboam limped over to the scraggly foliage and crashed to the ground. He nodded to sleep before his weight had even settled.

Shimei, Pashhur, and Doeg staggered out toward Colossae. It was not far, but the three could barely move. Pashhur pulled strips of dried dead skin from his cracked lips as they walked. Just inside the city wall, they came to a small fountain where children were playing. The three mustered what little strength they had and raced forward. Shimei dropped to his knees and slammed his face into the cool pool. He looked like a camel trying to drink the collecting trough dry. Pashhur and Doeg tore off their fighting tunics and dove into the fountain with the small children. Blood and grime quickly tainted the water. The frightened children backed momentarily away but then quickly resumed their play. Shimei continued to drink deeply.

After several minutes, Shimei too began to clean the dirt and blood from his arms and legs. Soon the three men started to feel human again. Shimei yelled to the others, "We need to be quick. The rest of the squad and spoil are still out there." Pashhur and Doeg reluctantly pulled themselves out of the cooling water and threw their fighting tunics back on. The beleaguered threesome garnered some curious stares as they squished and dripped their way through the city streets.

Shimei and the others were quickly pointed to the nearest livery and directed to its master. "We need a wagon and four or five horses," Shimei explained. "And we will pay in gold right now if the price is right." The master of the livery was a jovial older man, Ligio. He began his opening price, and negotiations were quickly underway. Shimei did not want to seem too eager, but the price was fair. He continued to banter with the livery master for a few more minutes. Just as he was about to close the deal, Doeg interrupted. "You $#&@#. Listen up. It's simple," Doeg sneered. "We need a wagon and a couple of horses. How %$@*& difficult is that." He shoved Shimei out of the way and put his hand menacingly on his sword. He stood, staring down the livery owner.

Even with the refreshment the cool water at the fountain had brought, Pashhur felt dazed and ready to collapse. He was done, and he too was not a man to trifle with. He pulled his sword and shoved it into Doeg's side. "Shut your %$@* mouth, or I will gut you right here." He shoved the tip of his blade firmly into Doeg's flank. "You heard what Jeraboam said." The sneer of Pashhur's face made it clear he was more than ready to kill Doeg and just move on.

Shimei pushed his way back in front of the livery man. "Here is the price we had agreed upon. My men are just exhausted from our travels. My apologies. Could you just show us the wagon and horses?" He pushed a bag of coin into the livery master's hand and nodded happily, as if the deal was done.

The nervous livery man looked appraisingly at the three unsavory men and then glanced into the bag of coin he had just been handed. The gold and silver coin within was sparkling and new. Almost all of it bore the mint of Philadelphia. He smiled up at the men. "It is a good price," he roared. "Come. Let me show you the quality of our horses. If you need more, you will know where to come." The livery master took the three men around the back. The wagon was quickly hooked to a pair of stout mares. Five nice horses were then brought out with new halters. They were not prize animals, but they were still of high quality.

Shimei saw some old waterskins hanging on the wall for the livery workers. "For an extra silver dinar, will you throw those in as well?" he asked.

The livery master reached up and threw the old skins into the back of the wagon. "Consider them a gift. But if you ever need to buy more horses, you must promise to come here." He laughed.

"Of course, of course," Shimei replied as he crawled into the wagon. Pashhur and Doeg quickly mounted their horses as the livery master secured the other three to the back of the wagon. The threesome whipped the fresh animals and rode off.

Back with the others, the waterskins were quickly emptied. The dead horse was stripped of its spoil, and the treasure concealed in some large wooden boxes in the back of the wagon. The other men were soon mounted on their horses or packed into the back of the wagon. The squad ventured into Colossae.

Just inside the city wall and past the fountain, they came to a mundane inn called The Red Tree. They needed a way to guard their spoil and stay out of view of any Romans. "We have little coin," Jeraboam explained to the innkeeper. "My men and I would just like to stay the night in the barn. We have gathered three silver dinars between us, if you will also provide us dinner tonight and an early breakfast in the morning."

The innkeeper quickly agreed. "I will have my wife bring the food out in an hour or two," he said happily. "We here at the inn is also early to rise and can awaken you at dawn. We can have breakfast ready and a-waiting as well." Jeraboam quickly handed him the coins.

Once in the barn, he sent Shimei to find a physician. Jehoiakim's fever was getting rapidly worse. He had almost fallen off his horse on the ride into the city. The bleeding had stopped from the deep wound in his belly the day after the fighting. But now his whole abdomen was as hard as a rock and agonal to touch. The belly wound was still open and poured out foul-smelling pus and stool. Jeraboam doubted he would live out the night.

By the time the physician arrived, Jehoiakim was lying on a bed of straw in a deep stupor and no longer arousable. The physician took a quick look at his belly and felt Jehoiakim's feverishly burning head. He shook his head solemnly. "Nothing more to be done here," he said. "This man will be dead by morning."

Jeraboam sat on a workbench near the wall and motioned toward his leg. The physician cleaned the deep gash out with some fresh water and put on a fresh bandage. "Keep your leg up whenever you are resting. If it starts to go pussy, another physician will have to open it and let out the evil humors. Otherwise, it should heal up fine. You will be left with a large scar and a limp for a while. But you should do well."

The healer's response to Nahash's injury surprised them all. The physician took down the large dressing Nahash had fastened over the socket. "The eye has been torn cleanly from its roots," he pronounced. "Believe it or not, that seems to be a good thing. I have seen this before—as long as you keep it covered with clean bandages, it should heal in fine. The socket will fill in with scar, and of course you will never see, but you will live." Despite Nahash's insistence that he was dying, the physician assured him that he too would survive, and departed.

The grand plan to go and celebrate vanished as quickly as did the old physician. Most of the men found a soft spot in the piles of hay and fell instantly asleep. Pashhur took first watch. Menahem too was exhausted, but his pride and desire got the best of him. "I will tell the ladies that you men were too tired for a visit," he roared. "But not to worry. I will make sure they do not miss you! Yaa-haa-haa-haaa!" The other men shook their heads and remained collapsed on the hay.

Menahem headed straight for the nearest brothel. He held the purse of freshly minted coins from Philadelphia that Jeraboam had given him tightly in his hand. Once inside the brothel doors, he held the bag of coin high in the air and loudly pronounced, "Call me King Menahem, for I have arrived home to my glorious kingdom!" He stood there waving the jingling bag back and forth for all to see. The prostitutes at the brothel were young and eager to please him. The wine was sweet, and the food hot and savory. Just as he had demanded, he spent his night as king of the brothel.

He did not bother to stir when the maiden on his right snuck slowly out of the bed. Nor did he lodge complaint when the one on his left departed with equal discretion. He heard his coin purse rattle as the two whores rummaged through his tunic to rob him. But what did he care? He had a hoard of treasure waiting for him back with the other men. Then one of the young whores grabbed his foot and shook it softly. He kicked his foot sharply. "I told you—wake me at sunrise, not before!" he roared. He felt his big toe being softly grabbed and wiggled. Then… "AAHHH!" He roared in agony as the great toe was suddenly yanked and broken backward. He rolled out of the bed onto the floor in searing pain. "What the &%*#@! I'm gonna…" He glanced up at the foot of the bed. The two young prostitutes were gone. There by the door stood six Roman soldiers with their swords drawn. One flashed his blade and grinned.

"Wakie, wakie…"

Philadelphia, Dryados's villa at the Acropolis

Jo-El and the others swept the refuse from the floor. They would work on getting the blood stains out of the tile and rugs later. The bodies of the raiders and dead Romans had already been dragged out of the house. The servants placed all the shattered pottery and destroyed housewares in some makeshift boxes and put them by the road to be scavenged by the city's poor. Jo-El and the others had heard the reports that the raiders had asked for Dryados by name. After the attack, they had searched the house but found no trace of his or Alesia's bodies. The only odd thing the servants had noticed was that the baby ceramic fox was missing from the backyard. Jo-El had also seen the rope at the bottom of the high wall at the back of the house that dropped down into the city park. He was not sure, but he had his suspicions that Dryados and Alesia had survived the attack and fled in that direction. Still, he and the other surviving servants told everyone they could that the two were murdered in the assault.

Cleaning the empty house took several days. Jo-El had searched the markets and replaced all the destroyed art. What could not be salvaged was donated to the city's poor. The kitchen pantry was restocked. The garden in the back was mended and the game of Foxes and Hounds set up, waiting for the young couple's return. Yet for Jo-El, the echoes in the house remained loud and somber. His efforts at the caravanserai were equally sullen. He told everyone he met about the terrible attack at the house and spread the rumor of Dryados's death among the caravans. Strangely however, when he spoke with workers in Dryados's secure storage area, they seemed…overly eager…to accept the couple's untimely deaths. He decided to explore the tragedy with the storage-area workers further, but with significantly more discretion. "Master Dryados's death is a great loss," he said as he helped several workers stack boxes. "Still, we should prepare for his return…I mean for… well, if he has any sort of heir…or something."

"Yes, well said," one responded. He looked questioningly at Jo-El. "But you are right. If he were to come back…I mean if he has a living heir…it is our job to ensure his businesses are run smoothly in his absence. That way when the master returns, whoever that is, we can approach him boldly knowing we have done as he would have willed and made the business even bigger than when he left."

"Exactly!" Jo-El seconded as he rubbed his lower back. "That is exactly what Master Dryados would have wanted. He has done everything for us. The least we can do is continue about his business until he comes back."

The two men looked cautiously at each other for a moment. "I have helped him here in the caravanserai with everything he has done," Fattore added cautiously.

"And I have done everything with him here in the city and at home," Jo-El chimed. "He has shown me everything I need to do to continue on with his work."

The two stood silent in the storage area for a long moment. Jo-El smiled at Fattore. Fattore smiled back. Both slowly put out their hands. Their handshake was vigorous and long. "OK, so let's get started."

Thyatira, Jezebel's mansion

Bera reached over to unbolt the door. Demas paused and wiped the sweat from his face, using the tunic he still held in his hand. He was exhausted.

As Bera slid the door open, he looked at Demas with a sly smile. "Jezebel was very impressed with your, ah…"

Demas laughed. "Well, I just wanted to make her proud."

Bera chuckled back. "Well, that you did…that you did. Even Daravaza was impressed, and that's hard to do."

Demas looked back inside the room at the various alcoves filled with bizarre toys, appliances, whips, feathers, masks... "I just had no idea..." He shook his head as he continued to stare. "Absolutely no idea." He looked back at Bera with a huge smile as more sweat dripped from his forehead. Then he started to chuckle. "You gotta admit, some of that is pretty strange..."

One of the young ladies he'd had earlier that night walked slowly past, running her hand softly across Demas's bare shoulders. Her face was still red and her eyes sensuously flirtatious. She mouthed a silent *Thank You* to Demas as she walked by. Once beyond the door she staggered down the hall, struggling to put her clothes back on.

"What was I saying?" Demas asked.

Bera mockingly shook his head. "I have no idea."

"Me neither..." Demas pushed his way out the door and raced down the hall after the young woman.

"Just a moment! Just a moment!" He sped down the long corridor waving his hand. He didn't bother to try to put his tunic back on.

The young woman stopped, smiled, and turned, waiting for him. She eagerly began to remove what little clothing she had regained as he approached.

About a half hour later the two walked up the stairs to the now empty great meeting hall. Both were completely disheveled and spent. Demas gave her a final passionate kiss as his hands made one more quick exploration of her body. "I look forward to our next fellowship meeting," he whispered.

"As do I," she said softly. She gently nuzzled her face against his neck and upper chest. "But Thursday I will be in the market. I usually spend the whole afternoon there. I will not be missed if I happen to leave and wander off someplace else."

Demas deeply breathed in the smell her hair. "Funny, I too will be in the market Thursday. I know a very private place not far from there."

The two went their separate ways. Demas stopped at one of the city fountains and washed himself up. He tried to comb his hair and straighten his tunic as best he could. He hoped his wife would not notice any of the stains on the garment. He hoped the night breeze would keep him cool so he would stop sweating. Still, he felt like he was roasting when he got home and walked in the door.

His wife, Vjeran, greeted him with a warm hug and kiss. "Demas...you are so hot. Are you all right? You're sweating."

"The fellowship meeting just went so late..." He edged his way farther into the house, loosened his tunic, and sat down. "Jakotrudi just drones on and on. I wish sometimes the man would just shut up." He shook his head. "I left as soon as I could and just ran the whole way home."

Vjeran sat down beside him. "Well, at least you're home." She snuggled closer. "The children are all asleep. It is just the two of us." Her tired eyes still managed a sensuous twinkle. "Let's just go to bed."

There was an inviting softness to her voice. Still, he was spent. "Honey, that's a great idea, but I am just really tired. It's been a very long day." He leaned over and gave her a kiss. "Maybe tomorrow." He got up and walked toward the bedroom, alone.

Colossae

It was still dark as the barn door slid slowly open. No one knew whose turn it was to stand guard duty, for all the men were collapsed and asleep on the floor and in the hay.

"Now! Take them! Take them all!" The soldiers crashed through the doors and leaped in through the windows. Before any of the beleaguered squad of men could even open their eyes, they were all captured, dragged outside, and put in chains.

As Jeraboam's vision cleared, he could see Menahem in the back of one of the many wagons nearby on the road. The man had been beaten so badly he was barely recognizable. But it was him.

"Throw them all in the back of one of the transports and take them to the main gate of the city!" roared the commanding centurion. The men were quickly jerked, prodded, and shoved into the back of a heavy barred wagon but were otherwise kept unharmed. Just outside the city gate, the back of the wagon was unbolted and the men thrown to the rocky ground. As their arms and legs were chained, they each crashed headlong into the dirt. The guards gave each a few quick kicks before they were each dragged to their feet. "Over here! Over here!" barked the commander. "I want them all to see exactly what is going to happen to them if we do not get the information we need." Then he stormed over to the separate wagon holding Menahem. "We will start with him!"

The soldiers tore Menahem from the back of the wagon and dragged him over to a spot where several tubular holes had already been dug into the rocky earth. The centurion raised his sword and pointed dramatically at a wagon with a large box on the end. Then he nodded. A squad of his men ran to the wagon, opened the box, and unloaded several long, narrow wooden shafts. Each had been cut to a needle-sharp point at one end. Jeraboam's whole body shuddered in terror. He could barely breathe. He had seen the victims of Roman impaling rods many times in his travels. The other men around instinctively started to back away, but they were held tight in the grips of their Roman captors. The Roman centurion nodded his head toward Menahem. Without another word, the Roman soldiers stripped Menahem of his clothing and impaled him with one of the sharp shafts.

It was not quick. Even though he already looked near death, his screams were hor-rific. The Romans seemed to drag the process out as long as they could. Menahem didn't stop moving until the shaft was hoisted up by several of the soldiers and finally settled into one of the tubular holes. The commander walked over to one of the wagons and took out a waterskin. He drank from it casually and splashed several handfuls on his face to freshen himself up. He gave the men plenty of time to look at their murdered friend.

"Now, it is very simple. You are small fish of no real value. We have already learned that the attack on Philadelphia was conducted by General Sargon, the Conqueror. We simply do not know where to find him. If you tell us reliable in-formation as to where he is going, we will set you free. As I have said, you are not the ones we seek. If you do not have this information, we will break every bone in your body and impale you here alongside your friend. We have made plenty of room here for a fine garden to show all who pass what happens to those who trifle with the peace of Rome." He nodded at the remaining rows of deep tubular holes in the ground.

Shimei jerked forward from the restraint of the guards. "He is the one! He can tell you!" Shimei motioned frantically toward Jeraboam. "He was one of his undercommanders. He knows exactly where Sargon is going. He was leading us all there. He can tell you. He can tell you!" The guards regained their grip on Shimei's frame but otherwise stood unmoving beside him, waiting for their commander to proceed.

The commander nodded at another one of his men. The soldier ran back to the wagon with the large box of impaling rods and returned with a heavy war hammer. He walked slowly toward Jeraboam, letting the stout war hammer swing menacingly in his hand. He stopped and glared into Jeraboam's eyes. "I will make sure my men break your bones so slowly you will think it is a career. And when we finally impale you, that too will take hours." He took a slow, deep breath. "Where is Sargon?"

Jeraboam stood silently. He had known Sargon for years. He was one of Sar-gon's most loyal and trusted men...

The Roman centurion turned slowly toward his men.

But not *that* loyal... "Sargon has a secret villa just outside the city of Akkad." Jeraboam told the Roman centurion detailed directions on how to get there, Sargon's security measures, travel routes, and everything else he knew. Then he waited.

"You have kept your part of the bargain, brigand. I shall also keep mine." The centurion took a few steps back. He smiled. "Well, at least part of it." He turned, facing his men. "You will not need to break every bone in their miserable bodies." He loudly commanded, "Impale them all!"

The centurion's men were fast and well practiced at their work. The horrific screams echoing off the city walls and large puddles of bright-red blood did not seem to faze them a bit. A fresh new Garden of the Dead rose quickly in the cool, early morning rays of sun. "Like flowers greeting the new day…" The Roman centurion beamed. Before he rode away, he watched as his men hoisted a sign above the garden that read "Violators of the Peace of Rome."

Less than a week later, a small army of Romans raided the villa outside of Akkad. All Sargon's men were killed, his fields burned, his treasures seized. His wife and six young—all murdered. But Sargon was not home. Before they left, the Romans positioned a bright Roman battle standard beside each of the family's dead bodies. Over each of their eyes they placed newly minted coins from Philadelphia.

Chapter 33

A Knock at the Door

Every morning, the sun shone straight in their eyes. Every evening it was at their back. Eastward they traveled, ever eastward. The road they navigated was small, rough, and dangerous. During the day they hid from every traveler passing their way. They watched for bandits and ambushes. Every night they hid their camp. No fires were lit. All food was eaten cold. The farther they traveled from Thyatira, the less Ascalon spoke. It was like the light of his soul had been left behind in that place.

Days passed. Then a week. Then two more. They never stayed in a village. They bought supplies and moved on. They gave no one their real names. The mountains were barren and rocky. The travel was arduous, even on the road. Alesia grew more and more anxious as the days passed. Her stomach could get no larger. She was due.

"No, we are staying in Nigidia. I am telling you, I can feel it. The baby has shifted lower in my pelvis. It is time!"

"No, it's not safe. Let's just see what Kayseri says when we find her." The road around them was dry and desolate. Dryados's eyes were sunken. Of the three, he had fared the worst on the journey. He never traveled well. Now his nerves were shot. He'd been battling diarrhea for days. Despite drinking as much water as he could, his urine was a brown sludge.

"You mean if we find her. If she is still in the area. If she even remembers Decima. And…if she believes us," Alesia said. "That is not a plan. Here is the plan. We stay in Nigidia! We find a midwife. And I have a baby! No, that *is* the plan! If you are going to do something else, then you are doing it alone." She scowled over at Ascalon. "And the same goes for you too!"

Ascalon looked blankly at Alesia and then stoically at Dryados.

Dryados felt so lightheaded. "I think that is a good plan, my love. And I think…I may also need a physician." He felt like vomiting. He was so hot. He was having a hard time even thinking. There were so many shadows around them…

Dryados slumped in the saddle. He remembered laying his head on the horse's neck. And that was all...

"Drink! Drink!" Someone was yelling or whispering or something. "Drink! Drink!" Dryados took several drinks of...something.

Why are they so angry? he thought.

"Drink! Drink!"

Dryados felt...wet. He took several large swallows of whatever was being poured in his mouth. It was pitch black all around him. *It must be nighttime*, he thought. *And...these people are just obnoxious.* Someone was still yelling. "Drink! Drink!" *Perhaps this is a dream.* He drifted off. He could feel the waves crashing against him. *Perhaps I have fallen overboard...perhaps this is what is like to drown.* Fear gripped him.

"Stop splashing! You're getting water everywhere."

Dryados opened up his eyes. The world was so dark. He was in a tub, in a room. Alesia was standing over him. He was in a tub full of water. He felt confused. "How did I get here?"

"The physician said you would be OK. You must drink lots and lots of water. He said we needed to cool you down as quickly as we could."

"I'm in a tub..."

"Yes you are, my sweet. A very lovely tub. Now drink some more of this." Alesia put a cup of cool water to his lips. "You must drink it all."

Dryados drank the goblet dry. He looked around the room. He had no idea where he was. "Are we in...where are we?"

"We are in Nigidia. We have found a nice room to stay in. When you are better, we will get you something to eat. Just keep drinking."

After what seemed like gallons of water going down his throat, Dryados started to feel better. He looked around the room. It was clean and...well, it was clean. The room had no distinguishing features. There was a tub, so that was a bit of a luxury. There was a bed and a table with a pitcher of water. "How long have we been here?"

Alesia put another goblet of water in his hand. "Keep drinking." Dryados downed the water. "We got here a couple of hours ago. Ascalon just left. He has a room down the hall." Alesia got up and refilled the cup from the pitcher. "We sent for a physician as soon as we arrived. He said you had some sort of a heatstroke and were horribly dehydrated. He said we needed to cool you down as quickly as we could. We got the only room here at the inn that had a tub." Alesia held the cup to his mouth again. "Here, drink some more."

"I'm really getting full..."

"That's OK. Just drink it anyway..." Dryados gave her a disgruntled look but continued to drink. "They have also sent for the midwife. She should get here any time."

"Nigidia?"

"Yes. We are in Nigidia. In a room. Where we will be staying for a while."

Dryados sat up in the tub. "Ohhh, I feel so much better." He took the cup from Alesia's hand and finished the water.

Alesia retrieved the cup and refilled it over by the pitcher. "Not so fast..." Dryados was trying to climb out of the tub. She hurried back over, putting her hand to his head. "Your fever is down, but you are not getting out of the tub until the pitcher is empty. Those were the physician's instructions. Now, here." She handed him the cup.

"I really have to go pee."

"Then I suggest you drink quickly. And the doctor instructed me to watch and see what color your urine is."

"What? That's disgusting," he moaned.

"Just drink your water." Alesia nudged him back down in the tub. Dryados drank the pitcher of water dry. Then stood to go outside. "No, you are to go here in this basin. The physician said he wants to see it when he gets back."

"What kind of healer did you get for me?" he groaned.

"A very good one. Now go pee in the basin." Alesia shoved the basin into his hand. Dryados begrudgingly stepped out of the tub and walked over to the corner. He still felt faint.

"That can't be good..." Dryados muttered. Dark blood-tinged urine filled the bowl. "I think I need to lie down."

The bed was soft, but he was getting cold. He reached down to grab another blanket.

"No, no, no...no more blankets. I wasn't supposed to give you even the one. The healer said you should not get chilled but that you still need to keep your temperature down."

Dryados sat up in bed. "I am really feeling much better."

"I know. Your urine was almost clear last time." She looked at him with a small smile. She was still worried.

Dryados didn't remember going pee. He didn't remember how he got in bed or drinking any more water. But sitting up in bed, he no longer felt dizzy. "How long this time?"

"We arrived in Nigidia the day before yesterday. You have been in and out of consciousness since then. But each time you have awakened, it has seemed to last longer, and you have become more and more alert."

"And Ascalon, where is he?"

"He has been discreetly trying to contact Kayseri. But he has had no luck. He says the people just look at him funny." Alesia poured Dryados some more water.

"The people here in the village may not want to reveal the location of a young woman to some stranger. Especially one as stout and rugged as Ascalon." She handed him the cup, which he quickly emptied. "To make matters worse, Ascalon continues to carry that big hammer of his strapped to his waist wherever he goes. Between that, his eye patch, and his arm brace, he looks like a crazed lunatic trying to pick a fight. Either way, I do not think Kayseri is going to come knocking at our door anytime soon."

The hours passed. Many people came to the room, knocking on the door, but none were Kayseri. The physician, Elazig, returned to reexamine Dryados. Elazig was tall, with a heavy black beard. His nose was thick and long, with a large hump. He wore his clothes like some of the desert people from the south. He never seemed to smile. Perhaps it was simply hidden beneath the thickness of his beard. Still, Dryados liked him immediately.

"And these herbs will help with the looseness of your bowels. They should be taken with food. The best foods for the next few days will be starchy roots and lots of bread." Dryados smiled and nodded. "And you..." Elazig turned, facing Alesia. "What was said by the midwife of the baby?"

"She thinks I still have a few days." Alesia blushed. "I have never met a midwife who did that...that exam."

"This is how things are done. The women here must know exactly how much time is left. There is much work to be done in a small village. If they have time, they can take the herds out to grazing. If not, they can stay and weave. The exam tells the midwife what is safe and how much longer the women can keep working. When did Tatavan say she would check you again?"

Alesia was redder than Dryados had ever seen her. She was a woman of the aristocracy. Speaking of such things, especially to a man, was unconscionable. "She said she would be back later in the week. Sooner if I needed her or my water broke." That was it—if her face turned any redder, it would have exploded.

"Yes, Tatavan seems very competent," Dryados interjected. He glanced at Elazig and tried to quickly change the subject. "Do you know her well?"

Elazig smiled, or at least Dryados thought he smiled. "Of course, of course. She is my brother's wife's cousin. We are very close. Her husband is a butcher, which makes it very convenient in her line of work."

Dryados had no idea what that meant. He glanced at Alesia. She had gone from apple red to white as a newborn sheep.

"Yes, yes...and, ah, have you lived here long?" Dryados stammered, trying again to change the topic.

"Yes, my whole life. Everyone in the village has lived here their whole lives. No one moves to Nigidia. Which makes me wonder, why are you here?"

"Well actually," Dryados said slowly, "we are looking for a young woman somewhere here in the area. Her name is Kayseri. We were told she might help us with a problem we have been facing. It's of a personal nature…you understand…"

"Of course, of course. It is just a little confusing to me…"

Dryados looked questioningly at Alesia. Alesia nodded back with a yes.

Dryados slowly added, "Well, you see, her name was given to us by a mutual friend. His name is Decima. He said we could find her here and that he thought she might be able to help us. We have come a long way to see her."

"Yes, of course I see, exactly, exactly. Well, if I hear of such a person, I will let you know." Elazig bowed multiple times as he exited the room. "And remember, eat lots of bread."

Dryados nodded politely as the doctor backed out of the door.

Alesia walked over and sat beside him on the bed, leaning against his shoulder. "I think he knows something. He seemed different after you mentioned Kayseri's name."

"He said he was confused." Which of course made Dryados feel confused.

"Yes, but confused means you know something. Even if it all doesn't quite match up." Alesia looked like she was in the middle of a game of Foxes and Hounds, plotting her next move, but was stuck.

"Do you think we were wrong to ask? You nodded like you thought it was OK."

"No, you did the right thing." Alesia nodded again. "He is the local healer. If anyone would know of her or her family, it would be him. Now I think we just need to wait."

The next day Tatavan returned early. She did the same shocking examination to Alesia as she had done before. Dryados had to wait out in the hall. When he was finally allowed back in, the midwife spoke casually. The baby within Alesia would arrive in the next few days. But mostly, she asked indirect questions about the three travelers. Sideways questions about their journey. Interesting things they had seen. Open-ended questions about their pasts, their jobs, where their relatives lived. Anything that would elucidate more about who they were. The three remained tight lipped. Ascalon, of course, was no mystery to anyone. He was a smithy. But who Alesia and Dryados were and why the three had come there seemed to have put some people in the community on edge.

A few hours after Tatavan's unexpected visit, there was another knock at the door.

Dryados opened the door only to be surprised to find a very old man standing alone in the hall. "May I help you, sir?" Dryados asked politely.

"Yes. I am Malatya. I am one of the elders here in the town. I would speak with you." His eyes were watery and his face drawn. The skin of his arms looked thinner than parchment.

Dryados looked questioningly at Alesia and Ascalon, who nodded their approval. "It would be our honor, sir. Please come in and sit with us." Dryados opened the door for the man to enter.

The old man shuffled slowly in, leaning heavily on his staff. "It is easier if I stand. If I sit, I will not be able to rise to my feet again without your assistance."

Alesia and Ascalon rose to their feet. "No, sir, you honor us with your presence. Here, please sit." Alesia tried to smooth out the pillows on the lounge they had just been seated upon.

"To steal the chair of a woman with child would be a horrible act. No, I thank you, but I will stand. But please...please sit back down that I may speak with you."

Alesia and the two men sat back down. The old elder shuffled closer. "Tell me in truth, why do you seek the woman Kayseri here in our village?"

Dryados answered, "As we have shared with others in the community, it is a personal matter. But we were told by a mutual friend that she might be able to help us. And we have traveled far to find her."

The old man looked as confused as everyone else by their seemingly bizarre request. "And who is the one that told you of her? What is his name? What does he look like?"

Dryados sighed deeply. Then he shared the truth of their benefactor and answered all the unanswerable questions. "Yes, as I said, he is a leper. No, I have never seen him. No, I have no idea how he made his livelihood in the past. No, I have no idea how long he has been with the colony." And on and on it went.

"It seems you did not know this man Decima very well at all, Master Dryados," the old man said disappointedly.

"Actually, I knew him very well in every way that matters. And we are here because I would trust him with my life." Dryados had never said those words out loud before. But as he thought about it, they were all true. Decima was a close friend. As close as Ascalon or Talmun. "And if this young woman, Kayseri, is anywhere in the village, perhaps you should ask her if she could give better testimony as to my friend Decima."

The old man nodded as he leaned on his staff. Then he turned halfway toward the door. "I would like to step outside for just a moment. I will be right back...I promise." The old man slowly shuffled out the door, closing it behind him. Dryados sat with his wife and Ascalon silently on the lounge, somewhat bewildered.

A few minutes later there was another knock at the door.

Dryados opened the door again to see the same old man standing there, leaning on his staff. Next to him was an equally ancient woman. She held a delicate cane and was as thin as the stick she used to walk. The two shuffled slowly in. Malatya held up the old woman's hand and smiled. "I would like to introduce you to my lovely wife, Kayseri."

Kayseri and Malatya were soon seated on the lounge. Ascalon made arrangements with the inn's staff to bring in some additional chairs, tea, and snacks. Dryados continued to drink water and to eat lots of bread.

"And you say all three of you spoke with him?" Kayseri's voice was airy and weak, but she always smiled.

"Yes," they all replied.

"And none of you ever saw his face?"

They shook their heads. "No."

"Perhaps you were not ready…" Kayseri slowly sipped her tea. "Yes, I'm sure that is it. It is, well, it is a sight, but of course you must be ready to see it. Some people, I suppose, never are."

"But he is still a friend," Dryados interjected. "His leprosy is not a barrier to that."

"So you say, but still…" Kayseri continued to nibble on a small honey roll. Her mind seemed to wander off. "You know, he has been a friend of mine for some time. I didn't even know my mother had gone off to Tyre and Sidon to seek help for me. Of course, in those days I wasn't aware of very much. The demon that had seized me was cruel. It was always there, dwelling next to my mind. Trying to destroy me. And I had no hope. None at all. All I could do was endure. I still remember it." She drank more tea and snuck another honey roll. "No, such things you do not forget. Then one day he was just there. Decima, I mean. And the demon was gone." She looked over at her husband, who smiled and squeezed her hand. "We traveled a lot back then, always on the move. Still, wherever we went, he would come and check up on me every few years. Perhaps in my agedness he feels that is no longer necessary. Still, I would love to see him…"

"A leper!" Ascalon interrupted. "A hundred paces away beneath a hood is fine with me."

Kayseri laughed. It was an old laugh. "Despised and rejected, even by those who love him. Just like the one my mother visited in Tyre and Sidon when I was a child. Still, I would love to see him again." She nodded at her husband. "It is time. We must be leaving." Her husband rose to his feet. After he had braced himself up with his staff, he began to help her up too.

Dryados jumped to his feet. "But we haven't even told you why we have come!"

"You told my husband you needed my help and that Decima has sent you." She shuffled to the door. "At my age, there is very little help I can offer. But still I am here for a purpose." She slowly looked back at Dryados. Her eyes were old and seemed to see through him. "Three visitors obviously on the run from someone." She spoke it as a simple fact.

Dryados nodded yes.

"You seek a secret place. Where you will be safe for some time."

Dryados again nodded yes.

"You will leave early in the morning. Bring everything you have. Tatavan will meet you on the north road, leaving Nigidia at dawn. She will take you to Der-inkuyu."

Chapter 34
Derinkuyu

"**A**smithy? Why would a smithy come to move here? We already have a smithy." The old peasant looked confused as he tried to answer the Roman's questions. "Don't think…"

"I did not say he was moving here. I asked if you had seen one traveling through here." The Roman commander shoved the peasant man off to the side. "And what of the rest of you? Have any of you seen a smithy pass through the area in the last week or so? He would be a big man with a large brace on his left arm." The people on the street remained silent. "He is a murderer and extremely dangerous." The Roman commander paced through the crowd. "Do not approach him. If you see him, contact us immediately. If it is the right man, you will be generously rewarded with twenty silver dinars. His name is Ascalon." The commander's men continued to search the street and nearby buildings. The commander looked back at the crowd. "It is possible that we may have gotten ahead of him. Keep a watchful eye, and Rome will reward you."

The band of soldiers moved farther down the road. They had arrived at midmorning. They had been marching all night trying to get to the city before dawn. They spread out rapidly when they arrived, searching the village for the murderous smithy.

The commander's squad approached the next group on the street, where he gave the same practiced announcement. "One of the other villages suggested he may be traveling with a blond-haired woman and another man. The woman is said to be very pregnant. Or may have a newborn child…" There were no answers from this group either. It was clear that everyone in the village was either in on the deception or simply had not seen them. "My men and I will be staying here the next few days. And remember, the reward is waiting for anyone who cooperates."

The Romans scowled at the villagers. "We have heard there are secret places hidden in the mountains where they might go."

One of the old men sitting at a table playing a board game laughed.

"You think that is funny, old one? You think it humorous to laugh at the power that rules you?" The commander stomped over and tore the man from his chair and hurled him to the street. The old man flew in the air like a tossed pebble and slammed onto the rocky road. He landed with a cry of pain.

"No, Great One, no. It is not funny. Not funny at all." He was bleeding from both of his hands. He cradled one of his arms up with the other. "It is just that we have heard these tales our whole lives—enchanted cities in the hills made of gold. Bewitched so that you cannot see them even if you are standing in the middle of them. Every empire and kingdom that has conquered these areas has searched for them. Every one of us here in the village at one time or another has wasted our time looking for them. Yet here we sit in our poor village. I meant no offense sir. Truly, sir, I just…"

The Roman commander turned and stomped down the street.

Earlier that morning, the north road

The horses snorted loudly in the chill morning air. It was still dark. Ascalon's horse seemed particularly unhappy about having to carry the heavy smithy so early in the day. "Ho there! Ho!" Ascalon nudged the horse on the sides a few times with his heels and pulled the reins tightly, but the horse continued to whinny and spin. Dryados's pack horse, which carried a much lighter load, stood placidly, obviously bored.

"I think the horse finds you to be a cruel master to put such a heavy load on its back," Tatavan said, half giggling.

"I would put a much harsher load on its butt if I had a switch. It is not my fault if I'm big," Ascalon said as he continued to spin in a circle with the befuddled horse.

Tatavan kicked her horse forward. "The horses will calm quickly as we ride. They do not like to travel in the dark, but it will soon be light." She led the way out of town on the north road.

The others nudged their horses forward and followed in behind her.

"How far is it?" Dryados asked.

"It is…as far as it is. Hidden places do not stay hidden by talking about them," she answered passively.

"But you haven't talked to us about it at all." Dryados shrugged.

"Exactly." Tatavan smiled.

The chill of the air quickly vanished as the sun rose. Less than a mile out of town, Tatavan took them off the road onto a narrow trail—steep and filled with switchbacks and back cuts. Sometimes, it seemed they plodded in circles. They took several breaks, usually stopping near the top of a hill. Tatavan would then dismount and creep to the top. She would peer over the crest to make sure the road ahead was clear. Other times, she would conceal them in the hidden cleft of a valley and then ride back and make sure they were not followed. The first night was spent in such a cleft. It was very cold, with no fire.

The next day began much like the first, but that soon changed. They stopped more frequently. Tatavan would be gone for longer intervals of time. As they rode, she pulled a sword out from her night roll and strapped it beside her. Her eyes darted in constant motion. Her altered demeanor was not subtle. Ascalon clung to his hammer. Dryados held his kukri hidden in his tunic. The morning passed, then noon, then soon the afternoon. Now it was dusk.

Tatavan raised her arm and brought her horse to a stop. She looked around again, searching their surroundings. She dismounted and signaled the others to do the same. They walked silently single file down another rocky goat trail, the only noise the occasional whinny of the nervous horses and the tumble of a loose stone off the path. Tatavan raised her arm and stopped.

"Take this." She handed the reins of her horse to Dryados. "Stay here and do not make a sound."

He nodded, and the three did not move.

Tatavan crept quietly up the trail and disappeared around the next corner.

The wind blew in the low brush around them. Beyond that, there was no noise. The minutes passed. The sky grew darker, but they could still see the empty trail in front of them. Ascalon unfastened the hammer he had secured to his waist. Dryados pulled out his kukri. There was the distant sound of loose gravel shifting down the hill in front of them. They remained frozen in their spots.

Tatavan crept back around the corner. She took the reins of her horse. "Our camp is just ahead." She led her horse silently forward. Ascalon followed next. He held his horse's reins in one hand and his hammer in the other. Alesia waddled next to her horse. Dryados brought up the rear, scanning behind them for any sign of being followed. He clenched his kukri tightly as he walked.

They turned up a wide ravine. Off to their left was a high rock face with a large overhang of rock. Under the overhang was a small shepherd's camp. There was a small goat stall off to the back. In the center was a small fire pit and on the right a place to lay blankets to sleep. It was old, grimy, and well used.

"The local shepherds are rarely here this time of year. The grazing is better lower down. Still, we must be watchful should any arrive tomorrow. But for tonight, it will be safe to stay here." Tatavan led the group in. The horses were quickly secured in the goat stall and a meal prepared. Tatavan allowed no fire. The meal of bread, cheese, and dried fruit was still filling. Dryados's diarrhea had resolved, but he still ate a lot of the bread just to make sure. Tatavan decided that she would take the first watch. The others gave no argument. Moments after the meal was finished, the others were asleep.

The only clue to the outside world of their location was Ascalon's thunderous snoring.

"Alesia, Alesia." Tatavan pushed gently on her shoulder. "Alesia, wake up."

It was pitch black. Alesia groggily regained consciousness. There was no sense of urgency in Tatavan's voice, so she remained calm. "Is everything OK?" she whispered.

"Yes, everything is fine. But it is time for us to leave. I think it will be safer if you wake up Dryados, and Dryados wakes up Ascalon. Men sometimes do not take well to be woken up in the middle of the night by an unfamiliar voice." Alesia nodded and pulled herself out from under the now warm blanket. After several unrestrainable yawns, she crawled over and woke up her husband. Dryados in turn woke up the hard-snoring smithy.

Tatavan gathered everyone together. "Now, we go to Derinkuyu," she whispered.

"It's pitch black. We are either going to need torches and let everyone know where we are…or someone is going to break a leg out there," Dryados whispered back. "We need to wait for a little more light. It's not safe for Alesia."

"No, I said we are going to Derinkuyu right now. So do as I say!" Tatavan walked over to the stall with the horses. She gently petted and quieted her mare. But then she walked to the back wall of the stall and started to kick away some of the manure stacked against the back wall. Dryados and the others moved closer to watch. There beneath the manure was an old hammer. She picked it up and gently began to tap the stone wall of the rock face behind them. It was a very specific set of taps and scratches. Then she held her hand up for the others to remain silent. From deep inside the ancient stone behind them…they heard someone knock back. Three loud taps. Tatavan motioned for the others to move to the side. Suddenly the wall of stone behind them moved. A section of the stone wall slid back into the mountain. As it moved away, a wide door became visible. "Now, move everything inside. Leave no traces."

"What about the horses?" Alesia asked.

"They will come too. The underground city is bigger than you might expect. Again, leave nothing behind." As she spoke, several men emerged from the passage dressed completely in black. Silently they helped move all their belongings inside the mountain. Once everyone and their goods were inside, they swept the area with some old brooms, removing every trace and footprint. Then they stacked the manure in the path where the stone door would slide forward. As the door slide back into place the manure again piled high up against it on the other side.

Like the sound of a giant cat purring, the monolithic door slid quietly closed. "Krrrrrrrrrr." Torches were then finally lit. The threesome stood in a large chamber. "The horses will be secured here for the night. We will move them to the main stables in the morning." The man speaking removed his black veil and put out a hand toward Ascalon, who was standing closest to him. "My name is Malakop. Welcome to Derinkuyu." He greeted Dryados and Alesia in turn. The three travelers remained silent as Tatavan gave her report to Malakop.

"The three of you will please follow my men. Ascalon, my friends will be taking you to the hall for the single men. They will show you where you can sleep and a place to put your things." Malakop's smile was wide and cheerful, even in the subdued light of the torches.

Ascalon wanted to scream. He wasn't single. He was married. He had a son! They had a life together! He sighed, and his body slumped as the excitement of entering the hidden city was drowned out by a tidal wave of despair.

Alesia watched as Ascalon's countenance fell. The movement of the child in her stomach reminded her instantly of everything Ascalon had lost. "No, Ascalon will be staying with us."

Dryados's face flashed with confusion.

"No, Alesia, that will not be necessary." Ascalon walked slowly toward his waiting guide. "He is right. I am a single man."

Dryados's mouth gaped as he suddenly grasped the unintended anguish Malakop's words had caused his friend. He started to say something, but stopped. He looked at his friend and began a silent prayer. "Oh God..."

Ascalon and his escorts departed into the darkness.

"And the two of you will be taken to your own quarters in the married section. I will come by later in the morning to take you on a tour." Malakop turned and started to lead them away. Then he suddenly stopped. He turned back, looking at Alesia. "Alesia, do not worry. We have had many children born here in Derinkuyu. Yours will not be the first. Nor do I think it will be the last. Tatavan has already informed me she will be staying until the baby is born." Malakop flashed his broad smile.

The path they took through the underground city was a maze of turns and pitfalls. "Be careful—the floor here is wet...stay to the left and watch your head. Ventilation shaft to the right...stay on the bridge...deep chasm on the left..." Dryados and Alesia hit their heads several times. Dryados also twisted his ankle after hitting his knee on a protruding rock. They arrived at their assigned quarters exhausted and slightly bruised.

Their dwelling area was much larger than they imagined. It contained a sizable living room with a smaller but separate sleeping room off to the side. Abundant storage alcoves were carved into the stone walls throughout both rooms. Several lamps had already been lit, so the rooms were easy to see. Malakop showed them around with the added light of his torch. "It is cold in the unoccupied areas here in the hidden city—worse at night. The smaller rooms will heat up fairly quickly and easily stay warm once they are. Still, you should put on some extra blankets." Malakop smiled one last time, then closed the curtain, which served as their door.

How it exactly happened they did not know, but soon their blankets were unpacked and they were next to each other, sound asleep on the floor.

With no sun to wake them, the city leaders allowed the new arrivals to sleep in late. Malakop's tour later that morning was impressively confusing. The three newcomers were impressed beyond measure with the size of the vast underground city, and totally confused by its jumbled maze of tunnels. The city was exactly that—a city. The first place Malakop took them to was the city's hospital. It had several beds, a fire shaft, shelves of bandages, and alcoves stuffed with herbs and healing remedies. Ascalon, of course, was most impressed with the main smithy and stables. "And I see you have brought your own hammer." Malakop laughed. "Perhaps you can put it to use here. There is much work that must be done, and we have no true full-time smithy of our own." Ascalon smiled as he clung to his hammer. He nodded but did not speak. They saw the bakery and small agora. "We have very limited shopping. Most everything here is shared communally. The coolness and dryness of the upper levels is ideal for long-term storage." Malakop flashed his ever-present smile. "We can house ten thousand people. With all the doors sealed closed, we have enough food to feed them all for six months." He beamed with pride.

"What about water?" Alesia asked. She was really struggling to climb up the short ladder Malakop had directed them to scurry up.

"The city goes down eleven levels." Malakop took Alesia's hand as she reached the top. "Below that is an underground river. We call it Vita et Mors, which means Life and Death. The river is a source of life to the city. There is never a need for water. Over the centuries, the city has been discovered from time to time by our enemies. Many have tried to starve us out and set ambushes at the nearby springs. None, of course, have ever known how big the city truly was or of the deep river. Obviously they never succeeded. Eventually they all departed, only for the city to become lost again…here we go. This way." Malakop led them along a thin passage and then down a steep incline. "We are now eight levels below the entrance. We only use the lower three levels in time of war. They can sometimes be damp because of their proximity to the river."

The group huddled in the circle of light created by their torches. Malakop continued to speak about the city and its history. "You see, the Hittites were the first…" Ascalon played with his hammer like a baby with its favorite toy. Dryados listened intently. Alesia's mind was lost as she stood there simply enjoying the feel of the baby kicking in her stomach.

"And so that is how we find ourselves here today," Malakop concluded. "Now, if you will follow me up, I think it is almost time for lunch." Malakop's torch flickered as he swung them back up the tunnel they had just come down. Alesia huffed and puffed up the steep path. She stopped. A flood of water gushed down her leg.

"We are almost there," Malakop said reassuringly.

Dryados walked up beside her. "Here, take my hand. I can help you the rest of the way."

"No, it's not that," she reassured them. "It's...my water just broke."

The three men stood in shocked silence. Alesia looked around at their white dumbfounded faces. "It's going to be fine," she said, smiling. "I'm just going to have my baby now."

She beamed with joy as she looked over at Dryados, who did not seem to be breathing.

"I think it might be best if we headed directly back to the hospital section," Alesia said calmly. "Malakop, do you think you could guide us there directly? Personally, I am completely lost."

"Of course, of course. We continue exactly the way we are going. Here..." Malakop started to hurry up the passage.

Dryados wrapped his arms tightly around his wife. "Let me help you."

"I'm fine—the baby is not coming this instant." She smiled at him again. "But the baby is coming."

To the men, the journey down the dark halls to the hospital seemed to take an eternity. For Alesia, it seemed it was just around the corner. She was only a little scared.

"I will fetch Tatavan. You just stay here and...and everything will be fine." Malakop spoke quickly. For the first time, his confident demeanor and broad smile seemed forced. He spun. In an instant, he and his flickering torch disappeared down a different passage.

Dryados and Alesia stood looking at each other. Their smiles each a facade to encourage the other. In the near blackness of Derinkuyu's hospital, they were both frightened.

"Perhaps you should lay down, my love." Dryados nudged Alesia toward one of the beds.

"I don't think I need to lay down. I feel fine. I have been having these contractions off and on for days." She stood smiling for a moment, and then another contraction hit. This one started in her back. Alesia winced, leaning forward and holding her stomach. It passed a few moments later. "Perhaps you are right," she groaned. Dryados grabbed her hand and helped her into a nearby bed. Then he knelt on the ground beside her. His face seemed whiter.

Ascalon shuffled forward. "I never saw my son born, so I don't know exactly how things are done. But if they need to use my hammer, well, here it is." He held his hammer up in the shifting torchlight. His serious look slowly changed to a small smile. His subtle chuckle grew into a hearty laugh.

Dryados and Alesia burst into laughter. It was Ascalon's first joke. They looked at each other, each one roaring. Alesia watched the big smithy. Tears rolled down his face. It made her smile even more.

"Well, it sounds like this is the right place to be—best party in the whole city," Tatavan joked as she entered the room. She looked over at Alesia. "Why are you laying down? You need to be walking." The laughter in the room slowly abated. "Well, since you are already there on the bed, let me take a look."

Ascalon and Dryados raced to the other side of the room.

"Perhaps I should be going. I really don't belong here," Ascalon said nervously.

Dryados placed his arm warmly on Ascalon's shoulder. "No, you are part of our family now. We would be honored if you would stay. Besides, you have never seen Alesia angry. We might need that hammer of yours after all." He looked at Ascalon with a smirk.

"No, I really must be going…" As the two men argued, Tatavan performed her examination.

Sitting on the bed, she smiled. "Well, you are farther along than I thought, but you still have a long way to go. As I said before, you need to be up walking." Tatavan stood up beside the bed. "You two men, please join us over here."

The two men scuffled hesitantly forward.

"Now Alesia, before the other women get here, does the blacksmith stay or go? It is up to you. But you must decide before Malakop gets here. He could escort him back, if you like."

Alesia looked up from the bed at Tatavan. "I don't know. Do you think we will need the hammer?"

"What?"

"I'm just kidding." She turned toward Ascalon. "I would love it if you would stay. As Dryados has said, over our travels together, you have become part of our family."

Ascalon smiled and nodded.

"Good. You will stay and help me. Dryados, you will walk your wife up and down that corridor until the other women arrive." She motioned to an area of blackness off to their left. "It is the widest and flattest. Stop when you come to the bridge. You can talk to her, sing to her, or whatever. But you cannot let her stop except for a contraction."

Dryados grabbed one of the lamps and began walking the corridor with Alesia.

"Now, Ascalon, I will need…" Tatavan seemed to enjoy ordering the big blacksmith about. She had him fetch supplies from the various shelves, light all the lamps and torches, and then to even start rearranging the furniture. Each time Dryados and Alesia returned from their circle down the corridor, she would flash them an obtuse smile, suggesting the work she gave Ascalon was completely unnecessary. In short order, the other women arrived along with a now smiling Malakop.

Tatavan thanked Malakop, Dryados, and Ascalon for their help. "But the rest of this is for the women and me. One of us will come and fetch you once the baby is born."

The men nodded and eagerly followed Malakop down a separate passage.

There was no window. There was no breeze. Even with the torches burning, it was clear Alesia was hundreds of feet below ground. When the women nearby spoke, their words were muffled, but they echoed in the strange hollow cavern. This was not how she imagined having her first child.

"Do not push! Do not push!" Tatavan yelled for the hundredth time. "It is too early. If you push now, you will tear. You must wait. Let the contractions slowly do the work."

With every fiber of her being, Alesia wanted to push. She was so tired. Every part of her body ached. Her back most of all. And it seemed the weight of the entire world was pushing down in her pelvis. Time dragged around her like a squirrel pulling an oxcart full of boulders. She concentrated on breathing. She breathed, and she kept breathing. Her whole universe existed in a simple rhythm—wait for the contraction to pass and then wait for the next one to begin...and breathe. It seemed like an eternity had passed since she'd lain on the bed.

"Don't hold your breath. If you hold your breath, you will want to push. Breathe...breathe..." Each contraction was like a winepress ratcheting down her stomach. Tatavan examined her again. She looked up, smiling. "You are ready." She nodded her head. "On the next contraction, you push, and we will have a baby!"

Alesia felt it building in her back. The muscles flexed. The contraction wrapped quickly around her like a passionate embrace. The whole world was in her stomach. She had to push...

"Now!" Tatavan yelled. "Now!"

Alesia pushed. It was as natural and effortless as breathing. It was something she was meant to do. Something she had to do...

There was a new sound that filled the chamber. The sound of a young child announcing his or her arrival to the world. And to Alesia, it was the most beautiful noise she had ever heard. The travail of the last several hours vanished from her mind. "Is everything OK?" Alesia propped herself up in bed. "Please, let me hold my baby."

"The nurse still needs to cut the cord. But *he* is fine."

"*He* is..." Alesia smiled.

"Yes." Tatavan nodded. "*He* is."

The nurses moved near the foot of the bed. The dim light of the flickering torches continued to conceal her son. Alesia couldn't see what the nurses were doing. "Is everything OK? Is he all right?"

"He is fine. They are just cleaning him up." The nurse handed the baby to Tatavan. Tatavan swaddled the baby in a clean blanket. "Here you go." She handed the infant to Alesia. "Be careful. He may still be a little slippery." Alesia took her son into her arms and began cooing and kissing his head. "And who is this young man who has made such a loud and boisterous entrance into the hidden city?" Tatavan asked with a big smile.

Alesia's face was worn and tired. Still, it glowed. "His name is Talmun Cleopas Titus Dryados," she said as she continued cooing and kissing her son. She did not look up at the others in the room. Nor did she hold her son up for their viewing. At that moment, nothing in the world mattered but the child she was gently kissing. "Talmun…baby Talmun…Mommy is right here…"

Dryados could see the flickering torch approaching down the passage. It moved steadily but not frantically. That was good. Malakop and Ascalon got out of the way so Dryados could speak to the courier. It was one of the women helping with the delivery. "All is well. Mother and baby are both fine. Your wife wishes you to come."

"And is it a boy or a girl?" Dryados blurted out.

The courier smiled. "Talmun Cleopas Titus Dryados arrived just minutes ago."

Dryados almost laughed. He was proud to have a son. But still, Alesia had insisted on four names. It was very *Roman* and aristocratic. But he still thought it was funny to actually hear someone say it out loud. They hadn't come to an agreement on the name until halfway through their journey from Sardis. He was sure he would never hear the end of it if he ever met up with Decima again.

"Can we all go?" Dryados asked.

"No, this is not a place for queasy-stomached men. The women are still tending her. Tatavan said you could come in for just a few minutes."

Dryados looked sheepishly back at his friends and then followed the courier down the slit in the rock. He twisted his ankle again as he hurried through the maze.

Chapter 35
Selah

The world turned time and time
    And the torches burned
    And the caverns were warm.

But there was no sun.

Chapter 36
Four Blood Moons

The black-clad assassin pulled the scarf higher on his face. The four guards the bandits had posted around the perimeter were killed over an hour ago. Their clothes had been stripped off and were now being worn by the men who had replaced them. The assassin had counted the bandit camp several times. Tonight, all twenty-three of the marauders were present. Now they were down to nineteen. Soon it would be time for the guards to change. Then they would be down to fifteen. After that, the invisible army would attack. Ten to one was the rule they followed. Ten to one. Two hundred and thirty men clad completely in black now encircled the encampment. They had all watched as the bandits slowly tortured and then killed a small squad of Roman soldiers. They could have intervened then. But what would have been the point? There could be no survivors of tonight's attack.

The ground around the camp was alive. It moved like a flowing sea of black as concealed men crawled closer and closer. The four new guards shuffled out to their posts. One was complaining about how %&# cold it was. As they approached their presumed comrades, the earth around them welled up. Black arrows flew through the air. Sharp blades fell and black spears stabbed. The four men were swallowed up whole by the engulfing tide of merciless men. There wasn't so much as an audible groan. A mountain owl hooted softly to signal the next phase. The flaps of the tents ruffled as a stream of black flowed inside each dwelling. The assassin on the outskirts of the camp adjusted his scarf once again. His blade was blackened with tar and invisible beside him in the moonless night. His heart pounded in his chest.

"*Rraaahhhhhh!*" The sounds of battle erupted from one of the tents. The side of tent collapsed outward as men crashed through its frame. Shadows danced around the screaming men. There was the sound of slicing and the deep thumps of hard blows. Their screaming quickly stopped. One of the bandits made it to his horse. The horse flew forward as black shadows jumped out of the way. The assassin breathed faster. He tightened his grip around the tarred blade. The horse and rider galloped closer now. Arrows bounced off the rider's chest. He wore armor. Black bolts slammed into the horse's chest and side. It coughed and snorted to a halting stop. The assassin leaped from the darkness of the concealing earth. The man was still high on the horse's back. The waiting assassin slammed the tarred blade into the man's thigh. As he screamed, another assassin shot a bolt through his neck while another jabbed a long black spear deep into his armpit. The rider lurched backward. The assassin slammed his tarred blade into the man's now exposed stomach. Bolts and spears continued to do their work until the man was unmoving on the ground. The horde of assassins took no chances.

The bandits were all dead. None of the assassins was seriously injured. The black-clad assassin began to clean the blood from the tarred blade. The blade itself had an oddly hooked shape and was thick on the back side, almost like an ax. The night warriors began to remove every sign of the bandit camp. Everything would be taken into the hidden city and sorted out. Any coin, gold, or silver would go to the city treasury. Food, clothing, weapons—anything that could be used, would be used. The bodies were always the hardest to dispose of. Leaving them stripped to rot would draw flocks of circling birds. The circling birds could draw attention. Instead, the bodies would be buried in shallow graves in the hard, rocky ground.

It was still dark when the last of the black cohort reentered the city. As the great stone door ground into place behind them, the assassin finally lowered his scarf. He stood motionless in the entry hall and let out a deep sigh. He stood there for several minutes as countless other silent men walked past him. That was the fourth raid he had fought in. The fourth time he had helped kill a man he didn't even know. He walked back to his room in near total darkness. He knew every corridor in the hidden city like he knew the smile lines on his wife's face. He no longer even needed a lamp.

He slid the curtain opened that served as a door. He placed the tarred blade on the shelf next to a dusty ceramic baby fox. Slowly he started to slip out of his black garb. Alesia came out of their room and started to help him undress.

"Are you OK?" she asked quietly. Baby Talmun was still asleep.

Dryados nodded. "Yes"

She squeezed him tightly and whispered, "I love you."

Dryados turned and kissed her on the forehead. There was a hint of a smile in his eyes, but not on his face. The smile she loved so much seemed to make its appearance less and less often these days.

Alesia wrapped her arms back around him. "Tomorrow, if the guards approve, let's take baby Talmun to the Chasm."

Dryados forced a smile. "That's a good idea. I just need to get some sleep." He pulled her close and gave her a small kiss. Then he went into their room, lay down, and slept.

Despite the heavy raid the night before, and the worrisome death of a squad of Romans, the distant perimeter guards detected no one approaching the hidden city. The city elders decided it was safe to grant the residents of the hidden city access to the Chasm. It was not like a valley that had an opening. Much as the name implied, it was more like a big hole, a great gauge in the surface of the earth. It was perhaps 400 yards long and 150 yards wide. Located on the plateau adjacent to the city to the west, it was easy to guard and completely concealed from the view of the outside world.

Dryados and his family walked among the large stones and heavy underbrush of the chasm's floor. Today they would go to the small pool at the far end. They had not been there for some time. The sun was high in the sky. Baby Talmun scurried among the boulders as they made their way to the pool. To ensure their secrecy, there were no trails cleared in the Chasm. Everything was left in its natural state. They found a nice flat spot not far from the pool. Alesia laid things out for a nice family picnic. As baby Talmun continued to play among the boulders, Dryados and Alesia snuggled by the pool. Dryados set up an old tattered board of Foxes and Hounds, his mind still distracted by the events of the night before. As always, Alesia played foxes. She gave Dryados no quarter and quickly beat him.

"That's not fair," he complained. "You're supposed to be nice to me. I had a rough night." He reached up slowly to touch her face. She let him gently stroke her hair. "If there were any flowers here in the Chasm, I would fill your hair with them." He gazed longingly into her eyes.

She smiled back. "Today, I would even let you." She leaned over and kissed him. Before he could respond, she stood up and walked over to the pool.

Dryados watched his wife as she walked slowly in the sunlight.

Being outside during the day was such a luxury. Alesia just enjoyed the warm sunshine on her face. She fiddled with some leaves on a bush as she walked casually around the large pool. She glanced at the smooth surface of the water. She stopped suddenly, her face filled with horror.

Dryados jumped to his feet and pulled out his tarred kukri.

Alesia turned slowly toward him, her face filled with anguish. "My hair!" she exclaimed. "It's…it's…brown!"

All the muscles in Dryados's body relaxed. "Yes, my love. Your hair is brown."

"No. No, it's not! My hair is blond! You love my hair."

"Yes, I love your hair. It doesn't matter to me what color it is." Dryados replaced the kukri back inside his tunic and walked slowly toward his wife.

"I wash it every day down in the underground river. I wash it every day!" She looked at him, almost distraught.

"I know you do. It's not that you don't wash it. I think it is just…" Dryados paused for a moment. "I think the underground river must have a significant clay component in it, just as do the walls of the underground city. I think it has just, well, sort of dyed your hair from the clay." He smiled and then reached up and kissed her hair. "It actually has a little bit of a red hue. It's just different."

She turned, looking at him with eyes of childlike sadness. Such a simple thing, but it had hurt her badly. Perhaps it was the sleepless night she had spent worrying that Dryados might be killed on the raid. Perhaps it was their lives living in perpetual darkness, always being dirty, buried inside a silent mountain, considering fire or sunshine a luxury. Perhaps she was just worn out.

"All right, let's just play another game, and I will let you win again," Dryados said with a mock smile.

The sadness fled from her eyes. She looked at Dryados and scoffed and marched back to the game board.

Perhaps she was madder than he thought. Each game went by faster than the one before. "All right," Dryads said confidently. "First one to six." He started to set up the game again.

"I have beaten you five times in a row," she said in proud fatigue. "Perhaps we need to take a break." Alesia moved to a better place in the diminishing sunlight. Dryados scooted over beside her. They watched baby Talmun playing among the boulders. He was almost there.

Dryados looked proudly over at his son's skills among the boulders. He weaved in and out of the tiny crevices. Both parents sat watching their scurrying monkey. He smiled and giggled as he played and climbed. "Look how fast he is," Dryados said, smiling.

Alesia nodded, her eyes crinkling, lying beside him in the sun.

Suddenly Dryados sat up. He looked stunned. His mouth was open, but he did not speak.

"Dryados, what's wrong?" Alesia sat up and grabbed Dryados's arm. Dryados continued to stare at the boulders and their son.

Slowly he turned toward her. "Talmun can't run," he said blankly. "He doesn't know how." Dryados's eyes remained fixed on his young son. Talmun smiled back as soon as he noticed the gazes of his parents upon him.

Alesia did not respond. She stared at their playing son.

Tired, they picked up Talmun and left a few minutes later. Their visit to the Chasm was not as restorative as they had hoped.

They ate dinner later that evening in the community hall. As was there routine, Ascalon ate all his meals with them. He too had changed over the many months. The raids were part of that. But there was much more to it. Dryados and Alesia had both seen it. The anger in his heart had changed. The despair that once filled his soul had changed. They were not gone. They simply existed inside his soul as something else. Dryados wasn't sure what it was for the longest time. Then he figured it out. It happened one day when he had visited Ascalon at the city smithy.

The smithy was a unique place in Derinkuyu. It had rules regulating everything that happened. No smoke was probably the biggest. The smiths worked mostly at night, and then only when the moon was small or it was cloudy. Days of low clouds or fog were also occasionally approved. The vent system was a complex arrangement of pipes. At the surface, the pipes spread out in ten or fifteen directions and went out fifty to one hundred yards from the main shaft. That way the smoke was spread out over a wide area and dispersed quickly by the wind. When Dryados had arrived that day at the underground smithy, Ascalon was already working on a piece of steel. The metal was stubborn. Ascalon used his brace as fluidly now as he did his own arm. Hours passed. Ascalon had his eye patch up to give him the depth perception he needed. It was then that Dryados first saw it in Ascalon's eyes. It was always there now—perhaps that was why it had been so hard to see. All those feelings and emotions had been remade. All the pain, sorrow, loss, anguish, and despair—all still there. But now they were changed into one immutable trait—resolve. Unfailing, unbending, unbreakable resolve.

They sat at the dining table as they always had. Alesia half played with baby Talmun as she nibbled on her dinner. Dryados ate mindlessly, as his thoughts relived the events back at the Chasm. Ascalon had stopped eating entirely and sat silently.

"Ascalon, is everything OK?" Alesia asked quietly. Baby Talmun was half snoozing now beside her.

"I will wait until Dryados finishes eating," he said.

That caught Dryados's attention. "I'm sorry? What was that?"

"No, go ahead finishing eating. It is not an emergency."

Ascalon's voice was even more stoic than normal. Dryados wolfed down the rest of his meal. "OK, what is it? Is everything all right?"

"Everything is fine," Ascalon said calmly. "It is just that I am leaving tomorrow night and would like to invite you all to come with me."

It wasn't clear whose jaw dropped the furthest, Dryados's or Alesia's. Alesia put her hand on Ascalon's arm. "But, Ascalon, what about the Romans? They will have you killed."

"That may be true. I do not know. But much time has passed, and the Romans have many enemies and many people they are trying to find. Perhaps my name has been lost among the myriads of others." Dryados noticed Ascalon's eyes had not changed.

"Still, it does not matter. I am leaving tomorrow night. I hope you will come. Oh, and I will also be going to Pergama to kill the governor." His voice was as placid as the still pond in the Chasm, and his eyes were like the steel that he made.

"What!" Dryados exclaimed. His loud proclamation brought absolute silence to the eating hall. Everyone turned, looking at them. Dryados shifted lower in his chair. He stared at Ascalon. Soon the low hum of people talking around them returned. "Are you out of your mind?" he whispered. "Don't you realize…" The rest of the conversation was like trying to stop an avalanche with an umbrella. Dryados and Alesia gave every rational reason why his plan was absolutely insane. They gave every passionate plea they could to save Ascalon's life. Ascalon would leave and die for nothing.

In the end, the result was the same. Ascalon was departing tomorrow night. And oh, by the way, he was also going to Pergama to kill the governor.

In the end, all Dryados and Alesia could say was, "We will really have to pray about that."

Dryados and Alesia took Talmun back to their room. Their discussion was long and troubling, but still they had no idea what they would do.

Bang! Bang! Bang! Dryados looked around the familiar blackness. The dream… But this was not a dream. He was in his room in Derinkuyu. *Bang! Bang! Bang!* Even though he was awake, it was still his dream. This was the same dream he had many times before. He got up and ran through the familiar blackness. The land-scape was not empty—it was the blank face of the stone passage walls. Now in the distance, he could see it. The great forge of Derinkuyu bursting forth with red power.

Bang! Bang! Bang! Ascalon stood there working at the forge. He pumped the bil-lows. Sparks of living fire filled the room. It was so hot. Dryados fell to his knees, sweating. Ascalon's hammer slammed against the heated metal. But this was no fine or delicate object of small instrumentation. It was big and round. *Bang! Bang! Bang!* Dryados turned to find Alesia kneeling on the floor beside him. She did not speak. Her eyes were transfixed by what was happening before them. The room was changing. There was a mighty flow of wind and energy. Figures began appear-ing around the room. They formed a great circle, with Ascalon and the forge at its center. Their faces were each covered by hoods of flickering red. No…they were not red. But the red power of the forge cast its glow upon their glimmering white-ness. As they watched, the hooded wings of the seven figures ruffled and spread open. Seven angels stood around the circle. Each wore a small filigree crown. One seemed to glance right at Dryados and smile. His crown was a pulsating deep carnelian red. They spread their wings to touch tip to tip like lovers holding hands. The circle was complete. Ascalon's hammer continued its unrelenting rhythm. *Bang! Bang! Bang!* The clanging of the hammer became the foundation beat of a new song. The angels began to sing. Like a song born deep in the earth, it was low like the river beneath them, Vita et Mors, Life and Death. Like the two choices the river offered, it branched out high and low in different choruses. The rhythm of the hammer did not falter, nor did the song. It swept through Dryados's and Alesia's souls as fluidly as the blood pumping in their veins. They watched as a single drop of sweat fell from Ascalon's brow. It exploded into vapor as it hit the metal. The loud sizzling *kaccchh* just added to the song like a small cymbal. The sound enfolded them like a thunderhead. But it was a familiar sound. A sound that tickled a memory deep within their souls. But the memory was not their own. It belonged to Ascalon and whisked them away…

Ascalon looked up, smiling at his father. They were at a smithy. His father wore the heavy black leather apron of a smith. "Hold the hammer low at the base. Then, just before it hits the metal, use the last bit of muscle in your wrist as well. The added speed will…" They could feel the love in Ascalon's spirit filling the memory.

The angelic song filled the room around them. The hammer lashed at the metal. The seven crowns of the seven angels burst with living color that danced across…everything. The light was a symphony of the visible proclamation of God's glory. It was like glancing at a written word and knowing what it said without thinking. The praise of angelic thought made visible.

Another drop of sweat hit the metal…

Ascalon danced with Sperta. It was his wedding day. They spun together like a pair of eagles on the winds of ecstasy. They were married!

Dryados's and Alesia's eyes opened to see filaments of power swirling from the angels and infusing into Ascalon's frame. The Shard of Light within him now pulsed to its own rhythm that brought a new layer of harmony to the song. As the hammer struck the metal, great bursts of energy leaped into it. The round disc he was now making glowed white like the sun.

Another drop of sweat…

Ascalon held his dying mother. "I will always love you…"

Another drop…

It was Ascalon's first day running the smithy. Doubt, fear, and sorrow permeated the memory. He couldn't do it…he wasn't the smithy his dad was, but…

A new sight confronted them. The Shard in Ascalon's chest smiled. It was like springtime within Ascalon's being. Green vines grew like ivy within him. His whole body glowed like a young green stalk of grass in the sun. Arcs of blue flame twisted up from the forge and cut the leather bonds holding the splint to his arm. He reached for a set of smithing tongs. As he did, he shook his arm, and the smoking splint fell to the ground. His arm was as big as the day Dryados had first met him.

The infusion of power in the room was growing blinding. Brands of fire burst from the forge and then slammed into Ascalon's thigh. Letters of pulsing red and blue emblazoned themselves there. Dryados began to cry. He could not read the words, but he knew what they were—a new name. His had been given to him on a white stone ages ago. Ascalon grabbed the glowing white disc with the tongs. Tools of every fashion seemed to appear and then disappear from his grasp. The angels around him moved. Their movements guided Ascalon's frame. Their skills flowed through him. An Opus Angelorum began to take shape. It was a shield.

Another drop of sweat…

Ascalon was talking to Sperta beside a fire. His eyes locked with hers as his fingers ran through her hair…

Another drop…

Sperta smiling…she was pregnant.

Another drop…

Lautus was born. The intensity of emotion was overwhelming.

Dryados and Alesia began to cry. Love, absolutely pure love poured into them. The love of a husband for his spotless bride. The love of a father for his spotless son. Love incarnate.

Another drop…

Another drop…

Green fire burst from Ascalon's eye. The eye patch above it disintegrated to ash. His whole body was white and green. Then he himself became part of the rainbow around him.

Another drop…

Another drop…

Ascalon ran with every ounce of strength and power he had to save them. Desperation! Absolute agonal desperation…

Another drop…

The room exploded around them. Sight and sound fled to perfect emptiness. The walls around them were the void before creation. Nothingness…

Then there was a spark of light in the distance. A glowing hand appeared above the white shield and began to write upon it. An image was etched deep into its substance. As the hand disappeared, swirls of eternal matter began to circle the white shield like a gathering storm. The sound in the room was like the crashing of many waters. Suddenly the circling swirls twisted and smashed into the substance of the metal and were absorbed. Each collision was like a wave crashing into a boulder. With each bursting impact, an image began to take color within the design honed into the substance of the shield. Like an enamel made for the fabric of existence. Red and green and brown…upon a background of snow white. The image was that of cherries on snow. A bride serving a son and a son killed by the sin of others. Then something came from Ascalon himself. It was not from the angel or the Shard. But it was like their reflection. It was something of his. His faith. And it made the shield shine.

Then Another entered the room. Dryados and Alesia covered their faces. They could not look upon Him. Terror gripped them as absolute love enfolded them. The angels kneeled and sang, "Sanctus…sanctus…sanctus…" He walked to the side of the room and grabbed a simple rod of iron from beside the wall. There was no inscription upon it. No infusion of angelic power or praise. He simply held it. As He did, the earth around them sighed. It was the sound of one being in love and being caressed by a lover. As He stood there, an essence appeared flowing from the rocks and stones around them. It snuggled into the iron rod like a cold child into the warm embrace of its father. It was the living memory of the inanimate world of its Creator. The acknowledgement of His absolute authority over everything. He walked over and handed the rod to Ascalon.

Dryados and Alesia were not sure if Ascalon was alive or dead, for he too had fallen motionless to the floor. The One of Power placed the rod into his hand. He spoke, though what He said was beyond comprehension. Yet they knew the rod was His and He had granted them His authority to use it.

The room around them had shaken and grown greatly in dimension, though its size did not change. Flashes of lightning and peals of thunder rose around them. Four living creatures hovered around Him in its center. Their eyes were fixed upon Him. The floor had melted like a sea of crystal glass. The angles sang. "Holy, holy, holy is the Lord God, the Almighty, who was, and is, and is to come." Power and love and holiness enfolded them. The moment persisted for what seemed an eternity. Then the One of Power departed.

The colors of jasper and Sardis lingered in the air. The angels continued singing "Sanctus...sanctus...sanctus..." long after He had left. Then they too faded through the fabric and were gone. Dryados and Alesia departed without speaking a word to Ascalon. What was the point? They needed to go back to their room and pack. They would be leaving with him tomorrow night.

Chapter 37
Very Soon

"And welcome to Seattle, where the local time is 4:25 pm. Baggage for this flight can be collected downstairs at baggage carousel number three. We hope you had a good flight. And on behalf the entire flight crew, we would like to thank you for choosing to fly with us today. Have a great time here in Seattle."

David and Philip collected their roller bags from the overhead and took the escalator downstairs. They collected their bags and called the hotel to send a shuttle. Soon they were both checked in and unpacking. The phone rang in David's room.

"Yes, Dr. Newman, there are some men here saying they are from a tour you have scheduled. They just shoved an envelope at me and asked what room. They didn't even know your name. It was just in the envelope. Is it OK if I give them your room number and send them up? They seem kind of…unprofessional."

"Yes, that would be fine." David hung up the phone and messaged Philip to come right over.

Philip, just three doors down, was there in moments. "Yeah, what's going on?"

"Come on in and have a seat." David closed the door. "I'm not sure, but I think we are about to meet our hosts."

"Our hosts?"

"I'm sorry. I mean our 'tour guides.'" There was another knock at the door.

"Oh?" Philip rose back to his feet.

David opened the door. Two men shuffled in without saying a word. One carried a long duffel bag over his shoulder. David put out his hand. "Hi, I'm—"

"Stop!" the taller man interrupted. "Don't say another word." He pointed his finger firmly in David's face. "First, a couple of ground rules. We are not at the Hedges. Anything you or I say can be compromised. No names. No personal information about who you are or where you are from. What little we need to know about you, we already know. Understood?"

Both men nodded.

"Good. I understand you are both here for some kind of a conference. Is that correct?"

Both men nodded.

The guide who had been doing all the talking grinned. "It's OK to speak. Just try to say as little as possible. My friend and I have been doing this for a long time. But we will need your help to pull this off."

The two surgeons stood silent and again nodded.

"Tomorrow will be just like any other day. With one exception. You will go, register, and attend your meeting exactly like nothing is happening. You will be social, but do not make any plans with anyone. Then you will return here to the hotel."

"And what is the one exception?" Philip asked.

The guide who had not yet spoken slung the long duffel bag onto the nearby couch. He unzipped the bag. "You will both carry long umbrellas with you wherever you go." He pulled out two long umbrellas. "None of the locals carries an umbrella. But a lot of out-of-town people do. When you come and go here at the hotel, the people at the desk will see the umbrellas. They may chuckle to themselves, but they will remember the out-of-towners needlessly carrying them. They will not notice your face. When we make the switch, all they will remember are the umbrellas coming and going."

"And when do we switch?"

The two guides did not answer.

The taller man continued. "You will then give us your conference IDs, credit cards, and rental car keys. We will have people go the conference, drive your car, and go out to dinner in your place to leave a perfectly normal electronic trail for you." He glanced at the two men. "Understood?"

They both responded in unison, "Understood."

"One final thing. What shoe size do each of you wear?"

"Twelve," Philip murmured.

"Same," responded David.

"All right, that makes it easy." The two guides left without saying another word.

The next day went exactly as planned. At the end of the day, David and Philip took the conference shuttle bus back to the hotel. As they walked toward the hotel entrance, a young woman playing with her cell phone bumped into David. "You will make dinner reservations at Bill's Steak House for eight p.m. tonight. Drive your rental car." As she pulled away, she politely apologized. "Oh, I'm so sorry. I wasn't paying attention." She continued to walk by like nothing happened. Philip didn't even notice.

"No, Philip, it has to be medium rare, or even rare."

"David, how can you eat a steak that way? You're a trauma surgeon. All that blood—it's just gross."

"It's not blood. It's juice—it's steak juice. It's absolute ambrosia. When we get inside, let me order for you. I will tell the chef how to cook you the perfect steak." He raised his finger to his lips, kissing them like he was a fancy connoisseur.

"No, I like my steak well done."

"Well done! That is a culinary crime. And if it was me, I'd have you arrested and throw away the key."

David parked the car in back of Bill's Steak House. The two men started to walk to the front entrance.

"Where's your umbrellas?" someone asked from behind them.

The two men turned. "I guess we left them in the car," Philip responded.

"You were instructed to bring those with you wherever you went." The man shook his head. "Act like you forgot something and go back to the rental car. My associate and I will join you in a minute." The man bent down to tie his shoe.

David and Philip kept walking. Philip suddenly stopped and pretended to search his pockets. "Uh, I think I left my cell phone in the car." The two turned and walked back to the rental car. They were joined a few minutes later by the two tour guides they had met earlier at their hotel. The two guides opened the doors and climbed into the backseat of the car.

"OK, room keys, cell phones, wallets, everything."

The two men did as instructed. "OK, while I do this, both of you search all your pockets again. I want everything, including your loose change."

The men handed the guide their loose change and other debris from their pockets. "Which one of you had the gum and which one had the Altoids?"

Philip raised his hand. "Altoids."

David sheepishly nodded. "Gum."

The man dropped the gum and Altoids into the appropriate separate paper bags. "Your replacements will use these as well." He continued to fiddle with their cell phones and then handed each of them a new one. "Your real cell phones will remain here with your replacements, for tracking purposes. I have forwarded all your calls to these burner phones so you can take all your calls just as you normally would. And lastly, I need the umbrellas." The one who was speaking handed the umbrellas and paper bags to his associate. "He will take these to your replacements, who are about to enjoy an amazing steak dinner…at your expense." He laughed. "You also need to know—they are big tippers." His large smile was visible even in the dark car. "Now, in just a minute you will exit the rental car and join us in the blue pickup truck over there. In the back you will find some very dark glasses. You will put those on. You will not be able to see anything. We will be going for a short drive. You can sleep if you like. Otherwise, I hope you like country music."

"Oh no," Philip groaned, shaking his head.

They arrived at their new hotel room about three hours later. They were instructed to leave the glasses on until they were inside. The hotel room was small and devoid of any identifying features.

After a quick shower the next morning, they were each handed a sweatshirt, sweatpants, and a pair of hiking shoes, size twelve. They put their black glasses on and were escorted into the backseat of the pickup. "It'll be about another hour or so from here." They were soon back on the road. From the flow of the traffic and lack of turns or stops, the two men could tell they were on a highway. No one spoke.

"OK, this is just getting ridiculous. We don't even know your names. We need to call you something," David said. The car made a right turn. It seemed to be going at a slower speed.

"Fine, let's just play a game," said the taller guide. "All right, you"—he touched David on the chest—"pick a number between one and one hundred."

"What?" David seemed confused. "Fine. Twenty-seven."

"Excellent, number twenty-seven, excellent. Now pick another."

"Forty-one," David mumbled.

"OK, fine. Number forty-one. Not as distinguished as twenty-seven, but a fine number."

"Oh, oh, now it's my turn," interrupted his partner. "OK, you"—he touched Philip on the shoulder—"same thing. Pick two numbers between one and one hundred."

"Sixteen and ninety-three." Philip sounded a bit annoyed.

"Perfect," exclaimed the taller guide. "Now that we have that settled, things should be much easier." The two guides stopped talking.

"We haven't settled anything. And you haven't answered my question," David snapped.

"Yes, we have, on both accounts," answered the associate.

"No, you haven't—"

"Yes, we have," answered the taller one. "And I believe you should be addressing me as 'Ninety-Three.' Although, I suppose if you want to keep things formal, or if you're mad at me or something, you could call me 'Number Ninety-Three.' My mother was like that. When she was mad, she would always say, 'Number Ninety-Three, you get right up here and clean your room. Just you wait until your father gets home. Number Ninety-Three, you are grounded!' Saint of a woman, my mother."

"What?"

"Until I tell you otherwise, my name is Ninety-Three. My associate is number Sixteen. From now on, I will be calling you number Twenty-Seven. And your friend here with the distinguished nose will be number Forty-One."

They suddenly drove onto a rough gravel road and traveled at a much slower speed. The road was steep and winding. "We're going up into the mountains," Philip said out loud.

"Number Twenty-Seven, I am the hired guide, so you will need to keep any commentary to yourself." They hit a big bump in the road. "Maybe we are in a city with terrible roads. Maybe this is some elaborated simulation and we are parked on a big warehouse on a conveyor belt. In any case, we will be stopping soon. There will be some signage nearby when we get out of the car that we do not want you to see. So I will guide you a little ways away from the truck before I take off your glasses. Then please keep your eyes down and focus on the trail in front of you. That's it. You do not need to see any local landmarks. Understood?"

"Understood."

The truck was parked, and as he had said, Ninety-Three and Sixteen walked the two men away from the truck and up a gravel trail. They pushed the two men's heads down and took off their glasses. "Just keep your heads down and watch the trail. We still have some hiking to do."

The trail was made of loose rocky gravel and went up a steep, narrow ravine. The dirt was much dryer here than in Seattle. No one spoke. About two hours later, they stopped.

"OK, Twenty-Seven and Forty-One, you can look up." David and Philip lifted their eyes from the trail. In front of them stood a barrier of shimmering blue-white. It was like arctic ice dancing on a wall. Ninety-Three and Sixteen smiled and then walked forward and disappeared through the translucent wall to the other side. David and Philip stood looking at each other. Then both walked hesitantly forward and entered the shimmering curtain. It was like getting a deep soothing massage of springtime. They each moaned as they exited out the other side. Their relaxed grins were instantly replaced with stunned eyes of wonder. Straddling the sides of the valley before them stood a great angel. He was several stories tall and held a great flaming sword. His garments were the same shimmering arctic blue-white as the barrier they had just passed through. His countenance was serious and undistracted by their arrival. His eyes remained unblinking as he gazed to what now lay behind them.

"His name is Gabriel. He is one of the Valde Beatus…an angel. He or one of the others is always there." Number Ninety-Three looked up in amazement at the sight he had obviously seen many times but still seemed to take him by awe.

"Does he ever speak?" David asked.

"Oh yes. In fact, when he is not on watch, he can be very talkative. Of course, he is not so big then. He's just normal size. Or I guess I should say, human size. By the way"—he walked toward David—"my name is Josh. And number…whatever over there…is my new pastor, Pastor Vern."

Vern put out his hand as well. "A pleasure to actually meet you for real. Just call me Vern." Then he turned and put his hand out again. "And your name is?"

"Philip. And I want to thank the two of you for what you have already done for us. We know you had to take a lot of risk to just meet with us." The four shook hands and made sure they had each other's names figured out. Philip looked out between the high mountains surrounding them to see a distant view of Puget Sound. "It seems warmer here than in Seattle, and the terrain is much dryer. Where exactly are we?"

"You are on the North Olympic Peninsula in a wilderness area just south of Sequim, Washington. Of course, before the war, when everyone was taken, Vern and I were just hiking buddies out here. A handful of the brothers here at the Main Archive were left behind with the rest of us. They obviously knew what had happened and began evangelizing here on the peninsula immediately. Before that, Vern and I had occasionally gone to this ministry downtown called The Upper Room. To be honest, we mainly went for the music and, you know, maybe a chance to meet some girls. But we did hear the messages. It wasn't long after the stewards starting sharing that we both became Iredenti. Some months later, they asked us both to join the order." Josh paused, looking at the two new additions. "So are you new Iredenti, like us, or are you witnesses?"

The question was shockingly blunt. The men's hearts stopped. The answer that swirled within them was laced with incredible emotion. Love, loneliness, joy, and heartbreak coalesced into its own feeling…of identity. Both men had never really came out and said it like that. The truth of the world crumbling around them seemed to suddenly collide with the reality of who they were. David and Philip both glanced at each other. "We are witnesses," David said softly.

"Which tribes?" Vern asked.

"Levi," David said.

"I am descended from the tribe of Manasseh," Philip replied. He could feel the redness and tears forming in his eyes, but he quickly hid it by turning to take in the view. "So exactly where are we headed?" he added.

"We are taking you to a place called the Tubal Cain Mine. It is safely hidden away inside the Olympic National Park. The only way here is by foot, donkey, or one of our helicopters. The order moved here back in the 1930s. By the way, where are you from?"

"Hartford," Philip responded. "We are both trauma surgeons there."

"Oh, that makes sense." Vern shook his head. "So have you been to a Hedge before? I think in your area that would be the Church of the Good Shepherd."

"Yes, it was amazing. But"—Philip chuckled for a moment—"but not like this." He pointed his finger at the great angel standing watch beside them.

"Well, the Main Archive here has always been a greater target. They tried to nuke the place back in the 1970s."

"What? What do you mean they tried to 'nuke' the place?" David interrupted.

"Exactly that. They sent a bomber with a nuclear weapon and tried to nuke the Great Archive. The weapon was of course neutralized by the angel and the plane destroyed. I'll show you some of the wreckage up here just off the trail. We'll be walking right by it on the way to the mine."

"I thought the Hedges were out of the purview of the enemy?"

"They are," Vern said matter of factly. "But that does not mean the enemy doesn't come knocking at the door every now and then to see if anybody's home. Satan will always test his limits and try to break them. That's a given."

David and Philip both looked up with a new understanding at the great angel's presence.

"Remember," Vern said, laughing, "you already know what is going to happen and how the story ends. So it's your job to be bold and courageous. Meek as doves and shrewder than serpents. And never ever forget who is in control." Vern had a big smile that made his eyes squint at the corners. "Now come on. We are almost there."

They hiked quickly up the valley. The trail flattened out and started to parallel a small creek. True to his word, Vern took them a little off the main trail and showed them the wreckage of the old bomber. "Of course, most of it has been taken over the years as souvenirs by the local hikers and hunters. We of course secured the nuclear weapon immediately."

"Of course," David said rhetorically.

Back on the main trail, they started to pass the rusting refuse of an old mining operation. Large pieces of rusty debris and cables protruded from the ground and off the surrounding hillside. There was really nothing left standing at all. It was just littered across the forest floor. A few more turns later...

"Here we are," Vern said with a cheerful grin.

The two men stared at the finish line of their great journey. It was a hole in the side of the hill. Hardly worth calling a cave, let alone a mine. It seemed slightly bigger than a door. They both thought roughly the same thing. *If this was a mine shaft, it was done by some miners on a very tight budget.* It was overwhelmingly unimpressive.

Josh put down the small backpack he carried and took out some flashlights. "I didn't bring any hard hats, as I didn't want to raise any suspicions or have to answer any unwanted questions if we were stopped, so watch your heads. The roof is low, and the mine gets wetter the farther we go in."

The four men skirted down the narrow shaft. Josh led the way. The only words shared once inside were, "Low roof," "Slippery rocks," "Wet floor," "The water is not that deep," "Ouch...watch your heads," and "Stay close."

The shaft got wetter and wetter. Within a few minutes they found themselves walking in an underground stream. Josh stopped and opened up his backpack. He pulled out a thick nylon climbing rope. "Here, strap yourselves onto the rope like this." Attached to the rope at eight-foot intervals were four simple clipped loops. "Unfasten the crampon, then wrap it around you like this." Josh put the two ends of the loop around himself. "Then reclip and tighten, like this…simple." Josh pulled the ropes tight and smilingly put his hands up in the air. Everyone else was quickly secured together. "OK, the waterfall is the really dangerous part, so just follow me."

Another hundred yards in, they could hear the waterfall in the distance. They pressed forward. It was freezing. The water was above their knees now. They continued to trip over the submerged refuse of the old railroad tracks now concealed beneath the water. Another fifty yards after that, they came to a dead end. It was a wide cavity with an icy waterfall off to the left, plunging into a black abyss deep into the earth. The walls of the cavity glistened with ice. The water seemed to pour directly out of the rock above them from an underground river. The heaps of water splashing off the walls flowed down the shaft they had just come up, and formed the stream. They were at the end of the shaft with no place to go.

The noise of the waterfall was deafening. Even yelling, it was hard to hear the guides. Josh seemed to just stand there. He didn't seem to be looking for anything, making any kind of a signal, or trying to find some hidden passage. He just stood there. Then Philip noticed there were only three flashlights shining on the cavity walls. He looked back at Josh. Josh's was pointed directly at his own face.

Several long minutes passed. Josh turned toward Philip. "They must be on a coffee break." Another two or three minutes passed. Philip could hardly feel anything below his knees. He was starting to think how he was going to get frostbite. Then they all heard a loud mechanical *clang*.

From directly below them, a platform slid out into the cavity of the waterfall. Two men ran out onto the platform and secured a metal ladder into some braced slots on the platform floor.

"OK, everybody, just stay hooked together and follow me." Josh turned and backed down the ladder. The others followed in turn. The ladder was made of a roughened metal that helped with their slippery grips and cold hands. The men on the deck helped them down as best they could. Directly below the shaft they had just traveled was another parallel shaft. They were quickly ushered inside. The ladder was removed and the platform retracted back within the shaft. The stone outer door was then resealed and the parallel shaft again made invisible.

Lights suddenly flashed on. The room was roughly honed out of the rock and contained some metal benches to sit on, a few old gym lockers, a big plastic garbage drum, and an oval metal door that looked much like what would be seen on a submarine.

One of the men from inside the mine moved to the center of the room. "Just take everything off, and throw it into the laundry bin over there. That includes your shoes. There are dry clothes in each of the lockers. But it's all pretty much small, medium, large, and extra-large. Here, let me crank the heaters up." He walked around, turning the knobs on a series of old space heaters stationed around the room. "That should help." He walked back to the center of the room. "My name is Kevin Spiro. I am a witness…as are all the remaining primary staff." He came over and shook David's and Philip's hands as he continued to speak. "This is the Great Archive of Nos Servo. I will be your main contact point while you are here. So if there are any questions or concerns, please speak directly to me." He walked over to Vern and Josh with a big smile. "Thanks for bringing them in. You guys always go the extra mile. We really don't have anything pressing for you, so just relax and enjoy yourselves while you're here. I would like to speak to both of you sometime after dinner tonight to go over some things, but otherwise just relax." He turned toward David and Philip. "I understand that Wednesday is the last day of your conference. Is that correct?"

They both nodded.

Kevin looked back at Vern and Josh. "So you will need to get them back to Seattle by late Tuesday night so they can make themselves visible again."

"No problem. We will hike them out Tuesday morning," Josh replied.

Everyone was soon dressed and in dry clothes. Josh and Vern seemed completely unfazed by their freezing arrival. David and Philip huddled together over a space heater.

"OK, if we are all set, let's go inside." Kevin walked over to the old submarine door and spun the large round metal valve at its center. The door was heavy on its hinges as he pushed it open. Beyond that was a clean, brightly lit white hall like in any office building. The floor was polished white linoleum with cerulean-blue strips along the sides. On the walls hung various framed pieces of artwork. They walked past a set of elevators. "The Great Archive is on the lower six levels. That will be violet floors one through six. You can get there by taking any of the elevators. The level we are currently on, blue level, is mainly administrative and offices. All levels are color coded like the spectrum and marked, as you can see. We have a fabulous research center on the level just above us." He stopped in the hall, as if thinking. "In fact, let's head up there now. There is someone there I would like you to meet." He turned around and pressed the Up button outside the set of elevators.

The floor they exited onto was much like the one they were just on, except that the blue highlights on the sides of the floor had been replaced by spring-green ones. "Here we go." Kevin stopped and opened one of the doors, ushering them in. The room was filled with a vast array of elaborate scientific equipment. A man stood inside, working. He looked up and smiled as the men entered. He had a friendly face. He was a big man, about six foot four, long light-brown hair, hazel eyes, with wide shoulders and large hands. He walked eagerly toward them and put out his right hand. "Hello, my name is Talmun."

SPECIAL THANKS

Thus ends book two of The Chronicles of the Seven Cities. Again, I would like to thank the stewards of Nos Servo for allowing me access to their Main Archive and antiquity depositories. I was especially honored to meet some of their primary staff. It is terrifying for me to see world events unfold just as they have been revealed. I pray we all hold true to who we are as Iredenti. I pray we all strive to bring the Rider where He needs to go. Time is running out.

Dear Reader,

Thank you for reading, Nos Servo. I hope you enjoyed reading it as much as I did writing it. As an author there is nothing more enjoyable for me then to hear from my readers, so if you have any comments or prayer requests please visit my website at: RobertWCraven.com

Knowing that God is there and that the battle continues to rage around us hopefully will serve as a trumpet sound that calls each of us to serve Him. For me, writing this book has been one way to do that. As an independent author, I don't have a marketing department or the exposure of being on bookshelves. If you enjoyed reading Nos Servo, please tell your friends and let people know on your Facebook page. The other big thing you can do is write a review on Amazon.com. The truth is that the only way this series will ever reach the lost people of today, is if we who are Iredenti tell them about it. And talking to people, is the doorway to serving them.

May God bless you and those of your house,

Rob Craven

If you injoing reading Cherries on Snow, be sure to look for book 2 in the series coming soon!

THE CHRONICLES OF THE SEVEN CITIES

The saga continves...

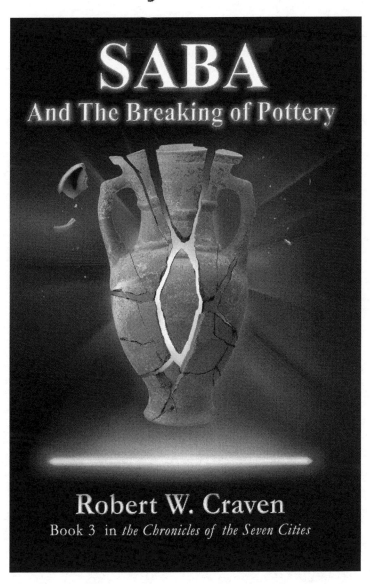

SABA
And The Breaking of Pottery

Robert W. Craven

Book 3 in *the Chronicles of the Seven Cities*

GLOSSARY

Abraham and his concubine. A story about taking matters into your own hands.

AkAk. Named after a real Kham warrior named KaKa, who served in the British Gurkhas. He later became a Christian and helped missionary Dave Waters translate the Bible into the Kham language. KaKa's son was shot and killed for his faith, and many of the Kham people were imprisoned.

Akkad. Capital of the ancient empire of Sargon, who reigned from 2334–2279 BC in southern Mesopotamia, Syria, Anatolia, and parts of modern Iran.

Alesia. A mysterious city in France, the whereabouts of which was unknown for centuries. Its conquest under Julius Caesar led to the end of the Roman war with the Gauls in 52 BC. In order to conquer it, the Romans had to completely encircle the city—not once, but twice. They had to build two complete and separate fortified rings of battlements completely around the town, fifteen kilometers and twenty-one kilometers long. Otherwise it was unconquerable. (The character is modeled after my courageous daughter Kristina, whom we all call "Rosebud.")

Amahanz (modified Cebuano). Amahan—father. I added the z on the end to get the A to Z in the name.

Aque et ignis communicatio. Roman ceremony of sharing water and fire to signify that a marriage is completed and the couple is now a new and separate family.

Ascalon. In church tradition, the name of the sword used by Saint George to slay the dragon.

Aurum (Latin). Gold.

Bellua (Latin). Monster.

Bellator (Latin). Warrior.

Bera. Genesis 14:2—the king of the sexually depraved city of Sodom.

Cantus Cresiti (modified Latin). Cantus—melody. Cresco—to grow.

Cellarius (Latin). Steward.

Cerulean blue (Latin). Derived from the caeruleus—dark blue or blue green. Derived from caelulum/caelum—heaven, sky.

Chaim and Jankel. Two of the most common Jewish names registered at Ellis Island between 1898 and1924. Number one was Abram.

Daravaza. Name derived from the fiery pit of Derweze in the Karakum Desert of Turkmenistan. Derweze is also called "the door to hell" by the locals.

Decima Grati (Latin). Decima—a tenth, or one in ten. Grati—thankful, like the lepers who were made clean.

Demas. Biblical character who abandoned the faith because he loved the world.

Chayot Ha Kodesh, Ophanim, and Erelim. There are different levels of angelic beings, each different in grandeur and power and purpose. These are the upper three most powerful classes of angelic beings.

Ecclesia Custos (Latin). A church angel.

Fattore (Italian). Steward.

Iredenti (modified Italian). Redeemed ones.

Ivoluntas (mixed English [I] and Latin [Voluntas]). I will. This is the singular expression of Satan, to have his will above God's.

Jakotrudi (Croatian—Jako-trudi). Trying too hard. A loving character who lets things slip by.

Jehoram. 2 kings 8:16–18—evil king of Israel, son of Jehoshaphat, married to Ahab's daughter. Did evil in God's sight.

Justinia. Catholic saint who would not deny her faith. She was martyred with a dagger in her throat by order of either Nero or Diocletian.

Lautus (Latin). Spotless.

Ligio (Italian). Observant. Turned Sargon's men into the Romans.

Nehushtan. The Israelite name for the bronze snake banner that Moses held up in the desert. God had it destroyed as a distracting idol (2 Kings 18:4).

Nicostrate family. One of the wealthiest families in Asia. Lucius Nicostrate and his youngest son, Nicostrat, built a stadium in Laodicea using their own funds and dedicated it to proconsul Marcus Trajan, father of Emperor Trajan.

Novitate Unum (Latin). The Unexpected One, the Holy Spirit. (Jesus Christ is the Long Expected One.)

Opus Angelorum (Latin). Great angelic work.

Otvoriti (Croatian). To open.

Pater, Prognatus, Pentral (Latin). Father, son, spirit—a literary allusion to the Trinity.

Parceida (modified Latin). Murderer.

Perpetua Occultis (Latin). Unending secret places.

Prochorus. Saint John's aid who went with him to Patmos and wrote down John's words as he experienced the revelation of Jesus Christ. A scribe.

Qui Malaam (modified Latin). Those that have chosen badly.

Qui Salvum (Latin). One who saves.

Sargon's fleeing squad of raiders. **Nahash** (1 Sam 11:2)—Ammonite king who threatened to pull out the right eye of every Israelite. **Doeg** (1 Sam 22:18)— Edomite who slayed eighty-five priests and then many more. **Shimei**—cursed David. **Jeroboam**—evil king who led the ten northern tribes astray. **Menahem** (2 Kings 15:14–22)—evil ruler who ripped open the pregnant wombs of his enemies' women. **Pashhur** (Jer. 20:1–6)—evil priest who persecuted Jeremiah. **Jehoiakim** (Jer. 36)—evil king who burned the scroll of Jeremiah.

Sperta (Latin). Bride.

Strange flesh. Joel, verse 7.

Suistus (Latin) Se iustus—self-righteous.

Temarius (Latin). Impulsive.

Tresdi Sintunus (Latin). Tres Dii—three gods. Sint unus—they are one. This is the fundamental nature of the Trinity.

Unda Cruciatus (Latin). Liquid pain.

Valde Beatus (Latin). Greatly blessed, the term used for the community of faithful angels loyal to God.

Vjeran (Croatian). Faithful.

Water of Galliae. Famous waters from France, high in hydrogen peroxide, used for centuries to help heal wounds.

Caravanserai, external walls, Islamic modified entrance.

Caravanserai, Hall and holding areas off the inside courtyard.

Caravanserai, Inside courtyard.

Caravanserai, Protected internal halls.

Thyatira, very limited ruins remain.

Thyatira, very limited ruins remain.

Philadelphia, ancient ruins with modern mosque in background.

Philadelphia, very limited ruins remain.

Gustave Dore, Original etching,
Biblical Illustration based on Herod's slaughter of the innocent,
Matthew 2:16-18

Made in the USA
Charleston, SC
18 May 2016